Sage felt almost lik the photocopied p Jenny's handwriting easy to read.

> *My dear papa,*
> *We've reached Lake Bennett safely as last.*
> *I have no words to describe the trip over the*
> *White Pass trail. The first day I thought*
> *I would die and every day thereafter I knew*
> *I couldn't survive.*

Drawn immediately and intimately into Jenny's world, amazed at the other woman's openness, Sage read on.

> *Papa, I'm so very sick at present and William*
> *is furious because I didn't immediately*
> *tell him of my condition, and now he's*
> *insisting I go back to Seattle, back over that*
> *murderous trail without him! He says he'll*
> *send Robert to accompany me, but, Papa,*
> *I don't want to go. I simply cannot go.*

Even on the photocopy, the tearstains were evident. Sage touched the marks gently, her heart hurting for Jenny, even though the other woman had been dead for years. She felt an immediate kinship with Jenny Galloway because she too had a secret she'd kept from her husband....

Bobby
Hutchinson

ECHOES

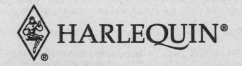

TORONTO • NEW YORK • LONDON
AMSTERDAM • PARIS • SYDNEY • HAMBURG
STOCKHOLM • ATHENS • TOKYO • MILAN • MADRID
PRAGUE • WARSAW • BUDAPEST • AUCKLAND

ISBN-13: 978-0-373-19854-2
ISBN-10:   0-373-19854-X

ECHOES

This edition published by arrangement with Harlequin Books S.A.

® and TM are trademarks of the publisher. Trademarks indicated with
® are registered in the United States Patent and Trademark Office, the
Canadian Trade Marks Office and in other countries.

www.eHarlequin.com

Printed in U.S.A.

BOBBY HUTCHINSON

was born in small-town interior British Columbia. Learning to read was the most significant event in her early life. Bobby married young and had three sons; the middle child was deaf, and he taught her patience. After twelve years of marriage, she divorced and worked at various odd jobs: directing traffic around construction sites, caring for challenged children and selling fabric, by the pound, at a remnant store. Following this, she mortgaged her house and bought the remnant store. Accompanied by her sewing machine, she began to sew one dress a day. The dresses sold, but the fabric did not, so she hired four seamstresses and turned the old remnant store into a boutique. After twelve successful years, Bobby sold the business and decided to run a marathon. Training was a huge bore, so she made up a story about Pheiddipedes, the first marathoner, as she ran. She copied it down, sent it to *Chatelaine*'s short-story contest, won first prize and became a writer. Today she has over thirty-five published books. She has four enchanting grandchildren and lives alone. Bobby runs, swims, does yoga, meditates and likes this quote by Dolly Parton: "Decide who you are, and then do it on purpose."

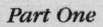

Part One

Chapter One

Humming a little under her breath, Sage Galloway filled her favorite china mug with coffee. With a small pang of guilt, she added cream and a heaping spoonful of sugar. Balancing the mug carefully, she walked out her door and into the breathtaking brilliance of the early Alaskan morning.

As usual, she'd left Ben upstairs snoring gently, his long, muscular body sprawled across their king-size bed. She'd paused a moment, watching him sleep, missing him even before he was gone. He was flying to Anchorage today, the first leg of a journey to Tanzania to hunt buffalo.

The thought of hunting *anything* made Sage shudder. She and her husband had different passions, different rhythms. She was morning, and he was night. After four years of marriage, Sage had finally stopped yawning her way into the midnight hours to keep Ben company. After all, she reasoned, he made no effort to rise at dawn with her. Marriage demanded compromise, but it ought to be an even balance—in a perfect world.

At 4:30 a.m., it was already full daylight outside. Even this early in June it was light most of the night, thanks to the midnight sun. The birds were singing a cheerful chorus, and the cow moose who'd been feasting on Caitlin's flowers took one guilty look at Sage, lowered its ungainly head and ambled off into the woods.

"Glutton," Sage accused under her breath. "You should be ashamed." Her mother-in-law's beloved marigolds were once again missing most of their heads. Caitlin would patiently replant from the seedlings she nursed all summer long in the wide kitchen window of the Lodge. She'd endlessly searched for a variety the moose and deer didn't fancy.

With her cup in one hand, Sage drew in a deep, delicious lungful of air that smelled of pine trees and ocean before she headed down to the dock. Off to her left, the Lodge and its inhabitants still slumbered. This was her own magical, private hour.

A fresh, cool breeze from Prince William Sound stirred the branches of the spruce trees that sheltered the four guest cabins. The cabins, too, were all silent, although she knew that every one was occupied. She did the bookings for the Lodge, keeping the complicated schedule of arrivals and departures in order, updating the Web site she'd designed, making certain there were live links to publicize this wild, beautiful place.

Along with the rest of the Galloways, Sage was proud that Raven Lodge had been voted best fishing lodge in Alaska by *Travel and Adventure Magazine* for the third year in a row. This June, the Lodge was filled to capacity, and booked solid for the remainder of the season.

The blinds on the windows of the long clapboard bunkhouse were still pulled down against the light, but Sage knew that within the hour the fishing guides would be up, readying the boats.

Raven Lodge was isolated, the only access by plane or boat from the small town of Valdez, and yet the Lodge and its cabins were filled with visitors eager to try their luck at catching the fabled king salmon for which Prince William Sound was famous. They came to fish, to experience what was known as the Last Frontier, and not least to sample the down-home delicious food Caitlin and her staff concocted.

Sage ambled to the far end of the dock and settled into the lawn chair she kept there, stretching out her long, bare legs and sliding her sunglasses down against the glare of sun on water. She savored her coffee as her brain ticked off items on her schedule for the particularly busy day ahead. She was down to the last mouthful of coffee, but far from the bottom of the to-do list, when a deep voice from behind her said, "Morning, early bird."

Sage squinted up at her father-in-law and smiled with pleasure and affection. Theo had lost muscle tone since his recent heart attack, and his formerly robust body was frail and thin. His baritone voice was the same as always—rich and strong and reassuring. "Theo, what are you doing up so early?"

"Couldn't sleep. Too excited, I guess. I just can't wait to meet these relatives of mine." He folded his tall, lean frame into the other webbed chair. "I was an only child, you know, and I used to long for brothers and sisters. Even cousins, but there weren't any. My only relative was my elderly aunt Martha, and she'd never married. No one talked much about these long-lost Australian Galloways. I only knew there'd been some kind of family quarrel and we'd lost touch with that branch of the family. Haven't been in touch for generations."

"That split was over your grandma Jenny, wasn't it, Theo?"

Sage was well acquainted with the story, but she knew Theo loved telling it. And she enjoyed hearing it.

"It certainly was. A real love triangle. The story goes that my grandfather William and his brother Robert both fell in love with Jenny," Theo said. "William had gone to Scotland and brought her back as his bride. He brought Robert over, as well. He'd gotten them both jobs with the Canadian Pacific Railway. But when they got to Seattle the gold rush had just begun. They went over the White Pass Trail to Dawson, must have been quite an adventure. I don't know any of the details about the fight they had, I only know it was over Jenny. I'm hoping Andrew can fill some of those holes in for me. I do know they split up in Dawson. Robert went to Australia and started a brewery. William came here, bought this land and founded the Galloway Salmon Packing Plant, right over there in the building we now use as the staff bunkhouse. They never spoke again."

"And William designed and built the Lodge as a home for his Jenny, didn't he?" Sage loved that part of the story. Having a house built especially for you had to be so romantic. She often wished Ben had built their house just for her, but he'd started it when he was still married to his first wife, Jill. It wasn't completed until after they'd divorced, though, so Sage was the first woman to live there.

Theo was squinting up at his home. "William was a talented engineer, and no slouch as an architect, either. The Lodge is well designed and built to last."

"And your father was born here," Sage prompted.

Theo nodded. "Dad's two sisters, as well, Martha and Emma. Emma died in her teens from tuberculosis, but Martha lived to a ripe old age. And so did William. I was ten when he died, he was ninety-two. He was a fine grandpa, took me fishing and taught me the basics of steam engineering."

Sage, who'd never known her grandparents, wondered what it would be like, growing up with extended family. If—when—she and Ben had kids, that's what she wanted for them.

"And Jenny? How long did she live, Theo?"

"Sixty-two. Apparently she died of pneumonia. I didn't know my Grandma Jenny. Unfortunately she was gone by the time I came along."

"That's too bad. She sounds like a fascinating woman." A portrait of her hung in the family living room. "She was very beautiful." Sage looked up at the Lodge. The family's history always reminded her of how many Galloways had lived and loved here, how many tragedies they'd lived through and survived. It was comforting, that sense of permanence. Sometimes she imagined their energy still permeated the air.

"Good thing your cousin Andrew got interested in genealogy," Sage remarked. "Otherwise, you two might never have made contact."

"I'll say," Theo agreed.

Andrew had written from Australia six months before, asking for information about the Alaskan branch of the Galloways. Theo wrote back, and the two formed a friendship that resulted in this much-anticipated visit. Andrew was bringing his wife, Opal, and they'd be staying for an extended period.

Theo said, "I gather that until he retired Andrew was like me, too busy raising a family and making a living to bother much about history. But then he got interested in genealogy, and that's when he first made contact." Theo reached over and patted Sage's arm. "Listen to me prattling on about my family like some self-centered old man."

"You could never be self-centered, Theo," Sage assured him, slipping her hand into his. "Besides, I grew up as an only child, too. I can guess how exciting it must be to get to meet close relatives. I was lonely, growing up." And that wasn't the half of it. "But I don't feel lonely anymore. How could I around you and Caitlin? You make me feel part of the Galloway family."

"Of course you're part of our family." Theo sounded surprised that she'd even mention it. "Caitlin and I are just grateful Ben had the good sense to marry you." His voice held rueful humor. "He learns the hard way, that boy, but he does learn. Eventually."

Sage knew Theo was referring obliquely to Ben's first disastrous marriage to Jill Redmond. Their marriage had been volatile, their divorce vindictive, and it must have been difficult for Caitlin and Theo to remain impartial. But they had, thus safeguarding their relationship with their granddaughters, Sophia and Lily.

The thought of Ben's daughters brought Sage a familiar sense of failure and frustration. Her period had come the day before, regular as clockwork. Once again, no baby. The latest round of fertility treatments hadn't worked. Ben hadn't said anything, but his expression had signaled his disappointment. And they hadn't made love, and now he was leaving for three long weeks, which meant there'd be no baby next month, either.

She didn't want to think about that. It made her feel depressed and desperate. Sage drained her now-cold coffee and got to her feet.

"Time to get cracking." She forced cheer into her voice. "I don't think Ben's finished packing, and I have to put the finishing touches on the guest room for the Galloways."

The Lodge and the cabins were full, so it was only logical the Galloway relatives should stay with Sage. And with Ben gone, she'd enjoy the company, she told herself firmly. In truth, she was more than a little apprehensive. The visitors were going to be here for the summer, and she couldn't help but wonder whether or not they'd be easy houseguests.

"Looks like Oliver's all packed and rarin' to go." Theo nodded toward one of the cabins where Oliver Brady, one of the guides and a friend of Ben's, was shouldering a backpack and heading up to the Lodge. Ben had invited Oliver along on the Tanzania trip, even though Theo hadn't approved.

"We're going to be shorthanded with both him and Ben away," Theo grumbled again now. "I only hope that new guide Ben hired knows as much about fishing as he says he does." He got to his feet. "Too bad Logan's so far away—it'd be good to have him to fill in at times like this."

Ben's twin, Logan, was a lawyer in Seattle. He visited only rarely, and Caitlin and Theo missed him. Sage liked Logan, but there was always an atmosphere of tension when he was around. Ben and his brother didn't always get along.

"Well, I should go shower and put on some decent duds myself," Theo said, getting to his feet. He'd had a serious heart attack a few months before, and Sage couldn't help but notice how it had slowed him down. "Tom'll be here in another hour. Don't want to keep him waiting."

Caitlin's brother Tom was a pilot, with a thriving

business called Up and Away. He ferried guests to and from the Lodge, which was accessible only by plane or boat. This morning he and Theo were dropping Ben and Oliver off in Anchorage and bringing the Australian relatives back.

"See you later." Sage waved a hand as she hurried along the dock and up the stairs, her mind once again listing the things she needed to accomplish.

Bottles of water and some chocolates in the guest room.

Check the bathroom when Ben's done. He always leaves whiskers in the sink.

Make sure he remembers to pack the bug repellent and the water purification tablets.

Beg some oatmeal cookies from Mavis so there's something for the Galloways to snack on.

The group in cabin three will be leaving tomorrow. Get their bill ready.

She quickened her step. If she kept busy enough, she wouldn't have time to dwell on her problems. It was a strategy she'd adopted so long ago she was no longer consciously aware of doing it.

In the house, Ben was up, drinking juice at the kitchen island.

Sage went over and kissed him, aware that his mouth didn't linger long on hers. "So, sleepyhead, all ready for your big adventure?"

"Ready as I'll ever be."

His gruff tone indicated he wasn't in the best of moods. "Did you happen to see Oliver when you were out?"

Sage nodded. "He was heading up to the Lodge with his gear. Your dad's up, too. He came down to the dock—he's excited about the relatives coming. Too bad you're going to miss them today."

"What's the big deal? They'll still be here when I get back. Dad's got his nose out of joint because I won't be around to help entertain them, but this trip's been planned for months, I can't cancel now." Ben swallowed the last of his orange juice. "Mavis and Mom want us over there for breakfast. You ready?"

"In a few minutes, you go ahead. Did you remember to pack the bug stuff and the tablets for the water?"

"Yeah, I did. You made me an idiot list, remember?" He sounded sarcastic, and Sage scowled at him.

"Why are you being so grumpy with me?"

"Sorry." He came over and gave her a quick, cursory hug. "Late night, too much beer. Those guys from Sweden really know how to party."

He released her too soon. "I'll go over and pound back a pot of Mavis's coffee—that'll help. See you in a minute, huh?"

He was gone before she could reply.

Sage watched him from the window as he loped along the path. Her stomach was cramping, and it wasn't just from her period.

Marry in haste, repent at leisure, the old saw went. Maybe there was a lot of truth to it. She'd only known Ben two months before their wedding. She met him at a trade fair geared to the hospitality industry, held in New York. She was looking for ways to promote the small hotel she worked for in Bend, Oregon. He was looking for ways to promote the Lodge.

From their first meeting, she'd seen the way the other women looked at him, and she knew exactly how they felt.

How could any healthy heterosexual woman not be attracted to him? Three generous inches over six feet, he had the kind of long, lean body that came from hard outdoor work. And he'd ignored the other women, concentrating all his attention on her.

Beautiful Ben. How could she have resisted him?

He and his twin had inherited the thick dark curls, high cheekbones and chiseled good looks of their Highland ancestors, along with their broad-shouldered strength. Ben had a charismatic personality, dancing green eyes and a teasing, flirtatious manner that had captivated Sage the moment she met him.

Ben could charm the birds out of the trees, his mother always said.

Certainly he could—and did—captivate everyone he wanted to impress. He'd charmed Sage from the very first moment he smiled down into her eyes. She'd accepted his invitation to dinner that first night; she'd made love with him the second night; she'd believed him when he said he'd fallen in love with her. She'd been ecstatic when he proposed.

At twenty-six, she'd had her share of love affairs, but she'd never before plunged headfirst, all the way, down to the depths and up into the clouds.

And he did love her, she knew he did. But even in the beginning, the signs were there, and she ignored them. She hadn't realized or wanted to believe that Ben wasn't by nature monogamous, that the concept of being faithful to one woman wasn't in his cellular makeup. She'd learned that the hard way.

She still wasn't certain how far his flirtations really went. There'd been lipstick on shirts, traces of perfume not her own, phone calls to their private number. He always laughed it off, and she didn't pursue it, even though the jealousy and anger and sense of betrayal made her physically ill.

But she'd never even considered leaving. She couldn't leave. Her marriage to Ben had given her the one thing she'd never had and always longed for—family. The thought of separating, of leaving him and Raven Lodge and Theo and Caitlin, brought such panic and intense emotional pain she could hardly bear even thinking about it.

Ben wanted a son. He adored his daughters, but he'd made it clear that he longed for a boy. If only she could give him that, Sage knew he'd settle down. She was almost sure of it. She folded her palms over her aching belly and mouthed a prayer.

Please. Please?

If only...

The sound of the approaching float plane brought her out of her reverie. She hurried through the chores and then trotted along the path to the Lodge for the family breakfast, reminding herself that she mustn't cry when Ben left. He hated it when she cried, and as he'd already reminded her, he'd only be gone three weeks.

Oliver's girlfriend, Grace Fulton, passed Sage as she reached the Lodge. Grace was a fishing guide, like Oliver, and she was carrying a load of gear down to the dock.

"Morning, Grace," Sage said, but Grace shot her a surly look and then turned away without a word.

Maybe she was upset because Ben was taking Oliver away for three weeks, Sage reasoned, staring after the pretty blonde. But it was open knowledge that Grace and Oliver hadn't been getting along—you'd think Grace would be relieved to have him gone for a while.

Well, she'd find out sooner or later what was eating at

Grace, Sage concluded as she went around the path to the kitchen door. The Lodge was like a small town where everyone knew everyone's business.

She opened the door into the huge old kitchen. Guests ate in one of the several dining rooms, but the family always had their meals here.

The smell of bacon and eggs, coffee and pancakes greeted her, along with familiar voices raised in animated conversation. She wasn't particularly hungry, but the group around the big old oak table drew her like a magnet. She slipped into her usual seat, between Ben and his father.

Her mother-in-law, Caitlin, gave her a warm, welcoming smile. Caitlin's mass of white hair shone like a halo in the light from the window.

Mavis Armitage was Caitlin's longtime friend and assistant. She poured Sage a mug of coffee. Sage mouthed a thank-you, and Mavis's scarred face twisted into a smile. In her midsixties, Mavis had been seriously burned years before in a kitchen fire, and because of her disfigurement, she was uncomfortable around anyone except family.

Theo patted Sage's hand absently, deep in a conversation with Tom.

Ben, who seemed in a better mood, turned and winked at her, and the cramps in Sage's belly eased a little. When he came home, she vowed, they'd talk. When he came home, she'd find the courage to bring up the secret that haunted her, the secret she should have told him long ago.

Chapter Two

It was late that afternoon by the time the plane got back from Anchorage with its Galloway cargo. Sage was working in her upstairs office at the Lodge, updating the week's guest schedule, when she heard first the familiar drone and then, through the open window, the excited voices of the Australians as Theo led them up the stairs and into the house.

She finished what she was doing and then hurried downstairs to meet everyone. Halfway down she heard Theo's voice from the living room, stronger and more dynamic than it had been since his heart attack.

It was such a delight to hear him sounding normal. As a result, Sage was beaming when she put out a hand to the tall, older man who was nearest the door.

"This is Sage, our amazing daughter-in-law," Theo said with a proud and loving smile, getting up to pour her a glass of the white wine he knew she enjoyed. "Sage, my cousin Andrew and his wife, Opal. Sage is the dynamo I was telling you about. She designed our Web site, got us into the twenty-first century on the computer and started the ad campaign that attracted the European market."

"And pretty as a picture, into the bargain." Opal had a wide, mischievous smile. "With that dark hair and those blue eyes, no wonder young Ben fell for ye, darlin'."

Sage thanked her, and then added, "I'm delighted to meet you both. Welcome to Alaska."

Andrew Galloway was a shock, because his features and Theo's were so similar. Sage couldn't stop looking at him. Taller and slightly more muscular, he still looked enough like Theo to be his brother. Thick, curly salt-and-pepper hair, the same elegant skull, high cheekbones, generous mouth. The Galloway stamp.

This is what Ben will look like in his sixties, Sage thought as she moved from Andrew to his wife, extending her hand. "I'm so glad you're here, Opal, welcome."

Every inch of Opal Galloway's almost five feet radiated exuberance and good nature. Nearly as round as she was high, her startling silvery blue eyes and full-lipped mouth were bracketed with laugh lines. She wore gauzy, feminine layers of pink chiffon that billowed around as she perched on the sofa beside Caitlin like a pretty, albeit oversize doll. Her tiny feet in high-heeled gold sandals didn't quite touch the floor. She was sipping what looked like sherry, but as Sage approached, she set her glass down and sprang to her feet.

"Lovey, it's a treat to meet all you long-lost Galloways in the flesh." She reached up and wrapped plump arms around Sage, holding her close. It was a little like being hugged by a goose down pillow that smelled like roses.

"Sorry we missed yer hubby. Imagine, him flying off to Africa. Quite the adventurer, isn't he? Now come sit down here beside me and Caitlin. I'll be the thorn between two roses, I will."

Sage did as she was told. There was something about Opal that made you want to be near her.

"Now, let's get this straight right up front," the little woman went on with hardly a breath. "Drew and I aren't here to be entertained." She wrinkled up her pert little nose. "After our tour of the Philippines we're that tired of sightseeing and eating out, aren't we, Drew?"

"We are that, my dear." Andrew's trademark green Galloway eyes softened when he looked at his wife.

Opal twinkled at him before turning again to Theo. "So how's about letting us pitch in and help wherever we can, cousin? Looks like you lot have your hands full, running a *skookum* place like this one. Tom told us how shorthanded you were on the flight up. And we're family, after all. Blood's thicker than water. I always say that, don't I, Drew?"

"You do, Dumpling."

Dumpling? Sage had to suppress a hysterical giggle, because the word so aptly described Opal. Another woman could have taken offense at the moniker, but Opal just blew her husband a kiss.

They were more than a little over the top, but it was apparent to Sage that Andrew was totally besotted by his vibrant, cheerful wife, and that she returned the sentiment tenfold. So here was another couple making the most of a relationship, just as Theo and Caitlin did in their very different, more dignified fashion.

At least some of the Galloways seemed to have found the secret of lasting love and happy marriage, she mused with a pang of envy. Maybe all it took was determination and time. Her glance went to the large painting she'd often admired, of Jenny and William Galloway. It hung over the mantel of the tumbled stone fireplace.

They were the pioneers, the couple brave enough to begin a new life in a new land. But it was impossible to tell from a painting whether they were happy or not.

Andrew, too, was looking up at the painting.

"That's Auntie Jenny and Uncle William?"

"It is," Theo acknowledged. "Looking at you, Andrew, I see the family resemblance."

"It's amazing how much alike you and Theo look," Sage remarked to Andrew. "You could easily be brothers."

"Not surprising, my dear," Andrew said. "Theo and I had grandfathers who were identical twins, aye, Theo?"

"We sure did," Theo agreed. "Robert and William Galloway. I know William's story, he built this house and started one of Alaska's first fish canneries right here. I don't know much about Great-uncle Robert, though."

"My grandpa Robbie," Andrew said in a fond voice. "He was a hell of a fellow, doted on me when I was a wee sprout. Died in a boating accident when I was fifteen. I missed him sorely." He paused and then said, "Did you ever hear the rumor that it was him who fathered your da, Theo?"

Shocked, Sage paused with her wineglass halfway to her lips. She'd certainly never heard any such rumor, and she was surprised when Theo nodded, unperturbed.

"Ridiculous, isn't it? That preposterous story was whispered about when I was little. I had an old, eccentric aunt who lived here with my parents until she died, Auntie Martha. She told me once in strictest secrecy that my father wasn't William's child, but Robert's. Said her mother,

Jenny, had told her so before she died. But I didn't believe her, she was more than a little off in the head by that stage."

Andrew said, "Well, you owe Auntie an apology post-humously, cousin, because it's true all right."

"I'll be damned." Theo looked astounded. "How can you be certain?"

"I have proof, from Jenny's own pen." Andrew looked smugly pleased with himself. "As you know, Opal and I went to Scotland just before we came here to find out what we could about the Galloway history. Your grandma Jenny—" he pointed up at the painting "—was a letter writer, bless her heart. She wrote to her father, Bruce Campbell, and when Bruce died, she wrote to one of her brothers. He saved all her letters and passed them on to his daughter, Robina. She allowed me to copy them, and the whole story's outlined in those thin pieces of paper. And it's a corker, I tell you. Puts those soap operas on the television to shame."

Theo had been listening closely, his face registering his amazement and interest. "So we're more closely related than I thought, Andrew, aren't we? What would we be? That would make Robert my grandfather, instead of my great-uncle. So you and I are first cousins?"

"Right on, mate. The letters lay it out plain."

Theo said, "I'd love to read them. You did bring them along?"

"Better than that, I made you a copy of them all, Theo. It's our common history, after all. I'll get them." He started toward the doorway.

"Sorry, but we're about to eat dinner," Caitlin interrupted. "Can the letters wait until later this evening?"

Andrew and Theo looked disappointed, but Opal said,

"Food first, by all means. We've all the time in the world to figure out blood ties and read old letters, right, Drew?"

"Righto, Dumpling." He didn't sound as enthusiastic as Opal, however.

Sage glanced over at Caitlin, and it was all she could do not to laugh aloud when their eyes met. The endearment Andrew used for his round little wife was priceless, and Sage could see her own delight and mirth reflected in her mother-in-law's soft gray eyes.

Dinner was a wonderfully cheerful meal. Opal kept everyone amused with her outlandish descriptions of small Australian towns with peculiar names—and the more outlandish relatives she had living in those towns. Even Mavis, always ill at ease with strangers, had warmed immediately to Opal.

Instead of pretending not to notice the scars on Mavis's face, like most people did, Opal went straight over and laid her palm against the other woman's ribbed cheek, studying her closely. "Well then, you've had a nasty accident, haven't ye, lovie? Me auntie Patsy, the one in Nar Nar Goon, has nearly the same scars as you, only on the other side of her face. She was frying fish and the fat caught on fire. She lost all her hair into the bargain, you're so lucky to have yours, fair dinkum it is, too, so long and thick and black. Patsy's me favorite aunt, y'see, she taught me how to cook. Makes me feel right at home, meetin' you, Mavis."

For one tense moment, Sage was unsure how Mavis would react. The little woman was fiercely proud and sensitive. Sage had never heard her mention the accident that had marked her face.

Mavis was silent for a long moment. "I'd like to meet your auntie Patsy," she finally said. Her eyes were shimmering with tears. "With me it was a pressure cooker." And from that moment on, Opal and Mavis were friends.

Sage was intrigued with what Andrew had revealed about Jenny Galloway. What kind of woman could she have been, to have gotten pregnant by her brother-in-law? Even in these more liberal times, it was shocking. What must it have been like in the early 1900s?

Curious to learn more about the Galloway history, Sage joined the others in the family living room at the Lodge that evening.

"Here you go," Andrew pronounced, ceremoniously handing a thick manila envelope to Theo. "Your grandma's correspondence."

"Thank you, Andrew." With subdued excitement, Theo reached inside and pulled out the letters. He handed Caitlin a random portion, gave Sage some, and put his reading glasses on to study the ones he was holding.

Andrew got to his feet. "We can discuss them later. Opal and I are going to take a little stroll down to the dock, and then we'll head over to that lovely room you've prepared for us, Sage. We're going to turn in early. We're feeling more than a little jet-lagged."

Sage said, "Make yourselves at home. There's cookies in the jar on the counter, thanks to Mavis. And milk in the fridge, or soda if you prefer."

"Be sure and use the bug repellent I gave you," Caitlin reminded them. "The mosquitoes and black flies are particularly bad tonight."

Andrew and Opal left, and Sage felt almost like a voyeur as she lifted the photocopied pages Theo had given her. Jenny's handwriting was beautiful, clear and easy to read.

The letter began,

My Dear Papa, we've reached Lake Bennett safely at last. Dearest Papa, I have no words to describe the trip over the White Pass trail. The first day I thought I would die, and every day thereafter I knew I couldn't survive. The trail crosses over a huge mountain, the temperatures drop to below zero, we encountered snowstorms and freezing weather, the incline is extreme, and I was in great pain because my feet blistered and bled. But oh, dear Father, I was also terribly ill because of the baby I'm expecting.

Drawn immediately and intimately into Jenny's world, amazed at the other woman's openness, Sage read on.

I didn't suspect that my stomach problems on the steamship coming over to America could have been pregnancy, but now I know that's what it was. Papa, I'm so very sick at present and most unhappy. William is furious because I didn't immediately tell him of my Condition, and now he's insisting I go back to Seattle, back over that murderous trail without him! I'd have to stay there alone until such time as he comes out of this wild North Country, which will be a year at least, as no travel is possible during the winter. He says he'll send Robert to accompany me, but Papa, I don't want to go. *I simply cannot go.*

Even on the photocopy, the faded tearstains were evident. Sage touched the marks gently with her fingertip, her heart hurting for Jenny, even though her rational mind told her the other woman had been dead for many years. She felt an immediate kinship with Jenny Galloway, because Sage, too, had a secret she'd kept from her husband.

Chapter Three

Sage had been holding her breath as she read, and she let it out in a slow whoosh. She looked up at the painting, suddenly seeing so much more than a little woman with a square, determined jaw and sky-blue eyes—Sage thought they were a much lighter blue than hers, if the painting was true to life.

Jenny's riotous coppery curls escaped from a chignon at the back of her head. It was silly, but that hair had long ago given Sage her first faint sense of kinship with Jenny. Sage knew all about impossibly curly hair. Her own chocolate-brown corkscrews had made her nuts until, in her late teens, she gave up on efforts to control the unruly mass and had it cut as short as possible. Later, she'd let it grow again, but with the assistance of stylists who cleverly shaped it into some sort of submission.

When she came here, Caitlin had recommended Luigi, the gifted hairdresser who had a shop in Valdez.

But Jenny wouldn't have had a Luigi at her beck and call. And if these letters were anything to judge by, she had much more important issues to deal with than her hair.

Sage's eyes were drawn once again to the letter. Jenny went on.

There is a woman in our party who seems to derive pleasure from causing me trouble. I believe I've mentioned her before, Kitty Fitzgerald. I was waiting for an opportune moment in which to confess my Condition to my husband, but Mrs. Fitzgerald viciously blurted it out in front of everyone this evening, and William is furious. I know he has good reason to be, I did deceive him, and it was wrong of me.

Oh, Papa, I simply had no idea that marriage could be this difficult. I miss you and the wee boys and home so terribly sometimes I feel I could die of loneliness. This country is harsh and cruel, it's taken all my stamina to get this far, and oh, Papa, I simply cannot go back to Seattle now. Quite apart from the terrible hardships of the trail, I would have to have this child among utter strangers, alone in Seattle. I have no doubt dear Robert would stay with me if I asked him to, but for all his kindness he is still a man. My only true dear woman friend is Mae Sundstrom, who will be going on to Dawson.

The story ended there. Sage's portion was missing an ending. She hoped it was in the bundle Theo held.

"I'm missing the last of this letter," she said, impatient to know what had happened. "Can you find it for me?"

Theo began flipping through the stack, reading a line here and there, looking for the pages she was missing.

Sage noticed that Caitlin was shaking her head and wiping her eyes.

"This poor child. This letter of hers makes me cry. She could only have been eighteen or nineteen, and she's telling her father about the loss of her first baby. It was a little boy, born prematurely by the sounds of it, and he died at birth. It's heartbreaking."

"Was she in Dawson, or in Seattle?" Sage had to know if William had sent her back.

"Dawson. What's in the letter you have?"

Sage explained briefly, and they exchanged letters.

"Dearest Papa," this one began. This time the writing was small, the letters formed by what Sage instinctively knew was a trembling hand.

I have sad news, my dear wee baby was born too soon and didn't live.

Sage's eyes filled with tears and she choked back a sob. This letter was almost too painful to read. Imagine carrying a baby and then losing him at birth. Her hand went to her own empty, aching belly.

His name was Jamie, I held him only for a moment but he was beautiful, with dark hair like William's and I think a forehead like yours, Papa.

Jenny wrote about the funeral, and William's new job building a railroad.

It's not the one he came to America to build, but it will make it easier to come and go from this far North Country, and for that I'm glad. It's to be called the White Pass Railroad, and William takes great pride in his work.

But, Papa, he's so far away and I feel so alone. Whilst he's gone, Robert is taking very good care of me, as is Mae. Her baby will arrive soon, and I pray all goes well for her. She is a dear and treasured friend to me in this barren place.

Obviously too emotional to continue, Jenny had ended this letter abruptly, expressing her love for her father and her brothers.

"Theo, was Jenny's mother dead by the time she came to America? Jenny never mentions her."

Theo thought it over. "I think she had a stepmother. Andrew would know for sure."

Sage thought of her own stepdaughters with a pang of regret. She'd tried her absolute best, but there was no closeness between her and Sophia and Lily, even though she longed to be on intimate terms with them. Ben claimed that Jill was doing her best to turn the girls against both him and Sage, and although she didn't want to believe that, there seemed no other explanation for their behavior.

Sage looked up again at the painting of William and Jenny, and she noticed that Caitlin was doing the same thing.

"It makes such a difference to read these letters, doesn't it?" Caitlin commented. "She and William are three-dimensional now instead of being an old family painting on the wall."

"They bring Jenny to life, that's for sure. I can't wait to

read the rest of them." Sage handed the one she held back to Theo. "Thanks so much for letting me share them." She yawned. "Whoo, excuse me. I should go home now. Obviously it's past my bedtime."

Theo took a sizable chunk from the stack and handed it to Sage. "Here, take these with you. I won't read much more tonight anyway. I'm wiped out from all this excitement."

"Oh, Theo, are you sure?" Sage felt drawn to the letters, to the woman who'd written them. She felt a strange and powerful sense of camaraderie with Jenny. "How about you, Caitlin? Maybe I should wait until you're done."

"Absolutely not. There's plenty for both of us, and I'm just as tired as Theo. I know I'll be asleep the moment my head hits the pillow."

"Thank you. It's like reading a fascinating book that you can't bear to put down, isn't it?" She kissed both Caitlin and Theo.

"See you in the morning, dear," Caitlin said. "Ben should be calling sometime tomorrow to tell us they've arrived safely."

Sage agreed. "He promised he would. I only hope it won't be in the middle of the night. He tends to forget about time differences."

It wouldn't have mattered that night, however. Ben didn't call, but if he had, Sage would have been awake. It was after two by the time she set the letters aside and turned out the light. She'd laughed out loud at times, and at other times she couldn't hold back the sobs that Jenny's words roused in her.

Over the next three days, Sage read her way through the entire bundle. The later letters had been written when Jenny lived right here at Raven Lodge—called the Big House in those days, by the workers in the cannery.

It was exciting and a little eerie for Sage, thinking of this other woman sitting with her writing box, perhaps at the old oak table in the kitchen, or at the ornate little maple writing desk in the corner of the living room. Several times Sage found herself glancing over her shoulder, thinking that she'd caught a glimpse of Jenny's ghost out of the corner of her eye.

Jenny's accounts of everyday life here were riveting, but it was the earlier story of her time in Dawson that fascinated Sage. The hardships the poor woman had endured were difficult to even imagine.

Out of all the letters, the one that had the most profound effect on Sage was the one in which Jenny wrote, with brutal honesty, about the tragic love affair with her brother-in-law, Robert, and the terrible quarrel that caused the fatal schism between William and his twin.

Dearest Papa, Jenny began, as she always did.

I hardly know how to put these words on paper, I am so mortified. But I know I must. I've done a terrible thing, and the consequences will likely bring me back to Scotland, a divorced woman. I make no excuses for myself, dear Papa. But neither will I allow my husband to make me totally responsible for what was at least partially his doing.

As you know, William has seldom been home in the past months. His work consumes him, and the distance between us is measured not only in miles. We have grown apart. William blames me still for

Jamie's death, and cannot find it in his heart to
forgive me. I long for another child, but with William
living so far away, that hope is futile.

He's insisted Robert stay here in Dawson to care
for me, and a kinder, more generous and caring
friend I could not find. I should have guessed that
Robert was developing feelings for me other than
those of family, but I was too lost in my own despair
to notice. As I told you in a previous letter, Mae and
her family had to leave because of Carl's poor health,
so I have been more alone than ever these past
months. I mourn my poor wee lost son daily, hourly,
and I cannot seem to regain my former health or
lightness of heart.

I told you once of Kitty Fitzgerald and her dislike
of me. I believe she is enamored of Robert, who will
have nothing to do with her, and consequently she is
jealous. She took note of the many kindnesses Robert
paid me, and she secretly wrote to William, telling
him that my relationship with his brother was that of
lovers. Which, at that time, it was most certainly not.

Sage could feel the tension in every word. It wasn't
hard to guess what was coming next, and the hairs on her
arms stood up as she read on.

But there came one night, Papa, when I was totally
desolate, and Robert expressed his feelings for me.
I was too hungry for human comfort to resist, and
William arrived home to find us in a most compro-
mising situation. There was a horrible fight. I believed that William was about to kill his brother, and

it was only with the most extreme difficulty I managed to prevent him. Robert has now left Dawson, going to far-off Australia, and I have told William I am leaving him, coming home to Scotland. His rage is all-consuming. But, Papa, please don't be concerned about my safety. Although he castigates me with words, William has not harmed me physically.

The only thing that comforts me is the thought of seeing you all again.

I will write soon and tell you which boat I shall be on.

A storm of emotions rolled over Sage as she read Jenny's tragic confession. Her loneliness, her sorrow and the emotional coldness of self-righteous William touched Sage deeply. No wonder Jenny had turned to Robert.

And through the cruelest twist of fate, she'd become pregnant that night, with Robert's child, who became Theo's father, Bruce—who was also Ben's grandfather.

Sage wondered what Ben would say when he heard about this long-ago scandal. She felt a little guilty, because the letters had taken her attention entirely away from her husband and the concerns she had about their marriage.

But she doubted he was spending much time thinking about her, either.

So far he'd called only once, to say that he and Oliver had arrived safely and were about to go out hunting with their native guide. The connection had been noisy, and after a few hurried sentences, Ben ended the call.

As usual, Sage was sitting on the dock early the next morning, enjoying the sun and the morning solitude along with her coffee.

She'd finished reading the last of the letters and she was thinking about them.

Sage wasn't sure how she felt about William. He sounded self-centered and judgmental. But Jenny was an extraordinary woman. And even long after her death, she was an inspiration and a comfort. Sage's own concerns about her husband and her marriage seemed less urgent now, after reading about Jenny's amazing life.

Enjoying her reverie, Sage felt a stab of resentment when Grace came walking along the dock. Grace was still not speaking to her.

Sage did her best to swallow her dislike. She manufactured a smile and said, "Morning, Grace."

"I need to talk to you," the woman blurted in a surly tone.

"Sure. Sit down." Sage gestured at the other lawn chair. She knew she didn't sound overly polite.

The other woman shook her head. "I'll stand, this won't take long."

It didn't, but by the time Grace finished what she had to say and walked away, Sage felt as if a bomb had exploded, shattering the world she thought she knew.

All that day, Sage felt as if the part of her that could feel emotional pain was far away, observing the calm way she worked at the computer, politely answered phone calls, and talked reasonably enough with relatives and guests. Somehow, she managed to act as if nothing at all was wrong, but that was because she really wasn't there.

Just before lunch, Ben phoned from Tanzania, and she blurted out what Grace had said.

"She's lying," he said in a vehement tone. She heard voices in the background, laughter, a male voice calling

Ben's name, and he said in a rush, "I can't talk now, there's people around. I'll call later. Don't be paranoid about this, it's nothing. I love you, Sage." And he hung up.

Paranoid? Nothing? Suddenly all her frozen emotions unthawed, and she was so furious with Ben her entire body shook with it. How dare he brush her off this way? But she knew why. Ben was a control freak; he'd talk to her when it suited him and not a moment sooner.

She couldn't sit still, so she went outside and attacked the rocky earth at the side of her house where Ben had promised to dig her a little garden. Except he'd never gotten around to it.

She kept frantically busy, all the while planning what to say to him, but he hadn't called back by midnight, and Sage finally had a bath and turned out the light. She didn't think she'd be able to sleep, but she fell into an exhausted stupor. At three forty-five when the phone rang, she was in the midst of a confused nightmare.

She snatched the mobile off its stand and sat up. In a sleep-blurred voice she said, "Ben? Ben, it's the middle of the night here—"

But it wasn't him. At first she had trouble understanding the man on the phone. His accent was pronounced. He explained that he was a police officer, and it finally registered what he was telling her. Ben had been shot in a hunting accident.

After he'd repeated everything twice, answered her stunned questions and finally ended the connection, Sage sat on the edge of her king-size bed in the balmy Alaskan summer night, shivering in her white eyelet nightgown.

She stared in horror at the telephone that had dragged her out of one nightmare and into another. She clutched the piece of yellow paper where she'd scribbled names and numbers during the call.

She had to phone Caitlin and Theo, but for a long moment, she couldn't remember her in-laws' phone number, as familiar to her as her own name. Her brain wouldn't cooperate. Her breath was coming in short bursts, her heart was drumming a terrified tattoo inside her chest. It was her fingers that finally found the rhythm and somehow pressed the right keys.

On the third ring, her mother-in-law's voice, thick with sleep, responded.

"Caitlin, it's—it's me." Sage had to gulp in air before she could continue, and her voice trembled, the words coming out in short bursts.

"Caitlin, I just got a call from a po-police officer in Tanzania. Ben's—oh my God, Caitlin, Ben's been shot. He's alive, but he's not conscious. He was—the man said Ben was—was shot in—in the head. He's in a hospital in Dar es Salaam."

Caitlin made a wordless sound of shock and horror, and in the background, Sage heard Theo asking in a sleepy voice what was wrong, who was on the phone.

"Sage. It's Sage, she says—" The rest was lost in a sudden burst of sobs, an indecipherable babble of shock and horror as the phone passed from one to the other.

Theo said into the receiver, "Can you come over, dear?"

"I'll be right there." Sage hung up and pulled on the first clothes she touched, a green terry tracksuit she'd worn the evening before when she'd hosed down the float boats. It was still damp around the sleeves and ankles, but she didn't care. As she crammed the piece of paper into the pocket of her jacket, her glance came to rest on the wedding photo she kept on the dresser.

For a moment, she stood absolutely still, hand pressed to her heart, staring at it. It had been taken four years ago. She'd been twenty-six, Ben thirty-four. Her dark brown curls had been much shorter then, hugging her skull. Her body was slimmer than it was now, the cream satin clinging to slender curves. She was looking up at her new husband with utter adoration, blue eyes feasting on his face.

A half sob caught in her throat. The young woman in the photo was gone forever, ideals smashed, hopes and dreams abandoned somewhere by the wayside. Suddenly she felt old, as if a lifetime had gone by since the photo was taken.

Ben hadn't changed at all, she was sure of that. Physically and emotionally, he was still exactly the same as he looked in the picture—tall and muscular, impossibly good-looking. He towered over her, even though she was wearing heels. He was looking at her with the satisfied smile of a man who'd gotten exactly what he wanted.

She turned the photo facedown, hurried down the stairs, pulled on her track shoes, and, belatedly remembering her sleeping guests, she closed the door of her home softly after her.

Sage sprinted toward the Lodge. Normally, she used the back door that led into the kitchen and laundry, but now she took the wide log steps at the front two at a time and wrenched open the heavy front door, desperate to reach Ben's parents. She'd never felt more alone, more terrified.

"Sage, honey." Caitlin, her slender body wrapped in a blue terry robe, was just coming down the winding staircase that led to the second floor where she and Theo had their bedroom.

"Come here, sweetheart." Caitlin hurried down the last few steps and wrapped her strong arms around her daughter-in-law. Her long white hair was loose, framing high cheekbones and stricken gray eyes. She was trembling.

Sage felt a measure of comfort as she hugged Caitlin. "I can't believe this," she whispered. "I feel like I'm having the worst nightmare."

"So do I," Caitlin said. "They did say Ben was still alive?"

Sage nodded. "But not conscious."

Caitlin shuddered. "I need to hear all the details, but Theo's coming down, we'll wait for him. Let's go make some coffee."

Sage thought of the major heart attack Theo had barely survived. She prayed this shock wouldn't cause another.

With her arm tight around Sage's waist, Caitlin led the way down the hallway to the back of the house. The big old kitchen had been modernized since William Galloway built this house for Jenny, but in size and character it remained the same—huge, homey, welcoming, the emotional heart of the huge log house.

How many other times had Galloways gathered here to deal with calamity? Repetition didn't make it easier. Sage felt as if she couldn't breathe, as if a vise was squeezing her heart.

Nearly an hour later, Theo once again punched numbers into the phone. He'd already called the hospital in Dar es Salaam, spoken to Ben's doctor, and now he was calling Logan's number in Seattle.

There was a long pause, and then Sage heard Logan's deep voice resonating from the receiver, and she swallowed back tears. Their voices were identical.

"It's your brother, son." Theo relayed the facts in a calm,

steady voice, but Sage could see what it was costing him. His hand was clenched tight around the telephone, his other hand balled into a fist, unconsciously tapping the table.

"You knew Ben was hunting wild buffalo in Africa? He and one of the guides, Oliver Brady, went over six days ago. Well, Ben's been shot, we have no idea how or why. He's in hospital in Dar es Salaam. He's in critical condition, a head wound. I spoke to a doctor there, it doesn't sound as if there's much they can do, there's a lack of equipment and trained surgeons."

Theo listened and nodded. "Please, Logan. As soon as you can. Some of us will have to go over there, bring Ben home. We really need your help."

He listened again, and his tension eased somewhat. "Thanks, son. As soon as you know your flight number, call us.

Caitlin said, "Logan's coming." It wasn't a question, and there was enormous relief in her voice.

"He is." Theo nodded. "As soon as he can get a flight. I'll call Tom now, so he'll be standing by when Logan gets to Anchorage."

Once again, Theo dialed and went through the painful explanations, this time to his brother-in-law. While he was still on the phone, Mavis came bustling into the kitchen.

"What's going on? Why's everybody up so early?"

She looked from one stricken Galloway to the next, and clasped her hands together over her heart. "Oh, my good gracious. What's happened?"

Caitlin got up and wrapped her arms around Mavis, explaining about Ben. Mavis began to sob. Never married herself, she'd known the boys since they were children and

helped Caitlin raise them. Sage knew that Mavis considered Ben and Logan her sons.

"Logan's coming," Caitlin explained, holding her friend
close. "And Theo's calling Tom right now."

"I'd best get some food going, then." Mavis blew her
nose and wiped her eyes; patting Caitlin's back she then
headed for the cupboards, her practical nature taking over.
"Everybody'll need food." She began to gather bowls and
flour. "I'll put up a batch of biscuits. There's pancake batter
in the fridge and yeast dough for cinnamon rolls. I'll get
bacon and ham sliced, and make fruit salad. And then a pot
of soup for later, when Logan gets here."

Sage suspected that if any of the others felt remotely as
she did, no one was going to want to eat much. Her
stomach was verging on nausea. But she also knew that
food was Mavis's only way of helping, of feeling useful.

Sage wished there was something similar that would
ease her own anxiety. In a short while, she made her way
back to her house. She needed to shower and dress, but she
also needed some time alone to try and make sense of the
news they'd just learned.

Chapter Four

At Anchorage International Airport, Logan Galloway strode quickly past the glass case containing the ten-foot-tall Alaskan brown bear. His eyes scanned the waiting area for his uncle.

"Just behind you, son."

Logan whirled around. Tom was limping toward him. Logan hurried over to him.

"Good to see you, young man." Tom wasn't the hugging sort, but he took Logan's right hand in a crushing grip and thumped his shoulder several times, his grizzled, handsome face somber, eyes worried.

"Hell of a thing," he said.

"Any news of Ben?" Logan had raced to catch the 10:00 a.m. Alaska Airlines flight out of Seattle, and he'd been on the plane three and a half hours. His imagination had run rampant the entire time.

It was a huge relief when Tom shook his head. "Not that I know of. Your dad phoned the hospital just before I left. There'd been no change in his condition at that point. You got any checked luggage?"

Logan shook his head. "Only these." He'd stuffed a random selection of clothes into a carry-on and a backpack.

"Good. We'll catch a cab back over to the float dock and be on our way."

Outside the airport, Logan slipped his sunglasses on. It was an Alaskan blue-sky day, hot and clear.

"Look at this sunshine. It was raining in Seattle when I left," he told Tom as they climbed into a cab.

"Time you came back to God's country, son," Tom growled after he told the driver where to take them. "Never did understand why you left in the first place. Lots of work for good lawyers right here at home."

It was a complex issue, not one Logan was about to get into with his uncle, or anyone else for that matter. "How's Dad holding up?"

"As well as can be expected, I guess. He doesn't look any hell, but he's still recovering from that heart attack. He'll be glad to see you—it's been a while."

Logan knew Tom was reprimanding him. He'd only been back to the Lodge once since Theo's heart attack the previous autumn. He'd flown up in March, for his parents' fortieth wedding anniversary. He'd planned to come back at Christmas, but Beth had bought them both tickets to Mexico, a Christmas surprise, and they'd gone to Cancun instead.

And that had been the end of that romance. He just couldn't seem to sustain a relationship.

"You don't have the faintest idea how to really love anybody," she'd screamed at him. She hadn't meant the physical part. He was pretty secure about that; he'd had lots of practice. Nope, she was talking about the emotional component. Which was all mixed up with his reasons for not coming home as often as he could have.

The flight from Anchorage to the town of Valdez took just under an hour, with another ten minutes flying to get to the Lodge. Tom set the plane down in the protected bay with all the casual finesse that years of flying afforded, taxiing up to the dock and then killing the motor.

As he tossed his bags up and jumped from the wing to the dock, Logan could see his father hurrying down the steps toward them, and there was a moment of shock when he saw how old Theo looked.

Theo grabbed the rope before Logan could reach it, securing the plane to the steel stanchion before he turned to his son.

"Logan," he said, wrapping his arms around him.

"Dad." Logan felt tears sting his eyes as he hugged his father, aware of the older man's fragility. Theo, who'd always been robust, was bone thin, and the arms around Logan lacked the hard muscle that had always been there. Logan had to swallow the lump in his throat.

Tom climbed up beside them. "Anything new on Ben?"

Logan held his breath, relieved when Theo shook his head.

"He's the same, I've been calling every couple of hours. This Dr. Shulani seems like a good guy—he gave me his cell phone number. But I get the impression there's not much they can do for Ben except keep him comfortable."

"We'll go and get him. You and me, Dad. I've got a travel agent making reservations for us."

Theo picked up Logan's carry-on bag, refusing to give

it up even when Logan objected. "You need a passport to get into Africa, don't you?"

"Yeah, you do." Logan shouldered his backpack and followed the two men up the stairs to the Lodge, noticing that even Tom deliberately slowed his pace to accommodate Theo. "You've got a passport, haven't you, Dad?"

Theo shook his head. "I've always meant to get them for your mother and I, but we never really needed them and I kept putting it off. We've never traveled outside the States. That one time to Mexico, but they accepted birth certificates. Sage has a passport. It's probably better if she goes with you anyhow, Logan."

What the hell could he say to that? He wanted to say no, he wasn't going anywhere with Sage, but what logical reason could he give?

Logan looked up at the Lodge. His mother was waiting outside the door, Mavis at her side. And just behind them was Sage, long dark curls gleaming in the sunlight.

Even now, with catastrophe spreading its ugly wings over his family, Logan couldn't help the violent emotion that boiled through him at the sight of her.

He took the wide steps two at a time, catching his mother up in his arms and holding her close for a long moment. He felt her tears on his face, and emotion welled up in him, as well. He swallowed hard, set her down and hugged Mavis, and then held out a hand to Sage.

"Logan. God, Logan, I'm so glad you're here." She ignored his extended hand and moved into his arms. She was short, five-six-and-a-half, and he had to bend his six-two frame to accommodate her. He let his arms close around her, shutting his eyes, drinking in the strawberry scent of shampoo in long, wild curls, alarmed by the feel of her voluptuous body pressed against his own. She was trembling violently. Her huge sapphire-blue eyes reminded him of a frightened doe.

"It'll be okay," he said inanely, letting her go long before he wanted to, wishing there was something else to say, or do, for her. For all of them.

"Let's all go inside and figure this thing out," he suggested.

When they were all seated at the kitchen table, Theo announced, "Logan's arranging for plane tickets for Dar es Salaam, and you'll go with him, Sage."

Logan saw the shock register on her face, but she didn't say anything.

Theo went on, "The two of you will bring Ben back. Tom and I will figure out how best to do that."

Tom nodded. "Maybe the military's the way to go. I'll call some people I know." Tom was a veteran of the Vietnam War. His limp was the legacy of that war, a piece of shrapnel that had permanently crippled him.

Mouth suddenly dry, Logan swallowed the first mouthful of food and realized he wasn't hungry anymore. He looked over at Sage. His fears seemed to be reflected in her eyes.

Africa was far away. His brother was unconscious, in critical condition. It was going to take a series of miracles, a small fortune and the most incredible luck to bring him back alive. He met Sage's gaze, and he knew she understood how slim their chances really were.

He glanced from her to his parents, and the hope and trust he saw reflected on their faces nearly broke his heart. He'd do his best, but who knew if his best would be nearly good enough to bring his brother safely home?

* * *

Two frantic days later, Logan and Sage were in the International Departure level of Seattle's SeaTac Airport, waiting to board a flight to London for the second leg of their grueling forty-three-hour journey.

It was midnight, and their flight left at 1:00 a.m. Logan had gone in search of juice, and Sage smiled up at him as he handed her a foam cup and a small bottle.

"You've probably saved me from being taken away by security. Any more coffee would send me screaming down the corridor."

"Me, too." Logan twisted the cap from his own juice bottle and tipped it up, relishing the cool, tangy taste. "It feels strange to be in Seattle and not be going home."

"I can only imagine."

"You like Seattle?"

"I really do. Ben and I have spent quite a lot of time here, at trade fairs and wildlife conferences." Rich color bloomed in her cheeks, and she looked embarrassed.

Logan guessed that Ben and Sage had been in Seattle much more often than he knew. The fact that his brother hadn't phoned him or come to visit was a telling comment on the way their relationship had deteriorated.

Their estrangement was partly due to their differing views on wildlife and conservation. Ben traveled the world in pursuit of big game. Logan worked for and supported organizations opposed to hunting. Despite their differences, it hurt Logan, knowing his brother had been to Seattle and deliberately chosen not to contact him.

He felt bad for making her uncomfortable all over again. Time to change the subject. "This is going to be the longest

I've ever spent on a plane. I've flown to Mexico, but that's the extent of my out-of-country adventures."

"The farthest I've been is New York." Her eyes had a distant look when she added softly, "That's where I met Ben."

Logan remembered. Ben had told him about that meeting the first time he'd introduced Sage, two days before their wedding. They'd met at the New York trade fair two months before they married.

Logan had come home for the wedding, wearing his lawyer's mantle and planning to caution his brother about marrying someone he'd only known for such a short time. After all, Ben already had an ex-wife and two daughters, costing him big-time in alimony and child support. He could ill afford another matrimonial mistake. Logan had had all the arguments prepared, and then Ben introduced Sage. Logan wondered what had taken Ben eight weeks to make up his mind.

"That's us, finally." Their flight was being called. Sage got to her feet, stuffing the magazines Logan had bought her into her carry-on bag. "Next stop, London, England," she said, trying her best to be upbeat.

Logan followed her down the tunnel and onto the plane.

Sixteen hours later, Sage came out of the restroom at London's Heathrow and walked wearily over to the waiting area, where the flight for Dar es Salaam would be departing in forty minutes. The thought of spending another twenty-six hours on a plane made her want to lie down on the carpeted floor and weep with exhaustion.

Logan looked as tired as she felt. He was sprawled in one of the chairs beside their carry-on bags, long legs extended, head resting uncomfortably on the chair back, muscular arms crossed on his chest. He looked so very much like Ben when he was asleep. Sage stood and looked at him, and her heart ached for her husband.

Logan opened his eyes and sat up, blinking sleepily and then smiling at her. When he was awake, the differences between him and Ben were obvious. Logan was consistently good-natured, much more tolerant and relaxed than Ben. He was also much less outgoing, content to stay at Sage's side. Ben would be striding around the airport, striking up conversations with strangers, complaining about the long waits between flights.

Logan patted the pocket that held his cell phone. "I tried to get through to the Lodge again, but no luck. The operator's going to call me back if he can get through before we board."

They needed to hear how Ben was doing. And Caitlin and Theo would be anxious about the two of them, as well.

Logan said, "Maybe we can sleep better this time." They'd both been unable to do more than catnap on the incoming flight.

Logan's cell phone rang, and he quickly answered the call. It took a few moments for the connection to be made, and then he said, "Hey, Dad. Yeah, we're at Heathrow, just waiting to board the flight. How's Ben?"

Sage clenched her fists and silently prayed.

"No change?" Logan was repeating what his dad said for her benefit. "Has anyone heard from Oliver?" He listened and then shook his head at Sage. "It's weird that the guy doesn't phone and say what happened. Anything new from the police?" He listened and again shook his head at Sage. "We'll try and call you the moment we land. Yeah, I'll tell her." His voice roughened. "I love you, too. And Mom." He closed the phone.

"Everyone sends their love."

A wave of homesickness washed over Sage, as well as a sense of anxiety. Had she left something important undone at the Lodge?

Sage did all the bookings. She'd had to spend hours with Caitlin and Theo, going over everything, making sure guest transportation was arranged from airports, updating them on the various computer Web sites that brought in much of their business and needed daily response to queries.

There'd been packing to do, and the phones at the Lodge rang continuously as news spread about Ben's situation. Theo and Caitlin were old-timers in the area, and their friends and neighbors wanted to offer support.

The first few hours on the flight to London had felt like a blessed reprieve. She'd longed to sleep, but she couldn't shut her mind off enough. She was as tired as she'd ever been—physically, mentally, emotionally exhausted. And her brother-in-law was being so kind and thoughtful and considerate it was all she could do not to burst into tears.

"You want anything before we board?" Logan got up and stretched, groaning as cramped muscles responded.

"Bottled water, please. Lots of it. They say it's one way to avoid jet lag. Of course nobody mentions lineups at the washrooms as a result."

"I'll bribe the stewardess to reserve one just for you. Besides, we're in business class, our sort of people don't pee as much as the hoi polloi in the back of the bus. Be right back."

She was smiling as she watched him walk away, but then she sank down in the chair as utter despair washed over her. She and Logan had carefully avoided saying it, but he, too, must wonder if Ben was going to make it. If he did, if they managed to bring him back alive, if medical intervention could remove the bullet in his brain, if he came out of it with all his faculties—if all that happened, then what would become of her marriage? She'd somehow managed to put her conversation with Grace into a locked compartment, but now it sprang out and enveloped her in despair.

God, she felt as if her brain were exploding. She needed to talk to someone she could trust. She could trust Logan, she knew that. If ever anyone was trustworthy, it was her brother-in-law. But could she bring herself to confide the most intimate details of her life with Ben's brother?

Chapter Five

They'd been in the air five hours. The food service was over, the movie finished, and the overhead lights dimmed so passengers could sleep.

Sage flipped through one magazine after the other without a single item registering. The events of the past few days were tumbling through her brain faster than the pages she turned.

"Wanna talk?" Logan's soft, deep voice brought her out of her waking nightmare. "I'm not going to sleep, and it looks as if you're not, either."

"Can't. For the first time in my life, I understand insomniacs." Sage impatiently shoved a thick handful of curly hair back and rubbed her scalp. Her head felt itchy, her eyes dry, her clothing soiled even though she'd changed at the airport in London.

"You're worried about Ben." Logan shifted in his seat, trying to find a comfortable spot for denim-clad legs too long for the space. "Me, too. We don't always see eye to eye, but he's my brother. More than that, he's my twin." He paused for a heartbeat. "And your husband." He turned a little more toward her, his voice suddenly intense. "The thing I don't get, Sage, is why Oliver isn't in touch. He's Ben's friend—why else would he be along on this safari? And even if the bullet was from his gun, it had to have been an accident. Right? So why isn't he phoning home, telling Mom and Dad what actually happened?"

Sage turned and looked out the window, blind to the darkness and the stars. She desperately wanted to tell him, but she couldn't compartmentalize it. One truth led straight to the next. What the heck, it was all going to come out soon anyway—pregnancy wasn't a thing you could disguise for long. Her indrawn breath was shaky.

"Grace Fulton says she's pregnant with Ben's baby." There, it was out. Saying the words eased something inside of her, and she sighed and felt her body's stiffness relax just a little.

"What?" Logan's horrified exclamation had the staid businessman in the seat across from them glancing over, the first time his attention had strayed from his computer.

Sage waited until he looked away before she spoke again. "She told me a few days ago. She's insisting on DNA testing through amniocentesis, so it's pretty hard not to believe her."

Logan used a four-letter epithet. Sage gave a sad smile. "Yeah, that's about how it would have happened, all right."

"Sorry. It's just—and of course Oliver knows?"

"I assume he knows Grace is pregnant. Whether he

knows it's not his baby, I can't say. See, Oliver wasn't meant to go on this trip with Ben, but the guy who had the reservation backed out at the last minute. He got shingles and couldn't travel. So Ben invited Oliver. He told me it was because Oliver and Grace were having problems and he figured Oliver needed to get away for a while. Put some distance between him and the problem, was how Ben phrased it. Now I wonder exactly what problem he really meant."

"God almighty." Logan shook his head. "Did you get a chance to ask Ben about Grace?"

"Not before he left, I didn't know then. But I did when he called me, after they'd arrived in Dar es Salaam. Grace had just told me, and I was—" Sage shook her head, and the memory of that day made her feel sick all over again. "I was—I was furious. Hurt, and betrayed, and so mad at him I could have—well, you fill in the blanks. So the minute Ben phoned, I told him what she'd told me. That she was pregnant with his baby, that she was havin DNA testing done to prove it. That—that he'd told her he was—" Sage's voice faltered, and Logan swore under his breath. He reached over and took her hand, lacing her fingers with his.

"Grace said that Ben told her he was in love with her."

She could see the effect her words were having on Logan. A muscle in his jaw clenched tight, and she could feel his anger escalating.

"That part at least is utter bullshit," he growled. "Ben loves you."

Sage was grateful for his support, but she didn't want to argue. The truth was, she and Ben had been having problems for some time now. Although he never said so, Sage knew he blamed her for not being able to get pregnant. He was increasingly intolerant of the procedures at the fertility clinic.

And there'd been women, flirtations with female fishing clients. When she confronted him, Ben had laughed off her suspicions, putting them down to an overactive imagination, plain old jealousy. And maybe he was right; maybe she was insecure.

Except that their sex life, once so passionate, had dwindled away to almost nothing in the past few months. Which made the whole baby issue laughable—except that she spent a lot of time crying instead. And Ben hated tears.

She couldn't tell Logan all that, how could she? He'd probably die of embarrassment if she started blabbing about periods and sex and ovulation and hormones. And damned if she was about to reveal Ben's flirting and his lack of interest in her. She had some pride left.

Had her husband fallen in love with Grace? Sage honestly couldn't say one way or the other. Ben was Ben, charismatic, changeable, as quick to anger as he was to laughter. Women loved him. He was incredibly generous, fun to be with and kind when it suited him. A natural leader whom other men looked up to. And utterly ruthless when he wanted something.

"She could be lying about everything," Logan said. "In fact, she probably is."

"I don't think so," Sage said. "I did at first, but the thing about the DNA scares me."

"Did you agree to it?"

Sage nodded. "Of course, I insisted on it. I gave her some hairs from Ben's brush, she went into Anchorage for amnio. The test will take a week or two, there's a new lab in the city. But the other thing that convinced me she was telling the truth was—well, she knew things about Ben."

Logan frowned and shook his head. "What sort of things?"

Sage shivered. "Details about his body. Things she couldn't have known unless they'd been intimate." She recited them exactly the way Grace had. The words were burned into her brain. "He has a scar near his groin, from an accident when he was a kid. There's a mole high up on the inside of his right thigh. His appendix scar is low down and jagged, it didn't heal properly." She was near tears, and her voice betrayed her. "He has this—this weird birthmark on his tailbone, shaped like a hand—"

"Don't." Logan spoke gently. "Don't torment yourself with it."

"I can't seem to stop," she whispered, letting out a shuddering breath. "I try, but its right there, every time I close my eyes, every time I think about him. And there's the baby to consider, as well. If it's his, he'll want it nearby. He'll want to raise it at the Lodge. He's paranoid about his kids moving away."

"What makes you think that?"

"Remember two years ago when Jill fell for that doctor from San Diego?"

"I remember Mom saying something. I didn't pay much attention."

"Well, the guy asked Jill to marry him and move south with the girls. Jill really wanted to go, but Ben told her he'd go to court and fight for full custody if she tried it. He said that he'd get it because courts paid attention to where the kids have family and a support system. He said he had the money for a drawn-out court battle and Jill didn't. He said you'd handle the case for him. He told her he'd make it next to impossible for Jill to ever see her girls again."

"And Jill caved." It wasn't a question. Of course Logan knew his brother.

"Yeah, obviously. She stayed in Valdez. I guess the guy has a lucrative practice in San Diego and wasn't willing to start all over again in Valdez. They broke up. She's still bitter over it."

Sage had only been married two years when that happened. Jill had been downright nasty to her every time they met—and still was—but in that instance, Sage had been strongly on her side. It shocked her to learn that the rugged, handsome man she'd married could be that cold and ruthless to his ex-wife. For the first time, but not the last, she saw the dark side of the man she'd married, and it had bothered her.

"Jill's not my favorite person, but she's a good mother," Sage went on, adding almost as an afterthought, "And Ben's a good father, too." *When he has time, and the inclination.* She realized that Ben wouldn't make a good single dad, and that thought always disturbed her. "He wants his kids near him. And he very much wants a son. We've been trying, but it hasn't happened."

Logan was silent for so long she turned to him.

He looked stricken. "God, I'm so sorry, Sage." The words were heartfelt, and she wondered how much of what she'd left out he suspected and was apologizing for.

Which was crazy, because none of it was his fault.

Lost in troubled thoughts, Logan stared out the window. When he turned to Sage again he found that she'd fallen asleep. Her head rested against the window, bent at an unnatural angle. He watched her a moment.

Her flawless skin was unnaturally pale except for the

dark circles under her eyes. Her arms were crossed on her torso, holding the airline blanket against her body like a suit of armor.

Remembering how cold she'd been, he tucked his own blanket close around her and then gently moved her head over so that it rested on his shoulder.

She sighed in her sleep and turned slightly toward him, her soft breath tickling his neck. Her hair spread in a wildwood tangle across his shirtsleeve. He could smell the faintest whiff of strawberries from her shampoo.

He didn't want to even imagine what awaited them in Dar es Salaam. Back in Valdez, there were monumental issues that would have to be faced. Calamity swirled around the two of them, but for these few moments in time, it couldn't reach them. Sage was asleep, and holding her, Logan was as much at peace as it was possible to be — knowing the circumstances.

Chapter Six

Many hours later, Sage stared out the airplane window as Dar es Salaam appeared beneath them, a sprawling morass of buildings arranged around a blue-black lagoon.

"Finally, we're here." Logan peered over her shoulder as the earth rose up to meet them and the plane's landing gear groaned into place. "Shall we check into the hotel first and then go to the hospital?"

"*Please.* I can't face another hour without a hot shower. We can call Theo and Caitlin from the hotel, they'll be wondering how and where we are." Logan had tried to place calls during the flight, but they wouldn't go through. Now that they were almost at the end of this journey, the nerves that had been blunted by the monotony of the endless trip once again twisted her belly into knots and made her throat dry.

"I hope Ben's awake by now."

He was somewhere nearby, in the Aga Khan Hospital. She'd thought she'd want to know how he was the moment they landed. Now, for some reason she was terrified. She wanted to put off knowing.

The plane taxied down the runway and came to a halt. After a time, the seat belt sign went off. Weary travelers stretched and hauled down luggage from the overhead compartments. Logan retrieved theirs and then they were outside.

The smell was heavy and foreign, thick and so hot and airless Sage gasped for breath, and the edges of her vision blurred. Dazed, she stumbled, and Logan dropped a bag and grabbed her arm.

"Hey, lean on me." He looked around for a place to sit, but there was none. "Hang in there, just concentrate on that shower."

Sage was so dizzy she was sure she was going to faint. "Take deep breaths. Give me that bag." Logan steadied her, picked up the small travel bag she carried and transferred it to his left shoulder so the right was free to support her. Holding her tight against his side, he got them inside the terminal, which was air-conditioned.

They had only their carry-on luggage. The customs lineup was long, but it moved quickly. Logan had the necessary visas. Keeping a close eye on her, one arm around her waist, he hustled them through.

Still feeling as if everything was far away and happening to someone else, Sage staggered into the cab Logan hailed, heading for the Holiday Inn where his efficient travel agent had booked them rooms.

"This is so stupid, having the vapors like some Victorian maiden," she joked weakly.

"And me fresh out of smelling salts," he said. He was holding her hand again, fingers interlaced with hers, and Sage imagined some of his strength seeping into her palm.

The moment they were in their suite, Sage closed the door of her bedroom, stripped off her clothes and turned the shower on full.

Hot water was seriously underrated as a luxury. She moaned with pleasure, shampooed and rinsed and then just stood there, absorbing the sensory comfort into her pores. At last she climbed out. Rubbing her freshly shampooed hair with a towel, wrapped in one of the hotel's exotically colored cotton robes, Sage opened the bathroom door and smiled at Logan, who was standing by their bags, which had been dumped in the middle of the room.

"I used all the hot water, sorry about that. I actually feel almost human again—" she began, stopping when the expression on his face registered. "Logan? Oh, God, Logan, what? What is it, what's happened?"

Instead of answering he came over to her and gently guided her to a chair. She sank into it, holding tight to the wooden arms, staring at him, waiting, knowing somewhere deep in her gut what he was going to say.

"I just called the hospital and talked to the doctor," Logan said. "Ben—" He swallowed hard. "Sage, Ben died two hours ago. He never regained consciousness."

"No." She shook her wet head, sending drops of water flying. "*Noooo,* that can't be right." But the desolate, stricken look on his face told her it was. She couldn't get her breath, and then she let out a howl.

"He's gone, Sage. I can't believe it, either." Logan fell to his knees and took both of her hands in his. She could see that he was struggling with emotion, fighting back tears. She knew she should feel something similar, but she didn't. She was hollow, and again she had the feeling this was all happening to someone else.

Theo and Caitlin. Dear God, they'd have to be told.

"Did you—were you able to get through to the Lodge?"

He shook his head. "Not yet. I can't yet. I'm trying to— to get my mind around this first. I'll call them in a few minutes." He bowed his dark head, and she could see his wide shoulders shaking. He let her hands go and put them over his face, stumbling as he got to his feet. "He's my twin." The words held agony. "How come I didn't know? Identical twins are supposed to know when one dies. But I didn't know, I didn't feel it. I didn't even feel him go."

"Logan. Logan, listen to me. It's not your fault." She got up and put her arms around him, repeating what he'd said to her not so long ago. "Logan, I'm so sorry. I'm sorry."

She held him, trying to figure out what this meant. Her husband was dead, the charismatic man she'd fallen in love with, married too quickly, thought she knew. She'd believed until lately they could work out their differences, grow old together. She'd longed to have his children. So many dreams, all gone.

"It's not fair," she whispered through frozen lips. "It's not fair. You and Ben—you're both only thirty-eight." It was too young to die. He had no right leaving her like this.

Shock and disbelief gave way to outrage. He had no right to do this to any of them, especially to her. He was leaving her with questions unanswered, problems to deal with that were *his* to solve—problems he'd created.

She needed him to tell her the truth about Grace, one way or the other. Closure, they called it. She wanted closure; she needed to know whether or not he'd had sex with Grace, gotten her pregnant. Whether—whether he'd told the other woman he loved her, as she claimed.

"Damn him. Damn him for doing this." Pain twisted in her chest, not the pain of loss for Ben, not yet, but the knowledge that her husband might have turned from her to another woman. "I needed—I needed to talk to him."

The DNA test would tell the scientific truth. What Sage needed was the emotional one, from her husband's lips.

Dead lips. The bastard.

The trembling had begun again, but instead of fear, this time it was anger, dry and hot, like acid in her chest. She pulled away from Logan. She had to move, do something, or she'd burn up with rage. She stomped unseeing through the small living room, into the far bedroom. She closed the door and leaned against it.

She heard the bathroom door close behind Logan and a moment later the shower started. She felt such compassion for him. And the most overwhelming, all-consuming rage at Ben.

Sage wrapped her arms around her torso, trying to contain the emotion that made her want to smash something. She opened the door again and paced up and down until Logan came out, wearing only his jeans.

He went over to the discarded travel bags and knelt, his wide bare shoulders and hair-dusted chest so dangerously familiar to her. He and Ben had both been blessed with beautiful bodies—lean, muscular, perfectly proportioned. She used to watch Ben dressing or undressing and think with a sense of awe, *He's gorgeous, this man. And he's mine.* What a fool she'd been to think marriage equaled fidelity.

"It's such a damned waste." She meant the love she'd felt for him. She didn't even realize she'd spoken aloud until Logan's head turned toward her, dark hair wet, eyes red and stark and empty.

"Yeah, it is a waste." He yanked out a clean blue button-down, got to his feet and thrust his arms through the short sleeves. "I'll call Mom and Dad now."

He sat down on the edge of the bed and began the tedious process with operators, and in the stark lines of his face Sage could see his heartbreak, the effort he was making to be strong for the people they both loved. And for her. He'd taken such care of her, every minute on this long, fruitless journey.

She sat down beside him, and he looked into her eyes and transferred the phone so he could grip her hand. She laced her fingers through his, and when the telephone contact succeeded, she felt every muscle in his body tense, anticipating the agony that her beloved in-laws would endure when they heard.

Sage thought of them, of the unconditional love they'd always given her, and pain lanced through her, empathy for their pain.

"Dad." Logan cleared his throat. "Yeah, we're here in Dar es Salaam, in the hotel, we got in about an hour ago. Dad—"

But Sage could hear Theo's deep, anxious voice, asking about Ben. She heard Logan swallow, saw his knuckles whiten as he clenched the phone.

"Dad, Ben died a couple of hours ago." His voice was thick, his face contorted, and the hand holding hers squeezed hard enough to make her wince. "Yeah, I know. I feel the same way, Dad." He bent forward and rocked a little to ease the pain. "No, the doctor said he didn't regain consciousness."

He cleared his throat and closed his eyes. "We're

going over there soon, I'll call you later today." He listened again, and Sage felt the tremor that went through him. "I love you, too. And Mom. Tell her—my God, Dad, there's nothing to say that helps, is there? Except that I love her."

Theo spoke again, but Sage couldn't hear the words. She was imagining the raw agony in the people she loved at the Lodge.

Logan said, "She's right here beside me. Yeah, I'll take good care of her. I'll tell her you said so. Bye, Dad."

Logan swallowed convulsively as he hung up the phone. He straightened his shoulders, but it was several minutes before he could speak.

"Tough one," he said in a gravelly voice, giving her a sad facsimile of a smile. "Dad says to tell you that love never dies."

She nodded. *Not unless it was dead already.* She needed to think about that, figure out whether she still loved Ben. But her in-laws' concern for her touched her heart. Theo and Caitlin were the parents she'd never had. She loved them with everything in her, and she could only guess at the depth of pain and terrible loss they were feeling at this moment.

"I feel so bad for them. But selfishly, I'm glad you're with me, Logan. I don't know what I'd do if I was here alone."

"I'd never have let you come here alone." They sat for a long moment, hand in hand. Sage was the first to move.

"I'll get dressed." What she really felt like doing was crawling into bed and pulling the covers over her head. "I guess we'll have to go to the hospital and—and make—make arrangements."

"To the police station, too." His voice hardened. "I'd very much like to talk to Oliver Brady, and the guide who was there when it happened. I'd like to know exactly what went down. Are you sure you want to come along, Sage? Because there's no real reason for you to go through this. You could stay here and rest."

She narrowed her eyes at him. "I'm coming."

"Okay. Good. I promise you we'll get this over with as fast as we can, Sage, and be on our way back home."

"It can't be too fast for me." Dread and a terrible fear rose in her. Would she be able to get through the next few hours without falling apart?

At the hospital they learned that the police were regarding Ben's death as suspicious, and insisting on an autopsy. Logan asked to see his brother.

"I need to do this by myself," he said to Sage in a stark tone, squeezing her hand in apology just before a nurse led him into a room and closed the door.

Logan didn't come out for some time. When he did, his jaw was set, his eyes closed. She made a move toward the door, and he caught her arm.

"Are you sure, Sage? Because—" He didn't finish.

She gulped and nodded. "I need to." Ben was—he had been—her lover. And, like Logan, she needed to see him. She steeled herself when the nurse led her into the small room and lifted the sheet away, but she could never have prepared herself for the grisly sight.

She gasped and then gagged, sickened by the damage the bullet had done. The room seemed to close in on her. Stunned and horrified, hands clasped over her heart, she looked at the wreckage of the man who had been her husband.

Ben's head was bandaged, but it was all too obvious a part of his skull was missing. Why hadn't they said so? Why hadn't someone told the truth, that a wound like this had to be fatal? It was a miracle he'd stayed alive as long as he had.

She gulped and told herself a person could get used to anything. Hesitantly, she stepped closer and took his hand in hers, the big, calloused hand that had touched her so intimately, so many times. The ring she'd given him at their wedding was still on his left hand. His skin was clammy cold, and the vital essence that had made him Ben was entirely gone. The body underneath the white sheet bore no resemblance to the vibrant Ben she'd known and loved.

She hadn't seen anyone dead before. It was a profound shock, and when she came out of the room she was shaking so hard she could barely walk. She made it into a bathroom, dropped to her knees on the tile floor and was violently sick, throwing up until nothing but bile was left.

"Sage, I'm coming in." Logan opened the door. She was kneeling on the floor, dizzy and disoriented, still sobbing and gagging, and he lifted her, supporting her as she retched, holding her hair back and murmuring wordless comfort into her ear.

When the spasms finally eased he wet a paper towel and clumsily wiped her face. It amazed her that she wasn't embarrassed. He was so matter-of-fact about it all that she couldn't be self-conscious.

"There's a pile of forms you need to sign before we can get out of here. They won't let me do it," he told her, and after a time she managed to get her wits about her and scrawl her name on the dozens of consent forms the administration insisted were necessary.

Through it all, Logan made her take sips of bottled water and when they left for the police station he instructed the taxi driver to cruise the city for an hour, to give her time to recover.

The driver was delighted, driving along narrow, congested streets with horn cheerfully blaring, giving them a singsong travelogue. With the horrible image of Ben's destroyed skull imprinted on her brain, Sage barely noticed the ramshackle colonial-era buildings, some with Moorish influence, complete with shuttered windows and gracious balconies. They rubbed shoulders with ugly modern concrete block monstrosities.

"Kivukoni Front, near harbor, very good for food. You try chicken, rice and *ugali* with sauce," the driver insisted, pointing out one restaurant after the other.

Sage shuddered. Her stomach balked at the thought of food, and she wondered if she'd ever want to eat again. She gave Logan a questioning look and he shook his head.

At the police station, Logan introduced them to the clerk and asked to see the chief. Within minutes, a gigantic African man appeared. He topped Logan's six feet two inches by another half foot, and was easily a hundred pounds heavier. His blue uniform was pristine, and he greeted them graciously, inviting them into his office and offering icy bottles of soda along with his sympathy for their loss.

Logan, polite but direct, said, "We'd like to talk to Oliver Brady. Could you tell us where he is?"

Akello Jumbe's ebony eyes went slowly from one face to the other, searching. Sage stared back at him, wondering what Oliver had said, how much he really knew about the tangled mess Ben had left behind. Had Oliver even known about Grace's pregnancy? It seemed likely. And what was Jumbe looking for in her face?

"You know Mister Brady well?"

Logan nodded. "He's a fishing guide, he works for my father."

"He is a friend?"

"He's an acquaintance," Logan said. "He is—he was my brother's friend, though, and we'd like to have him explain to us exactly what happened to Ben."

"You are a lawyer." Jumbe had done his homework. "Will you be representing Mr. Brady should he need a lawyer?"

"Does he need a lawyer?" Logan sounded casual, but Sage understood the importance of the conversation.

"Not at this time," Jumbe said slowly. "Mr. Brady has been helping us with our investigation. There are no charges right now." There didn't seem to be any irony in his tone. "He's back at his hotel, I will give you the address." He printed in big block letters on a piece of foolscap, tore it off and handed it to Logan.

Logan took it and tucked it into his pocket. "Does he know that Ben—that my brother died today?"

"He was here when the hospital called. He was very upset by the news."

"I see. Now, Chief Jumbe, can *you* tell us exactly what happened to my brother?"

Jumbe again looked slowly from Logan to Sage and then back again.

"Until the autopsy determines which gun the bullet came from, I know only what the guide, Towanga, and Mr. Brady have told me."

"And what is that?" Logan was still polite, but it was clear he was also growing impatient.

"Unfortunately Towanga was suffering a severe stomach upset when the—accident happened, and didn't see the actual shooting."

Sage heard the hesitation. She glanced at Logan, but he was paying close attention to Jumbe.

"Tawonga was squatting in the underbrush about twenty yards away when he heard your brother call out to Mr. Brady telling him to run, that a buffalo was charging. Before Tawonga could move he heard two shots in quick succession, one he thought from Mr. Galloway's rifle and one from Brady's. Tawonga then saw the buffalo, which was indeed charging—very dangerous, a charging buffalo. He shot at it, wounding it, not realizing at that point that your brother had been injured. He shot a second time, killing the animal, and only then became aware that Mr. Galloway was down and unconscious. Tawonga is trained in first aid. He did what he could and immediately radioed for an air ambulance."

"And what was Brady doing while this was going on?" Logan's tone was soft.

"Mr. Brady was shocked and horrified. And remains so," Jumbe said with just a trace of irony. "He has great difficulty in explaining the exact sequence of events."

Logan said in an even softer voice, "Do you think he shot Ben?"

Jumbe shrugged massive shoulders. "My opinion is not of value. As I said, an autopsy will determine where the bullet came from." His eyes moved back and forth like a metronome from Logan to Sage, and for a panicked moment she wondered if he could actually see into her mind.

Then Jumbe said, "Do *you* think so, sir? Do either of you have any thoughts as to why Mr. Brady might want to shoot Mr. Galloway?"

"No." Logan sounded positive. "If the bullet is from Brady's gun, it had to be an accident."

Sage stiffened when Jumbe turned to her. "And you, Mrs. Galloway? What are your thoughts?"

Sage knew what Logan was doing, and why. If Oliver was arrested, it was unlikely Ben's body would be released anytime soon. And from what Jumbe had said about the situation, it would be next to impossible anyway to prove that Oliver had fired purposely. They were in a foreign country, a court case could keep them here for an undetermined period. She thought there was a good chance Oliver had shot Ben, but saying so could mean an endless delay. All she wanted was to go home. Nothing would bring Ben back, what was the purpose of dredging up suspicions that might also have no real basis in truth?

"I agree it would have to be accidental." Was she covering up for a man who might have murdered her husband? But even if he had, there was no positive method of proving it. What good would her suspicions do?

She said, "Oliver Brady and my husband were friends." That, at least, was the entire truth.

"Just so," Jumbe agreed. "Exactly what Mr. Brady himself has said repeatedly."

"We would like to return home with—" Logan had to stop and clear his throat, and Sage saw the flash of despair that came and went across his features "—with my brother's body as soon as possible. When the autopsy is completed, your department will not object?"

"As long as all the necessary documents are in order, you are of course free to leave Africa."

They left the police station, and Logan asked if Sage was up to going to Oliver's hotel. "I can drop you at the Holiday Inn and go by myself," he offered, as he had before. "I need to talk to Brady, the sooner the better."

"I'll come." Sage was exhausted, wrung dry with emotion, but she had a horror of being alone in that hotel room.

And she, too, wanted to know what Oliver would say about Ben's death.

"With your permission, Sage, I'm going to question him about Grace and the baby. About…about Ben's involvement. Are you okay with that?"

Sage wanted to say no. She didn't want to even speak of Grace, or the baby, in the same breath as Ben. But she also realized how important it was to both her and Logan to try and find out the truth.

She sighed. "If it's really necessary, then do it."

"Thanks, Sage." He took her hand again, and she clung to it.

The taxi drew up in front of a cheap rooming house. Dark, sinister faces peered at Sage and Logan from behind half-closed doors, and there was a uniformed policeman lounging outside number ten, Oliver's room. Obviously, Jumbe was taking no chances.

Logan knocked, and after a long while Oliver opened the door.

For a moment, Sage didn't recognize him. Always rangy, he'd lost at least twenty pounds. His face was skeletal, no remnant of his blond good looks remaining. He hadn't shaved in some time. He stared at them from red-rimmed, wild eyes. "Sage? Logan? I wondered if you'd come." His face crumbled and he started to cry, great heaving sobs that he didn't try to hold back. "You—you know about Ben?"

"Yeah. We've just come from the hospital." Logan took Sage's arm and led her inside, closing the door after them.

The room was small and none too clean, with an iron bedstead and a curtain hiding a toilet and washbasin. It smelled strongly of body odor, and Sage's stomach roiled.

Oliver pushed the curtain aside and splashed water on his face from the sink. When he came out, he seemed unable to make eye contact. His hands moved restlessly, tucking in his shirt, straightening his khaki trousers, plowing through his greasy hair.

"God, I'm so sorry," he kept repeating. "I'm so sorry." He sank down on the bed, and Logan motioned Sage to the only chair.

She sat, wondering how much longer this endless day could possibly last. It was terribly hot in this small room, and she felt sweat trickle down her temples. She felt light-headed, acutely uncomfortable and nauseous again, but everything seemed remote, as if a semitransparent screen was between her and what was happening. Extreme fatigue and shock had blunted her emotions.

"Can you tell us what happened, Oliver?" Logan's voice was firm and cool, the kind of voice Sage imagined he would use to query witnesses.

Oliver shook his head. "I wish I knew," he said in a trembling voice. "One minute there was a charging buffalo, and the next—" He gulped. "I fired at the buffalo. I ran over to where Ben was, and he was lying there, with that—that hole—in his head."

Sage shuddered and gagged. She clamped a hand across her mouth. The memory of Ben's shattered head had imprinted itself on the backs of her eyelids.

"You okay, Sage?"

She shook her head, swallowing hard. Logan took a bottle of water from the small fridge and opened it for her. He gave it to her, and then stood beside her, his palm on her shoulder.

Sage sipped, finding comfort and reassurance in his touch. He said, "Have you spoken to anyone back at the Lodge?"

Oliver shook his head, keeping his head bent, eyes down. "I couldn't. I—I can't. I know I should have called, but—but how can I tell Mr. Galloway that Ben—that he—"

"Oliver." Logan's sudden change in tone brought Oliver's head up. Sage stared at her brother-in-law, aware for the first time of the power he kept so well hidden. "You do know that Grace is pregnant."

Chapter Seven

Logan's words hung in the air and Oliver's gaze skittered away again. His shoulders folded in. After a long time he nodded.

"Then you also know that Grace says the baby is Ben's."

Again, it was a long time before Oliver responded. His tone was belligerent. "That's not true. She's lying, to—to make me jealous. Ben said it was a lie."

"And you believe him?" Logan's voice remained steady and calm, but the fingers on Sage's shoulders tightened.

Oliver bristled. "Of course I believe him. He's—he was—my best friend. I—I know he'd never do anything like that. Not with Grace, anyway."

The casual disclaimer made Sage catch her breath. *Not with Grace.* With other women, then? Oliver had spent a great deal of time with Ben.

The wife is always the last to know. She had the sudden absurd urge to giggle at being such a cliché.

Oliver was saying, "Besides, Ben knows—he knew—how much I love Grace. I want to marry her. I will marry her." He looked squarely at Logan. "That baby's mine."

Logan studied the other man for several moments in silence before he said, "Have you spoken to her since the—the accident?" Logan's voice hesitated, just as Jumbe's had done.

Oliver shook his head. "I can't talk to anyone right now. I mean, the police would let me, but I—I break down. It's—it's embarrassing."

"You know there's a cop right outside the door."

"Yeah, I know." Oliver sounded resigned at the surveillance. "They've had one watching me ever since—ever since the helicopter brought us out of the bush. They—they think—" his face contorted, his breathing audible in the small room "—they think I shot Ben."

"And did you?" The words were so soft Sage wondered if she'd imagined them.

"*No.*" The denial was loud and forceful. "No, I didn't. I shot at that bloody buffalo. It was coming straight at us."

"And was Ben in your line of fire?"

"Damn it. Damn all of you!" Oliver sprang up, startling Sage. His eyes were wild, his muscles tensed, and for a moment she thought he might strike out at Logan, who moved swiftly in front of her, blocking her from Oliver.

But after a moment, Logan moved aside again, and Sage saw that Oliver had put his hands flat on the table, arms braced, leaning over them with his head down, back turned toward them. She could see his shoulders trembling.

"I don't know," he said at last in a tormented voice. "I can't—I can't really remember, it happened so fast."

Sage noticed the things he wasn't saying.

"We're going home as soon as Ben's body is released," Logan said next. "We don't have reservations yet. When are you planning on flying back?"

Oliver said. "We were booked out next Friday, I've never changed it. Just in case—in case they decide to let me go."

"Jumbe is waiting for the autopsy report."

"Yeah," Oliver muttered. "So am I."

When they left, Sage was sweating. She was also irrationally angry at Logan. He flagged a taxi, and when they were inside, she turned on him.

"You know as well as I do that Oliver had good reason to shoot Ben. What if he killed him deliberately? He didn't sound very convincing to me. Why didn't you push him, ask him more questions?"

"Because there's absolutely no way of knowing for sure what happened out there, Sage. Sure, he had motive, if he believes Grace's baby was fathered by Ben. We can go back to Jumbe, tell him the whole story, everything we suspect. We could wait here until the DNA comes back, and if Ben's the father, all we still have is circumstantial evidence. No real proof. Jumbe's going on about the autopsy report because he needs it to prove he did everything by the book. There's no question that bullet came from Oliver's gun, but there's no certain way of proving intent. I don't think a case like this would stand up in court, and neither does Jumbe. He's going to have to let Brady go."

"Do—do you think he murdered Ben?"

Logan stared at the back of the cab driver's head for a

long time, and then he laid his head back against the seat and closed his eyes. "I honestly don't know, Sage. I wish I did. What do you think?"

The anger was gone, and once again she was numb. "My gut says he did, but that's all I have to go on."

Logan heaved a long sigh. "Gut feelings are usually right. If so, Brady's getting away with murder. It burns my ass, but I just can't see any way to prove it in a court of law. Especially not here in Africa."

Hours later, unable to sleep and haunted by nightmarish images of Ben's destroyed skull, Sage padded barefoot into the tiny kitchen. The door to Logan's room was ajar, and she tiptoed past it, not wanting to disturb him.

She opened the small fridge, found a tin of orange juice, emptied it into a glass. The hotel was on a quiet side street, but a block away, Sage could hear cars honking and voices calling back and forth, even though it was past midnight.

"Jet lag?" Logan came out of his room, track pants slung low on narrow hips, white T-shirt hanging loose, jaw sprouting tomorrow's beard.

"Something like that." She gestured at her glass. "I needed a drink. You want some?"

"Yeah." He got a can from the fridge, pulled the tab and drank. "Good. And I'm hungry now, finally." Earlier, neither of them had been able to eat the rice and sauce the taxi driver had insisted they pick up on the way back to the hotel. Logan got the containers out of the fridge and slid them into the microwave, then put generous helpings on two plates.

He set one in front of Sage and handed her a fork. "No arguments, lady. Eat. You're getting thinner by the second."

Sage gave him a look. "That's not bad news."

"Yeah, it is, when you're perfect to start with." He tossed off the matter-of-fact compliment, concentrating on his food.

"Thank you, Logan." He sounded as if he meant it. And after the past few days, her extra pounds didn't seem as important anymore.

"You're welcome." He forked in food. "This stuff isn't too bad, y'know. A little spicy, but nothing like that Thai place I go to in Seattle."

"You like spicy food?" She realized how little she really knew about him.

"Sometimes. But only with beer." He smiled and rolled his eyes. "And afterward I'm always sorry, but I never learn. How about you? What kind of food do you like best?"

"Normally, I just like food, period. Ben teases me all the time—used to tease me—" there was a hitch in her voice "—about my appetite." With a pang, she realized she'd have to get used to using the past tense.

Logan whistled. "Lucky him. Most guys go nuts trying to figure out where to take a woman to eat. These days they're either vegans, or raw food fanatics, or following Atkins or South Beach or Suzanne Somers."

"Wow, a guy who knows all the popular diets. Sounds as if you get around a bit, Galloway."

"Nope. I just work out at a gym where the guys gripe a lot."

Sage actually laughed. And lifted the fork and started in on her rice and whatever. "You're right, this *is* good."

Logan scooped up the last of his helping. "Mavis wouldn't consider this fit to eat, but I won't tell her if you don't. So what kind of stuff did your mom make, Sage?"

"My mom? Oh, she didn't cook. She didn't clean, or

sew, or do any of the things mothers usually do. Her entire contribution to mothering was in providing an apartment for us."

"You have brothers and sisters?"

Sage shook her head. "Only me. Probably a good thing, because Mom wasn't cut out for family life. She was divorced from my father—he was a drinker who walked out on us. She was really pretty, she dated a lot. She was a nurse, a lot of the guys she dated were doctors." *Alcoholic doctors.* Lucy had been a magnet for anyone with a drinking problem. "She died ten years ago. Cancer."

"I'm sorry, I didn't know." He was paying close attention. "What about your dad? You ever look him up?"

Sage gave the nonchalant shrug she'd perfected over the years when anyone asked about Murphy. "I did, I was curious. I met him twice. He—he was pretty much a write-off." She remembered his purple nose, the smell of alcohol, the sad realization that both of her parents were drunks.

And both of those times he'd asked for a loan.

"So you can see why I totally adore your folks, Logan. They've treated me like a daughter, made me part of your family. I didn't know what a family really was until Ben introduced me to yours. I fell in love with them as well as with Ben." It helped to say his name, to talk about him.

He smiled at her. "Why wouldn't they treat you well? Anybody'd be proud to have you in their family."

She hadn't really cried all day, but now tears trickled down her cheeks and into the rice on her plate.

"Hey, hey, sweetheart." He got up and pulled her to her feet, wrapped his arms around her. "I didn't mean to make you cry." He used his palms to wipe the tears away, then swiped his hands nonchalantly on his pants, which horrified her. "You—don't do that, Logan." She sniffed hard. "I'm covered in snot, I need a tissue."

"We're fresh out." He went into the bathroom and came out trailing toilet tissue. "Use this. Come and sit over here on this couch, and I'll make you laugh. Promise. I'll tell you lawyer stories about my clients that'll make your hair stand on end. Or else put you to sleep."

He was a natural storyteller, something else she'd never known about him, and he had a wonderful sense of the ridiculous. For the next few hours he actually did make her laugh with his wild tales of a cross-dressing farmer who wore his wife's best underwear to drive tractors, and a divorcing couple who ran up astronomical legal fees over who got to keep the dog's ashes.

Until the golden African dawn shone through the windows, he distracted her. And with the darkness gone and a new day outside, she found she could sleep, knowing he was nearby, knowing that whatever the next day held, Logan would be there to help her handle it.

Having Ben's body released and making arrangements for shipment of a casket back to Alaska was a clerical and technical nightmare. After two days of utter frustration, Logan finally contacted a legal firm, spoke to a lawyer and hired him to help in wading through the incomprehensible forms and legalities required.

On the third morning, Sage was asleep when the phone rang.

Mixed in with her dreams, she could hear Logan's husky voice talking with someone. She came awake slowly, listening to his voice, unable to make out the words. Groggy, she thought of getting up and then dozed off again.

"Sage? Wake up a minute, sleepyhead." Logan stood in the connecting doorway with a cup of coffee for her. He'd pulled jeans on, but that was all he wore. His hair was tousled with sleep, his face creased from the pillow. "Man, I was really zonked when that phone rang." It was the first night since they'd arrived that either of them had slept more than a few hours at a time.

She sat up, groggily straightening the oversize T-shirt she wore as a nightgown.

He came over to the bed, handing her the coffee and then perching on the edge.

"Thanks." The coffee was hot, lightly creamed, heavily sugared, just the way she liked it. She sipped at it and yawned.

"You awake enough for some news?"

"Good or bad?"

"Good and bad. That was Chief Jumbe. The medical examiner says the bullet was definitely from Oliver's rifle."

"Oh, dear God." It was as much prayer as anything. "You said it would be. So what happens now?"

"This is the good part, I think. He also said they just don't have enough evidence to charge Oliver. They're calling it an accidental death. Oliver's free to go, and so are we."

"It can't be too soon for me." Sage had been clutching the cup as if it might fly away. She loosened her grip and gulped the rest of her coffee.

"They're releasing Ben's body today. I'm calling the lawyer right now. If he's managed to get the proper forms signed, I'll try to get us on the first available flight."

"Oh, Logan, I hope you can." Sage felt her body go slack with relief. "I so want to go home. I know this is a beautiful country but I hate it here because of what's happened. I'm sure under other circumstances it would be different, but all I can think about right now is getting out of Africa."

She needed to bury her husband. She needed to find out the results of the DNA testing. And there was something else she was going to do as soon as she got back, something that she'd told herself she'd never attempt. She'd given it a lot of thought, and the decision had crystallized.

Logan said. "I'll do my best, Sage. I feel the same as you. This is like being trapped in limbo." He got up and stretched. His jeans hung low on his flat belly. His broad chest had a mat of dark hair arrowing down to his navel. Sage could smell him, a heady male mixture of sleep and sweat and soap. And suddenly she felt aroused. The jolt of sexual feeling horrified her.

What was wrong with her? What kind of woman would be sexually aroused when her husband had just died? And attracted to her husband's brother? Shame filled her, disgust at her response to Logan. It must be his uncanny resemblance to Ben.

But part of her knew she'd never mistake Logan for Ben. They might look alike, but Logan had compassion and thoughtfulness that Ben was sadly lacking. When had Ben ever made her coffee and brought it to her in bed? She'd always been the one doing things like that for him. Not that she hadn't wanted to. Just that she appreciated it when Logan did it for her.

And in that moment she thought of Jenny, of her descriptions of how kind Robert had been to her. How strange, that Sage's life should hold echoes of the ancestor who wasn't even a blood relation.

She remembered as well that Jenny had found Robert sexually attractive.

Logan must have noticed the hot flush that spread upward from her chest to her cheeks, but he didn't comment.

"More coffee? Or should I go out and get us some fruit and bread?"

"Yes, please. That sounds wonderful." She needed space, but she was also hungry all of a sudden. Her appetite, which had all but disappeared, seemed to be back with a vengeance. *All her appetites.*

"I'll make the call to the lawyer, and then I'll scout us out some food. Stay put, relax. You look comfortable, and there's nothing to jump out of bed for." With the smile she'd come to rely on, he went out, and Sage lay back on the pillows. The room was comfortably cool, thanks to the air-conditioning, and she pulled the sheet up and closed her eyes.

As usual, Logan was taking care of everything. It was becoming a habit, letting him pamper her. Well, she'd get over it soon enough. These were unusual times. She slept again.

By some miracle—and a great deal of help from the lawyer—Logan was able to get them on a flight leaving the following evening. There'd be an overnight stop in London this time, and he booked them into a small hotel. At least this way they'd get a decent rest, although Sage had somehow mastered the art of sleeping deeply on a plane. Logan had refused the meal service so as not to disturb her. His arm had long since succumbed to pins and needles where her head rested.

He was equally aware of Ben's coffin, somewhere in the belly of the plane, and Sage, warm and weary, sleeping on his shoulder.

Thou shalt not covet thy neighbor's wife.

What about your brother's?

It was agony to be so physically close to her. The days they'd spent in Dar es Salaam had progressed on two levels, one being the management of his brother's death, and the other, the constant, subliminal awareness of his feelings for the woman at his side, feelings he'd suppressed since the moment he'd first laid eyes on her. Being with her, even in circumstances like these, had made the attraction more intense.

He found her beautiful, even when her nose was red and her eyes swollen with crying, or her face puffy and drugged with sleep as it was now. She had a dignity about her that he admired. She'd cried some, but thank God, she didn't do hysterics. Logan had enough of hysterical women at work.

Sage met each challenge head-on, discussed the problem, negotiated if her opinion differed from his. She was strong, strong willed, and at the same time, vulnerable. It was a heady combination. The best and safest thing for him would be to scuttle back to Seattle as quickly as he could manage, and then stay there, out of the reach of temptation.

One more week, he promised himself. There'd be the funeral, and he wanted to spend time with his parents afterward. There was the whole god-awful issue of Grace and the baby and the DNA. A shudder went through him, and Sage lifted her head from his shoulder, untangled her hand from his, stretched and yawned. "Was I asleep long?"

"Nope," he said, relieved that she was awake, that conversation would take his mind off things he'd rather not think about. "A mere seven hours or so," he teased. "You missed the movie and the food, the only real highlights of air travel. But never mind, we'll be landing at Heathrow before long. Are you hungry?"

"Starving. I can't believe I slept for seven hours." She yawned again and grimaced. "Maybe I caught sleeping sickness in Africa."

"And maybe exhaustion and stress are catching up with you."

"What about you, Logan? Were you able to sleep?"

"I napped some," he lied. He'd spent the hours remembering happy childhood escapades with his brother, wondering sadly when exactly he and Ben had grown so far apart. Close or not, losing Ben was like losing one of his limbs. They'd shared real estate before they were born, and regardless of how often they saw one another or how violently they disagreed, Logan had always known Ben was somewhere on this green planet, a part of him in ways he could never explain.

Not anymore. That was going to take a lot of getting used to.

"I'll go wash my face and try to brush my hair into some sort of order," Sage decided, gathering up her makeup bag. "Don't want to freak out the poor customs officials."

As soon as she was gone, Logan buzzed the stewardess and asked for coffee and some food for Sage and for himself. He figured there were a couple of perks when traveling business class, namely food on demand and having almost enough legroom so that he wasn't permanently crippled.

He desperately needed exercise. If it wasn't pouring rain in London, maybe Sage would agree to a long walk. For the first time since they'd left Alaska, there was nothing urgent either of them had to do. And the less time he spent with her in a hotel suite, the better.

They were in luck. During the forty-minute cab ride from Gatwick into Central London, the sun came up, and

Echoes

by the time they checked into the Gainsborough Hotel, the morning was balmy.

"This is funky, I really like it," Sage declared, walking around their Victorian-style suite. "How did you know about it?"

"A lawyer friend stayed here when he came on a trial. I remembered the name." He pointed at the window, where the sun was beaming through the draperies. "Care to go walking?"

"Sure. If I even remember how, after sitting on that plane for so long. I need to shower first, though." She yawned, obviously still bone weary.

"No rush, take your time. You want food?"

"Love some. You order, anything's fine with me."

By the time she came out of the shower, room service had delivered a full English breakfast and a large pot of coffee.

Logan handed her a plate, and Sage filled it with bacon, egg, sausage, a scoop of baked beans, topping it off with hash browns.

Afterward, they walked.

But Sage found that after three hours of exploring land-marks like the Victoria and Albert Museum and wandering through Harrods, she was too exhausted to make it back to the hotel. She was trying to be as upbeat and cheerful as she could manage, for Logan's sake, but the effort depleted her. Inside, there was a black hole of sadness, compounded by the issue of Grace and the DNA.

Logan hired a cab, and she limped into her room, shucked off her clothes and climbed into bed. As she slid into sleep, it occurred to her that in spite of her sorrow, on some level, she was beginning to accept the fact that Ben was gone. For small moments at a time today, she'd forgotten.

The nap revived her. They ate dinner that evening in the dining room, and when they were once again back in their suite, Logan ordered a bottle of wine.

He poured them each a glass. Sage had brought one basic black dress which she'd worn to dinner. She kicked off her heels and curled into the soft cushions on the overstuffed settee, tired all over again. Her stamina was low.

Logan was on the phone to Raven Lodge, talking to Caitlin. When the call ended, he said, "Dad's not doing well. Mom says he's not eating and he can't sleep. They've planned the funeral for the day after we arrive. It'll be from the church in Valdez. Oliver is due back tomorrow—he finally called Grace. Dad wants to talk with him, he wants to know exactly how Ben died." He swallowed his wine in one gulp, adding in a bitter tone, "Don't we all."

The funeral was going to be an ordeal, and Sage dreaded it.

Besides the horror of burying her husband, there would be Grace to deal with. She'd undoubtedly be there, as well as Jill, Ben's ex-wife.

And at some point Sage was going to have to tell Theo and Caitlin about the baby. The thought made her shudder. If it was Ben's they'd naturally want Grace to stay nearby, because the baby would be their grandchild.

Even the thought of having to face a pregnant Grace day after day made Sage's heart constrict. It was going to be horribly lonely when Logan, her support—her friend—left Raven Lodge.

"Are you going home right afterward, Logan?"

"In a week or so, yeah. My partner's taken over my cases, but he can't handle the whole business for long on his own. What about you, Sage? Have you thought about what you'll do?"

She knew he was thinking about the baby, too, and all the terrible side effects of Ben's death.

"Not really. Not yet." But for the first time, Sage dared to even think of leaving the Lodge, finding a job somewhere else. Theo and Caitlin loved her, but the ramifications of Grace's pregnancy changed things. A terrible emptiness and a sense of utter desolation came over her at the thought of leaving the only real home she'd ever known, the people she'd come to think of as her parents.

She finished her wine and Logan refilled her glass and his own. Maybe it was the wine that gave her courage and loosened her tongue.

"I've never told anyone this, but I had a baby when I was fifteen," she blurted on a shuddering breath. "A baby boy. I—I gave him up for adoption."

Chapter Eight

The old pain threatened to break her heart all over again, and she pressed a hand to her chest, the same unconscious gesture she always used when she thought of her son. "He—he was such a beautiful baby. I only ever held him once, right after he was born. Anyway, I've—I've decided now to try and find him. He'll be fifteen this coming October 3."

"Jesus, Sage. What a hell of a thing to go through." The compassion and caring in his voice was almost more than she could bear. "That must have been tough for you. Must *be* tough, all those years thinking about him, wondering how he is."

He understood. My God, he understood. The relief was overwhelming. "How—how do you know? That I think of him all the time?"

He shrugged, his dark eyes gentle. "I guess because I would. If I knew I had a kid out there—" He stopped abruptly.

She couldn't interpret the look on his face. "What is it, Logan?"

He opened his mouth and closed it again. "Nothing. It's nothing. How are you going to go about searching?"

She was eager to share what she'd kept secret for so long. "I know of an agency that traces family members. I used them to find my father. I'm going to ask them to find my son."

"And if they do, then what? Will you try and get him back?"

"No." She shook her head. "No, I'd never do that, it would only hurt him. I just want to know that he's okay, that—that the people who adopted him love him, that he's—he's happy." The wine made it so easy to say the things she'd kept bottled inside.

"And you never told Ben about this?"

"No." The denial was forceful. "I wanted to. I planned to, when we were first together. But I kept putting it off, and then—well, I told you what Ben's like—what he *was* like—about his kids. I realized he could never have given any child of his away, and I knew he'd think less of me for doing it. He wouldn't have understood how I could ever have given my son up for adoption. And we had so many other issues between us—I was a coward. I couldn't bring myself to tell him."

Logan rubbed a hand through his hair. "You were only fifteen, for God's sake. A year older than Sophia. I sure as hell can't imagine her with a baby, can you?"

Sophia, Ben's oldest daughter. His girls were beautiful, and Sage had been thrilled at the idea of being a step-mother. But from the beginning, Jill had caused problems for Sage with the girls, telling them that Sage had taken their daddy away from them, that it was her fault when Ben didn't keep the promises he made. As a result, Sage had never managed a close relationship with either Sophia or her younger sister, Lily, even though she'd longed for one. As the girls grew older, they tolerated her, but it was a long way from the friendship she dreamed of.

"No," she agreed. "The last thing I'd want to see is Sophia with a baby. Any fifteen-year-old, for that matter. A fifteen-year-old girl isn't ready to be a mother." Sophia was still a baby herself in so many ways, just as Sage had been at her age.

"You were a pretty smart kid to figure that out when you had your son."

Sage's laugh had no humor. She shook her head. "Smart was the last thing I was. My mother had a boyfriend that year." Sage shuddered at the memory of Cliff, with his hot eyes and cruel hands. "Mom didn't want me around, and I was scared of the guy. He tried to—he used to come into my room at night, when she was working. Well, anyway, I told her, and she blamed me. So instead of dumping Cliff, she arranged with a friend of hers, Louise Armitage, to let me stay at her place in exchange for doing the cleaning and shopping and stuff."

Sage finished her wine, her mind on that long-ago summer.

"Louise had a brother, Dean, who stayed there sometimes, as well. He was twenty, he worked in construction. He had blond hair and a white convertible. I fell hard for him. He also had a girlfriend, an older girl, but sometimes he took me out for rides at night. I was such a stupid kid. When I told him I was pregnant, he got in that car and drove away. I never saw or heard from him again."

"Nice guy. A real prize."

"Mom found this home for unwed mothers—they specialized in private adoptions. I stayed there until he was born." She rubbed absently at her chest, the spot where the pain had been so intense she'd thought she'd die of it. They blamed it on milk fever, but even at fifteen, Sage knew it was the loss of her baby that was hurting her so badly.

"There's this schmaltzy country-and-western song, I think it's called, "He Would Be Fifteen." It's about a girl giving up her baby. I heard it once, and it tore my heart out. I can't stand to listen to it, I turn the radio off if it comes on." Her eyes filled with tears.

Logan was sitting in an armchair across from her. With a wordless exclamation, he set his wineglass down, got to his feet and pulled her up and into his arms.

Surprised, and then grateful for the human contact, her arms slid around his torso. With her head on his chest, she could feel the rumble of his voice, the beating of his heart.

"You didn't get a certificate for a happy life, did you, Sage?"

"Maybe nobody does." It was something she'd wondered about, why some lives were carefree and others not.

She stood in the circle of his arms, feeling the solid, male warmth of him, breathing in the smell of his aftershave, the subtle aroma of his body that she'd become familiar with. It felt so safe, being in Logan's arms.

It was several minutes before she was aware that his heart was hammering away at double-time under her ear. At the same moment she felt his erection, pressing urgently against her belly.

Shocked—doubly so because of the instant, urgent response her own body telegraphed—she stepped abruptly away, knocking the nearly empty wine bottle over and tripping over the low table behind her.

"Hey, careful there." He caught her by the arm, holding on only until she got her balance. He growled, "I'm not going to apologize, Sage."

"I don't expect you to." She couldn't meet his eyes. "It's the wine, I should know better. I'm going to bed. We have to be up early in the morning, and I'm still wiped. Night, Logan."

He didn't reply.

Moving fast, she headed toward her bedroom, shutting the door behind her, collapsing on her bed. Her breathing was ragged, her heart hammering. What the heck was going on with her? Was this a stage of grief nobody ever talked about, being sexually aroused days after your husband died? She didn't know, and there sure wasn't anyone she could ask.

It was the second time she'd felt that powerful, primal response to Logan. She was attracted to him, but she kept telling herself it had to be because of his uncanny resemblance to Ben. As for him—he was a man, first and foremost, a young, healthy man in the prime of his life. Getting an erection was perfectly natural. It wasn't her, as a person, he was aroused by, she assured herself. It was simply because she was female, and they'd been in close contact for days, trapped in a foreign country, with no one else around to distract either of them. That was it—wasn't it?

She wasn't sure. She wasn't sure of anything anymore, except that when she got home, back to Valdez, back to Raven Lodge, then everything would look different. Maybe not better, but different. And she'd be in familiar surroundings, able to think more clearly. And she'd see that this thing between her and Logan was just raw emotional overload.

One more long day's flying, that was all she had to endure. And then soon after that Logan would be gone, back to Seattle, back to his life.

A feeling of desperate loneliness swept over her. Did he have a lover? She'd wondered often, but never quite got around to asking. Of course he did. He was the kind of man women dreamed of. He probably had his pick of women. Now why should that make her uncomfortable? No doubt about it, the sooner she was back home, the better.

But there was little comfort to be had at Raven Lodge.

Two days later and badly jet-lagged, Sage sat in the front pew of the small Valdez chapel, Theo on one side, Caitlin on the other, each holding one of her hands. Logan was on his mother's far side, and beside Theo were Ben's daughters. Andrew and Opal were one pew back.

Only a few feet from Sage was the casket, the huge, heavy, ornately carved box that she and Logan had bought in Dar es Salaam.

The chapel was packed to overflowing, with latecomers standing at the back and along the sides of the room. The Galloways were one of the pioneer families in the area, well liked and respected by everyone. A number of the Lodge's guests were present. Many of them were regular visitors to Alaska who'd met Ben in previous years.

Jill sat a few pews behind on the opposite side of the chapel, with Grace beside her. Sage could sense their malevolent energy, and prickles ran down her spine. She hadn't realized they were friends.

The service began. Ben hadn't been a churchgoer, and the young pastor didn't really know him. He was relying on the notes Sage and Logan had made that morning, and she realized he was reading them verbatim. When he was done, he invited the congregation to participate.

One by one, young men filed to the front, awkward and ill at ease, but touchingly determined to convey their admiration for Ben. They spoke of hunting and fishing trips, Ben's physical bravery, his penchant for practical jokes, his gift of leadership.

Sage listened, recognizing her husband in each clumsy eulogy, painfully aware that they were describing only a part of Ben. Conflicting emotions caused turmoil in her brain. No one mentioned that he was an unfaithful husband, careless enough to father a child with a woman not his wife.

She'd found out for sure that morning.

She hadn't been able to sleep past three. Crossing time zones had screwed her inner clock. She'd made a pot of coffee and taken it outside, grateful for the Alaskan summer, which meant it was already full light.

The sun was high over the water, and Sage wandered down to the dock, grabbing a folding lawn chair on her way. She set it up and settled into it, sipping her coffee and finding a measure of peace in the vista of ocean gleaming gold in the rays of the sun, rainbows of light glinting off the glaciers that surrounded the Sound, and the music of gulls swooping overhead, always hopeful for a meal.

Grace had found her there and shoved an envelope into her hand.

"I told you it's Ben's," the younger woman said in a smug tone. "Proof's right there. Science doesn't lie. Thank God for DNA, huh?"

Sage realized at that moment how narrow the gap was between control and mayhem. She wanted to physically attack Grace, slap the half smile from her pouty mouth.

Sage longed to push her off the dock, to shatter the illusion that there was anything civilized about this situation.

"Are you gonna tell Logan?" Grace lowered herself to the dock and dangled her bare legs in the water.

"He already knows." Sage got up and walked away, back to her house. She climbed the steps, the envelope clutched in her hand. Inside, she ran up the stairs to the second floor, closing and locking the door of her small office, even though she was alone in the house.

Only then did she let herself react. Dry, heaving sobs erupted from her throat. She opened the envelope, knowing what she'd find, needing to confirm it with her own eyes.

And it was there, some ridiculously high percentage of matches between the hair sample and the amnio fluid.

Ben's baby. In another woman's body.

Chapter Nine

It was all Sage could think of as she showered, dried her hair, put on the black skirt and short-sleeved jacket she was wearing to the funeral.

It was all she could think of now as she listened to the endless words of praise for the man who didn't deserve them.

After the funeral service, there was the drive out to the cemetery, the religious blessing, the finality of handfuls of earth falling on the casket before it was lowered into the ground.

Caitlin, who'd been strong all day, broke apart and wept uncontrollably. Theo, pale and trembling, held her close. Logan's jaw was set in a rigid attempt at control. Mavis was a round black wren standing stoically beside her friends, her black veiled hat hiding her scarred face entirely in the manner of the Kennedy women. Opal and Andrew bracketed the family group, offering silent, compassionate support.

And directly across from Sage, Jill wept as if it was her beloved instead of her ex-husband to whom they were bidding goodbye, sobbing aloud and wiping her streaming eyes on a series of tissues she dug from her handbag. Grace, standing beside her, was also weeping uncontrollably.

Sage watched them, wondering at this show of grief, particularly from Jill, who'd seemed to despise Ben.

Oliver, who seemed to have aged twenty years, stood beside Grace, but Sage noticed she shook off his arm when he tried to hold her.

Sage, dry-eyed, drained and numb, wanted it only to be over. She tried not to look at Grace, but the woman drew her eyes like a magnet, and Sage thought that the other woman looked more like the grieving wife than she did.

After what seemed like half her life had passed, the graveside service finally ended. Logan took Sage's arm and led her to the van that was driving them to the docks for the boat trip back to the Lodge.

Theo and Caitlin had invited anyone who cared to come back to Raven Lodge for lunch. Mavis, with Opal at her side, had been up half the night preparing a feast, and the moment the Galloway boat landed the two of them hurried off to check on the serving girls and make certain everything was ready. Other boats bringing friends and neighbors were close behind.

Ben's daughters and his ex-wife pulled up to the dock in another of the Lodge's boats, piloted by Grace. There was no sign of Oliver, which was a good thing; Sage knew that Theo and Caitlin could barely tolerate the sight of him.

They believed, as did she and Logan, that Oliver was somehow responsible for Ben's death. Neither of them wanted a scene on the very day their son was buried, but Sage knew Oliver's days as a guide at the Lodge were numbered.

Jill and Grace hurried past Sage and Logan with barely a nod. Jill held tight to Sophia and Lily.

"Hey, girls. Got a hug for your old uncle?" Logan called to his nieces. They smiled, but Jill held firmly to their hands, and the two women didn't stop or turn. In a quiet voice, Logan said to Sage, "What's biting their asses? And I wonder where Oliver got to?"

"Maybe he's bringing another boatload."

"I don't know about you, but I need a drink," Logan said, gently tugging her up the steps to the Lodge. "There's real common sense to the idea of an Irish wake. Liquor numbs feelings, and mine could stand some numbing right about now."

Inside, Theo poured Logan rum and Sage a glass of white wine. Andrew stayed beside Theo, lending support by his presence.

Theo and Logan talked about the service, but Sage was only half listening. From the corner of her eye, she could see Grace Fulton, at the back of the large room, talking intently to Jill. Until today, she hadn't known they were friends. She wondered if Grace was confiding in Jill about the baby.

Whatever they were talking about, Sage hoped they'd both keep their distance from her today. She might be able to overlook Jill's constant rudeness, but Grace was another matter. If the woman said anything suggestive to her, Sage was afraid she'd attack her, both verbally and physically. She was running on empty as far as emotional resilience went, and the last thing Theo and Caitlin needed today was a scene.

Theo glanced toward the door. "There's Tom now. I'll get him a drink." He headed off to greet his brother-in-law.

"Dad isn't looking too good, is he?" Logan was frowning after his father. "I was going to leave tomorrow, but I think maybe I'd better stick around for a few days."

"I'm sure both Theo and Caitlin would appreciate that." She glanced reluctantly toward the door of the Lodge. "I guess I should go talk to people. Why do people hang around after a funeral? It seems the wrong time for socializing."

"Me, too, but we're the minority," Logan said. "I'll go give my nieces jobs to do. They need something to distract them." He added softly, "Cross your fingers that the neighbors will go home soon. Not that I don't appreciate the support and the sympathy, but peace and quiet would be awfully good right about now."

Sage heartily agreed.

But peace and quiet didn't come for hours. People lingered, and of course there were also the Lodge's guests to tend to. Everyone ate Mavis's food and drank Theo's liquor, settling in small groups on the soft sofas and chairs, wandering through the gardens, congregating on the decks.

Midsummer in Alaska brought no twilight, no natural ending to the long day. It was close to midnight by the time everyone finally left.

With each passing hour, Sage grew more exhausted.

Finally, with the last of the Lodge's guests straggling upstairs to their rooms or out to their cabins, Sage and Logan helped gather up dirty plates and glasses while Mavis and Opal unloaded and repacked the dishwasher.

"I'm absolutely wiped, I'm going home now." Sage hugged Caitlin, and kissed Theo on the cheek.

"Good night, my dear. It's been a long, difficult day," he said. "See you in the morning."

Logan said, "I'll walk you over to your house, Sage. I could use some fresh air."

The sun was still bright, and Sage pulled her sunglasses from her bag and put them on, squinting even through the lenses, because the sun was low and glinting beams of molten silver off the ocean. A man was sitting on the dock, head bent forward and resting on his knees. "Is that Oliver?"

"Yeah." Logan's voice hardened. "He looks pretty dejected, and maybe he deserves to. I noticed Grace wasn't having much to do with him today."

"She's not so dejected. The DNA tests came back, she made a point of telling me this morning, before the funeral. The baby is Ben's. She probably told Oliver, too."

Logan stopped. "Damn it. Damn her straight to hell."

"I only wish," Sage said. "She was pretty smug about it. I saw her talking to Jill. I wondered if she was spreading the news."

Logan swore again. "I don't want Mom and Dad to hear gossip. We're going to have to tell them ourselves, before she has a chance."

Sage gave a weary nod. She felt as if her legs wouldn't carry her much farther. "It's me that has to tell them, it's not your responsibility. But I appreciate the support more than I can say."

"It's a family affair. I want to be with you on this."

"Okay. In the morning?"

Logan nodded and swore viciously under his breath. "What a bloody mess."

They were at the deck leading to Sage's front door, and all she could think of was a long, hot bath, and the softness of her bed.

Logan said in a strained voice, "Look, Sage, there's something I need to tell you."

"Can it wait till morning?" Her hand was on the doorknob. "I'm tired. I just can't deal with anything else today. In the morning, okay? I'll feel better then. We all will."

He hesitated, but then he nodded. "Yeah. Yeah, of course. It's been a brutal day all round." He came close and gently touched her shoulder. "It'll keep till morning. Sleep well, Sage. I'll see you at breakfast."

She wished for an instant she could turn into his arms, rest there. And then the pressure of his fingers on her shoulder made her aware that Logan's arms wouldn't be restful. There was that powerful undercurrent of sexual desire that had sprung up between them. It was there now, and she knew from the expression in his eyes that he was every bit as aware of it as she.

"Night, Logan." She opened the door and stepped inside, hot and agitated, turning so she faced him.

"See you in the morning, Sage."

She waited until he'd turned away before she closed the door. She leaned against it, not at all curious as to what he wanted to tell her. Instead, she wondered what kind of cruel and wicked fate would make her long to have her brother-in-law make love to her on the eve of her husband's funeral.

Chapter Ten

Sage had just stepped out of the shower early the next morning when the phone rang. She wrapped herself in a towel and with some difficulty located the mobile she'd left under a book on her bedside table.

It was Mandy, one of the maids from the Lodge, and she sounded breathless.

"Logan says to tell you Mr. Galloway's had another heart attack, and the medevac is on its way, and could you please come right away?"

Sage threw on shorts and a T-shirt and went racing over to the Lodge.

Theo was lying on the sofa in the living room, propped up on several pillows. His face was ashen, and although he was shivering, a sheen of sweat covered his skin. Caitlin was at his side, and Logan was kneeling on the floor, holding his father's hand. Several guests hovered around, concern evident on their faces.

Logan turned worried eyes on Sage.

"I'm fine," Theo insisted in a faint voice when he saw her. "Just a little dizzy, is all."

"He was passed out on the floor of the bathroom when I found him," Logan said. "Any sign of that medevac yet?"

Sage shook her head. "I'll get blankets." She ran upstairs, snatching a soft comforter from the first open room she came to.

Downstairs again, she tucked it around Theo. He was breathing fast and shallow. She heard the whirring of the medevac landing on the helipad outside the Lodge.

Two medics came running in, and Sage felt enormous relief when they took charge. It seemed only seconds before Theo was on a stretcher, oxygen mask clamped over his face, being wheeled out the door and hurried over to the copter, Caitlin right beside him.

"I'll call," she promised Logan as he raced alongside the stretcher.

"Don't worry, we'll take care of everything," he assured her.

For the next hour, Sage pounced on the phone every time it rang, praying it was Caitlin with good news, but it never was. She worried sick about Theo in between explaining to guests what had happened, doing her best to manage incoming bookings, getting bills ready for guests leaving, arranging various fishing expeditions and making sure guides were available.

When Sage picked up the phone for the twentieth time and it was Caitlin, she said, "Oh, thank goodness. How is he?"

Caitlin sounded weary. "Not wonderful, but at least it wasn't major this time."

"Oh, I'm so relieved. Do you want to speak to Logan? I think he's down at the dock."

"Don't bother, dear. Just give him the good news. Theo's doing fine. The doctors aren't sure yet if it was a heart attack—the tests are coming back negative. They think it might have been a reaction to extreme stress. They're doing an EKG, blood tests and he's scheduled for a nuclear scan, but depending on the results, they'll release him in the morning. How are things at the Lodge?"

"Absolutely fine, but I'm glad you're coming home."

Sage was familiar with the business side, but the social aspect of running the Lodge was very much Caitlin and Theo's area of expertise. She was finding it really difficult to be upbeat and sociable all the time, especially when all the guests insisted on talking about Ben and the funeral and asking for the dozenth time how she was coping. She kept smiling and reassuring everyone, but as evening approached she felt like snarling, "Will you just *shut up* now?"

Also, she tried not to be pessimistic, but she couldn't help wondering what calamity was going to befall the family next—the past two weeks had been one long series of nasty and tragic surprises.

And fortunately, she hadn't had to talk to Grace yet. The woman was out with a fishing party at a nearby lake today, and Sage had sent Oliver out with another party to fish for salmon. She'd asked Logan to discuss Grace's schedule with her.

Throughout the serving of dinner, the clearing up and the enforced conversations with guests, there hadn't been a quiet moment, but at last things settled down and Sage headed for home, so drained she could barely put one foot after the other.

"You look tired," Logan said. He was carrying a load of fishing gear down to the dock.

"Yeah, I'm beat." She gave a huge yawn and they both smiled. "It's been a long day. I'm so glad Theo is okay. And I hope your mom is holding up. This has been awful for her." Sage had thought all day of her mother-in-law, enduring one calamity right after the next.

"She's one marvelous lady, my mom," Logan said, and Sage could hear the tenderness and love in his voice. "You know what always astounds me? The love those two have for one another. They seem to operate as a single unit. They always did, even when Ben and I were kids."

Sage nodded. "It's rare and beautiful. If I hadn't met them, I'd never have believed that romantic love could endure through a lifetime."

"They're living proof, all right. If you wait while I dump this stuff off, I'll walk you home. You can fill me in on what needs to be done tomorrow."

Sage waited, and he joined her a moment later. "I haven't had a chance to draw up tomorrow's guiding schedule yet, and I really don't want to have to deal with Grace. I was sort of hoping—"

"Of course I'll do it. Just tell me who wants to go where and I'll assign the guides."

"Thanks, Logan." Sage was relieved and grateful. "I was dreading having to talk to her. I know I'll have to sooner or later, but…I'd rather it was later."

Logan nodded. "Did you ever get around to contacting that agency, Sage? About your son?"

"Yeah, I did, the very day we got back from Africa. They said I'd be hearing from them soon."

"Let me know the minute you hear. I meant to ask you sooner, but the pace around here has been just a little hectic."

"No kidding. But now that all the panic's over, what did you want to tell me the other night, Logan?"

She glanced at him and saw him tense, and she was suddenly apprehensive. He glanced around, making certain they were alone. They'd reached her house, and he sighed and sat down on the step, gesturing for her to join him.

When she was seated, he said, "There's no easy way to say this, Sage. But Grace's baby could be mine instead of Ben's."

Chapter Eleven

Shocked speechless, Sage could only stare at him.

He looked and sounded miserable, but he met her eyes without flinching. "I made a call to a DNA testing lab today, and one of the techs there said that it's nearly impossible to differentiate between DNA from identical twins."

"You—you were…with…you had…sex…with Grace? I can't believe…you—you made love to—to her."

"Yeah." He sighed and shook his head. "I wouldn't call it lovemaking, exactly. And being stone drunk is no excuse, either. But, yeah, I was…with Grace. In March, it was a one-night stand. The night of Mom and Dad's anniversary party."

She counted back. The timing was right. A confusion of emotions rolled over her—relief that Ben had maybe told her the truth, growing anger that Logan hadn't told her sooner, and a strange sense of renewed and painful betrayal. And something else powerful that she rejected out of hand.

She couldn't possibly be jealous, she told herself.

"I feel rotten about this, Sage."

"You should." She felt sick, but her mind was racing. "But—but then why would Grace claim the baby belonged to Ben? And—and how would she know about the scar, and the other marks on his body?"

"I don't know. I've tried to figure that out and I can't. I'd planned to grill her about it before I spoke to you, but Dad had this attack and there wasn't an opportunity. And I wanted you to know that she could be lying about Ben. I'm going to confront her tonight."

Her voice was hard. "*Could be. Might be.* But there's no real way of telling for certain, is there?"

"Not unless she talks, there isn't. I'm sorry, Sage."

"I'm so sick of people saying they're sorry." Her voice was vehement, her hands clamped tight around the wooden arms of the chair. "I can't believe you didn't tell me sooner. You knew how much it hurt me, believing Ben had an affair with her."

"I wanted to tell you, the minute I heard about the DNA. And yeah, I should have told you right up front that I'd been with her, but damn it all, Sage, I was ashamed. I *am* ashamed. And I kept thinking she was bluffing, that the baby probably belonged to Oliver. So did he. You remember what he said when we talked to him in Africa."

"But you also thought that Ben *could* have been with her, didn't you?"

He started to deny it, and she cut him off.

"Don't lie to me, Logan. I deserve the truth." She tried to hold on to her temper, but it was too late. She felt totally betrayed. She got to her feet and stood over him, trembling with fury, arms crossed protectively over her heart.

"Ben was unfaithful to me before this thing with Grace. I know it now, and you did, too, didn't you? That's why you didn't say anything sooner. And for all we know, the baby *is* his, isn't that true?"

"Sage, don't. Don't do this to yourself." He was on his feet now, too. "I don't know any such thing." He reached out a hand to her, but she smacked it away.

"Don't touch me." She was breathing as if she'd been running hard. Her voice went up and down and she couldn't control it.

"I trusted you. I confided in you, and the whole time— my God, it's so ironic, both of the Galloway brothers, making out with the same woman, not even bothering to use protection. It would be funny if it weren't so pathetic."

He stood still, letting her rage break over his head.

"So what are you going to do now, Logan?"

He didn't answer for a long moment. When he did, he looked her straight in the eye. "Whether the baby was fathered by Ben or by me isn't the major issue here," he said. "The kid is. He or she deserves to be supported. I'll do that, in every way I can. Which means making sure Grace is taken care of."

Sage gaped at him. "You—you're going to—to… *marry* her?" She'd thought she couldn't feel any worse, but that did it.

"No." His denial was vehement. "Absolutely not. It would be wrong, I have no feelings for her."

Sage drew a deep, relieved breath.

He said, "That would make a bad situation one hell of a lot worse. I'll make certain she's financially okay. I've seen way too many pregnant mothers deserted by the guys responsible, struggling financially, living on social assistance. I won't let that happen to a Galloway."

In spite of herself, Sage felt a tiny spark of admiration for him.

"And will you stick around and be a real father to the baby?"

"I don't know." He ran a distracted hand through his hair. "I haven't had a chance to think this through yet. I'm taking it one step at a time, and the first thing I need to do is talk to Grace."

"I'll let you get on with that, then." Sage felt as if she was on a roller coaster, going from one heart-stopping dive straight into the next.

She ran up the stairs and into her house, shutting the door forcefully behind her. She needed time to think this through, time to figure out how she really felt about it all. Most of all, she needed to be alone.

Logan watched her go. He started after her, and thought better of it. What could he say that would make it better? He'd watched her, seen shock, disbelief and then betrayal flash across her face, seen the hurt and disillusionment in her eyes, and hated himself for being the one to cause it.

The best thing for him to do right now—the only thing— was to shoulder responsibility for the running of the Lodge, try to sort out the truth with Grace, and forget about getting back to Seattle anytime soon. His parents needed him.

He watched Oliver pull up to the dock with a boatload of guests, and as they got out, angry male voices carried clearly in the warm evening air. Oliver was having a heated argument with one of the guests.

Now what? Logan wondered. If he was a superstitious man, he'd honestly think right about now that someone had put a curse on the Lodge and everyone in it.

With a sigh of resignation, he headed down to the dock and spent fifteen minutes calming down a furious guest whom Oliver had insulted.

When that was over, Logan headed for the bunkhouse.

Might as well finish off an altogether lousy day by finding and confronting Grace, he decided. How much worse could a damned day get?

But after a quick tour of the property revealed no sign of her, he headed for the kitchen. If Mavis was still up, she'd probably know where Grace was. Mavis knew pretty much everything that went on at Raven Lodge. He found her in the kitchen, wiping down the counters and the stove.

"Oh, *that* one." Mavis's tone revealed what she thought of Grace when he asked, and it wasn't good. "She left, didn't even bother with supper. Or her wages, either. What does that tell you?"

"Left? What do you mean, *left?* Where was she going?"

Mavis shrugged. "Away. And good riddance, I say. She had a big fight with that Oliver late last night. I heard them hollering at one another. She took all her gear and borrowed one of the boats, said she'd leave it at the public dock in Valdez. Asked her where she was headed, but she wouldn't say. Only reason I know she's gone is I caught her sneaking boat keys off the board again after she'd brought her last load of tourists in. I asked what she thought she was doing. Hope we don't see the likes of her around here again. I wish Brady would leave, as well."

Logan let out a long, weary breath. Grace had flown the coop, and wasn't that just the end of a perfect day? No chance now to get to the bottom of the whole thing with him and Ben and the pregnancy.

"Thanks, Mavis."

"I hear Theo's doing okay."

"He's going to be fine." Logan had to believe that. Something good had to come of all this tragedy.

"So you gonna stick around here for a while? Because we're awful shorthanded, especially now that *she's* gone. Your dad needs you." Mavis slapped a thick roast beef sandwich and a bottle of beer down on the table and pointed toward it. "Sit here and get that down you, you look peaked."

"Thanks, Mavis. And don't worry, I'll stay until things get sorted out." He was going to have to call his partner and arrange for more time. He was going to have to see Sage every single day, knowing she hated him now.

"You're a good boy, Logan."

Mavis had told him that all during his childhood, and Logan felt a rush of affection for this taciturn, childless woman who'd been around most of his life. He stood up and wrapped his arms around her, and by the force of the hug she gave him back, he knew she was worried and hurting, just as he was.

She filled a coffee cup and sat across from him while he ate, waiting until his sandwich was gone and the beer almost empty before she said, "You know, I think that Brady fellow shot Ben on purpose."

Logan looked at her. "What makes you say that?"

"She's pregnant, that floozy, right? With Ben's baby."

Logan choked on a mouthful of food. It was several minutes before he could answer Mavis.

She waited patiently.

"Yeah, she is." Time for total honesty. "But the baby

could be mine. Or Ben's. There's no real way of telling. The only one who knows for sure is Grace." There was no point trying to hide anything from Mavis. He and Ben had learned that when they were toddlers, and why would he think things had changed? Shame overwhelmed him, but it was also an enormous relief to talk about it with someone who wasn't involved.

"It was the night of Mom and Dad's anniversary party. Oliver was away on a three-day guiding trip, and Grace and a couple of the guides asked me to come to the pub in Valdez with them. We took one of the boats."

Sage had been breathtakingly beautiful that night. She was wearing something blue and snug and short, revealing that voluptuous body and her long, curvaceous legs. She'd been funny and vibrant and sensual, and Ben kept giving Logan sly looks that said, *eat your heart out, bro—she's mine.*

"I got stone drunk." And Grace had rubbed against him like a cat in heat. "I ended up in a two-bit motel with her. I felt like shit when I woke up in the morning. I hired a boat, brought her back here. It was really early, I hoped nobody saw us."

"I watched her shining up to Ben, too." Mavis's scarred face was sad. "That boy never could keep his pants on. And he has the best wife a man could have, too." She wiped tears from her eyes with the corner of her apron and then gave him a ferocious glance. "I saw you that morning you slunk in with that Fulton baggage in tow. I wanted to take a strap to you, being so foolish."

They were silent for a moment, and then she sighed. "So what's to be done now?"

"I'll have to find her." For one cowardly instant, he

wondered if Grace was considering abortion. It would be a way out for all of them. And it would haunt him the rest of his life. "There's the baby to consider. And I'll have to tell Mom and Dad. That's going to be the worst part."

"They've survived worse. We all have. Wait till your dad is home again and feeling better."

"I intend to."

"You go on to bed now." Her voice was gentle. "A good sleep works wonders. Tomorrow's another day, and goodness knows, there's more than enough for all of us to do around here."

Four days later, Logan could only think what an understatement that had been.

It was the height of tourist season, and every spare bed in the entire Lodge was filled. With Grace gone, they were short of guides, so Logan was forced to take tourists out on fishing expeditions. The fact that his guests caught their quota was pure blind luck, because it had been years since he'd done much fishing.

The one big advantage to the frantic pace was that he hadn't seen much of Sage. Over hurried meals in the kitchen, they discussed necessary business. She was polite and distant, and the rest of the time she kept out of his way.

Logan told himself it was for the best. The sooner he could get back to Seattle, the better—for more reasons than one.

He'd spoken to his partner, Jake Armstrong, and it sounded as if the woman Jake had hired to fill in for Logan was doing a phenomenal job. She'd taken over Logan's caseload so successfully that, if he stayed away much longer, Logan figured Jake might just decide to form a partnership with her and dissolve the one with Logan.

He was thinking about all of that as he emptied the boat, preparing to hose it down. It took a few moments for the sound of angry voices to penetrate. He heard Sage, speaking in a reasonable tone, and he realized the voices were coming from the side deck.

"—demand my money back," a male voice insisted at full volume.

Sage's reply was too low for Logan to make out, but a moment later he heard another man.

Oliver. Insulting a guest again. And the language he was using had Logan sprinting up the stairs and around to the side deck.

Chapter Twelve

Sage stood between Melvin Volenski and Oliver, horrified by the tirade of foul words the guide was spouting, not only at the guest who'd complained about the day's botched fishing trip, but now also at her because she'd tried to defuse the situation. She was all too aware of two other guests, standing at the end of the deck, staring at the three of them, wide-eyed and shocked by the violence of Oliver's anger.

"Stupid frigid cunt," he spat at her, narrow eyed, face twisted by rage. "You'd take his word over mine, can't even tell when you're being jerked around by a lying idiot like this one. Well, that figures, doesn't it? No bloody wonder you couldn't keep your husband from screwing other women."

Sage gasped. The cruel words were like arrows in her heart. She felt humiliated and dreadfully ashamed. She wanted to turn and run, but she was trapped.

Volenski was now staring openmouthed at Oliver, his own anger subdued by the vitriol Oliver was spewing. "Hey," he said. "Hold on there, no need to talk like that to the lady."

Oliver ignored him. "You think Grace was the only one? She had to take a number, that's how many there were. Everyone knew it but you—isn't that a laugh?"

Sage didn't hear Logan coming. She jumped and cried out, pressing a hand over her mouth when he appeared right in front of her, putting himself between her and Oliver. She didn't see his fist draw back and land on Oliver's jaw. She heard the sickening impact, though, and the grunting sound Oliver made.

He staggered backward, crashing into a deck chair, sprawling on hands and knees on the wooden deck. Logan took two steps toward him, grabbed handfuls of the back of his shirt and yanked him upright.

"Get out of here, Brady," he growled, shoving Oliver step-by-step toward the stairs. "Get out and don't ever come back."

Oliver whirled suddenly and took a swing at Logan. Logan ducked, grabbed the other man's arm and twisted it around and up behind his back, forcing him toward the stairs at a quick march. Oliver squealed in pain, but he stopped struggling and began grabbing instead at the railing with his free hand.

Logan gave him one last shove and let him go.

Staggering, rubbing his jaw and cursing, Oliver careened down the stairs and headed at a half run toward his cabin.

Logan stood for a moment with his back to them. Then he turned and came toward Sage and Volenski.

Even through her own burning humiliation, she could only imagine the effort it took for Logan to say in a quiet, reasonable tone, "Sorry about that, Melvin. My apologies. If you'll come see me later this evening in my office, I'll make certain you're reimbursed for your stay. Sage, could I speak to you privately, please?"

She shook her head. Inside and out, she was shaking. "I—I need to go home."

"We're on our way." With a hand on the small of her back, he guided her down the steps and along the treed path toward her house.

She couldn't believe her legs were actually working. They felt rubbery and weak. She realized she was making small, agonized sounds in her throat, but she couldn't stop.

Logan must have felt the tremors that raced through her, because he murmured, "Just keep walking, you'll be home in a minute. Just keep going, that's right."

Up the steps to her door. She staggered and he steadied her, arm now around her waist.

"Locked?" His mouth was close to her ear.

Sage shook her head, and he opened the door and then closed it behind them. She stopped just inside the door, and her knees began to give way.

Logan enfolded her in his arms, cursing himself, cursing Oliver.

"That bastard. That murdering bastard. I'm an idiot, I knew I should have fired him. I knew it was a mistake to keep him on. This was my fault, all mine." His voice gentled. "You want a drink, Sage? Some tea, maybe? Water?" He half lifted her toward the sofa. "Come sit down, sweetheart, that's right. Let me get you something, just tell me what you need."

His concern, his protectiveness, were what undid her. She'd dammed up her emotions behind a locked door, and suddenly they broke free.

She gasped, fighting it, but then she started to cry, and try as she would, she couldn't stop the sobs, or the tears pouring down her cheeks, or the awful, keening noises she was making.

She wanted him to go away. She didn't want anyone to see her like this, especially not him. He'd been with Grace, Ben had been with Grace. She hated him for it.

But she wanted him to hold her, exactly the way he was doing, cradling her head against his chest, smoothing one big hand slowly up and down her spine.

"There, honey, cry it out, you'll feel better for it."

She couldn't stop, regardless. She cried until her chest hurt, her nose was stuffed solid and her face burned from the salt. And through it all, he held her while she kept wondering when Logan would lose patience and walk out on her, the way Ben had whenever she cried. He'd hated tears, had no time for them—or for her, if her emotions were anything but upbeat.

She had no idea how long it was before tears gave way to dry, racking sobs and then to the sort of peace she hadn't felt since before Grace dropped her bombshell.

"I...feel...so betrayed."

"I know you do, sweetheart. I'm so sorry. For everything." Logan gently released her and got up.

She felt bereft, but he simply went into the bathroom and doused a washcloth in hot water. He was back in moments, handing her fresh tissues, gently mopping her face as if she were two years old, holding her chin in one big fist. His knuckles were bleeding, she noticed.

"Thank you." The words were muffled because her nose was swollen.

"Better now?"

She nodded. She felt drained. She closed her eyes,

curled against his shoulder. She must have fallen asleep, because when he gently released her, the light had changed. It was softer, more hazy, the way it was late in the evening.

He'd pulled a soft throw up and over her. "Sorry, Sage. I hated to disturb you, but I have to go. I told Volenski I'd meet him this evening. He saw me coming over here with you, and I don't want any gossip."

Sleepy, so exhausted she could barely move, she made a soft sound of assent.

"Go back to sleep." He tucked a pillow under her head and then bent and kissed her on the cheek. "I'll lock the door on my way. Andrew and Opal are staying with her."

She was asleep again before the door closed behind him.

Logan loped along the path back to the Lodge, the feel of Sage, the intoxicating scent of her skin, indelibly printed on his mind. He'd wanted to really kiss her, to take her in his arms and strip off her clothes and his. The urge had been almost irresistible.

The only thing that stopped him was knowing how vulnerable she was. She'd been hurt enough by Grace and Ben—and by him. The problem was, he didn't know how much self-control he could muster up. He shouldn't be alone with her. He was going to have to keep his distance from now on, that was all there was to it.

Sage figured she must be more than a little slow, because it took three whole days for her to figure out that Logan was deliberately avoiding her. Granted, there was a lot going on at the Lodge, but she still should have realized sooner.

She'd spent the morning frantically rearranging sleeping rooms to accommodate the ten guests arriving within the hour. First Grace, and then Oliver's departure had left them drastically short of guides, which meant reshuffling of schedules. A party of eight left that morning, which kept her busy settling bills. It was after lunch when it finally dawned on her that there was something different about Logan.

She'd found him in her upstairs office checking registrations on the computer.

"Hey." She closed the door of the small room after her. "Long time no see," she joked feebly. They'd eaten lunch an hour before with the rest of the family, but it was the first time she'd been alone with him since her total meltdown, and she wanted to thank him for being so kind and thoughtful.

She wanted to let him know that, in spite of feeling horrible about it, she had no right to judge him for sleeping with Grace. He was single, after all. His love life was his own business. She felt shy about bringing it up, but it had to be said.

"Hey, Sage." His smile was warm, but his eyes were panicked. He got to his feet before she could say another word and edged past her to the door. "Gotta go get the boat ready," he blurted. "I'm booked to take the Texans out this afternoon and I'm late."

She knew it was a total lie; she'd made up the schedule. He had another forty minutes before he had to leave. She opened her mouth to say so, but he was already hurrying down the hall, racing down the stairs as if the hounds of hell were on his heels. She stared after him, and then slowly, it dawned on her that he'd been deliberately avoiding her. Ever since the night she'd fallen asleep in his arms, exhausted from crying.

She felt confused, hurt, and finally, angry. So it hadn't

been coincidence, not seeing him alone. Mortified, she wondered if he'd thought she was coming on to him that evening. Did he actually believe she'd do such a thing?

Raven Lodge was a microcosm. Isolated by water and mountains and woods, there was no way of avoiding anyone. Before Grace left, Sage had wanted nothing to do with her, but in spite of her feelings she was forced to see her half a dozen times a day. Now Logan wanted distance, and it was going to be an impossible situation all over again.

She was enmeshed with the Galloways. When Ben was alive, that was exactly what Sage had wanted. Now, however, everything was different. Maybe she needed to be more independent. Maybe she needed to begin thinking of a time when she'd even leave Raven Lodge.

The thought scared her, depressed her. The people she was closest to in all the world were here—except for one.

For years, she'd been telling herself that she'd made an irrevocable decision long ago and she had to live with it, no matter the pain.

But Ben's death had changed everything. Jenny's letters, too, had left a deep and lasting impression. Both had made Sage painfully aware of how short life could be, how important the blood bonds of family are. If she were to die tomorrow, the one thing she would regret with every ounce of her being was not having made the effort to find her son.

She hadn't heard back from the agency she'd contacted to find him. She was scared to death to hear what they had to say, but she was even more afraid of letting another day go by without making contact.

Checking that the door was locked, she picked up the phone and dialed.

Chapter Thirteen

"Ms. Galloway," the woman with the upbeat singsong voice said. "This is such a coincidence, I was just about to phone you. My name is Carol Bernard, I've been assigned your file. I have news for you."

"Please, call me Sage." Now that the moment was here, she was terrified, knuckles white where she clutched the phone. "Did you—have you found out anything about him? About my—my son?" That's the way she'd always thought of him, as her son, even knowing he belonged legally to another mother.

"I've prepared a report for you, Sage. I'll be mailing it today, but I can give you the information over the phone as well if you'd like."

"Yes. Yes, please." It wasn't overly hot in the room, but she was sweating. She found a tissue and swiped it across her forehead, down her cheeks. "Who—where is he? What's—what's his name?" His other name. She'd named him David, because of the biblical story of David and Goliath. She'd needed to pretend he'd grow up strong, because how else would he survive, knowing his mother had given him away?

"His name is Tyler, Tyler Milani. He was adopted by a wonderful couple from San Diego who loved him very much."

"Tyler." Sage breathed the name, wondering what he looked like. She felt enormous, overwhelming relief, knowing he was alive, that he was loved. That he'd been loved all these years. Which is why Carol's next words came as such a shock.

"Unfortunately, the Milanis died in a car accident two years ago. Their only relatives were in Italy, and although an uncle there offered to take Tyler, it was his choice to stay in the U.S. He's been in foster care ever since."

Stunned, it took Sage a moment to respond. "Oh, no. Oh, my God. In foster care?" To be given away by your birth mother and then lose your adoptive parents—what would that do to a kid? Abandonment, not once but twice. Guilt and a terrible sense of betrayal flooded through her.

And then the possibilities began to register. "Does this mean...could I...is there a chance I could—" her voice dropped to a whisper "—maybe I could get him back?"

"I must caution you here, Sage." Carol's voice was compassionate but firm. "I'm not a lawyer, and I'm sure you understand there are legal issues involved here, and also emotional ones. I do know child care agencies focus only on the needs of the child. According to this report, Tyler has adapted well to his foster family, and they love him.

They're a professional couple, older, who never had children, and they're very attached to Tyler. In fact, they've applied for permanent custody with a view to adoption."

A welter of emotions filled Sage. "But—but I'm his birth mother, I'm now in a position…I—I mean, I'm single, I was widowed recently, but—but money's not an issue, there's insurance. Surely I could try…I must have some rights…legally?" The words tumbled out. "I want him so much. I—I love him. He's—he's my son."

Carol's voice was kind, but noncommittal. "I can't give you advice on that matter. I'd strongly suggest you consult a lawyer."

Sage swallowed hard. "Can you…could you at least give me his address so I could write him a letter?"

"Contact would have to be Tyler's decision, Sage. We'll certainly notify his social worker, asking her to tell him we've been in touch with you and that you're eager to meet him. You can write to him in care of this agency, but he has to make the decision as to whether or not he wants to hear from you. If he agrees, then we'll forward your letter."

"I see." It was such a good news, bad news situation. Sage, hungry for every detail she could get, asked what he looked like, what grade he was in, what sports he liked, how tall he was.

"Is—is he a happy boy? I understand he'd have been terribly upset when his—his adoptive parents died. But generally…is he good-natured? Intense? Cheerful? He's—he's not depressed, is he?" He had every reason to be. Her heart fluttered, waiting for Carol's reply.

"All the reports indicate that he's a well-liked, socially adjusted young man. That's about all I can tell you—I haven't met him myself. I have a photograph, though, and I'll do my best to describe him for you."

Sage listened so hard her ear hurt. Afterward, she thanked Carol for everything and hung up. She folded her arms across her chest, holding in the fact of her son, the reality of him.

Tyler, she whispered. Six feet tall, curly blond hair, blue eyes—like hers? Lighter, darker? In grade ten, tall and rangy, a football player. It was so hard to imagine. Her only memory of him was of a newly born little bundle, curled up in a ball, naked and red, black baby hair glued wetly to his skull. She'd kissed his hands and feet, his little scrunched-up purple face. She'd closed her eyes and smelled him, that indescribable new-baby scent.

She thought he had her ears, flat against his skull, with distinctive long lobes. She'd wanted to memorize every single thing about him, but they'd taken him away too soon.

Did he ever wonder about her? Did he despise her for giving him away? Lost in bittersweet memories, Sage jumped at the knock on the door.

"Sage?" It was one of the maids. "The guests in cabin three are ready to leave. They're looking for you."

"I'll be right there." If only things weren't so busy. She needed time to digest this, to figure out what course was best, what she should do, what steps to take first. There was no doubt whatsoever about wanting her son with her. She longed for him, ached to get to know him, to watch him grow the rest of the way into manhood. But just as Carol had suggested, she needed good legal advice. There were lawyers in Valdez, but she hated the thought of baring her soul to someone she'd never met—but who undoubtedly knew a lot about the Galloways.

Logan was a lawyer. He knew the full story. Could she put hurt feelings aside and ask his professional advice? Could he give her the advice she needed? His specialty was divorce, but surely he knew something about adoption, as well.

She longed to find him and tell him everything, but instead she had to plaster on a smile and attend to business.

The opportunity to speak privately to Logan came that evening. The day had been relentlessly busy, one thing right after the next. It was after eight by the time Sage finally headed for home. Halfway between the Lodge and her house, she saw Logan coming out of one of the guest cabins. He waved, and she expected him to hurry over to the Lodge. Instead, he loped over to join her.

"Plumbing problem," he explained, gesturing at the box of tools he carried. "Mrs. Littler dropped her wedding ring down the bathroom drain."

"Did you get it back?"

"Absolutely. Makes you wonder about the psychological implications, though, doesn't it? She's here on her own, no sign of Mr. Littler. She was wearing a bathrobe and not much else, and she stuck awfully close to me while I was working. I think I'll keep out of her way for the duration of her visit."

"Is that what you're doing with me, Logan?" Sage had started walking again toward her house, and she figured this was as good a time as any to clear the air. "Are you keeping out of my way?"

"Yup." The ready admission made her stop and whirl around to face him.

"But with you it's a little different, Sage," he went on, voice pitched low and husky. "See, if I allow myself to be alone with you, I won't be able to keep my hands off you.

I can barely manage it with people around. I want you, haven't you guessed that?"

"I...when...how long?" She was stammering like an idiot.

"Since the first moment I met you. Ben knew. It's one of the reasons I stayed away."

"Ben knew?"

"Of course he did. We're—we were—twins. Why the hell do you think I ended up in a sleazy motel room with Grace? You were so beautiful that night."

She gaped at him, speechless.

He held up his hands, palms out. "Don't worry, I plan to keep my distance, because the way people talk around here, you'll be the brunt of some nasty gossip if I don't." He took a half step closer, his green eyes telegraphing desire and frustration. "But only for a while, Sage. We need to let some time go by, before..." He paused. "You notice I'm not asking you how you might feel about me. I know it's way too soon. I just want you to know up front that I care, and when the time's right, I plan to take my chances."

Her mouth was hanging open, and she closed it with a snap. He was protecting her? He cared for her?

"I thought—I thought you didn't—" She gulped, trying to figure out what to say. "Thank you." It was the only thing she could come up with. She felt stunned.

"Welcome. So now I'd better head for my own cabin and a cold shower." His grin was rueful.

He was already turning away when she found her voice.

"Logan? Logan, I've found my son. And I need legal advice."

He didn't answer right away. She thought he was going to refuse, but then he sighed and said, "Okay." He looked around. "How about that picnic table over there?"

Sage nodded, knowing he'd chosen it because it was in full view of the Lodge and several of the cabins. When they were seated across from one another, Sage repeated exactly what Carol had told her.

Logan listened closely. "So what exactly is it that you want, Sage? Custody?"

She'd thought that was it, but now the word made her think of a prisoner, and she shook her head. "Tyler's fifteen, he's not a little boy anymore. He'd have to make his own decisions about who he wants to be with. I guess what I want more than anything at this stage is to meet him, get to know him." Her eyes filled with tears. "It's way too late to be his mother. I know I relinquished that right a long time ago. Now, I'll take whatever contact I can get."

"Smart thinking." Logan nodded approval. "I'm not an expert in this stuff, but I know a lawyer in Seattle who is. I'll get in touch with her and ask questions. In the meantime, you write that letter and we'll see what comes of it."

"Okay. Thanks." She started to get up, but he reached across and put his big hand over hers, and she sat down again. He gave her such a sense of security.

"Sage?" He looked into her eyes, and she caught her breath. How could she have doubted him? His feelings for her were there, in his eyes and on his face, naked longing.

His voice was gentle. "I'll do my very best to help you. Tyler's a lucky kid, to have you for a birth mother. I'm glad you found him. And when he gets to know you, he's going to be glad, as well. Maybe you can bring him here so we all can meet him."

She'd been thinking of leaving the Lodge, even though the idea gave her a sinking sensation in her stomach.

"Don't do anything in a hurry." It was almost as if he'd

guessed what she was considering. "It always helps to have family around you at a time like this." He gave her hand a final squeeze and got to his feet. "Sleep well, beautiful lady. I'll see you in the morning."

It took everything he had to walk away. He longed to pick her up in his arms and carry her to his cabin. But just as he'd told her, it was way too soon. For both of them.

For Sage, there was her son. And for Logan, there was Grace and the baby. That horrible mess was haunting him. He needed to find Grace, and in order to do that, he needed to locate Oliver. There was a chance the man would know where Grace was. One of the other guides had seen him in Valdez, drunk and trying to pick a fight in a bar.

He'd go into Valdez tomorrow, Logan decided. Much as the idea repelled him, he'd find Brady and do his best to get the truth, not just about the baby and Grace's whereabouts, but also about his brother's death. He was convinced now more than ever that Oliver knew much more than he'd told anyone.

Chapter Fourteen

"What the hell d'you want, Galloway?" Oliver was slumped on a stool in the only pub in Valdez open at eleven in the morning. "Go away. I don't work for you anymore, remember?" His voice was thick and belligerent, and the look he gave Logan seemed filled with hate.

Logan was shocked at the other man's appearance. Oliver's hair was greasy and lank. His thin face was roughly bearded, and the hand holding the glass shook uncontrollably. He looked as if he'd been on one long drunk since leaving the Lodge.

"I want to talk to you." Fortunately, the pub was deserted apart from the rotund bartender, busy stacking crates at the other end of the room.

"Yeah, well, tough luck, asshole, 'cause I don't want to talk to you."

"You might want to reconsider that. You either talk to me, or I'll hound the authorities into reopening the case against you in my brother's death."

Logan knew it was impossible—if there hadn't been enough evidence to lay charges in Dar es Salaam, there certainly wasn't going to be enough in Alaska. But he was banking on the fact that Oliver didn't know that, not for a certainty.

"Go ahead and talk to anybody you please, I don't give a shit." But this time he sounded only weary.

"Where's Grace?"

Pain flickered across his ravaged face. "How the fuck would I know? She didn't exactly invite me along, did she?"

"You must know where her home is, what relative she'd be most likely to run to."

"Why are you so interested, Galloway? Or were you sniffing around her as well as Ben?"

Logan had to control the sudden rage that made him want to flatten the other man. "She's having a baby. She needs help."

"Not my concern. Not my kid, apparently," Oliver sneered as he emptied his glass. "She had no family, none she was close to. Grew up in Portland with some old aunt."

"Okay, so who was she friends with here in Valdez? She must have had a woman friend, somebody she talked with. C'mon, Oliver, think."

"That Redmond woman's the only one I know of. Your brother's first wife." He waved at the bartender for a refill. "Keep it all in the family—that's the Galloway motto."

"Jill? Grace was friends with Jill?" It came back all of a sudden, the day of Ben's funeral, the two women talking intently in a corner. So much had happened since that day Logan had almost forgotten.

"They were tight there for a while. That's all I know."

"Okay. Thanks."

Jill would probably be at work at Valdez Medical Center. Grateful that everything in town was within walking distance, Logan set off to find her.

"You know that Grace is pregnant." Logan stirred creamer into the coffee Jill handed him. He wasn't sure if Jill knew or not, but statements were always better than questions. They were in the nurses' lounge, which fortunately was empty. "She's claiming the baby belongs to Ben." He watched Jill closely for a reaction.

"Sure, she told me that." Jill was a tall, statuesque blonde, cool and controlled. Her gray eyes showed not a hint of emotion. "Didn't surprise me in the least. He screwed around on me while we were married. Why would he change his ways?"

"Did she also tell you that the baby could easily be mine, instead of his?"

"Oh, it's Ben's all right. Grace would know, and she told me it was definitely his."

But Jill knew that he'd had sex with Grace, as well, Logan mused. Her lack of reaction to his admission was a dead giveaway. Now why would she be so convinced *he* hadn't fathered Grace's baby?

He decided to let that go for the moment. What he needed to know was how to contact Grace. "She left Raven Lodge right after the funeral, Jill, probably because of a fight with Oliver. Do you happen to know where she is?"

She sounded bored, and she lit a cigarette in spite of the

No Smoking signs on the wall. "Nope." She took a deep drag and shrugged. "Haven't a clue."

"But the two of you were friends. She must have said something to you, at the very least told you she was planning on leaving. I saw you having a long conversation with her the day of the funeral."

Jill's gaze was directed over his shoulder. "It was an emotional time. We'd both been hurt by Ben. We had a lot to discuss."

Logan was certain she was lying. He'd never liked Jill, and now his dislike grew even stronger. He tried to suppress it, to make her see what the real issue was here. "Look, there's a baby to consider. Whoever its father is, the kid deserves a decent life."

Jill's tiny smile was smug. "And what makes you think Grace won't provide that? I'm a single parent, I manage pretty well. My girls are just fine, thank you."

"But you get a healthy amount every month for their support."

Logan knew exactly how healthy; he'd been the one to draft the agreement. "It would be a lot harder without that money, Jill, and without the constant emotional support my parents give you. The girls also had Ben. Maybe he wasn't the perfect father, but he was on the scene. Sophia and Lily know they have family around, and that's important for kids."

Logan set his coffee aside and leaned forward, trying to force her to look at him. "Oliver told me that Grace doesn't have family. So she'll be entirely on her own, and as far as I know, being a fishing guide isn't much in demand away from here. How's she going to support herself, Jill? What if her pregnancy isn't easy, what if she can't find work? Living on social assistance is tough."

Jill's eyes had narrowed, and she crossed her arms on her chest. Her gaze met his and glanced away again, but he saw the bitterness and anger there. "Even if I knew where she was, I wouldn't tell you, Logan. See, unlike you and your brother, *I* keep my word. *I* don't betray a confidence. *I* don't take advantage of other people." She got to her feet. "Now, I have to get back to work." She turned on her heel and strode out of the room, leaving Logan angry, frustrated and unsure what to do next.

He thought about it all during the boat trip back to the Lodge, and he was still trying to figure out a plan that evening.

Dinner was over, and he and Sage were with his parents and Andrew and Opal in the living room. Theo held the thick folder with the copies of Jenny Galloway's letters.

"I can't thank you enough for these, Andrew," he said. "They put a whole new spin on Galloway family history."

"I thought so, too. The thing about the letters that I find so touching and surprising is Jenny Galloway's honesty," Andrew replied. "She speaks of intimate matters, like her affair with her husband's brother, and she doesn't try to excuse herself."

Sage's glance flickered toward Logan, and he saw the guilty color stain her cheeks. He could guess exactly what she was thinking. He, just like Robert Galloway, had fallen in love with his sister-in-law. Was he simply following a path set out long ago by dead relations? He was relieved that the others were too absorbed in the letters to notice the energy between himself and Sage.

Andrew said, "She writes down exactly what's going on. It must have taken great courage to be that open with her father, especially at a time when things like pregnancy and lovemaking weren't ordinary topics of conversation, to say nothing of adultery with her brother-in-law."

"She believed that her son, Bruce, was Robert's child," Theo was saying. "Which backs up what my aunt Emma told me before she died. I never understood till I read these how Jenny could have an affair with Robert, but her letters explain how and why she turned to him."

"And wouldn't you just know she'd get preggers, poor child?" Opal shook her head. "Makes you think the powers that be have a twisted sense of humor, don't it?"

"But in her later letters she emphasizes again and again how William totally accepted Bruce as his own," Theo said. "My father was their only son, too. They had the twins, Martha and Emma, but no more boys."

"She lost that first baby, which was a boy," Caitlin reminded them.

Opal clicked her tongue. "Poor wee soul, she was only a child herself. And William no support to her, the blockhead. Reading those made me want to give him a good boot right in the nether regions."

Logan hadn't read the letters. He listened to the discussion, intrigued by the complexity of his family's history, but not absorbed by it the way his parents were. They didn't realize yet that current events were unfolding which were every bit as complicated and emotional as the story of Jenny Galloway. Soon now they'd have to know about Grace and the baby, and his shameful role in the whole mess. He wasn't looking forward to telling them, but it was going to have to be done.

Mavis was serving tea and chocolate chip cookies when the knock came on the living room door.

Mandy opened it and stuck her head in. "Sorry to disturb

you, but the cops are here." Her eyes were huge in her narrow face. "They want to speak to you, Logan. They're in the entrance hall."

"Aha, your checkered past is catching up with you, lad," Opal teased, winking at him.

Sage and Caitlin looked anxious.

"I'll come with you, son." Theo was getting to his feet, but Logan shook his head.

"No, please stay here, Dad. It's probably a formality."

The two officers were standing inside the wide double doors.

"I'm Sergeant Jensen," the taller one said. "And this is Detective Mulvaney. We're here because of Oliver Brady. I understand he was an employee at the Lodge until very recently?"

Logan wondered what kind of trouble Oliver had gotten himself into now. "Yes, he worked here as a guide until three days ago. In fact, I was in Valdez earlier today and I spoke with him. What's the problem, officer?"

"What time would that have been, Mr. Galloway?"

"When I saw Oliver? Oh, about eleven. I got back here at five-thirty."

"Did he contact you again after you spoke with him?"

"Nope." Logan shook his head. "He was in the pub and he was drinking pretty heavily. I went over to the medical center, and when my errand there was done, I went down to the docks and brought my boat home. I didn't see Oliver again." He paused and then said, "So what's this about?"

Jensen said, "Mr. Brady left the pub, went to his rented room and shot himself two hours ago. He left a note for you."

"Shot himself?" Stunned and shocked, Logan stared at the policemen. "Oliver committed suicide?"

"This is the note." Mulvaney handed Logan a sheet of paper enclosed in plastic. "Read it through the covering, please."

It was written in pencil, the writing small and irregular. It was only a few sentences long, and reading it made Logan nauseous.

"Logan Galloway," it began. Oliver's anger clearly showed. The pencil had gone right through the paper.

I shot your brother, and if you were here right now
I'd shoot you. I love her, and she's gone forever. It's
all your fault, you and Ben.

The officers watched him as he read and reread it.

"Can you tell us what this is about, Mr. Galloway?"

Logan needed to sit down. He needed more privacy than the entrance hall provided; any of the guests could wander through. He gestured down the hall toward the kitchen door, and the officers followed him.

The kitchen wasn't empty, however. Mandy, obviously curious, hovered by the counter, and Logan was forced to ask her to leave. She did, closing the kitchen door with a bang. Logan led the way to the big wooden table and sat down. The two men took chairs across from him, and as succinctly as possible, Logan told the police the whole story.

They already knew about Ben's death in Dar es Salaam, and that Oliver had been detained afterward. Logan told them the rest, including the fact that Grace's baby could possibly be his. It was humiliating, but he knew it had to be done. Keeping secrets was no longer an option. Two men were dead because of Grace, and that was enough.

Jensen and Mulvaney made notes in small black note-books, and Logan was hugely relieved when they finally left.

Every eye focused on him when he walked back into the living room.

"Oliver Brady shot himself this evening." There was no easy way to say it. Logan heard his mother's indrawn breath and Sage's gasp, but his eyes were on his father. He'd been delaying telling Theo the whole truth, but now there could be no more delay.

Opal said, "Is he a friend, this Oliver?"

Logan shook his head. "He worked here as a guide. He was the one with Ben when Ben was shot."

Perceptive and thoughtful, Andrew got to his feet. He sensed that Logan and his parents needed privacy. "Opal and I'll be going to bed now," he said. "Come, my dump-ling. Got to get our beauty sleep."

They said good-night, and as soon as they were gone, Theo said quietly, "Come sit here beside me, Caitlin."

She did, and Theo put a protective arm around her shoulders, as if he sensed that she might need his support— or maybe he needed hers.

Logan wished with all his heart he could do the same with Sage. She seemed so alone and vulnerable, sitting in an armchair facing him, her lovely sapphire-blue eyes filled with the same dread he was feeling.

"Now, son, please tell us exactly what the police said."

If only that was all there was to it. Logan hated having to reveal Ben's weaknesses. He hated having to admit to his own. And it wasn't only his intimate life he was going to reveal; it was also Sage's.

She was looking at him.

He asked her, "Do I have your permission to tell my parents everything?"

Color drained out of her face, but her nod was certain. "Absolutely. They need to know."

He drew a deep breath and began.

Chapter Fifteen

When the full story was finally told, Sage felt an enormous sense of relief. She'd dreaded telling her in-laws, and she was grateful to Logan for doing it.

Her hands had stayed locked together in her lap as Logan quietly explained the reason for Oliver's anger, his rationale for shooting Ben and then committing suicide. Logan repeated Grace's claim, that the child she carried belonged to Ben. He told his parents about the DNA report, and finally he spoke of his own uncertainty as to whether or not the baby was actually his instead of Ben's.

"It's nearly impossible to differentiate between the DNA of identical twins," he concluded. "But regardless of who fathered Grace's baby, the fact is I'm responsible for his or her welfare." He met Sage's eyes, his own gaze remorseful but steadfast. "I'm going to tackle Jill again tomorrow.

I had the feeling she wasn't being honest with me. She knows where Grace is. Maybe she'll see things differently now that Oliver is dead."

Sage felt admiration for his straightforwardness, his bald honesty in admitting his role in the situation. Watching him, seeing the effort it cost him to admit what he'd done, she couldn't deny that she had feelings for him.

But what if he was more like Ben than she realized?

It hurt her to see the effect of Logan's words on Caitlin and Theo. They'd listened without interruption, but Sage saw the color drain from Caitlin's cheeks, the involuntary tightening of Theo's jaw and the disillusionment and sadness in both of their eyes when Logan was done.

"I'm so sorry, Mom, Dad." Logan's apology was made with love and dignity, but Sage could hear the anguish in his voice. "I guess all of us wish we could go back and do things differently. I sure do."

"I'm sorry, too." Theo heaved a deep sigh. His disappointment in his sons was obvious, and Sage tensed, wondering if he was about to vent his feelings on Logan. But all he said was, "You're right, Logan, about that child. Whoever is responsible, it's our grandbaby. Difficult as it will no doubt be on all of us, you're going to have to find Grace and bring her back."

"I plan to do exactly that."

Sage became aware that Caitlin was watching her.

Her mother-in-law said, "How horrible this has been for you, Sage, knowing about the baby, feeling so betrayed. I know how much you've longed for a baby. Losing Ben was bad enough, but to have to deal with all this at the same time—you're very strong, dear one. I'm so proud of you."

With a sinking feeling in her gut, Sage knew the time had come for her own confession and she wished to God she didn't have to make it. But Logan had paved the way, and the thought of her son gave her strength. She glanced up at Jenny's likeness. It must have been just as difficult for her to tell the truth in her letters.

"There's something else you need to know," Sage began, voice trembling. "Fifteen years ago, when I was fifteen, I had a son." She related her story, understanding all too well exactly how Logan must have felt a few moments before. But in spite of her shame, she told them everything she knew about Tyler.

She ended by saying, "I always wanted you both to know. But I was a coward, afraid Ben would despise me if he found out, because he wanted—he wanted his own son so desperately." She swallowed hard. "And—and I wasn't able to give him a child."

She hadn't realized until that moment how much she'd wanted to please him. She now saw the flaw in that desire. What was it in her, what terrible depth of insecurity, that had made her view pregnancy primarily as a way to make Ben happy?

"You must bring him here to meet us," Theo declared. "He'll need to know you have a family, that we're all pleased to welcome him."

Caitlin nodded agreement. "Yes, Sage, you have to do that. We'd love to have him here. And he'd enjoy it. You know how much the teenage boys that come with their fathers like to fish."

They were so loving, these Galloways, so generous and kind. Sage's eyes filled, and the room swam through the haze of tears.

"Thank you," she managed. "Of course, I'll have to wait and see if Tyler even wants to meet me."

"Of course he will," Theo assured her. "Every child wants to know who his birth parents are. I'm sure if my own father had read those letters Jenny Galloway wrote, he'd have wanted to go off to Australia and meet Robert. And vice versa. Robert never knew he had a son, poor guy."

The reference to the letters seemed to ease the tension in the room.

As Sage headed home in the warm summer evening, she thought about what a blessing it had been for Andrew and Opal to arrive when they had, just before all hell broke loose at the Lodge. They'd unwittingly brought a reminder that tragedy could give way to change that ultimately brought happiness.

If only that would happen to her. And to Logan. And Caitlin and Theo. She looked up at the brilliance of the sky, thinking over the events of the day. The Alaskan sun was making its sweeping, shallow dip into the ocean. There were still questions Sage desperately needed answers for. If Logan had fathered her child, then how did Grace know all those intimate details about Ben's body?

Logan walked into the nurses' lounge just past noon the following day. One of the orderlies had told him Jill was on her break, and he hoped to find her alone.

"You again?" She stirred sugar into her coffee, not bothering to offer him any this time. "I told you yesterday I couldn't help, so why come back, Logan? You're becoming a nuisance."

"You heard about Oliver." He knew the news of a suicide

would have swept through the entire village, and everyone in the medical center would definitely know.

"Yeah, I heard. It's a shame, but it's got nothing to do with me."

"Well, you're wrong there." He doubted the police would have revealed the contents of Oliver's note. "He wrote a suicide letter, addressed to me. In it he admitted he shot Ben on purpose. Oliver killed him, Jill. Over Grace. And then he killed himself."

Jill was expert at hiding her emotions, but he saw the shock in her gray eyes. He pressed his advantage.

"Two men are dead now because Grace said that her baby was fathered by Ben. Why would she be so certain, Jill? And if she had been with both of us, how would she know who was the father, when DNA from identical twins is almost impossible to differentiate? Wouldn't it have been a lot better for her to claim the kid was mine? I'm single, you'd think it would make more sense to tag me as the father."

He saw the tension in her body, the way her eyes wouldn't meet his. Her mouth trembled slightly.

"C'mon, Jill. Why was she so insistent it was Ben? And where the hell is Grace now? You know way more about all this than you're telling, and I'm not letting up on you until I get the truth."

"Give it a rest." She sneered, but there wasn't much conviction in her tone.

"I could tell the cops you were involved in Ben's death. I think they'd be interested in knowing exactly what led up to Oliver's suicide." They did know, because he'd told them. But she didn't know that. And Logan was sure the police had likely already written it off, one more case off the books.

But Jill was the only chance he had at finding Grace.

"Ben was your children's father, Jill. Didn't you think of that?"

Watching her defenses crumble was like watching ice slowly melt.

She swallowed and cleared her throat. "I—I didn't...I only wanted to hurt him, the way he hurt me. The way he hurt the girls, always making promises, never keeping them."

Logan nodded encouragement. He knew that part was true. Ben had played that game with him too many times when they were young, promising and then never delivering.

"I—I didn't know that Oliver would...I didn't even think about him. See, Grace was in love with Ben. I don't know why Oliver didn't see that, because everybody else did. She was obsessed with him, everyone knew it. And Ben reveled in it." Her voice was bitter. "His ego was a black hole."

"So what happened, Jill? How did all this start?"

She shook her head and blew out a breath. "Grace came here for a pregnancy test. We knew each other a little, she confided in me because she knew how I felt about Ben's new little wifey." She sneered. "Grace couldn't stand her, either."

The slur at Sage made Logan want to decimate her, but he kept his mouth shut, focusing on the end goal.

"She told me the baby was yours. She'd had sex with Ben, but he'd used a condom and the dates didn't quite match up. Not that Ben would ever know the kid wasn't his, not unless you told him you'd been there, as well. And I figured the chances of that happening were pretty slim. You and your beloved bro weren't exactly best friends. Everyone in the family knew that."

Logan swallowed hard. It was one thing to suspect, and quite another to know for certain. My God. *He was going to be a father.*

"I did some research, found out about the DNA thing. I saw a way to get back at Ben big-time. If Sage figured the baby was Ben's, she'd likely leave him. He'd fooled around on her before, and she's so sanctimonious, I figured she wouldn't stand for it again. So I convinced Grace to go to her and say the baby was Ben's. We timed it while he was in Africa, so she'd have lots of time to stew."

"And you told her about the marks on Ben's body."

"Sure." Jill was quickly regaining her confidence. "It was perfect. I had Grace convinced that Sage would leave Ben, and she'd have a clear field. Grace isn't exactly Nobel Prize material. I told her if the baby was a boy, Ben would be so thrilled he wouldn't give Sage another thought. Everybody knows she's a dried-up prune who can't get pregnant."

The urge to reach out and shake her made him take a step back. He wasn't done here yet. He needed to control himself.

Jill said in a disgusted tone, "I never dreamed that idiot Oliver would go psycho. How could anybody guess that?"

Logan stared at her, appalled that she seemed annoyed at Oliver rather than sickened by her own actions. Because of her, Ben's daughters were without a father, his parents had lost a son. Sage was a widow, Logan's twin was dead. And Oliver, as well. The man must have relatives, parents who'd mourn him. And this woman took no blame for any of it.

Jill revolted and horrified him. He felt faintly nauseous even being near her. He needed to get out, breathe in clean air, rid himself of the thoughtless evil she'd brought on him and on his family.

"So where did Grace go?" His tone was harsh. He needed to know, and he was ready to shake it out of her if he had to.

Jill hesitated, and then shrugged. "Oh, what the heck, what difference can it make now? She's staying with some old aunt in Portland, the one who raised her. Margaret somebody or other, I've got the number in my address book." Jill went over to a bank of lockers and retrieved her handbag. She flipped through a small red notebook.

"Here it is, Margaret Peters. Her number's 503-555-9252. But I wouldn't count too much on being a daddy, Logan." Jill's smile was feral. "Grace told me at Ben's funeral that she was going to have an abortion."

He needed to know. Either way, he needed to know.

"Stop by and see the girls, why don't you? They miss—" She caught herself. "Family."

He knew she'd been about to say Ben. He looked at her, holding her cool, dispassionate gaze for a long moment. No matter how much he despised Jill, her daughters were his nieces, and he knew she was reminding him of that, smug in the knowledge that he couldn't rid himself of her.

Mavis often said, *You can choose your friends, but you're stuck with your relatives.* He'd never been more aware of that than he was at this moment.

"I will. As you say, they're my nieces. They're Ben's daughters, Jill. Too bad you didn't think of that sooner." He turned and strode out, wishing he never had to lay eyes on Jill Redmond again.

He hurried down to the docks and reclaimed his boat. Away from Valdez, he skirted the coastline, squinting up at the blue glaciers that formed a backdrop for the rocks and trees, watching a heron swoop and soar. At some point he came to a decision without consciously thinking about it.

He waited until early that evening to knock at the door of Sage's house. He knew Opal and Andrew were still with his parents in the living room of the Lodge, and he needed to see Sage alone.

It took a few moments before she came to the door. She was wearing denim shorts and a rumpled pink T-shirt, and she looked as if she'd been sleeping, blue eyes heavy lidded, curls rumpled and flattened on one side.

Tenderness overwhelmed him. He longed to take her in his arms and hold her close. Would the time ever come when he could follow through on his impulses?

"Logan. Come on in." She yawned, wide and long. "Oh, excuse me. I came home after dinner and conked out on the sofa." She led the way into the living room. "You were in Valdez today. How's life in the big city?"

He could tell she was trying to keep things casual. As always, there was a heightened sense of energy around her, a gravitational pull as basic as the moon and tides. He deliberately sat away from her, where it might be possible to keep his thoughts straight.

"I talked to Jill. Or rather, she finally talked to me." He quickly outlined the scheme the two women had concocted, the fact that Jill had been the one who coached Grace on the scars on Ben's body. "Grace told her the baby's mine, Sage. Ben was telling you the truth."

And so was he, as far as the baby was concerned. There was no need for Sage to know that Ben had been with Grace. There was already more than enough pain to go around.

Her eyes widened, and a visible tremor went through her. She slowly folded over like a rag doll, head touching her knees. He could hear her breathing, ragged and erratic. When she sat up again, there were tear tracks on her cheeks, and she rubbed them absently away with the palm of one hand.

"Oh, my God. It's such a relief to know he wasn't lying to me. I can mourn for him now without wanting to kill him myself," she said with a heart-wrenching sad attempt at a smile. "Thanks, Logan. More than I can say. Did you find out where Grace is?"

"Yeah, she's in Portland." He hesitated, because this next part would be hard for her. God knew, it was hard for him. "I'm going to phone her in the morning. I wanted to talk to you first, before I did anything else. I'm probably going to try and get her to come back here, Sage. I need to know that she's being taken care of, that the baby has every chance for a good beginning."

She looked stricken, but she nodded.

"There's also a strong possibility that she's aborted the pregnancy. Jill said she was planning to."

He saw the swift play of emotion on her face, and he understood exactly what she was thinking. If there was no baby, things would definitely be easier. Having Grace here would be enormously difficult, particularly for Sage.

From his conversation with Jill, Logan knew the depths of Grace's resentment toward Sage. And there was also Jill to contend with. Grace was her friend; she'd probably be around more than she usually was.

"Would that be a relief for you, Logan? If she aborted? Or would you be disappointed?"

"You ask really tough questions, lady." He sighed. "Some of both, I guess. It's not a situation I've ever been in before, so I don't really know."

"Have you changed your mind about…are you planning to—to marry Grace?"

It was so far from his thoughts that it took him off guard.

"Good God, no. Like I said before, I have no feelings for her whatsoever, except concern that she's cared for while she's pregnant, and that the baby is supported." It was time to broach the other thing he wanted to say to her. "The only woman I'd ever marry is you, Sage."

He heard her gasp.

"You do know I'm in love with you. Or if you don't know, well then, darling, I'm telling you now." *Keep it light, Galloway.*

He'd taken her by surprise. Rich color bloomed in her cheeks, and her thick lashes dropped down so he couldn't see her eyes. He plowed on regardless. "I think I told you before that I've loved you since the first day I met you. I always thought that old saw about love at first sight was pure garbage, but the minute I laid eyes on you, I became a believer." It felt good to get it out in the open, although his heart was hammering like crazy. He had no idea what her reaction might be, but at least the need for pretense was over. "I want to marry you eventually, Sage. I want to make a life with you. I know it's way too soon to bring all this up, but the way things go around here, I'm scared each time I go to Valdez that I'll come back and you'll be gone."

She shook her head, still not looking at him. Her voice was soft.

"I thought of leaving. I'd pretty much made up my mind. And now, knowing Grace will be here—I can't forgive her for the pain she's caused me—not yet. It's still too fresh."

Now her eyes met his. Her look was challenging. "I decided to stay, at least for the time being, for very selfish reasons. I think it'll be easier for me if I have a home and a family if—when—I get to meet Tyler."

"You're right, it will be." He knew that wasn't her only reason. He knew the depth of her love for his parents, for this wild frontier. He knew that she'd made Raven Lodge her home, and leaving it would mean leaving half her heart behind. But if she wanted him to believe she was capable of coldhearted reasoning, he'd pretend.

She held his gaze and he dared the next part. "So tell me, do I have a chance with you, Sage?"

She was silent so long he lost all hope.

"I—I care about you, so much it scares me." The words were barely above a whisper. "But what if—what if you're like Ben? You're—you were—are—identical twins. What if one woman isn't enough for you, either? I know now that even if Grace hadn't been lying, Ben and I wouldn't have lasted. He—there was something in him that was ruthless, and I didn't see it until after we were married. He didn't really consider anyone except himself. Sooner or later, my pride, my self-esteem, would have forced me to leave him."

Logan wanted to stand up and roar, "But I'm not Ben."

Instead, in a quiet voice that took every ounce of his self-control, he said, "All I'm asking for is time to prove myself. I want you to get to know me, all my good points and all my bad ones."

"That'll be pretty hard to do when you go back to Seattle, won't it?"

"I'm not going back." He hadn't realized until this moment that he'd already made the decision. "I'm going to look into opening up a practice in Valdez. I'm calling my partner right away and asking him to begin dissolving the partnership."

She was shaking her head even before he finished speaking. "I really don't want you to do that on account of me, Logan."

His voice was firm. "I wouldn't do it for that reason. It puts way too much pressure on us both, and I don't want that." He stopped and gathered his thoughts. "Dad always wanted both Ben and I to take over the running of the Lodge. He wanted us to be partners, but I knew at an early age that wasn't going to be possible. We disagreed on a lot of basic principles. Ben loved it here, he had no desire to go anywhere else. And we didn't get along, so I left. Don't get me wrong—I love my job, I like Seattle, but this is my home. If I could work part-time in Valdez and spend time helping Dad manage this place, it would be the best of both worlds for me."

He left unspoken the fact that Theo was no longer strong or healthy, that he might never be again. With Ben gone Caitlin would have to shoulder far too much of the responsibility for the Lodge and its functioning. He was needed here.

Logan knew Sage understood that; she'd also been doing all she could in the past week to ease the burden.

"Okay, I accept that you're not moving here for me. And I'm glad of it, because I can't make any promises." She met his eyes straight on.

He wanted to snatch her off the sofa, kiss away her uncertainty, carry her up the stairs and into a bedroom where she hadn't ever slept with Ben and make incredible love to her. But Andrew and Opal were using the spare room, and he had the distinct feeling that caveman tactics wouldn't exactly impress Sage.

"I'll go now. It's way too hard to keep my hands off you when we're alone like this. See you in the morning." He blew her a kiss and hurried out the door.

Striding across to the Lodge to say good-night to his parents, he sent up a heartfelt prayer that things would work out for the two of them. He knew better than to think they deserved it. Life had taught him that, rather than getting what he deserved, he usually got what he worked hard for.

And he planned to work as hard as he could to convince Sage they had a future together.

Chapter Sixteen

Logan's declaration of love kept Sage awake most of the night. She alternated between elation at knowing how he felt to relief that she hadn't leaped into his arms and said to hell with the consequences. Because for one mad moment, that's exactly what she'd wanted to do.

But she'd told him the absolute truth. Knowing he loved and wanted her scared her about as much as it also thrilled her. She knew she wasn't anywhere near ready for another commitment.

As a result of her nearly sleepless night, she didn't wake at her usual time in the morning. Breakfast was long over by the time she made her way over to the Lodge, and it was a relief to find Mavis and Caitlin in the big kitchen, having midmorning coffee while they worked out the menus for the coming week. Mandy and one of the other maids flitted in and out as well, bringing down breakfast trays from guest rooms and refilling water jugs.

"Where's Opal this morning?" Sage asked. "She and Andrew were gone by the time I came downstairs." She'd grown fond of both of her houseguests. "They leave my kitchen cleaner than I've ever seen it and the bathroom's always shining. I'm going to miss them when they go."

"Luckily that won't be for a while," Caitlin said with a pleased smile. "They've decided to stay and help out for the rest of the tourist season. They want to experience a little of an Alaskan winter. Andrew's great with guests and familiar with boats, so he can take the sightseeing trips out to see the glaciers as soon as he gets familiar with the territory. And Opal insists on working with Mavis on meals, which leaves me free to supervise the cleaning and spend time with the guests."

Sage poured coffee for herself and refilled the other two mugs. "I'll be updating all the bookings this morning on the computer. I've gotten behind."

Caitlin nodded. "I wonder if you could help me take stock in the storeroom first. We're running low on some staples, and I want to have a list ready when you go into Valdez this afternoon with Logan. If you want to, that is."

"Me? Go to Valdez? Are you sure you don't need me here?"

"Positive," Caitlin said. "It'll do you good to spend a couple of hours away from here. You've been working far too hard the last while. Logan has to pick up those people who drove up from Canada, Joyce and George Cunningham. Apparently she's terrified of flying so Tom can't bring them. All you'll have to do is the grocery shopping."

Sage was grateful to Caitlin for arranging the trip. She

thought of the boat trip to Valdez, alone with Logan. Privacy was a rare commodity for them, and now, knowing how he felt, things were different.

Sage followed Caitlin into the huge storage room, pen and paper in hand to mark down the necessary supplies. But instead of counting tins of tomatoes, Caitlin closed the door behind them and put a hand on Sage's shoulder.

"I wanted a word with you in private, and around here the storeroom is the only sure place," she said with a rueful smile. "I had a talk with Logan this morning." Caitlin's smile vanished. "He told me that the baby is definitely his, that Grace deliberately lied just to cause trouble. I'm so sorry, Sage, for the pain all this has caused you. I'm sure you feel as betrayed as I do. I can't believe Jill was at the bottom of all this. It's going to be very hard for me to forgive her, and I intend to tell her exactly how I feel. But I also know that if Grace comes back here as Logan wants her to, it'll be very difficult for you. For all of us, but especially for you." She drew in a long breath. "Sage, I've never put this into words before, but you are the daughter of my heart." Tears glistened in Caitlin's lovely gray eyes. "I've already lost my son. I couldn't bear to lose you, as well."

"Oh, Caitlin." Sage wrapped her arms tight around her mother-in-law, breathing in the comforting scent of Caitlin's lavender perfume. "I love you and Theo more than I can say. I can't promise that I'll always be here at the Lodge, but I'll always love you."

And how would Caitlin react if she knew Logan had feelings for her? Sage wondered with a sense of disquiet. She had the feeling that everything was moving too fast, that she needed time to adjust to the changes in her life. She was going to have to make absolutely certain Logan understood how she felt.

Chapter Seventeen

"I do understand that you need time." Logan narrowly avoided a deadhead in the water that could have sunk them. He maneuvered around it and then looked over at her. "But I also need some indication that you don't find me entirely repulsive."

"Not entirely," she teased. "I've noticed how kind you are to old people and animals."

He shot her a look and she became serious again. "You know I'm physically attracted to you. But getting involved physically is easy, and it blurs a person's thinking. We need to talk first, really get to know each other."

Frustration filled him. "I thought we did talk. On that trip to Africa, that's about all we did." In spite of the fantasies that he couldn't, even then, suppress.

She shuddered. "That was a horrible time. We were

both upset, not really ourselves. We need ordinary days, lots of them."

"Okay. Okay, I hear you. So here we are, with half an hour before we get to Valdez." And talking was definitely his second choice, but beggars weren't choosers. "Let's use it to good advantage. Tell me something about you that nobody else knows."

She shoved the sunglasses up with a forefinger, thinking it over. "I stole lunches from other students in high school."

Logan looked at her to see if she was joking, but by the seriousness of her expression, he figured she wasn't. "How come? Were you hungry?"

"Nope. I think it had something to do with thinking that everyone had something I didn't have. A father, maybe. Love, probably. By stealing their lunches, I must have felt I could get a little of whatever it was."

He knew she was looking at him from behind her dark lenses, trying to gauge his reaction. Her face was flushed far more than the ocean breeze and sunshine warranted. She was ashamed, but she'd still confided in him.

"Oh, sweetheart." He reached out with one arm and pulled her close to his side. "I'll make you a promise, and I'll never break it. If you give me a chance, I'll fill your life with such love, you'll never have to steal lunches again. Ever."

"Hope to die?"

"Hope to die."

She was breaking his heart, without even knowing she was doing it. He wanted her at his side for the rest of their lives, he wanted her with every bone in his body, every drop of his blood. And he'd have her, he'd win her, even if it took half a lifetime.

Which, by all indications, looked probable.

* * *

Two weeks passed, endless, stifling hot days filled with the work that came with the busy tourist season. Logan telephoned Grace, learning that she hadn't aborted the baby. He told Sage that he was planning to fly to Portland as soon as business at the Lodge slowed a little.

Sage was in her office, preparing the layout for a new brochure one August afternoon when the phone beside the computer rang.

"Hello, Raven Lodge. Sage Galloway here. How may I help you?"

There was silence, and she said hello again, impatiently this time, her attention on the mock-up on the computer screen.

And then a young, nervous male voice said, "My name is Tyler Milani. I think, umm, they said that you—like, I got this letter where you said you might be my birth mother?"

Sage honestly thought that her heart stopped. Her mouth went dry, and for a second she couldn't reply or breathe or think.

"Hello? Are you there?"

Terrified he'd hang up, she croaked, "Tyler. Tyler, I'm so glad you called." Her voice was shaking, every nerve in her body was vibrating. She felt as though she was about to explode with excitement.

Her son was on the other end of the line, the voice she'd tried to imagine so often was right there in her ear. "Give me a minute here. I'm so excited, I can barely put two words together.

"Big shock, I guess, having me phone you."

He sounded so young, so unsure. It was exactly how she felt.

"They said it was okay, the woman at the agency. They said that you were cool with me calling, if I wanted."

"Oh, God, yes." She was crying, and she sniffed hard and babbled, "I can't tell you what it means to me to actually speak with you." There was an awkward silence while Sage struggled to control her tears. Then they both started to talk at once.

"I don't know what to—" he said.

"I can't think of all the things—" she said.

They both stopped, and they each laughed a little. It helped, because some of Sage's nervousness melted.

"You go first, Tyler."

"I don't know what I should call you."

"Sage. Call me Sage." Pain twisted her gut into knots. She'd abdicated her rights to anything else long ago, hadn't she?

"Okay. Your turn, Sage." He sounded so shy.

"Tyler, I want to know so many things about you. But first of all, just hearing your voice is incredible. In fifteen years, I don't think a day has gone by that I didn't think of you."

"Then why did you give me away?" There was more than a little aggressive resentment in his tone.

It was the question Sage had dreaded the most, the one she'd always feared she'd have to answer someday. She swallowed hard and closed her eyes, praying for the right words, wondering if hearts actually could break.

"It wasn't because I didn't love you, Tyler. It was because I did, because I knew I couldn't give you any sort of a life." She drew a shuddering breath. "I was fifteen and a half, eight months older than you are now. You're probably more mature than I was, though."

"So who was my father?"

This was the place where she'd have to tread very carefully.

"His name was Dean Armitage. He was twenty, he worked on construction. He was very good-looking, and smart." He might have been. She'd never had any in-depth conversations with him.

"Twenty. Isn't that kinda old for a fifteen-year-old kid to be dating? Or were things different in those days?"

He sounded stern. Sage would have smiled if she wasn't fighting off tears. "It wasn't appropriate, no. Even in those days."

"So didn't your parents say anything about it?"

Here was another thorny area. He needed to know about his heritage, but she hated having to tell him. "There was only my mother, Tyler. My dad left us when I was a baby."

"So where'd he go?"

"I still don't know, he never said. I only saw him twice more, years later, and he couldn't answer a lot of my questions."

"What were their names, your folks?"

The raw hunger in his voice scared her. Just for a minute, she thought of making up something good about them, something that would make him proud. But the truth was what he needed, however harsh. Not now, though, not all of it unless he specifically asked.

"My mom's name was Lucy King. My dad was Murphy Callahan. Lucy was a nurse—she died ten years ago. I traced my father the same way I looked for you, Tyler. Like I said, I found him, but it was—it was disappointing."

How disappointing would she be for this boy? What dreams had he concocted about her that she could never fulfill?

"How so? Disappointing in what way?" He was relentless, and she was so proud of him for that. He was strong, he demanded answers.

"He was an alcoholic. He was already very sick when I met him. He died quite young, fifty-four." She'd paid for his hospital care and for his funeral. There'd been four people there besides herself, two of them nurses from the hospital where he'd died. Sage hadn't even asked her mother if she wanted to go; Lucy would have laughed and called her a silly fool for spending money on a lost cause.

"Tyler, this call is costing you money. Is there a number where I could call you back, so you wouldn't have to pay?"

"It's okay. My foster mom said I could call you. I'll pay her back from my own money. I work at this pizza place, its called the Flying Wedge. But I also have my own money that my parents left me in trust, for my education." Such pride in his tone.

"Tyler—" This was so hard, but she had to know. "Tyler, are—are you really okay? I—I know about your adoptive parents. Their death must have been so very hard on you. Is there—is there anything at all I can do for you?"

Please need me, for something—for anything.

"Nope, I'm fine." There was bravado in his voice. "See, I lucked out and got these neat foster parents. Elaine and George Berzatto. They're in their fifties, never had kids. They're awesome folks, they treat me really well."

"I'm so glad." Sage had to swallow hard, had to accept that these strangers already had rights that she didn't. "Do you—do you think there's any chance we could stay in touch? Be—be friends, maybe?" Her heart was bleeding, she could feel it.

"Sure. Well, I guess. It's pretty weird, this whole thing. I mean, I always knew I was adopted. Mom and Dad were open about it—they always said I was, like, the biggest gift they'd ever gotten." He stopped and she heard him gulp and swallow several times. "They even said it when I was being a total jerk, y'know? I had the best parents a kid could hope for." His voice was thick, and Sage knew there were tears in his eyes.

It hurt more than she could have imagined to hear him struggle with his emotions, to sense the depth of his love and the enormity of the loss he felt for his adoptive parents. And she was endlessly grateful to them, she reminded herself, because they'd loved and cared for her son.

"D'you, like, have e-mail up there in Alaska?"

"Yes, believe it or not, we actually do." This time she did smile. Funny, the illusions the lower forty had about Alaska. She gave him both her personal e-mail address and the one at the Lodge. In return, he gave her his. She scribbled it down in frantic haste, even though everything about the conversation, about him, was indelibly imprinted on her brain.

"I'd really like to see what you look like, Sage. Can you send me a photo? Like, over the Net?"

She smiled again. "I think I can manage that." Sage looked at the sophisticated mock-up she was working on. "And you, too, Tyler. I'd love to see a photo of you."

"Sure thing. I'll send one. My foster dad, George, got me this really hot little laptop for Christmas. It's loaded up." He paused, and she could hear a woman's soft voice in the background, telling him that someone was at the door waiting for him.

He was going to hang up. Sage gripped the phone so hard it was a wonder she didn't crush it. It was irrational, but she felt as if she was once again severing all connections with Tyler.

"Gotta go now. Umm, Sage? Thanks for talking to me."

"Thank you for calling me. Please call anytime, Tyler, call me collect—" It took a minute before she realized she was talking to empty air. He was already gone. It took both hands and three tries to hang up the handset.

Waves of emotion pulsed and receded. Most of what she felt was incredible joy, immense excitement. It was like winning the lottery, and she had to tell someone.

That person had to be Logan. She raced down the stairs and tore out the door. He'd been fixing a leaky roof on one of the cabins last time she'd looked, and he was still there, balanced on a ladder, doing something to the shingles.

"Logan!" she shrieked, running toward him at top speed. "Logan, Logan, you'll never believe, listen to this—"

He turned too fast and she watched in horror as the ladder teetered and then slowly came away from its perch against the roof. Logan hollered and then jumped free as the heavy ladder toppled to the ground.

Sage screamed.

He landed with a thump on his back in the flower bed.

"Oh, lordie, Logan, are you okay? Oh, please be okay." Sage threw herself down on her knees beside him. "Logan, are you all right? Did you—is anything broken? No, no, don't move, lie absolutely still, I'll get somebody."

He was a greenish color and he was making a horrible noise, a guttural, gasping sound, and she tried to get up to go for help, but he grabbed her hand and held on.

"Oh, God, Logan, you've broken something." She was terrified it was his spine. "Let go, I'll go get Andrew."

"Uuuuu…uhhhhh." He labored for breath, and after what seemed an eternity, he finally managed to draw in a short gasp, and then another. He panted hard for a few minutes, and Sage was relieved to see some of his color returning.

"Damn," he said weakly. "Knocked the wind…right out of me." He propped himself cautiously up on an elbow.

"You shouldn't move. What if you've broken a vertebra?" She put an arm around his shoulders, trying to ease him back down. Instead, he struggled to a sitting position.

"I'm okay, nothing broken." He rubbed at his ribs and groaned. "Bruised, though. Phew. See, I can take a deep breath." He did, to prove it.

"You scared me half to death." She brushed dirt off the back of his cotton work shirt and sat back on her heels.

He scowled at her. "Yeah, well you scared me right off that bloody ladder." He sounded irritated. "What's wrong, what's happened now?"

"Nothing's wrong, I'm excited, and I wanted to tell you. Oh, Logan, my son phoned me! From San Diego, just now."

"He did?" A wide smile spread across his dirt-smeared face. "Hey, that's fantastic. No wonder you were shouting. What did he say?"

She related the conversation almost word for word. He listened intently until Opal came sauntering past with a basket of clean sheets.

"Fell off the roof, did you, son? No harm done, I hope." She winked at Sage. "Nothin' like havin' a handsome bloke fall hard for ye, love." She waved a hand. "Cheerio, then. Carry on."

Sage suddenly realized they were sitting in the middle of Caitlin's delphiniums, and had been for some time. She scrambled to her feet, holding out a hand to help Logan up.

He took it, but made it up without her help. When he was on his feet, he gathered her in, giving her a huge hug.

"Logan." She was scandalized. "Everybody can see us."

"What the hell. I just looked death in the face, I refuse to sneak around. If I want to hug you, I will. As long as you want to be hugged."

"I do, but I could live without the dirt." She looked down at what had been a pristine white T-shirt. It was filthy. But then so were her blue chino crop pants. She'd have to run home and change. "You're sure you're okay, Logan? No pain anywhere?"

"Pain everywhere." He lifted one leg, and then the other, and grimaced. "But nothing serious, I'll live to fall another day." He squinted up at the roof. "Law school didn't include courses in roofing, unfortunately." He grinned at her. "Does Tyler want to meet you?"

"No. Well, maybe. He wanted a photo, though. And I don't have any recent ones. I don't like having my picture taken because I'm not photogenic."

"Says who? I have a digital camera, I'll be happy to take some wonderful shots of you." He glanced around and lowered his voice to a suggestive whisper. "Wearing lingerie. For my own private use, of course."

"Dream on, perv. But maybe you could snap a couple of me fully clothed?"

"I'd be happy to. Later this evening?"

"It's a date."

"The first of many," he said with a wink.

Laughing, she hurried off to change, feeling more than a little surreal. Unexpected things were happening so fast she could barely keep up. And she was excited and hopeful, two emotions she hadn't felt in a long time.

She was already trying to compose an e-mail to Tyler. She mustn't sound too eager or intense. She couldn't sound needy, she knew enough about males to know that sent them running. She had to strike exactly the right note, caring, but casual.

Dear Tyler, Sage wrote later that evening.

Thank you again for the phone call, it made my day.

It made my life, she amended to herself, staring at the computer screen. But of course I won't say that. It was so hard to write a letter when you cared this much, when you were terrified the other person might take your words the wrong way. How had Jenny managed it?

There wasn't time to ask you the ten million questions I have. I'll start with just three. What's your favorite subject in school? Are you left- or right-handed? Your father was a leftie. I always wonder if such things are inherited.

Tyler, there's so much about him I hope you didn't inherit.

Any idea what you'd like to do when you're finished high school?

I'll tell you a bit about me, hope I don't bore you. I'm newly widowed, my husband, Ben, was killed six weeks ago while hunting wild game in Africa. I live in the house my husband and father-in-law built for us, near a fishing lodge run by my in-laws, Theo and Caitlin Galloway, whom I love very much. I work for them, doing advertising and publicity, keeping track of bookings, and pretty much whatever else needs doing. It's isolated here, the only access is by boat or plane. The nearest town is Valdez, forty-five minutes away by boat.

In case you're wondering, I have no other children of my own. I have two stepdaughters, but they live with their mother in Valdez.

She got stuck there, writing and rewriting that sentence. It was so hard to know how to word it.

Attached is a photo a friend took today. You can see Raven Lodge in the background.

She got stuck again when she got to the end, finally settling on Very best regards, hope to hear from you soon.

She reread it a few times, came close to deleting and then pushed Send. Would he write back? She went to bed still wondering.

In the morning, she opened her e-mail before she brushed her teeth, knowing it was stupid to think there might be a response so soon. But there it was. Yo, Alaska, the subject line read, and her heart thumped.

It took all her courage to open it.

He used abbreviations she wasn't familiar with, and he had an easy way that suggested he used e-mail to communicate more than she did.

Got yr missive, interesting stuff, thanks for the pic, got any photos of my brth father, grandparents, etc? Re queries, yeah, I'm a leftie, looking at oceanography re career. Schoolwise, biology rocks. Hey, is there medical stuff I oughta know, like anything congenital? I'm real healthy so far. Sounds like grndp's on your side died young, how about brth father's. Any way to trace him? Hey, does the sun really shine all night up there? Gotta go, work tomorrow. Stay in touch, Ty.

And in a separate file, there was the photo of her son.

It was like food after a long fast, water after a drought. Sage feasted on the carefully unkempt streaky blond hair, spiked into peaks on top, the eyes that uncannily reflected her own back at her, set in a face surprisingly like her father's. If only the superficial resemblance was all he'd inherited from Murphy Callahan.

The cheekbones were high, the chin strong. He wasn't smiling. His mouth was wide and narrow, and here she saw the man who'd fathered him.

Tyler—did he prefer Ty? She'd have to ask him. He wore a guarded look in eyes shaded by long, curly lashes. Her eyes, her lashes.

She pressed a hand over her mouth, overcome with delight, and pride, and gratitude. He was going to be not only devastatingly handsome, but interesting looking. Her son, blood of her blood.

All the years she'd missed, the plump and smiling baby, the toddler learning to walk, the little boy just learning to read, the first clumsy signs of puberty.

"Tyler. Ty." Sage touched the screen with her fingertips, caressing the first and only image she had of him. "With all my heart and soul, I love you, Tyler."

And then she wrote back, easier now, less constrained, able to sound more like herself, but still careful to tread softly, to sound casual, so as not to overwhelm him with the magnitude of her feelings.

And for the next three weeks, e-mail was the first thing she raced to check in the morning and the last thing she looked at before she went to bed.

Chapter Eighteen

September was known as the shoulder season in the Alaskan tourist business, a bridge between the hectic pace of the high season and the long dark days of winter when tourists were few and far between.

By the middle of the month, bookings at the Lodge were beginning to slow, and by the end, they trickled in. There was time now in the long autumn afternoons to linger over iced tea on the sun porch, and Sage was doing just that when Logan joined her.

"How about coming to Portland with me next Tuesday?"

He took the chair beside her, lifted her glass and took a long drink. "I know I should get my own, but it's sexier to drink yours."

"Apparently." Sage felt the familiar surge of awareness and pleasure that being near him always brought. "You're going to see Grace?"

She still didn't have any desire to be around the other woman, but time was slowly dulling the sharp resentment she'd felt a couple months ago. And Jill hadn't been back to the Lodge since the funeral. Tom had brought the girls a few times for a visit, but obviously Jill wasn't in any hurry to face Caitlin and Theo. She certainly wasn't missed.

"There's only one room booked here after the Texans leave." He reached over and covered her hand with his. "It's time we had a few days to ourselves. And I thought we could hop a flight from Portland to San Diego. You could meet Tyler in person."

"That's a scary thought."

"How so?"

"What if he doesn't like me?" She knew she sounded immature, but that's exactly how she felt at the idea of meeting Tyler. Immature, inept, unsatisfactory—the list was endless. "What if I'm a big disappointment to him?"

Logan gave her an incredulous look. "C'mon, Sage. You've talked to the kid twice a day on the computer for over a month now, you've chatted on the phone every week, surely by this time he knows how fantastic you are." He leaned over and pressed a quick, hungry kiss on her mouth.

She glanced around to see who might be watching.

"I want to get you alone in a hotel room with a lock on the door and nobody we know within a fifty-mile radius," Logan declared. "In a place where there's no chance of a moose wandering out of the bush and staring at us."

She wanted that, too—of course she did. Privacy here was at a premium. They'd spent time together, as he'd promised, but with Andrew and Opal still happily ensconced at her house, the Lodge and cabins filled with guests and no darkness to cover any sneaking around, lovemaking was impossible. And part of Sage was still reluctant. Becoming lovers would mark another ending, another beginning. She wanted to be certain she was ready.

He kissed her again. They were alone—except for the view from the kitchen window. She turned her head and caught a glimpse of Mavis, ducking back out of sight.

"You told me Tyler said he'd like to meet you," Logan reminded her.

"He did, in his usual offhanded fashion. What he said exactly was, 'If you ever get out this way, we'll have to get together.'"

"So there you go. As much of an invitation as you can expect from a teenage guy." Logan stroked her forearm with two fingers, making the fine hairs on every inch of her body stand at attention.

"Okay. I'll check with him. If he agrees, I'll go."

Logan sank back in his chair and closed his eyes. "Thank you, God," he breathed in a fervent tone. Then he sat upright again, gave her a sexy wink and drank the rest of her tea.

They decided to fly first to San Diego, in case Logan was able to persuade Grace to come back to Alaska with them.

It was a rainy California afternoon when Sage took a cab to the coffee shop where Tyler had suggested they meet. It was in La Jolla, a twenty-minute ride from their hotel in downtown San Diego.

The cabbie went on and on about the rain, how unusual it was, how much they needed it, how he hoped it wouldn't turn into a downpour and flood his house. Sage barely heard him. She was a bundle of nerves. She didn't notice the palm trees or the glimpses of ocean.

Logan had offered to come along, but Sage knew she had to do this alone.

"Here ya go, lady. The Coffee Cow, right over there."

She thrust some money at the driver and got out. Across the street was a tiny storefront with a red awning under which groups of teens gathered. Music blared out the door, some kind of rap. Surfboards were propped against the inner wall. She crossed the quiet street, scanning the faces of the young people, wondering if Tyler would take refuge in a group, hoping he wouldn't.

He wasn't outside. She went in, and one glimpse of a spiky blond head sent her to the booth at the very back.

He stood up before she got there. He was tall, tanned, broad shouldered, perfectly proportioned, with the long, hard muscles of an athlete. He must have been watching for her. For just a moment he looked as scared as she felt, and that gave her courage.

She was the adult here; she was the one who needed to put him at ease. Longing to enfold him in her arms, instead she held out both hands, trying not to cry when she touched her son for the first time in fifteen years.

"Tyler. It's wonderful to meet you in person." She'd rehearsed those first words over and over in her mind, in the bathroom of the hotel, silently in the taxi, and still she couldn't control the wobble in her voice.

And her son, bless him, smiled an incredible smile—his teeth were so white, so even against his bronzed skin—and said easily, "Hey, Sage. Good to meet you, too. C'mon, sit down. I, like, got you a cappuccino. I hope that's okay?"

"Very okay. Thank you." The thoughtful gesture nearly released the tears she was trying so desperately to hold back. She took a sip from the tall glass, scalding her tongue, fighting for composure, unable to take her eyes off him. God, he was beautiful.

"Guess I've changed since the last time we met, huh?" He had a quirky grin that she'd seen sometimes in photos of herself.

"Quite a bit. You were twenty inches long and not quite eight pounds." She was able to smile now, still shaky but awed by his self-possession, his effort to put her at ease. "And you were howling."

He wrinkled his face in disgust, but he said, "I was born in Los Angeles, right?"

"Yes, at Mercy Hospital."

"That's what my mom told me, but I always wondered. If maybe that was just where they picked me up." He flushed and looked uncomfortable. "My adoptive mom told me."

"Your mom," Sage said firmly. "I was only there when you were born, Tyler. She's the one who did all the work of raising you." And had all the joy, but of course Sage wouldn't say that.

"You look pretty young," he said next, and it thrilled her to see admiration in his blue eyes.

Again she was able to smile. "Thank you. Fifteen years older than you, actually." She was glad she'd worn the trendy jeans and brightly patterned cotton jacket Logan had bought her. She fitted in here, without looking as if she was trying to.

"Do you live near here?" The question popped out, and she was instantly sorry. Of course she knew his address, but she didn't want to make it sound as if she was prying.

"Yeah, a few blocks away. George and Elaine have a great place one block from the beach. Most days I go for a swim before breakfast."

"The Lodge is right on the ocean, too, but the water's too cold for swimming now. It's not bad in the middle of the summer."

"I'd like to see what Alaska's really like. It's sort of the last frontier, isn't it?"

Here was her opportunity, far sooner than she'd expected.

"I was wondering, would you like to come and visit me?" Once the words were out she couldn't seem to stop talking. "Anytime you like, maybe Christmas, you're off school then—or whenever it's good for you. You tell me when and I'll arrange the ticket. You'd fly to Anchorage on a commercial flight and then Tom would pick you up in the copter or the float plane and bring you to the Lodge." She'd introduced him via e-mail to all the people at the Lodge and all their relatives and friends.

"Wow, people fly all over the place up there, huh? Instead of, like, taking the bus or a train or driving a car?"

"There aren't that many roads in Alaska. And you can't get to the Lodge by road, so you're stuck with a boat or a plane. Tom is Caitlin's brother," she reminded him.

"Yeah, that's cool. I remember. Maybe I'll come see you at Christmas, then. I'll have to, like, talk it over with my social worker first."

Afraid to hope, Sage told him how much she'd enjoy it. She asked him about football, and he went into detail about his last game, play by play.

She tried to follow, but she was going to have to really study up on football.

He asked about fishing, and she explained how the Lodge had started out as a fish-packing plant. She told him a little of the Galloway history, mentioning that Logan and Ben were twins and that Logan was traveling with her. She prayed that she wouldn't blush when she said it. He seemed to take it as a matter of course, asking only if Logan was also a big game hunter, seeming relieved when she said no.

"I don't believe in hunting animals," he said. "It's pretty barbaric. We sure don't need them as food any longer."

She agreed and asked where he planned to study ocean-ography, if he decided to go that route, and his blue eyes shone as he told her about Scripps Institution of Ocean-ography, right there in San Diego, one of the world's oldest, largest and most important centers for global scientific research. He described the courses he wanted to take at the University of San Diego. He was amazed that she'd never heard of Scripps. He described the aquarium, gesticulat-ing with his hands, explaining the expeditions the scien-tists made to far corners of the world.

"They study volcanoes in Japan, and go down in a sub-mersible in the North Atlantic. It's like having the entire world as your lab."

Sage was amazed that this remarkable, interesting person had actually grown inside of her. Two hours sped by, and when she noticed and got up to leave, Tyler was the one who gave her a quick, embarrassed hug.

"Think about Christmas and let me know," she said.

"I will. Thanks for coming to meet me, Sage."

"Believe me, Tyler, it's been my pleasure."

Chapter Nineteen

"Logan, you're going to like him. He's so intelligent, and he's polite—they taught him good manners. He bought me a cappuccino—"

She'd been talking nonstop ever since she got back to the hotel. Sage knew she was babbling, and she didn't care.

Logan was lounging on the bed, propped against pillows, arms behind his head. He grinned up at her.

"I need to learn about football—he really likes football."

"I can help you with that. It's a sport I really enjoy. Contact sports, now, I like those a lot." He sprang up and wrapped his arms around her. "You're so cute when you're excited and happy."

"Oh, Logan, if only he comes for Christmas."

"Of course he will. He's a guy—guys love Alaska. He'll want to see what it's like north of sixty, and what these other weird Galloways are like up close and personal. And he's going to want to know you better, Sage. I'll bet he's already proud of you."

"He gave me a hug when I left. It was so much more than I expected."

"Your problem is, you don't expect enough." He tipped her chin up and kissed her.

She could feel him trembling, aroused, and her arms went around him. They'd arrived only that morning, and all she'd been able to think of was the meeting with Tyler.

Now, she was filled with awareness of this wonderful room, and Logan. Tomorrow morning they'd fly to Portland. She was dreading that, but here and now, they had an entire afternoon and evening ahead of them—and the privacy they'd both longed for.

"Maybe I'll just slip into something more comfortable," she whispered, batting her lashes at him, kicking off her shoes, unbuttoning her jacket, sliding it off so that the silky ivory camisole she wore underneath was revealed. Teasing, holding his gaze, she toyed with the fastening of her jeans and then slowly snaked them down her hips, watching him watching her as she stepped out of them.

"You're making me crazy," he breathed, tracing the outline of her breasts with his palms, sliding his hands down the satiny scrap of matching panty.

"Good," she said, working his T-shirt up and over his head, undoing the snap of his jeans. He tugged them off, underwear and all, and she fitted herself against him, hands on his shoulders, full, firm breasts against his chest. His mouth found hers, and she stood entranced, allowing her love for him to well up and overcome her. Sensation, poignantly sharp, made her close her eyes as he lifted her to the bed and settled himself beside her.

There was no need to hurry. They had all afternoon, all evening, all night. She relished this privacy, this gift of precious time.

"I love you, Sage. I will always love you." He slid the camisole to the side and kissed his way slowly down her throat, breasts, belly, using his mouth to prolong things to the point of delicious agony. "I want to see you this happy, I want to see you glowing this way, every day, for the rest of our lives."

She had no strength to help or resist, and at last he rose above her, looking down into her eyes as he filled her.

Tender, so thoughtful of her, showing her with every breath and movement how much he cared, he brought her to ecstasy once and then again before he allowed himself to follow.

The next afternoon, Sage held the memory of that room, those hours of miraculous pleasure, firmly in her mind as their rented car turned into the street in Portland where Grace was living.

Logan's hand gripped hers as he pulled the car to a stop in front of a ramshackle green shingled house.

"This is it," he said. "Doesn't look too promising, does it?"

Sage thought it looked like a dump. The yard was overgrown, what had been a lawn overrun by weeds. With great reluctance, she followed Logan up the cracked sidewalk.

She hadn't wanted to come here. She'd asked him to take her to the airport, where their flight would leave that evening for Anchorage.

"I want her to see, right up front, how it is with you and I," Logan had argued. "Even if I tell her, it won't have the same impact as having you at my side when I go there. Please, Sage. I need you with me."

He'd never asked her to do anything for him—except marry him. This was definitely the easier of the two.

So here she was, staring at a red-haired emaciated old woman who'd opened the door when Logan knocked. Makeup was thick on her wrinkled skin, her garish lipstick not quite matching the outline of her lips.

A cinnamon-colored cat wound itself around Sage's ankles and then slid through the door.

"Mrs. Peters?"

"Yeah, but whatever you're peddling, I don't want any," she rasped, and tried to close the door.

"Mrs. Peters, wait, please." Logan grasped the edge of the door and held on. "We're here to see Grace Fulton."

"Oh, yeah? What about?"

"My name is Logan Galloway. This is Sage Galloway. I'm here because I'm the father of Grace's baby."

"Hmph." The old witch gave Logan a scathing look, but all she said was, "Why didn't you say so in the first place?" She let the door open wider and stood back. "It's costing me a fortune having her here. If the kid's yours, wouldn't hurt you to pay me a little for Grace's keep."

Sage caught a powerful whiff of whiskey fumes as she followed Logan inside, but it was quickly overpowered by the smell of cat, so strong her eyes watered.

"Go on in there." A bony finger pointed at a dingy room with a sofa, a television and a beaten-up armchair. There were cats on each piece of furniture.

"I'll get her, she's in bed. All she does is sleep and eat."

Logan shooed a gray tabby off the sofa so they could sit. There was so much cat hair on the fabric it was hard to see the pattern of the upholstery.

According to Jill, Grace had grown up here. Sage

couldn't help wondering how a child could develop in an environment like this one. She thought about a baby living here and shuddered.

It took at least ten minutes before Grace came in, and when she did, Sage felt stunned. The other woman was wearing gray track pants with a gaping hole in the leg and a stretched-out, washed-out T-shirt that had once been white. It didn't cover her belly, which had grown big and round, belly button poking out in a hard knot.

It was obvious she'd been sleeping. There were lines on one cheek from something ribbed. She looked pale and sick. When she'd worked at the Lodge, she'd been pretty in an all-American girl kind of way, short white-blond hair cut close to her head and spiked, lithe, long slender body, pale blue eyes and always a becoming tan.

The tan had faded to a sickly yellow. She looked ten years older, eyes puffy, a huge zit on the side of her nose. Her hair hung around her face, greasy and lank, brown roots showing. She'd lost an alarming amount of weight on her face and her arms and legs were skeletal. The huge belly was a shock; the last time Sage had seen her, at Ben's funeral, there had only been the slightest hint of a swelling.

"Hi, Logan." She didn't glance at Sage or acknowledge her. "How's it going?"

"Sage and I are fine," Logan said pointedly. "We came to see how you're getting along."

"Oh, you know." Grace shrugged. "Or maybe you don't. Anyhow, this gig gets old real fast." She rubbed her stomach. "I'm not feeling too good, don't feel like eating much except for stuff like fries and popcorn." She shot Sage a malicious look. "So, are you two an item now that Ben's gone?"

"We're together," Logan said firmly.

"That was fast work." She sneered.

Logan ignored her sarcasm. "What are you planning to do when the baby comes, Grace?"

"Get it adopted, what d'you think I'm gonna do?" Her eyes filled with tears, and the words came out in a stuttering flood. "I can't even support myself, never mind a kid. I can't work, I'm sick all day. Aunt Margaret isn't happy about me being here, either, but I had no place else. I wanted an abortion, but by the time I got around to it, it was too late."

In spite of herself, Sage started to feel sorry for Grace. She was trapped, and there was a note of desperation in her voice.

"I've got a suggestion," Logan said. "I want to raise the baby. My family wants to help. Come back to the Lodge with us now, and we'll all take good care of you. If you still feel the same way when the baby's born, that you don't want anything to do with it, then I'll make sure you have money enough to make a fresh start. But a kid needs to know both parents, so maybe down the line you'll want to be part of his or her life. That option's always open."

"Come back to the Lodge? And have *her*—" she glared at Sage "—and all the other *Galloways* looking down their noses at me?" She snorted. "Not a chance. I'd rather stay here."

Sage leaned forward. "I promise you that won't happen, Grace. I was angry with you, but that's over now." It wasn't entirely, but she could pretend. "Caitlin and Theo are eager to have another grandchild. They'll welcome you and make you comfortable."

"I won't stay in the Lodge," Grace said in a belligerent tone. "I'd feel trapped there. Could I have one of the cabins? I always wanted to stay in one of the cabins."

"Absolutely," Logan agreed. "The cabin I'm in is winterized, I'll move into the Lodge and you can have it."

Grace was quiet for what seemed a long time. Finally, she gave a weary shrug. "Okay. I guess. But I can't go right this minute, I have to get my shit together first."

"When can you be ready, then?"

Sage knew what Logan was thinking. If he arranged a ticket for her at some later time, she'd likely change her mind. It was imperative that she come with them now.

"Tomorrow probably. Yeah, I guess tomorrow's okay."

"Morning? There's a flight out at eleven. If I can get us tickets we'd have to be at the airport by ten at the latest."

Grace's eyes traveled around the shabby room. The gray cat on top of the television was licking its fur and hair drifted down, caught in the sunshine pouring through the dirty windowpane.

"Yeah, okay, I'll be ready."

"We'll come by for you around nine."

Grace nodded, not looking at him.

"Okay, see you in the morning." Logan got up and deliberately took Sage's hand. "Do you need anything right away, Grace? Do you need money for anything?"

"Aunt Margaret—" Grace jutted her chin at the other room. "She says I owe her rent."

"How much?" Logan had his wallet out.

"Five hundred should do it." Margaret sidled through the door, a half-filled glass in her hand. "Food's expensive, and I lost the boarder I had when she decided to come back."

"Two will have to do, that's all the cash I have on me." Logan peeled off hundred-dollar bills, handing them to Grace. She gave them to her aunt.

The old woman snatched them and scuttled out of the room.

"See you in the morning, Grace." Logan led the way out the front door.

There was no answer. Sage glanced back. Grace was curled into a ball on the sofa.

When they were back in the car, Logan looked at Sage and shook his head. "What a bloody nightmare that was. D'you think she'll stand us up in the morning?" He started the car and accelerated down the street.

Sage had the window down, trying to get the smell of cat out of her nostrils. She brushed at the hair on her jeans. "I don't think so. Surely she's got enough sense to compare Raven Lodge with what she's living in now. I think she'll be waiting for us."

"Y'know the real upside of this?"

"That she agreed to come with us?"

"Nope. We get one more night together in a nice hotel that has a Do Not Disturb sign."

She whined, "Ahhhh, do we have to?"

He turned and gave her a look. "Well, there are a few moves from the *Kama Sutra* that we haven't tried out yet. But if you're really dead set against it—"

"As long as you're sure none of them involve cats, it's a deal."

Chapter Twenty

"This works really well for us." Sage was sitting in the middle of the king-size bed, wearing a white hotel bathrobe and eating a slice of pizza.

"Eating pizza?" Logan took a third slice from the box. He'd pulled on a pair of jeans, but his chest was bare. "Yeah, if we practice we could probably get into the Olympics."

"Sex, idiot. We're really good at sex." She took a gulp of the wine Logan had ordered along with the pizza. "I think two people are either lucky that way or they're not. We're lucky. We're good together."

"Good is an understatement. Try superlatives like *fantastic* and *mind-blowing*." He chewed for a moment. "And it's not just sex. We're good together in all the ways that matter, sweetheart. Which is why I think you should marry me."

She paused in midchew and looked at him. "Are you proposing?"

"You want me to kneel? Okay, I can do that." He slid off the bed.

"Stop." She'd been relaxed, totally at peace, her body humming with satisfaction, her stomach with hunger. She'd said the first thing that came into her mind, not thinking where it would lead.

"You know I love you." He sounded reasonable and patient. "You've told me you love me back. I want to spend my life with you, surely marriage is the next logical step?"

"It is. At least, it should be." The thought of another marriage scared her witless. "You've never been married— you might not like it. People change, there's no guarantee it'll work."

"You're the only woman I've ever thought of marrying, Sage." He'd set his pizza down. His voice was serious, and she could hear the undercurrent of impatience. "You're the only one I've ever proposed to. I wish you'd stop comparing me to Ben. We were twins, we were alike in a lot of ways, *but I'm not him*."

"How can I know that for sure?" The words burst out of her, things she hadn't even realized she was feeling. "Love and trust are two separate things. We're here right now because another woman's having your baby. For all I know, you have an entire stable of women in Seattle."

"Don't be ridiculous." He glared at her, but she didn't stop.

"And that's fine, because you're single. And this—" she waved a hand at the rumpled bed, their underclothes scattered on the carpet "—how do I know if sex with you is only this good because it's new, a novelty?" Her deepest reservations came tumbling out. "Maybe in a few years you'll get bored with me."

Ben certainly had. "I've read reports that said men aren't

by nature monogamous. I just can't take that chance, Logan. I can't rush into something and then realize I've made a mistake. It happened with Ben. It hurts too much."

"*Ben.* Goddamn it, I'm sick to death of paying for his mistakes." Logan hurled the wineglass he was holding against the wall. Splinters of glass scattered everywhere. Sage jumped and cried out.

"Yes, I got Grace pregnant," he said in a rage. "I wish to God I could change that, but I can't. I'm doing my best to be responsible, even though the idea of being a father makes me want to run far and fast. What the hell do you want from me, Sage? I can't give you any written guarantees, nobody can. I've told you how I feel, I've been as honest as I know how to be." He grabbed a sweatshirt and pulled it on, shoving his feet into his loafers. "I'm going for a walk. Leave the damned glass, I'll clean it up later."

The door closed behind him. Sage stared at it, wanting to throw something at it. Instead, she avoided the glass on the rug, filled the tub with hot water, and climbed in.

Was she being unfair? The hot water soaked away some of her anger, and she had to admit that Logan was right—she was comparing him to Ben. But a good part of the irritation she was feeling had to do with Grace, with knowing that all during the long winter ahead, she'd have to be around that woman. Despite what she'd told Grace, it wasn't that easy to forgive and forget the pain she'd caused. A part of Sage she wasn't proud of wished that Grace wouldn't be waiting in the morning, that she'd have disappeared somewhere, anywhere—and that she'd stay gone.

Sage stayed in the tub until the water got cold. She crawled into bed, and when Logan came in she pretended she was asleep. She lay there, trying to breathe regularly, sick at heart because she remembered so many other times she'd pretended the same thing when Ben came tiptoeing in, careful not to disturb her, dreading the questions she might ask about where he'd been and with whom.

But Logan didn't tiptoe. He turned on the bedside light and scooped her into his arms, holding her close against his chest. She could smell cigarette smoke and beer and chilly fresh air.

"I'm sorry, I'm so sorry, babe. I promised you time and then I get impatient. I guess my feelings get hurt when you don't jump at the chance to marry me, stud that I am. Forgive me?"

"Oh, Logan, I'm sorry, too. I know I'm being unreasonable. Just give me time."

"I will. I promise."

When they were both naked, he made love to her with an intensity that healed almost all of the lingering hurts either of them had.

In spite of Sage's assurances, Logan was certain the next morning that Grace wouldn't be there when he pulled up in front of the house. He was about to get out and go knock on the door when it opened and she appeared.

She was wearing jeans and a loose top that covered her belly. She was pulling a huge suitcase on wheels, and he hurried to help her. She closed the door behind her and got in the backseat of the car while he stowed the case in the trunk.

There was no sign of Margaret, which Logan considered a blessing.

He got back in the car and they drove away. He said, "I got hold of Tom. He's going to pick us up at Anchorage."

Neither woman responded.

Sage had gotten quiet as the time neared to pick up Grace. She'd turned and said good morning when Grace got in, but Grace hadn't responded.

Logan did his best, yammering on about Portland, the traffic, the weather, but he could tell it was going to be a long, tense flight. And he also had a gut feeling it was going to be a long, tense winter.

Her very first winter in Alaska, Sage had fallen in love with the months of arctic darkness. It was a time to regroup, to relax, to read the books she stockpiled during the busy summer, catch up with friends, use the exercise equipment in the Lodge's gym without having to relinquish it to guests.

During October and early November, she worked at the Lodge every day because bookings still arrived steadily—hardy souls who came solely to experience the Northern winter.

Advertising needed to be updated, any indoor repairs to the Lodge and the cabins had to be scheduled, and there was always bookkeeping to do, but the pace was relaxed, with frequent breaks for coffee, cookies and gossip with Caitlin and Mavis. This year, however, Grace was there, so Sage spent much more time in her own house or closeted in the office.

Grace was living in one of the cabins as she'd asked, but she spent a good percentage of her day at the Lodge, and Sage preferred not to be around her.

Sage had to admit Grace wasn't lazy; she searched out jobs to do, peeling vegetables in the kitchen, cleaning whatever needed it. She'd started feeling better almost immediately, and everyone had made her welcome. Mavis even made a special effort to find out what food tempted her.

Sage knew it was probably as hard for them as it was for her to be polite, knowing that Grace had played a major role in Ben's death. But her in-laws were mature, wise people, concerned about the well-being of their grandchild. And they were kind. Logan had told them about the disgusting house in Portland, and Grace's money-grubbing aunt Margaret.

The baby was due in mid-December. Because the Lodge was remote and the weather unpredictable in winter, plans were being made for Grace to move into a hotel in Valdez for the last two weeks of her pregnancy.

"Why doesn't she go to Valdez now and stay with Jill? I thought they were such good friends," Sage said to Logan, trying not to sound as bitchy as she felt.

"Apparently not. Grace feels Jill manipulated her, which is pretty accurate. It bothers you a lot, having her stay here, doesn't it?"

Sage sighed and nodded. "I have a hard time with her. When she's certain no one can overhear, she's snippy and outright rude with me."

That was true, but Sage knew part of her frustration came not from Grace, but from not having a chance to be alone with Logan. He'd awakened a powerful sexual hunger in her, and the privacy they needed to enjoy intimacy was almost nonexistent.

"It's only for another month or so," he reminded her. "She'll be gone around Christmastime, if the baby comes when expected."

Grace was still insisting she wanted nothing to do with the baby, but Sage had begun to wonder if she'd change her mind. Sage knew from personal experience exactly how hard it was to give up a baby.

"What if she decides to stay here and raise it herself? She's obviously decided to fall in love with you." My God, she sounded like a shrew. *Good going, Sage, men really like this attitude. Keep it up and he's liable to think Grace isn't so bad after all.*

Logan had said it before, but now he said it again. "I've told her in simple sentences that you're the woman in my life. But she's very single-minded."

"I'll say. Maybe lock your door at night." Sage had watched Grace touch Logan every chance she got, ask his advice on everything from exercise to maternity wear, sit beside him, insist he accompany her on her bimonthly trips to the doctor in Valdez.

Logan had nicely outmaneuvered her on that one by insisting that Sage come along. But seeing Grace's obvious efforts at getting his attention was infuriating. Sage hated to think she was jealous—but wanting to slap a pregnant woman senseless could hardly be interpreted any other way.

"All we can do is support her as best we know how," Logan said in a reasonable tone.

"Yeah. Believe it or not, I do understand that." Sage knew he was doing the best he could in a really difficult situation, but she was feeling on edge and irritable. And taking it out on him.

Andrew and Opal were still staying with her, and she loved having them, but it meant even her house wasn't really her own. They'd put off going back to Australia, planning now to leave the first week in December so they'd be home for Christmas.

And as he'd promised, Logan had moved out of his cabin and into his old room on the top floor of the Lodge, giving Grace the cabin. So for Sage there could be no passionate visits with him in the middle of the night.

At the moment they were down on the dock, taking inventory of the boathouse and the boats, making certain the safety equipment was up to code—and snatching kisses whenever they were reasonably sure they wouldn't be interrupted by one of the guides. It was below zero today with a windchill factor, and they were both wearing layers of clothing, so the relative privacy of the boathouse made kissing the only thing viable. And when your lips were numb, it wasn't very satisfying.

At least Jill hadn't been to the Lodge since Ben's funeral, Sage thought. The girls came often to visit their grandparents, but Jill stayed away, and for that she was thankful.

She knew she wasn't alone in feeling frustrated. Logan didn't say much, but she could sense the same raw hunger in the way he looked at her, and in the kisses they stole.

"Did you get your e-mail from Tyler today?" Logan knew Sage and her son were in contact almost daily.

"I did." Sage's smile was spontaneous and wide. The ongoing contact with her son was the one thing in her life that was perfect. "He made the football team, he has a science teacher he looks up to, and the new social worker isn't as bad as he thought at first."

"Did he say anything about coming for Christmas?"

"Nope. His foster parents want him to go with them to Mexico, they have a time-share there. He's trying to decide, but I know he'll choose the Mexican Riviera. Who wouldn't? Sunshine and warm water versus snow and ice and darkness." And even though she'd be disappointed, what she wanted for Tyler was whatever he wanted for himself. Maybe that's what love really was, she mused.

"If you want, we could go to Mexico on our honeymoon."

She shot him an exasperated look and he held up his gloved hands, palms out. "Just kidding. No pressure."

But she knew he wasn't just kidding. And neither was she, she didn't want him pushing her in any way. Although the idea of marriage was becoming more and more appealing to her, for what she thought were all the wrong reasons. You didn't marry someone just because you wanted to go to bed with them.

Time to change the subject, she decided. "How's your office renovation coming?"

"I'm having the windows changed, two of them leaked. And after that they'll have to put some new drywall up before they paint. It's a major overhaul."

To his parents' delight, Logan had sold his share of the Seattle practice in favor of opening a legal practice in Valdez. The only lawyer in town was known to have a serious drinking problem, and there were certainly enough domestic disputes, land claims and personal injury problems to keep more than one lawyer busy. He'd rented a main floor office space with living quarters above, and hired a local decorator to paint and refurbish the entire place. He wasn't planning to open for business until the New Year. When the time came, he'd spend four or five days working and living in Valdez and the remainder at the Lodge.

In the meantime, Sage knew there were more than enough challenges to keep him busy, and there'd be the baby to consider—if Grace left. If she did, Logan had told Sage he was planning to hire a nanny.

And she'd almost said there'd be no need, that she'd

adore taking care of his baby. Which she would, but she'd bitten back the offer.

Leaving him would be a thousand times worse if she fell in love with his baby, as well. And the longer she was in contact with her son, the more thought she gave to moving to California.

Two weeks before her due date, the day before she was scheduled to move into Valdez, Grace's labor began, and two hours into it her water broke.

The worst blizzard of the season was raging. It was six in the evening, twenty-eight degrees below zero and black dark outside. The wind and snow were howling like demented demons outside the windows.

At first, Caitlin had assured Grace that she was having false labor, but the pain had steadily increased as the afternoon progressed. Sage had kept in constant contact with emergency services by phone, explaining their predicament, but was told that sending a medevac was out of the question.

They were now trying to get in touch with Grace's obstetrician, and had promised to call back right away.

Caitlin and Mavis settled Grace in one of the guest bedrooms, and after a nerve-racking hour of listening to her scream, they joined everyone downstairs in the kitchen for a panicked conference, leaving Logan upstairs holding her hand. When the first pains began, she'd insisted he be with her.

Opal said, "So what's the plan here?" She sounded nervous.

"There's no possibility that the medevac can get through tonight, or Tom, either," Caitlin said with a frown. "We certainly can't take her into Valdez in one of the boats, and nobody's going to be able to come out here in one."

Sage saw the apprehensive looks the men exchanged.

"I've brought my share of lambs into the world, and a calf or two, but never a baby," Andrew said.

"Or me," Opal added. "I'm out of me depth here, I'll tell you that up front."

Caitlin tried for optimism. "First babies usually take a long time, so chances are good by the time she's ready to deliver the storm will have died down and the doctor will get here. I was in labor eighteen hours with the boys."

Everyone nodded hopefully.

Sage couldn't remember how long the pain had lasted. It had seemed like an eternity. She felt real compassion for Grace, besides being scared half to death along with everyone else at the thought of actually helping deliver the baby.

"You two had babies, at least you know what we're looking at here," Mavis said to Caitlin and Sage. "The only thing I know is what I've seen in movies, and that's boil lots of water."

"I've never understood why," Caitlin said. "What would they use all that water for? I don't remember them needing hot water when the twins were born. They don't bathe new babies right away, and goodness knows the poor mother isn't going to get up and jump into a bathtub."

"Women have been having babies forever, it's a natural process," Theo observed with a show of bravado. "How hard can it be?"

All four women turned in unison and glared at him.

"I need a pad and paper." Sage was again on the phone with emergency services. "Grace's obstetrician is in Anchorage this week, so they're going to transfer me to another doctor."

Ominous glances passed to and fro at that news.

"He'll give us the info we need now, just in case the phone lines go down." The Lodge had radiophones, as well, but reception on them wasn't always reliable in a storm, either.

"Please, God, no," Opal murmured, clasping her hands over her chest. "A bit of excitement is one thing, but delivering a baby is another."

There was a short wait, and then a confident-sounding man with a deep, reassuring voice introduced himself to Sage as Dr. Hunter. She again explained about Grace's water breaking and the labor pains beginning.

She listened closely as the doctor went through a detailed list of instructions. She scribbled every word on a pad of paper, shivering at words like *hemorrhage* and *resuscitate*.

"But of course none of those things are going to occur," he said in a hearty tone. "I'm simply giving you the worst-case scenario. Most births are completely uneventful, apart from the miracle of birth. I'll stay on the line as long as there's service and talk you through the whole thing," he promised Sage. "The most important thing is not to panic."

Logan came dashing down the stairs just then, and *panicked* was the best word to describe him. "Don't leave me alone with her up there, for God's sake. She says she has to push. Does that mean anything?"

"Oh, my dear God. It means the baby's in a hurry." Caitlin hurried upstairs, trailed by Mavis and Opal and Sage, who was clinging to the handset of the phone as if it was a life preserver. Halfway up the stairs they could hear Grace screaming, and when they reached the bedroom, the noise she was making made it hard to hear.

Grace was clearly hysterical, alternately bearing down and screaming.

"Your first job is to get your patient calmed down," Dr. Hunter was hollering in Sage's ear. "Talk to her quietly, reassure her that everything's going to be fine."

Sage thought that was pure optimism. "We're trying, but she doesn't listen well." She couldn't hear the doctor's reply, so she went out in the hall and shut the door.

"Dr. Hunter, she's totally hysterical, none of us know what to do, and this baby's coming fast." Her voice was shrill. She'd told him that Grace's due date was still two weeks off. "Will the baby be okay?" She was too frightened to ask if Grace and the rest of them might survive.

"Babies come on their own schedule, two weeks isn't early at all." His calm, quiet voice was reassuring. "She may well be full-term, I have her chart here in front of me. The baby was quite large three weeks ago at her last examination. But we'll cross that bridge if we come to it, for now let's just concentrate on getting this baby born. Tell me exactly what's happening."

"Well, you must be able to hear her screaming." Sage went back in the bedroom, wishing she was anywhere else on earth. "Her pains are about three minutes apart now," she hollered into the receiver. "There's some blood coming out."

Caitlin and Opal were trying to talk calmly to Grace, but it wasn't having any effect. Between contractions, she was out of control, screaming for Logan, cursing, threshing around like a madwoman.

Logan had prudently stayed downstairs with Theo and Andrew, and Sage couldn't blame him for it. This was like a scene from hell.

Mavis, always short on patience, finally had had enough. "You stop that right now or I'll smack your bottom," she thundered at Grace. "We're all in this together.

We're trying to help you, and you're not doing yourself any good with this screeching and rolling around. Now shut up and calm down so we can hear ourselves think."

Amazingly, Grace responded. She quieted, and when the next contraction came she didn't scream quite as loud as she had been doing. When it was over she whimpered, "I'm scared, I'm scared, I know I'm gonna die. It hurts really, really bad."

"Having babies hurts, I do remember that," Caitlin assured her. "Here, you hold my hand when the next pain comes."

"And you're not going to die, we won't let you," Sage said with a confidence she was far from feeling. "I'm on the phone with this wonderful Dr. Hunter. He says to tell you he's delivered over a hundred babies, and everything's going to be fine. He's going to talk us all through this."

"But I don't know him," Grace wailed, and another contraction came, lasting longer than the previous one. Grace was now bearing down hard, making a deep grinding noise during the worst of it. When it was over she whimpered and Caitlin wiped her face gently with a warm washcloth, murmuring comforting words. Opal took her other hand, wincing when Grace squeezed it hard.

The next contraction came almost immediately.

Mavis, who was at the foot of the bed, hollered, "The head's coming, oh my God, the head's coming. I can see it. It's coming out *now. What do I do?*"

Sage relayed this to Dr. Hunter.

"Mavis, is there a loop of cord around his neck?"

"I don't see any. Should there be?" Mavis was more agitated than Sage had ever seen her. "It's facedown, the baby's facedown."

"It's good that there isn't a cord," Sage repeated. "And

he says it's normal the face is down—it'll turn by itself."
She listened to Dr. Hunter and told the others, "The baby's
body is going to be born with the next contraction."

Excitement was taking the place of panic and fear.

"Make sure you have a stack of warm towels ready.
It's really important to keep the baby warm," Dr. Hunter
instructed.

Sage raced out to the landing and shouted down, "We
need warm towels up here."

Logan came running to the bottom of the stairs. "How
do we warm them up?" He sounded frantic.

"In the dryer, turn it on and put in big bath towels."

"They'll never be ready in time," Caitlin said. "Grab a
flannel sheet from the hall closet," she called to Sage. "Lay
it on the heat vent."

Sage did, and she was barely back in the room when a
red-faced, blood-spattered baby popped like a cork out of
Grace's body and into Mavis's unsteady hands.

Chapter Twenty-One

"It's a boy," Mavis crowed in a high-pitched voice. There was an instant of tense silence, and then a wavering cry filled the room.

"I can hear that. He's sounding great," the doctor said in Sage's ear.

He sounded as relieved as she felt.

"Describe him for me," Dr. Hunter ordered. "Tell me if he seems to be having any problems breathing, what color he is, whether everything's in the right place."

By now the baby was wailing in short, outraged bursts. Sage described him, adding that there seemed to be no problem at all with his breathing.

"He's howling away, but he's still hooked to Grace by the cord," she said. "What should we do about that?"

"Nothing, until the placenta is delivered. I'll tell you

what to do about it then. For right now, just describe what's happening there with baby and mom. Is there any heavy bleeding?"

"Just a little blood. He's crying hard. Oh, he's pouting. Look at that sweet little face. And he's turning pink, oh, he's so beautiful. He's got a full head of black hair, and these beautiful little ears," she enthused, realizing that she was crying, and so were Mavis and Caitlin and Opal. Grace lay panting, exhausted from her ordeal.

"Put him to Grace's breast, it'll calm him down," Dr. Hunter instructed. "Even if he sucks a little, it'll help stimulate the release of the hormone that helps the placenta get delivered."

But Grace shook her head and turned her face away when Caitlin laid the baby on her chest and told her what the doctor had said.

"I'm not feeding it. I don't want it sucking on me. Take it off."

Sage saw the shock on Caitlin's face, and on Mavis's. Caitlin immediately lifted the baby in her arms again, and in a few moments, Grace grimaced. "I'm having pains again," she gasped. "Owwww."

"That's good news," Dr. Hunter said into Sage's ear. He gave clear advice, and shortly the placenta was delivered and deposited in a bucket, to be kept and examined as soon as medical help arrived.

Then he gave Sage precise instructions for the severing of the umbilical cord, using string sterilized in the microwave and scissors doused in alcohol. Sage repeated what the doctor said word for word, and Caitlin cut the cord as Mavis and Opal tended to Grace, sponging her gently and fitting her with sanitary pads. They helped Grace into a clean gown, changed the sheets and tucked a warm blanket around her. Mavis stroked a gentle hand down Grace's cheek.

"You did real good, dear. I'm proud of you. I'm going down to make you some nice tea and toast now, with honey."

"I'd like that." Grace sighed and closed her eyes, lying back on the pillows.

Caitlin had rewrapped the baby snugly in a fresh sheet. She said softly, "Do you want to hold him now, Grace?"

Grace kept her eyes shut and shook her head. "You keep him." And in a voice drained of everything but terrible weariness, she added, "I'm so sorry, Caitlin, about Ben. I didn't know Oliver would do that."

Sage saw the shock on her mother-in-law's face. Caitlin put a hand to her lips, struggling not to break down. She swallowed hard and cuddled the baby closer to her breast, bending her head down to his, pressing her mouth against the mop of black baby hair. After a moment, she said in a not quite steady tone, "You don't have to do this, Grace. It's okay to love your baby. Don't punish yourself for what's past."

But Grace shook her head again. "I want him to be a Galloway. I don't have anything to give him except that. I'd like it if Logan names him Ben."

Sage felt an enormous tide of sadness wash over her, because she realized at that moment that Grace was deliberately not bonding with her baby. She knew now that Grace would take the money Logan had offered and leave the Lodge. It was a relief, but it was also heartbreaking. For the first time, she felt real affection and empathy for Grace. Sage knew exactly how it felt to walk away from childbirth with an empty belly, empty arms and an even emptier heart.

She'd almost forgotten that Dr. Hunter was still on the

line. He asked a few more questions, wished them well and congratulated them all on a job well done, assuring Sage that the moment the storm abated, he'd be there with a medical team to check on baby and mother.

Sage had just thanked him and hung up when she heard Logan and Theo and Andrew on the stairs. They came and stood hesitantly in the doorway, stacks of white terry towels in their arms. They all looked profoundly uncomfortable and out of place. It was both funny and touching.

Caitlin took the baby over to them, handing him to Logan. Logan dropped his load of towels on the floor and let out a squeak of panic as the baby settled into his arms.

"Meet your son," Caitlin said, her voice choked with emotion.

Logan shifted his hold awkwardly, staring down at the tiny face and one miniscule hand, all that was visible in the midst of the fluffy flannel sheet.

"He's got blood on him, is he okay?" He sounded terrified. "I don't know how to hold him, you'd better take him, Mom."

Caitlin smiled and shook her head.

"You're doing just fine." Her face was luminous as she watched her son with his son. "He's absolutely fine, as well. He's wonderful. He just hasn't been cleaned up properly yet. Take him downstairs, keep him wrapped up well and make certain it's really warm in the kitchen. I'll come down in a minute and we'll wipe him off properly. Sage, you go with them, please, dear. I want a moment alone with Grace."

Sage closed the bedroom door and followed the men, her heart overflowing with both overwhelming joy for Logan and his parents, and poignant sadness for Grace.

* * *

The storm died out by early morning, and just before noon Tom brought Dr. Hunter in the copter. From his deep, beautiful voice, Sage had envisioned a tall, slender, sophisticated man, and she did a double take when Dr. Hunter walked through the front door of the Lodge and held out a pudgy hand for her to shake.

He was five four, round and bald as a basketball. He examined Grace and the baby and pronounced them healthy as horses. He complimented Sage and the other women on a job well done, and he devoured with gusto the fresh yeast buns Mavis provided with tea.

Tom had brought a small mountain of baby supplies. Caitlin had stocked a meager supply of the essentials, like diapers and formula and tiny terry sleepers, but Tom had raided the stores in Valdez that morning.

"Does he need that much stuff?" Logan jiggled his son, propped on his shoulder. The baby had been crying off and on all morning, and Logan was looking both frenzied and haggard.

"All that and more. We'll move another dresser into your room to hold it all," Caitlin said. Grace had made it clear she didn't want the baby near her—she was planning to move out to the cabin later that day—so Caitlin had Logan go up in the attic and bring down one of the twin's cradles. They'd set it up in Theo and Caitlin's bedroom that first night, but Caitlin made it clear to Logan that from there on in, the baby was his responsibility.

That first day was chaotic, and it was clear to Sage that the pattern of life at the Lodge was about to change drastically. The baby's needs came first, and Logan was trying his best, but it was obvious he'd need help, at least until he became more familiar with basics like diaper changes and baths and feedings. Which was fine, because everyone, including two burly bear hunters from Arkansas who'd arrived three days before, were vying for a chance to hold the baby.

"Have you decided on a name for this fine fellow?" Dr. Hunter asked after examining the baby. He was deftly fitting matchstick arms and legs back into a white terry sleeper.

"Benjamin Hunter Theodore Galloway," Logan said, watching the doctor with envy and great respect. He'd tried to dress his son earlier that morning, and had accidentally snapped one of the baby's legs to his chest. "We couldn't have done it without you, Doctor."

"That's very generous of you, but it's nonsense. Birth is a natural procedure. And he's a fine boy, perfect in every respect. I'm honored to have him carry my name." The little man glowed with pride. "I'll keep a special eye on little Benny Hunter, you can bet your bottom dollar on that."

The abbreviation stuck, and by nightfall the entire household was calling the baby Benny Hunter, as in, "Please, Benny Hunter, stop crying and go to sleep." He had just a touch of colic, Caitlin declared with admirable understatement.

Late that evening, Sage made her exhausted way through the snow to her own house. The air was icy cold and the sky was clear. Over the mountains, the aurora played its eerie rainbows of color, deep green fading to rose, changing to yellow. She stood a moment and watched, entranced as always with the mystery of the Northern Lights, overwhelmed with the enchantment of Logan's screaming son.

Every vow she'd made to herself about not getting attached to the baby had been broken. She could smell him on her clothing, the sweetness of new baby, the sour smell of spit-up. She could feel him against her chest, even though he hadn't rested there for more than an hour. In her mind's eye, she could see the affronted little face, the quivery chin, the ridiculous mass of black hair, the tiny legs and arms that curled into his torso as if they were held there with magnets. His strident cry was already familiar, and the echo reverberated in her heart. She was in love with him, and there wasn't a damned thing she cared to do about it.

At home, she hadn't had a chance to turn on the computer the previous day, so it was the first thing she did when she got upstairs.

She was hoping for a message from Tyler, and it was there. She opened it, excited as always to hear from her son.

Yo, my lady Sage, it began.

If it's still cool with you, I'd like to come for Christmas. Hope it's not too late to arrange a flight. I could come on the 21st, and stay till January 2.

Sage let out a whoop, forgetting that Opal and Andrew were already in bed in the next room. Her son would be with her for almost two full weeks! Fingers flying over the keys, she assured Tyler that having him come for Christmas was phenomenal, fantastic, incredible! Then she told him about seeing the aurora, and about the arrival of the baby.

Three miracles in one day, she wrote, too excited to hold back the intensity of her feelings the way she usually did with him. I feel like the luckiest woman in the universe.

She pushed Send and sat for a moment, a huge foolish grin on her face. Things didn't get much better than this.

Chapter Twenty-Two

By Christmas Eve morning, Sage wondered if things could get much worse. Tyler had been with her a week, and every day seemed longer than the last. From the moment he arrived, she could see that Alaska was a big disappointment for him, and in spite of her best intentions, she was losing patience with him, something that she'd never dreamed could happen.

When he left San Diego, he'd been looking forward to the helicopter ride Sage had promised him from Anchorage to Valdez, but the weather had been too overcast and stormy for Tom to fly.

Hasty arrangements were made and a friend of Theo's, who sometimes worked in Anchorage, picked Tyler up at the airport and brought him by car to Valdez through a howling blizzard. Sage and Logan were waiting there for him, and they took him to the Lodge in the largest of the boats.

The sea was rough, and Tyler got seasick. In spite of their assurances that it was completely normal, the boy was humiliated.

The weather cleared the next day, and Sage's spirits lifted. She'd planned an excursion on a tour boat out to see the Columbia Glacier, but Tyler refused to go. He wouldn't admit it, but Sage suspected he was afraid he'd disgrace himself by being sick again.

Tyler asked, "When are the Northern Lights scheduled?"

Sage had to explain that the aurora put on a show only when weather conditions allowed. She actually prayed that it would clear, but as if to taunt her, another storm rolled in. That meant that flying was once again out of the question, so there went Tom's offer to take Tyler up on a sightseeing flight.

Logan's plan to take him out on snowshoes to ice fish was also canceled due to weather. A friend had a dog team, and he'd offered a ride on the dogsled, but while the storm raged everyone was confined to either the Lodge or Sage's house, and instead of feeling cozy, she realized for the first time how imprisoning the northern winter could be.

Tyler, more dejected and morose by the hour, moped around and spent most of every day on Sage's computer, e-mailing friends in California. Sage knew he was wishing he'd gone with his foster family to Mexico, and God help her, she was beginning to wish the same thing. A miserable teenage boy was beyond her coping skills.

Christmas Eve morning, Theo offered to play chess or checkers after breakfast, but Tyler politely declined and went back to Sage's house and the computer.

"Tom's bringing the girls over this morning. He just

called," Caitlin announced. "Visibility's improved, he'll be here in an hour. Jill wouldn't come, but she's letting Sophia and Lily stay over," Caitlin said as she and Sage cleared the dishes away. "Maybe having other young people around will cheer Tyler up."

Sage had already told Tyler that Sophia and Lily would be visiting. His reaction had been much less than enthusiastic.

"They're *girls,*" he'd said, sounding as though Sage had suggested he babysit them.

"The weather's supposed to clear by this afternoon, and stay clear until New Year's," Logan announced. He was sitting in an old rocking chair, wearing milk-stained gray sweats, giving Benny Hunter a bottle and yawning hugely every few seconds. The baby woke up every two hours, round the clock, to eat.

Sage's heart always melted at the sight of Logan. There was something about a big, disheveled man holding a tiny baby. Especially when you were in love with both of them.

Grace had disappeared a scant five days after Benny's birth. Logan had made certain she had plenty of money, and Theo had also given her a generous check. Logan told her again that Benny needed her in his life, but Grace ignored him.

So far, no one had heard from her, and she hadn't told anyone where she was going. As far as Sage knew, she hadn't held Benny even once. In spite of her compassion for the other woman, Sage was glad she was gone.

Andrew and Opal also left, but this time the parting was tearful for everyone. Theo and Andrew had grown as close as brothers, and Mavis and Opal had formed a close bond, as well. If Theo's health permitted, he and Caitlin were planning a trip to Australia the following winter, and to everyone's amazement, Mavis said she thought she might join them.

Sage finished stacking the dishwasher and pulled her boots and coat on. "I have gifts to wrap," she said, forcing a smile. "See you all later."

Outside, it was gray and the wind was still gusting, although it had stopped snowing. The path that Logan had shoveled earlier that day was drifted over, and as she waded through the snow Sage decided to ask Tyler to shovel it out. She hadn't really asked him to do anything since he'd arrived. Maybe some exercise would help his mood.

He was at the computer, playing one of the video games he'd brought with him. He glanced up, gave her a tiny wave and went back to the screen.

"I wonder if you'd mind shoveling out the paths, please, Tyler? The one to our house is filled in again. And Tom's coming soon in the copter. The cement landing pad needs to be cleaned off, maybe do that first."

With great reluctance, he ended the game and pulled on the parka and warm boots Sage had given him. She told him where to find a shovel, noting his rebellious expression, wincing at the way he slammed the door behind him.

She made a cup of tea and sank down on one of the stools by the kitchen island. She'd been avoiding it, but she had some difficult choices to make.

This visit was showing her plainly that if she wanted anything more than e-mail contact with Tyler, she was going to have to move to California. Any fantasies she'd had about him coming to Alaska for a prolonged length of time were exactly that—fantasies.

She was going to have to choose between Logan and her son, between watching Benny learn to talk and walk, or seeing Tyler graduate. Either choice would bring her joy and break her heart.

She'd lost Tyler once. She couldn't bear to lose him again. In three short years, he'd be in university, an adult who wouldn't want his birth mother hanging around. Until then, she wanted to be as much a part of his life as he allowed. She longed to see him make the transition from boy to man.

But by choosing California, she'd gain a relationship with her son and likely lose the man she loved. Would Logan wait for her? Three years was a long time. Common sense told her their lives would go in different directions. His life was centered here with his parents and his baby son.

She'd tried not to notice that he'd stopped proposing.

And Benny—she faltered when she thought of Benny Hunter. He was already so dear to her. She'd miss out on so much, all the precious milestones she'd forgone with Tyler.

The heavy thrumming of the copter interrupted her thoughts. She ran to the front window in time to see the machine settling on the pad. Snow blew up in blinding sheets and then settled again as the blades slowed.

Tyler was leaning on his shovel some distance away, watching as the copter door opened and first Sophia and then Lily hopped down. Tyler, always polite, if obviously reluctant, stuck the shovel in the snowbank and slowly made his way over to them.

Sage watched Tom secure the copter. The three teens stood in a little group. Lily, blond like her mother, stood back, shy, kicking at the snow, but Sophia was standing near Tyler, talking animatedly, gesturing with her gloved hands.

Sophia was getting tall, Sage noted. She'd always been a pretty girl, dark haired, with the Galloway green eyes. Curls peeked from under her zany red hat, and her snug little white jacket showed off slender curves. Something

Tyler said made her laugh, and the way she tipped her head back reminded Sage of Ben at his most charming.

Tom was unloading a small mountain of luggage and gifts, and he must have hollered at them to come and help because all three teens hurried over and loaded up, heading for the Lodge. Tyler's shovel sat in the snow, forgotten.

Sage finished wrapping her gifts, loaded them into a canvas bag and hurried over to the Lodge. The Galloways always exchanged gifts at midnight on Christmas Eve, after a long afternoon and evening spent decorating the tree, listening to carols and devouring the feast Caitlin and Mavis provided.

The Christmas would be bittersweet, Sage thought as she trudged along the path that Tyler had only half finished shoveling. There was much to mourn and much to celebrate.

There was a healthy baby to be thankful for. Logan was home at last, to stay. Theo was improving slowly. And for Sage, there was the miracle of having her son with her, their very first Christmas together. But even that was a mixed blessing. Tyler's attitude was wearing her down.

She vowed to put her concerns away for the rest of this special day and just enjoy the blessings. She opened the kitchen door to the smell of pumpkin pies baking, the sound of Benny howling and the sight of her tall son and her stepdaughters hunched over a board game at the kitchen table.

Tyler let out a whoop of triumph, Sophia punched him on the arm, and Logan, fitting the top on a baby bottle while balancing his screaming son on his shoulder, tipped his head at the three teens and gave Sage a huge wink.

She hardly dared hope, but it did look as if things were improving with Tyler, and to her amazement they continued to improve all afternoon.

The skies cleared and the sun actually made a brief appearance, which prompted Tyler and the girls to head out to the hill behind the Lodge with the old toboggan Logan dug out of the shed.

They came back two hours later, red-cheeked, exhilarated and famished. They wolfed down the cheeseburgers and fries Mavis made them to order, along with dozens of cookies and tarts. They disappeared upstairs with a bag of nachos, a box of chocolates and a case of soda. Soon the sound of rap music escaping from the girls' boom box had Mavis muttering under her breath and turning up the volume on the carols.

Over dinner, Tyler asked if Sage would mind him coming to stay in the summer. "Would six weeks be pushing it?" His blue gaze was anxious as he looked at her. "Mr. Galloway—umm, Theo—said if I wanted, there are lots of jobs around here in the summer. I wouldn't expect you to support me."

Sage almost choked on a mouthful of turkey.

"Please, please say yes, Sage," Sophia begged.

It was the first time her stepdaughter had ever asked her for anything except to go away and leave her daddy alone.

"He needs to see the Salmon Derby," Sophia pleaded. "And then there's Gold Rush Days and the Soapy Smith celebration. And Logan says you guys could take us camping. And Mavis told me I could work here, too, if I wanted."

"You'll both have to get up in the morning, no lolling around in bed till noon," Mavis warned dourly. "You'll have to take orders with no back talk."

"We will, we promise. Please, Sage? Is it okay?"

"Yes, I think that would be fine," she managed, resisting the mad urge to get up and snatch Sophia into her arms and dance around the table.

After dinner, with much horseplay and showers of tinsel, the teens decorated the tree. The gifts were brought out and stacked underneath, waiting for midnight.

Sage and Caitlin talked themselves hoarse as they diapered and fed the baby, then settled him in a quiet corner to sleep.

The men relaxed in front of the fire with glasses of brandy. Theo was nodding when Mavis noticed the glow of the Northern Lights through the living room window.

Tyler and the girls raced outside without coats, but everyone else, conscious that it was twenty-two below, bundled up before heading out to the deck.

The incandescent glow lit the sky in magical, shimmering waves of green and rose and eerie silver and violet. A shiver went up and down Sage's spine at the spectacle. No matter how many times she saw the lights, her sense of awe never diminished.

"They're putting on a real show tonight," Logan whispered in her ear. He was standing close behind her, hands on her shoulders, and he leaned forward and kissed her neck.

Sage shivered with delight, but she also glanced around, apprehensive as always about who might see. But everyone was staring up at the sky, involved in the magic.

"I love you, my darling." Logan's breath tickled her ear. She longed to turn into his arms, feel his lips on hers, but as always, she held back.

Tears came to her eyes, a reaction to the beauty above her, but also regret for the many opportunities like this that she'd resisted, the times she'd turned away from him for one reason or another. Good, valid reasons, all of them.

The reasons were still there: Tyler, baby Benny, the problems of geography and the uncertainties of their complex lives. But as the lights danced and shifted from one iridescent shade to another, something also shifted inside of Sage.

There was no way of predicting when the lights would choose to stage this magnificent show. There was also no way of predicting what challenges life would hold. The gift of the lights had to be enjoyed in the moment.

Sage looked around. On every beloved face, she saw the indelible marks of the same powerful emotions the aurora stirred in her: tears, laughter, joy, sorrow, hope. Awe. Appreciation. Fear of the unknown?

How many generations of Galloways had stood here like this, watching the lights, reminded in these fleeting moments of the sheer beauty of simply living their lives? Sage remembered the letters Andrew had brought, the poignant story of a pregnant girl who'd made mistakes, taken chances, been forced into hard choices.

Jenny Galloway must have been afraid, and yet she'd refused to let fear determine her destiny. Sage didn't have Jenny's blood in her veins, but at this moment, she could feel the other woman's spirit, almost hear her voice across the years, echoing down through the eerie sounds of the northern night.

Living takes courage, she seemed to whisper to Sage. Loving takes faith. Sometimes you just have to trust.

Sage turned to face Logan. He'd asked her more than once. It was her turn to do the asking now.

"Will you marry me, Logan Galloway?" Her voice was shaky.

She'd caught him unaware, and his beloved face first registered astonishment and disbelief. After a moment he stammered, "Say that again?"

"Okay, but this is your last chance," she teased. Her voice was strong now. This was right.

By now, Caitlin and Theo and Mavis were shamelessly listening, but Sage ignored them.

"I love you," she said, loud and clear. "Will you marry me, Logan Galloway?"

"I will," he roared, picking her up in his arms, kissing her as Caitlin clapped and the Alaskan sky rained ribbons of blessing down on everyone.

* * * * *

Part Two

Chapter One

July 8, 1897

Steam billowed up as the train finally pulled to a stop at Union Station in the downtown heart of Seattle. Jenny Galloway held her dusty skirts down with one hand and with the other clutched the small gold locket at her throat, a poignant reminder of her father. He'd given it to her in Edinburgh on her wedding day, six weeks before, and she hadn't taken it off since.

She could see that the station was filled with people. The crowd was boisterous and loud, and when she stepped from the train to the platform, she looked around in amazement and grabbed for William's arm, afraid of being swept away in the milling mass of bodies.

"It's worse than New York," she said to her husband in a voice raised enough to carry over the din, but neither William nor his brother Robert heard her. They were doing their best to keep tabs on the luggage.

"Something's goin' on," William declared. "There has to be something that's driven this mob to a frenzy." He stopped a young newsboy nearby and asked what the fuss was all about.

"Gold," the emaciated fellow shouted, waving a newspaper aloft.

Exasperated, Jenny sighed. There was no getting away from it; it seemed every time she turned around someone was gabbing about gold. That awful man on the boat had talked about it nonstop, until she'd longed to stuff a napkin in his gob.

The newsboy went on, "These miners came in a couple days ago from the North, brought a million dollars' worth of gold with them. They found it at this place called Bonanza, in the Canadian Yukon. We're all going—we're gonna be rich. Read all about it, sir."

William handed him a coin and the boy thrust the paper at William and hurried away. William turned the paper to the cover story. Jenny, who'd lost all track of time, took note of the date. It was July 8, 1897.

The headline shrieked, GOLD! GOLD! GOLD! 68 Rich Men on the Steamer Portland. STACKS OF YELLOW METAL!

William stuck the paper under his arm, seized Jenny's hand and led the way out of the station. Robert stayed behind, guarding their small mountain of belongings.

The streets outside were teeming with people hurrying toward the docks. William somehow located a hack, and when the three men had retrieved Jenny's trunk and the rest of the luggage, he gave the driver the address of the small waterfront hotel he'd stayed in previously. He studied the newspaper while the vehicle lurched along.

But when they arrived, the hotel was full, as was the next one the driver took them to. He explained that people were already pouring into the city from outlying areas, eager to head out on the first available steamer heading north.

"Don't worry, gov'ner, I knows a lady runs a clean rooming house," he said. "Not fancy, but serviceable. And she's got two rooms empty, drove the gents as was stayin' there to the station, earlier today. They was headin' fer San Francisco, goin' ta ship out on a boat headed north."

The rambling house was near the docks, and Jenny could smell the saltwater and hear the gulls screeching as they pulled up in front.

The extremely stout landlady, Mrs. Graves, greeted them cheerfully and led the way to two rooms on the second floor, the halves of her broad backside pumping up and down. She was puffing like a dray horse when she reached the top of the stairs. As the hack driver had promised, the rooms were clean, if sparse. In each there was a washstand in one corner, a double bed and a single padded chair.

"Rents are by the week or month," Mrs. Graves said when she'd recovered her breath. "Which'll it be?"

"We'll pay for a week," William decided, and Jenny felt like singing. One whole week in a bed that wasn't moving! Somewhere to wash away the grime of travel. There'd be time to take the stack of soiled clothing to a laundry, time to get the weariness out of her bones. Time to lie in bed with William in privacy and peace.

"Three dollars a week for each room. Toilet and wash-room down the hall, one bath a week each person permit-ted, clean the tub after use," the landlady recited as William paid her. "Breakfast and supper included, supper at six precisely. I expect my guests to be prompt, no one seated after six-fifteen." She ran out of breath and heaved in another one, making her breasts rise and fall like the deck of the steamship that brought them across the ocean.

Jenny shuddered at the memory. She'd been horribly seasick, and she never wanted to lay eyes on a boat again.

"There's a tavern down the street, McCloskeys, serves a ploughman's dinner," the landlady was explaining. "If ye're late here go straight there without stopping at my dining room, no exceptions to my rules. Breakfast from five to eight," she added, double chins wobbling. "Packed lunches extra."

She eyed Robert and William with her head on one side. "You're a brawny pair, never knew no twins before. As like as two peas in a pod, ye are. Which of you's is the married one, again?"

"Jenny's my wife." William put a proprietary arm around Jenny's shoulders.

Mrs. Graves gave her a lurid wink. "Better go careful, my girl. Easy to get confused betwixt the two of these, I should think. Not that that would be a tragic thing. Not at all, at all." She gave Robert a coquettish look from under stubby eyelashes and waddled out, chuckling.

Jenny giggled. She'd grown accustomed to having women admire her husband and her brother-in-law. The Galloways *were* handsome. Big brawny Scots, broad shouldered and narrow hipped, they both had their dark curly hair tied in a clout on their necks. Each had high cheekbones and strong jaws, eyes identically green as summer grass. Jenny liked to think they had the look of their wild Highland ancestors. There were tiny differences between them, but they weren't immediately apparent. Robert's chin was deeply cleft, while William's had only the faintest indentation.

Their ears were differently shaped. Robert's had a distinctive fold at the top which William didn't have. But the pair of them turned female heads wherever they went. Obviously, Mrs. Graves was smitten.

Robert waited until the door had closed behind their landlady. Then he raised his eyebrows and gave a silent whistle. "She's no one to trifle with."

William punched him on the arm. "Best lock yer door tonight, laddie. Ye might have a bed partner otherwise. Though the bed might'nt stand the strain." He laughed as his brother turned crimson. Without looking at Jenny, Robert picked up his bag and went next door to the smaller room.

Jenny started to unpack. The bags were in a terrible state, dirty clothes mixed in with clean, things shoved in every which way. She wrinkled her nose at the stale smell.

William had no patience for domestic duties. "While you get settled, lass, I'm going out to explore the city a bit, see if it's changed much since last I was here," he said. "Robert will come with me—we'll no be long. Back in plenty of time for supper, we dinna want to aggravate canny Mrs. Graves the very first day." He drew Jenny to him for a kiss that lasted longer than she expected. He cupped her face with both palms, tracing her jaw with his thumbs and ringing her lips with his tongue, making her shiver. When he released her his eyes were half-lidded and sultry, his voice husky. "And then we'll retire early, shall we, lass?"

"Aye." Suddenly shy, her cheeks grew hot, but she smiled at him and nodded. The bed was wide and clean, the pillows soft, and the comforter looked warm. Best of all, it was stationary.

"I'll tidy here a bit and then I'd like a wash," she said. "D'ye think Mrs. Graves would mind if I took my weekly bath now?"

"Go ahead, lass. If she says a word to ye, I'll deal wi' her." He found his hat and patted her bottom before he went out the door.

Jenny quickly sorted out the clothing, putting one huge stack aside for laundry, folding the much smaller stack of clean garments onto the shelf in the cupboard. She found her soap, took the towel from the rack by the washstand and stuck her head out the door.

She could hear raised angry voices, male and female, from the room across the hall, but there was no one in sight and the door to the washroom was open. She scuttled along the passageway and closed and locked it after herself.

The tub was rusted tin, and the water that trickled out of the faucet was barely warm. When there were only several inches of water in the tub, it turned icy cold and stayed that way. Set on bathing, no matter what, Jenny hurried out of her clothing, struggling with the hooks of her corset. She climbed in, shuddering at the chill. At least she wasn't tempted to linger.

Teeth chattering, she washed her long chestnut brown hair first and then the rest of her, rinsing with cold water from the tap, muttering curses she'd learned from the sailors on board ship.

The towel was threadbare, and her thick, unruly hair was still dripping as she struggled back into her clothes. Remembering the landlady's orders, she scrubbed the tub and rinsed it out, wondering if anyone else even ventured to use it.

She was halfway down the hall when a door flew open and then slammed shut. A short, very slender redhead, hair escaping from a braided bun, stormed down the hallway toward her.

"*Bloody* men," she fumed in a lovely deep contralto as she drew abreast of Jenny. "*Why* can't they make up their minds one way or the other and stick with it?" She suddenly stopped, put her hands on nonexistent hips and studied Jenny. "Sorry to be so rude, I'm that mad at Carl Sundstrom I'd forget my head if it wasn't tacked on. I'm Mae Sundstrom, Mae with an *E*, not a *Y*. I heard you arrive, and I also heard old lady Graves overcharging your husband. The rooms are only *two* dollars a week. She's a sly one, she'll take advantage if you don't watch her like a hawk."

Jenny, not knowing what part of the tirade to respond to first, settled for a smile. She shook the small hand Mae extended, responding to the warm, wide grin that, along with the lovely voice, were the other woman's only claims to beauty. She had a long, narrow face. Freckles were so thick across her nose and cheeks that her skin seemed to be two separate colors. Her pale blue, lashless eyes almost disappeared when she smiled, and her large nose had a distinctive arch to it. Her red hair was straight as a stick, which made Jenny a bit envious. Already, her wet mop was beginning to curl like the tail on a piglet.

Mae wrinkled her nose and shook her head. "There, I'm talking too much again. I'll button my mouth now and give you a chance to introduce yourself."

Jenny laughed and said, "How'd'y do? We were that glad to find a place, we'd no argue with Mrs. Graves even had we known the price ahead. Y'see, the hotels are all filled, it's this gold folderol, ye ken." She added, "I'm Jenny Cam—sorry, Jenny Galloway." She flushed at the slip. She still forgot at times that she'd left her maiden name far behind, along with everything else dear and familiar. "Pleased to make yer acquaintance, Mrs. Sundstrom."

"Oh, call me Mae, *please*. I've only been married two months myself, it makes me feel *ancient* to be Mrs. Sundstrom. I just turned twenty last week, that's not quite doddering."

Jenny was barely seventeen herself. Mae was the first woman she'd met in the New World who was close to her own age.

"Pleased to make your acquaintance, Jenny Galloway. I *love* your accent, by the way, I'm a sucker for accents. It's what first drew me to Carl, heaven help me. He came from Norway two years ago. He still makes me giggle sometimes when he says *Yah* for yes and *Yam* for jam. When I'm not furious with him, that is." Mae waved a hand at the wet towel Jenny was holding. "I'll bet there was no hot water for your bath. She makes certain there's none, she's that worried about the cost of heating it, as if an extra stick of wood for the boiler is going to send her to the doss-house, the wicked old tightwad."

Jenny glanced over her shoulder and lowered her voice. "Two inches, lukewarm and then like ice. I washed me hair and rinsed in cold. It's a wonder ye dinna hear me screamin' and cursin'." There was something about Mae that invited confidences.

Mae giggled. "I'm sure you *did* hear me screaming and cursing. Carl and I were having the most stupendous quarrel." They both giggled at that, even though Jenny figured it wasn't really polite to laugh at a quarrel. But Mae's forthright manner was engaging. Jenny felt instantly at ease with her.

"I'd offer you some hot tea to warm you up," Mae said, wrinkling her nose, jerking her thumb back in the direction of her door, "but Carl's still in our room, and I'm not speaking to him at the moment. I'm avoiding him."

Jenny nodded, unsure of what the proper response might be to that. She hadn't yet had a quarrel that called for not speaking to or avoiding William. Her husband had a temper, and she wasn't quite sure how that would go over. She settled for, "Thank ye anyhow, but William will be back directly, and I have to dry my hair and dress for supper. I'm that afraid o' bein late, ye ken. Mrs. Graves made it sound as though it was a major offense."

Mae blew a raspberry. "Her and her stupid rules. The old battle-ax, she runs this place like a home for wayward girls. Which actually would be lots more fun, don't you think?" She didn't wait for Jenny to answer. "Well, I'll see you at table, then, Jenny Galloway. I'm going to hide out in the backyard till Carl gets good and worried and comes looking for me. Oh, and don't have any of the chowder at dinner. It's made from fish that was already going bad yesterday. Give you a proper bellyache, it will, and there's only one bathroom per floor." She sailed on down the hall, making more commotion than her tiny form warranted as she went clattering down the stairs.

Jenny smiled all the way to her room, and once inside she laughed aloud, delighted with Mae Sundstrom and her outspoken opinions. She hadn't known many girls her own age, not since she'd left school at twelve to help out at home. Feeling elated about this chance meeting, she changed her damp clothing and tried to get a comb through her wet, wayward curls.

When William came in just before six, she told him about Mae, and although he seemed to listen, murmuring he was glad she'd made a friend, Jenny could tell he was thinking about something else. His face was flushed, his eyes bright.

Her heart sank. He'd bought two more newspapers, and she suspected he was thinking about gold.

She remembered what Mae had said about men changing their minds. While William was splashing water over his face and putting on a clean shirt, she decided to meet whatever this was head-on.

"And what did ye learn about the gold, William? Is the city gone quite mad about it?" Might as well get it out in the open.

"It has, and with good reason." His deep voice rang with enthusiasm. "This gold strike is no just a rumor, Jenny. Men who came in on the boat the other day are millionaires, swearin' there's plenty more where theirs came from. Robbie and I talked wi' one of them, Joe Bergeoin, he's called. He was havin' a pint in the saloon round the corner. Used to be a logger, he came out wi' fifteen thousand in gold nuggets, says he's goin' straight back for more."

Jenny thought she'd like to see the nuggets before she believed a story like that, but she didn't say it. "And where exactly is this Klondike place?"

"In Canada. Dawson City is fourteen hundred miles up the Yukon River. Klondike is the name of the river that joins the Yukon at Dawson."

Which was so much gibberish to her, except for the distance. "Fourteen hundred miles." Jenny was shocked. She couldn't imagine a country where you could travel such a distance. "And how do ye get there, William? I doubt there's railways, aye?"

William laughed at that. "No railways, Jenny. No roads, for much of the way, either. The way Bergeoin tells it, ye travel from Seattle by steamer up to a wee place called Skagway in Alaska. Then ye either pay exorbitant amounts for packing services, or ye carry yer supplies on yer back over the mountains to the goldfields. After that, it's another five hundred miles by water to reach the place. It's no an easy journey, gettin' there."

"Easy? More like impossible." The vast distances were inconceivable to Jenny. And carry supplies over the mountains on your back? The train trip across the continent had given her some idea what mountains were like over here. The gentle rolling hills of her native Scotland had nothing to compare with them.

"It sounds doubtful, William." It sounded bloody ridiculous, not to say totally mad, but she was determined to be tactful. "And what if folks get there and the gold's all gone?"

"Ahh, Jenny, ye're a wee doubtin' Thomas, are ye not?" He laughed harder than before, which annoyed her because it had seemed a perfectly reasonable question. "From the sounds of it, there'll be gold for the takin' for many years tae come, for as many as can make the journey."

She wanted to say maybe it was wisest to wait, then. If the gold would be there years from now, then it made sense to make certain it was more than wind and dreams. Give it time, she wanted to say. But again she curbed her speech, warned by the glitter in William's eyes, the passion in his voice when he spoke of the gold.

The next question was a hard one. "And are ye thinkin' ye might go after this gold, then, William?"

He waited a long heartbeat before answering. "Aye," he finally said. "I'm givin' it some thought. From what I've heard, mining for gold is hard work, it would take both Rob and I to make it a success."

A flicker of anxiety shot down her spine. He wasn't saying a word about her. What did he plan to do with her if he set off on some wild-goose chase? He couldn't very well send her back home to wait for him, could he? Surely he wouldn't think of leaving her somewhere, like a bundle of laundry to be claimed when it suited him?

Jenny tried to hide her alarm.

He turned and looked at her, his expression unreadable. "Would ye mind over much if we changed our plans, Jenny? I'd no ask ye to come along to the Klondike—God, no, it's nae place for a woman from what I hear. I'd leave ye here in Seattle safe and secure, with plenty of money to go on. And I'd no be gone all that long, just enough to see what the prospects are."

It was her worst fear, to be left alone in a strange country where she knew not a soul. Her heart skipped a beat and she suddenly felt icy cold. Surely he wouldn't do any such thing. Didn't he realize how alone she'd be, how lonely?

She felt like screaming at him, but instead she forced herself to say in a reasonable tone, "And did Robert say he'd go wi' ye?" If only Robert would say he didn't want to go—maybe then there'd be a chance William would stick to the original plans. He was an engineer, he'd been offered a fine job building a railroad in British Columbia, in a place called the Crowsnest Pass. And there'd be laboring work for Robert, as well. She'd been looking forward to the lodgings the company supplied.

"Aye, I'm sure Robert would come, though I havena

asked him yet, not right out and fer certain. We'd need to study on it, see if it's somethin' we could make a go of together, Jenny."

And suddenly she knew Robert's opinion wouldn't matter if William decided for it. Robert wouldn't object— he went along with whatever William decided. She was that proud of having an educated man for a husband, but in some ways it made William more than a bit overbearing.

Her belly knotted, and this time it wasn't from hunger. "Have ye already made up your mind, then, William?"

He shook his head. "No, no. I'm considerin' possibilities is all." His voice softened. "And I wouldna do it if ye were right dead set against it, Jenny."

She was right dead set against it, and then some. She opened her mouth to say so and closed it again, because she didn't want to sound like a harpie. She needed to be cautious here, not go into a flaming rage and lose the battle through temper. But it was the maddest thing she'd heard in all her born days, and it was nearly choking her to hold her tongue. "It would take some thinking on," she finally managed to sputter.

Lord, if she didn't deserve a medal for discretion.

William didn't notice anything amiss. "The talk is that even if a man doesna have a claim of his own, he can make fifty to a hundred dollars a day working for someone who does. We'd soon have enough to buy land, Jenny. Workin' fer wages it would take me a full year to save as much as I'd make in a week in the goldfields. And if we staked a claim and found gold, why, we'd all be on easy street, lassie." His green eyes sparkled with excitement.

Easy street? "But it's a gamble, William, is it not?" Bloody certain it was. Anyone with a cool head could say that much. "And surely not everyone who goes finds gold." She was becoming more alarmed by the second.

"Aye, yer right, Jenny." William stroked his chin and nodded, as if he was actually considering her words. "It is a gamble, sure enough, although the word is that the Klondike is the richest goldfield in the world. It seems worth taking the risk, ye ken." He took out his pocket watch. "We'd better go down, or Mrs. Graves will refuse to feed us."

Dinner would give her time to figure out how best to go about this. And she remembered something else. "Mae Sundstrom said she's overcharging us for the room, it ought only tae be two dollars a week."

William nodded. "Aye, I guessed as much, but if the rumors are even half-true about the numbers of men heading here, Seattle won't have a bed free in a few days, so it's wise to pay the old bisom what she asks. It's said men from every corner of the country will be coming here to board a ship for the Klondike. And we'll need a clean, safe place for you to stay while I'm away North."

Chapter Two

Jenny was speechless. So he was already planning to leave her here with fat old Mrs. Graves. So much for not having made up his mind.

"And when would you be leavin', William? You and Robert?"

"There's a steamer, the *Falcon,* leaving tomorrow evening, but I doubt we could get our supplies ready that fast. We'll need to hurry, though, so we're well on our way before the big rush really begins. So I suppose in a week at the latest, if we can book passage."

Jenny didn't say anything, because if she opened her mouth she'd shriek at him and not be able to stop. Did he not understand anything at all about women? They'd left Scotland two weeks after their wedding, and since then she'd been on either a boat or a train. She'd so looked forward to staying in Seattle for a week, having time to relax before she again climbed on something moving. Sure, he planned on leaving her behind, but she was having no part of it.

And he had no idea how distraught she was. He said in a mild voice, "Did ye want to brush your hair before we go down, lass? It's a wee bit wild."

Jenny moved to the wavy mirror on the wall over the washstand. Her reflection showed a girl with flushed cheeks, wide mouth tightly clenched, dark angry blue eyes narrowed and smoldering, and a wild mass of chestnut hair standing out all around her head in stubborn corkscrew curls that defied her efforts at containing them in any reasonable fashion.

She used the brush as if it was a currycomb, dragging it painfully through her hair, clenching her teeth because now instead of screaming at William she felt like crying. When the mess was as tidy as it would ever be, she wound it up and pinned it, shoving the pins in as if she was driving nails into her skull, glaring at her husband through the mirror.

Of course William didn't even notice. His head was bent over the newspaper, checking out ships heading for Alaska, no doubt.

"I'm ready." The words came out in a high, squeaky tone because she was struggling with the sobs that followed the anger.

William tapped on Robert's door, and it was obvious he'd been waiting for them.

"Ye're lookin' bonny, Jenny." Her brother-in-law smiled at her and led the way down the twisting staircase. She followed on William's arm, wondering why Robert was the one to compliment her while her husband seemed hardly to notice her unless she was wearing her nightdress. If she'd married Robert, she'd bet he wouldn't think of leaving her in a foreign city on her own so he could go chasing a dream.

The dining room was small and noisy. It seemed crammed with people all talking at once, but the noise quieted as the Galloways entered the room. Every head turned their way.

Mrs. Graves was seated at the top end, and she beckoned to Robert, indicating he was to sit next to her. She'd obviously been holding a seat for him.

William edged his way along the wall to the only other two empty chairs, holding one out for Jenny to be seated before he took his own.

Directly across the table, Mae Sundstrom wriggled her long fingers and smiled her wide smile at Jenny, and the gesture was calming. She wasn't the only one having issues with this gold nonsense, Jenny assured herself. Mae was fighting a similar battle.

Mae was seated beside a short, balding man with a ruddy complexion. He looked far too old to be her husband, and Jenny glanced around the table, trying to figure out which of the other men might be Carl. There was a huge, broad-shouldered man with side whiskers and a beard seated two seats away from Mae. That must be him, she deduced. Mae was probably still angry and refusing to sit beside him.

"Everyone, these are our new guests," Mrs. Graves announced in a loud, unctuous voice, placing one plump hand on Robert's forearm.

Jenny saw him wince, and some of her anger suddenly turned to amusement.

"This is Robert Galloway," Mrs. Graves simpered. "And

his twin brother, William, and William's wife—now what did you say your name was again, dearie?"

"Mrs. Galloway." Jenny was in no mood for the landlady's cattiness. Across the table she saw Mae stifling a giggle. "Jenny Galloway," she amended after a moment.

Mrs. Graves used a forefinger to indicate the diners, one by one.

Jenny nodded as each was introduced, making an effort to remember their names. Letitia McPhee looked to be seventy, wispy and wrinkled in her black bombazine dress. Bertha Snider sat beside Letitia, thin gray hair pulled into such a tight snood she looked perpetually surprised. Zachary Crawmire, a stooped, elderly gentleman with round spectacles and a nervous habit of clearing his throat every few minutes was on William's far side. And Evan Smith was the young man Jenny had decided, wrongly, it turned out, was Mae's husband.

"And Carl and Mrs. Sundstrom," Mrs. Graves concluded, giving Mae a smarmy smile.

So the small, older man beside Mae was her husband after all. Jenny stole another curious glance at him, and he smiled at her. Like his wife, he had a wide, capricious smile that lit up his face and made it endearing.

"How do you do, Mr. and Mrs. Galloway? Pleased to meet you." His lilting Norwegian accent made the words sound like music.

"And now that we all know each other, please bring in the soup," Mrs. Graves said. When that didn't bring a response, she hollered out in a booming voice, "Susie? Bring the soup, *now*." Under her breath she muttered, "Lazy slut."

A blond girl with rosy cheeks and a checkered apron

hurried in carrying a tureen. She placed it in front of Mrs. Graves, who ladled out a generous scoop into bowls which she then handed down the table.

The soup was creamed fish, and the smell made Jenny's stomach turn. She looked up and caught Mae giving her a tiny head shake, and suddenly her spirits lifted. She had a new friend, one who would understand this impossible business of the goldfields—hadn't Mae been quarreling with Carl already over that very thing?

"And where are you from, Mrs. Galloway?" It was Letitia McPhee who leaned past her neighbor to inquire.

"Scotland," Jenny replied. "The outskirts of Edinburgh."

"Are you here on holiday?" This time Letitia turned her attention to Robert, who was looking profoundly uncomfortable. He seemed to be trying to edge as far away from Mrs. Graves as possible without toppling out of his chair.

"No, we're emigrating," Robert said. "That is, Jenny and I are, Willie's been in America for four years already. He's an engineer. He'll be building the new railroad across Canada."

"Aye, but I'll need joost a wee bit a' help wie it, ye ken," William added, emphasizing his brogue and making everyone laugh.

"What made you return to Scotland after four years, Mr. Galloway?" Letitia was fluttering her eyelashes at William.

"I'd promised wee Rob I'd come for him, soon as a job in the New World seemed likely," William explained. "And I fancied a bonny Scots lassie as a bride," he added. "Not that the lovely ladies in the New World are lackin' in any way," he said with a broad wink at Letitia. "It's just comfortin' ta have a wife who kens yer brogue."

Everyone laughed again, as he'd intended.

"So you and your brother are not going to the Klondike, Mr. Galloway?" Evan Smith directed the question at Robert. His voice didn't suit the rest of him. It was a boy's voice, like one of Jenny's small brothers, surprising coming from such a bear of a man.

Robert looked over at William and shrugged, turning the question over to him.

"We've no decided as yet," William said. "How about yerself, Mr. Smith? Are ye goin'?"

"Indeed, I am. It's the chance of a lifetime. I'm getting my pack together but it's a slow business because it seems every man in Seattle is doing the same thing, so supplies are dwindling."

"Expensive enterprise, I gather," Zachary Crawmire said in a dry, cracked voice, clearing his throat before and after he spoke.

"Five hundred dollars for a complete outfit," Evan said. "And steamer tickets are a hundred each. Packing services over the mountains are another three hundred, making a total of nine hundred in all just to get there."

"It costs money to get rich, no endeavor for a poor man," Zachary said, and then cackled at his own humor.

Appalled at how much money was needed to go north, Jenny looked across at Mae, who rolled her eyes and pulled her mouth down in a disgusted expression.

"It's a gamble, ve can't know ahead if it's vorthvhile," her husband said.

Jenny was amazed when Mae snapped, "But it's a chance to get rich, how many of those come along in a lifetime?"

Could it possibly be Mae who wanted to go north, and Carl who was against it? Jenny could hardly get her mind around it.

And all the men at the table agreed with her, nodding and murmuring assent. They all began to talk at once, detailing what was needed for the trip, relating gossip they'd heard that day on the wharves and in the saloons, generally agreeing that a man would be a fool not to go.

Jenny was shocked at how she'd misinterpreted the quarrel between the Sundstroms. She thought about it as she pretended to eat the soup, not swallowing a single mouthful.

"Sophie," Mrs. Graves bellowed in a few moments. "We're done with the soup, bring in the roast."

Jenny noticed that none of the women had done more than stir the soup around, while the men, engrossed in their gold talk, had devoured every drop. She figured there'd be lineups for the toilet tonight, and a glance at Mae made her think her friend was considering the same thing. Mae's eyes danced with glee.

Sophie staggered in with a platter far too large for one person to handle. It held an immense pot roast and roasted vegetables, and it was followed by a steamed plum pudding and hot sauce. Mrs. Graves might be stingy with the hot water, but she didn't stint on the food.

Jenny ate, but her appetite wasn't as healthy as usual. She kept hearing her father's voice, warning her that William was a wandering man.

A wandering man? Try a gambling man, which to her sounded much worse. If Bruce had suspected that, he'd have forbidden her to marry William. Bruce was very opposed to gambling. His own father had been well-off, with a large house and an inheritance, but he'd lost everything he owned by betting. As a result, Bruce had had to leave school early and take a job on a nearby farm.

No doubt about it, Bruce didn't know the half of it

where William was concerned, and there was no way her pride would ever allow Jenny to tell her father the truth about her husband.

Chapter Three

"They've all gone gold mad, every last one of them, except for my husband," Mae pronounced two mornings later. "Why can't he see that opportunity is banging away at our door? He does make me quite annoyed, does Carl Sundstrom. There's a time for caution, but goodness me, this isn't it."

She and Jenny were sitting cross-legged in the middle of the bed in Mae's room, drinking soda and eating cream puffs Mae had bought from the bakery around the corner.

"Ye're right about them goin' mad," Jenny agreed, licking powdered sugar from her fingers. "Klondike fever, they're callin' it. William's dead set now on goin' and Robert with him, as soon as they can get tickets on a steamer."

In fact they were off this very minute getting their supplies together, along with most of the male population of the city.

If it weren't for Mae, Jenny figured she'd be locked in her room bawling her head off. She'd made a trip to the post office, praying for a packet of letters from her father, but there wasn't a single piece of mail for her. She'd mailed the letters she'd written, but it had felt a little like dropping them down a rabbit hole, knowing it would be a good month before she could even hope they'd reach Scotland.

Mae was still talking about the Klondike. "Carl's going, damn his hide, even if I have to drag him kicking and screaming. He'd rather stay here and work in a *sawmill,* can you believe that?" Mae reached over and plucked another cream puff out of the box and bit into it. She chewed for a moment, took a sip of her soda, and said, "He wants to take all our savings and buy a house, rather than have an adventure and go off searching for gold."

It was the very thing Jenny would do in his circumstances, but she didn't want to alienate Mae by saying so. Why couldn't William be a little more like Carl Sundstrom?

"He says it's no place for a woman, that even if he wanted to go—which he doesn't—he'd leave me here. Can you believe that? As if I'd ever agree to stay here alone… We couldn't afford it anyways. And the last thing I'll do is go back to Daisy's, her and Jake tried not to show it, but it was a relief to them when I married Carl and they got to be by themselves for a change. And as for begging my job back, or getting another one here in Seattle…" She shuddered. "I think part of the reason I married was to get out of teaching. It's not the children I minded, it's the school trustees. Horrible men, with not an ounce of imagination between them."

Mae had told Jenny how her father and stepmother had died from influenza three years ago, just after Mae quali-

fied as a schoolteacher. Since then she'd been living in
Portland with her married sister, helping care for her four
nieces and nephews when she wasn't teaching primary
classes at a nearby school.

Carl had met Mae's brother-in-law in the cigar store
where Jake worked, and he'd liked the Norwegian and
brought him home for supper. The rest, Mae said with a
sigh, was history.

"He's not the most handsome man, but he's funny and
kind and sweet, and he adores me. I love him, I'm certain
I do—most of the time, at least when he's not being a pig-
headed idiot about prospecting for gold."

"Are there only men goin' ta this Klondike place, do ye
know, Mae? Is there some rule against women goin' along?"

"Not that I've heard. Although, I haven't really met any
women planning on going. Except me. I wonder what the
men think they'll do about meals and such? Carl can't boil
water without scalding himself—he has no idea about preparing food. He'd starve to death in a full pantry. And as for
laundry, well, forget it. He shipped his out until we married."

Jenny had no idea whether William could cook or not,
or Robert, either. It wasn't a question she'd ever thought
to ask. She added it to a mental list she was making. If she
could ever make William stay still long enough, she
planned to get answers to every single query.

"It would only make sense to take us along to this
Klondike place, wouldn't ye say?" she said thoughtfully
to Mae. The idea had been gestating since the previous day.
If there was no rational way to stop William from going,
then the only thing to do was go along.

"I'm no overkeen on another boat trip," Jenny added with
a shudder. "And I'm certainly no so keen as you about the

Klondike, but I think I'd prefer anythin' to stayin' here wi' Mrs. Graves, which is what William has in his mind fer me."

"She'd far rather have Robert stay than you," Mae said, and then sputtered crumbs all over the spread when she giggled.

Jenny laughed, too. Robert had been mortified because he'd confided to William that both evenings at dinner, the landlady had put her hand on his crotch under the cover of the tablecloth while he was trying to eat.

After they'd made love, William hadn't been able to resist telling Jenny, and they'd laughed together about it. And today she hadn't been able to resist telling Mae.

"He's that afraid of her, poor man. He says he'd rather starve than sit beside her again at a meal," Jenny told her new friend.

"I don't blame him. Can you imagine her and a man in bed? The poor fellow would have a terrible time locating the necessary places in the midst of all that fat."

They dissolved in scandalized giggles again.

"Joking aside, old lady Graves is a bold one," Mae said when they finally sobered. "She can't be bothered to remember your name, but she's ready to fiddle with your brother-in-law. She's got good taste, I'll say that for her. He's a handsome fellow. If I weren't head over heels for that idiot Carl, I'd flirt with Robert Galloway myself."

Jenny was too fascinated by Mrs. Graves to think much about Mae flirting with Robert. "What ever became of her husband, d'ye think?"

Mae shrugged. "Chances are she never had one. There's no law says you can't put *Missus* in front of your name, you know." Mae dropped her voice to a whisper. "I think she was a woman of ill repute before she started running this place."

"A *prostitute?* Ye think so?" Jenny had only learned what the word meant recently. She'd asked William about such women, after he'd made a remark about someone on the ship. "How can ye tell?"

"Well, she pretends to be genteel, but what lady would be so familiar with a man as to feel his privates under the table? I can't see a respectable widow doing a thing like that, can you, Jenny?"

Jenny shook her head, but she felt herself blushing because of some of the things she did do with William. He'd taught her things she'd never dreamed were even thought of, and assured her they were fine between man and wife. She didn't know what was the truth, but she found them so exciting and pleasurable she wasn't about to question anyone and find out he was fibbing to her.

"William says the only sort of women who'll be goin' ta the Klondike are the ones who are prostitutes." Late the previous night, Jenny had suggested that maybe she'd go with him rather than stay in Seattle, and that had been his immediate response.

"Balderdash." Mae smacked a fist down on the comforter. "Excuse my French, but Carl said the *exact* same thing, that decent women wouldn't be going because they wouldn't be strong enough to make the trip, blah blah blah, and it makes me livid to hear it. Why would prostitutes be able to stand hardships and women like you or me not be able to? We're young and strong. And smarter than the average prostitute, I'd bet money on that."

Jenny agreed. "I'd rather suffer any sort of hardship than have to stay back and wait for William and Robert to come back and collect me like a—like a carpetbag they'd forgotten."

"So we're agreed, then, Jenny?" Mae sprang off the bed and stood tall, small hands on her nonexistent hips. "We'll stand firm and tell our husbands we want to go to the Klondike. We'll refuse to be left behind. We'll persevere until they see reason and give in."

"Aye, we will so." But Jenny felt a little anxious about standing firm with William. She hadn't really disagreed with him over anything so far, nothing serious at any rate— oh, she'd been sick and cranky on the ship, but that wasn't really a disagreement, was it? And this would be.

"I'm going to take a stand with Carl the moment he walks through that door," Mae promised with a determined look on her face.

"Aye, and me, as well." Their eyes met as they heard the clatter of boots on the stairs and the sound of excited male voices. "Here they are. Are we in this together?" Mae held out a hand and Jenny put her own in it, even though her heart was hammering with nervousness. They shook on the vow.

"Aye, we are so. William's a reasonable man, he'll see it's the only thing," Jenny declared with far more conviction than she felt.

"Be reasonable, woman," William thundered a short time later. "Ye dinna ken what such a trip will be like, a fair bit o' it's on the water and were ye no sick nearly te yer death comin' o'er on the steamer? And that'll be a bed o' roses compared to the trip to the Klondike, I grant ye. Even Rob isna overjoyed at the prospect. The steamer takes from five to seven days to reach Skagway, and that's only the start of it. Then we hike over the White Pass Trail, a forty-two mile walk up and o'er the mountains wi' all our supplies.

This is no an easy trek even for strong and able men, never mind a frail woman, fer the good Lord God's sake."

Jenny bristled at being labeled frail, but she was learning to pick her battles. "It's no fourteen days on a heavin' ocean, either, William." This was harder than she'd anticipated, standing up to William. It was some consolation to hear the raised voices across the hall, where Jenny knew Mae was taking her stand with Carl. It gave Jenny added courage, knowing she wasn't in this alone, even though Mae was trying to make Carl go and Jenny would far rather William stayed back.

She narrowed her eyes at her husband, feeling squeamish and not a little frightened, but refusing to let him know she was intimidated by his bellowing. "I do recall our marriage vows said fer better or worse, in sickness and health, did they no?"

"All I'm tryin' tae do is care fer ye, the best way I know how, Jenny," William fumed. "What would yer da say, were he tae know I'd dragged ye over snowy mountains and along raging rivers, tae reach a place so back a' beyond there's nae even a decent shop? He wasnae exactly overjoyed at the idea o' me marryin' ye, to begin with." As usual, his brogue became thicker when emotion was involved.

"Me da isna here to say anythin' at all, William, is he?" The knowledge wasn't comforting for her, either. "As yer wife, surely I have a say in what we do and where we go? Ye did say ye wouldna go north at all if I were dead against it, ye do remember sayin' that?"

She could tell she'd scored a point when he muttered an oath and looked away from her.

"Now I'm no tellin' ye not to go, am I, William?" Only because it wouldn't make a whit of difference. "All I'm sayin' is, as yer wife I want to go along wi' ye. Fer better or worse. As is a wife's due."

He didn't answer straightaway, and she knew she'd won when he heaved a heavy sigh, rubbed a hand through his thick hair and sank down on the bed.

"All right, Jenny. All right. I'll make the arrangements first thing in the mornin'."

It made her light-headed, to win an argument with him.

"Robert and I are already booked on the *Utopia,* set to sail in seven days. I'll have tae get an outfit together for ye, a pack animal and all, no one is allowed on the trail wi'out the right supplies. It'll no be easy, mind. Ye're dead certain, now, this is what ya want tae do?"

A shiver of excitement combined with a shudder of foreboding. The last thing in the world she wanted to do was climb on board another boat or clamber over mountains, but she nodded, pretending certainty. "Aye, it is. I want tae be with ye, William." Only because being left behind would be worse, she was certain of that.

"I hope ye don't come tae regret it, Jenny." He gave her a narrow-eyed look. "Nor me, either, come to that."

She hoped not, but even if she hated every moment, she vowed to herself not to complain even once to William.

The days until the ship sailed passed in a frenzy.

Carl, too, had given in to Mae's urging, and with much discussion with the Galloways he set about getting the necessary supplies together.

The two women spent their time frantically trying to decide what sort of clothing would be suitable for the trip. There were lists published in the paper, but Jenny and Mae agreed they sounded excessive.

They needed warm clothing, certainly. The problem was that long skirts and stays made walking difficult even in the city. Climbing over mountains wearing the restrictive garb didn't sound practical or even possible, they agreed.

It was Mae who discovered bloomers.

"They're perfect, Jenny," she enthused, holding up the pair she'd found in a store that sold bicycles. "We can shorten our skirts and wear these underneath, they'll keep us warm and allow much freer movement. I found flannel dresses for sale in the market, too, good practical ones that are made to be worn without stays."

Jenny, who'd always hated corsets anyway, enthusiastically agreed with Mae's choices, and she was delighted when William had no objections.

"It doesna make sense ta struggle through the wilderness laced so ye canna breathe," was his considered opinion. He handed her money and a list. "This is what is recommended for women ta take. Go out and buy it all, Jenny."

Jenny thanked him and gave him a kiss. He may have his faults, but William wasn't tight with his money.

Carl wasn't, either, and she and Mac shopped for what they thought they needed. When the day of their departure arrived and they walked onto the *Utopia*, their daringly shortened skirts showed voluminous bloomers that reached to their ankles. The shocking sight caused both men and women on the dock to gasp and point and frown and whisper.

Taking her cue from Mae, Jenny tipped her chin high and marched up the gangplank, ignoring the scandalized comments of those who weren't heading north. She tried to also ignore the sick roiling in her belly. Just the sight of the huge boat rocking in the swell made her nauseous.

Jenny and Mae parted company once they were on

board, but they promised each other they'd meet as soon as they were settled in. Carl and Mae were short of money. They'd managed to put together a basic list of supplies, but as a result of the expense they were traveling steerage.

William had paid an enormous sum for a cabin for himself and Robert and Jenny, but when they arrived belowdecks, he was furious to learn they'd be sharing their already cramped quarters with another couple.

The Fitzgeralds had also booked a private cabin, and were just as perturbed as William when they found out that the miniscule space had been hastily converted to hold two double bunks as well as the single one where Robert would sleep.

William and Mr. Fitzgerald stormed off together to complain to both the purser and the captain, leaving Jenny and a very blond and pretty Mrs. Fitzgerald alone with Robert. Far from wearing pantaloons, Mrs. Fitzgerald was dressed in peach silk, her generous skirts taking up a great deal of the limited cabin space, and by the miniscule size of her waist, Jenny knew she was wearing tightly laced corsets. She tried not to look at the other woman's chest where a shocking amount of plump white flesh bubbled out of a bodice rather too small to contain it.

"Where ya from, kid?" Kitty Fitzgerald addressed Jenny in a husky drawl, but from the corner of her eye, she was watching Robert as he hoisted his carpetbag onto the bed.

Amused at being called *kid* by a woman who looked not much older than she was, Jenny said, "We're from Edinburgh, Scotland." She introduced herself and Robert, explaining that he was her brother-in-law. "And you, Mrs. Fitzgerald? Where are ye from?"

"Just call me Kitty, dearie. As to where I'm from, I started out in New York, but I've been around and about. Traveled, you know. Worked in Seattle the past six months. I was there when the *Portland* docked. Made up my mind then and there I'd make my fortune in the Klondike."

Maybe she was older than she looked, Jenny speculated. She noticed that Kitty didn't mention Mr. Fitzgerald, and although she was curious, it would have been impolite to ask where he'd been when the *Portland* docked.

"So you got the gold fever, too, did ya?" Kitty had turned to Robert. "What you plannin' on doin' when you make your fortune, hon?"

"Willie and I will buy land," Robert said.

"Farmin', aye?" Kitty made a disgusted sound. "Hard work for no money, that's what farmin' is. I should know, I grew up on one." She lowered her chin and batted her long, dark eyelashes at Robert. "Maybe ya oughta set yer sights a little higher, handsome bloke like you."

Robert smiled and shrugged, then said to Jenny, "I'll just go and see how Willie's makin' out." He picked up the cap he'd just taken off and edged past Jenny and Kitty. When the cabin door closed behind him, Kitty let out a belly laugh.

"He's a bit of a babe in arms, yer brother-in-law, ain't he?"

"Robert's twenty-two."

Kitty laughed again. "I meant, he hasn't been out and about much."

Jenny had no idea what she was talking about. The sound of the boat's heavy engines had increased in volume, and the rocking motion of the floor beneath her feet and the queasy sensation in her belly warned her that the portion of the journey she dreaded most was beginning. Why couldn't the trip to the Klondike be on dry land? She felt sweat bead on her forehead as the musky, oily aroma in the small cabin made her stomach heave.

"If ye'll excuse me, I think I'll go out and get some fresh air." She started for the door. The dizziness was getting worse. Everything began to go dark, and she stumbled against the table and would have fallen if Kitty hadn't caught her.

"Hey there, chickadee. Sit here and put your head down between your knees. That's the ticket." She pushed Jenny's head down and held it there, and slowly the dizziness eased.

"Better now?"

Jenny managed to nod, swallowing hard against the bile rising in her throat. Unable to stop herself, she gagged, and Kitty snatched up a basin and held it as Jenny retched.

When the sickness passed, she felt weak and teary eyed and ashamed.

"Here ya go." Kitty gave her a clean cloth to wipe her mouth with and pressed a cool, wet handkerchief to Jenny's forehead. "Take deep breaths, if you can. You're not laced too tight, are you?"

Jenny managed to shake her head. She didn't have energy enough to even explain that she wasn't wearing a corset.

"Best not to lace tight when you're in the family way, I've been told," Kitty said in a matter-of-fact tone. "What are you, a couple months gone?"

Jenny started to shake her head and then, like a thunderbolt, the truth struck her and took her breath clean away.

Chapter Four

With all the traveling, Jenny had totally forgotten about her courses. They'd come two weeks before her wedding, but since then, nothing. She counted in her head, and she could feel her heart begin to pound. She was now more than three full weeks overdue. And she didn't want a baby, not now. She'd had enough of smelly clouts and whining wee ones, taking care of her five younger stepbrothers. She'd secretly hoped it would be a good long time before she fell.

"You've got that look about you," Kitty was saying, squinting at Jenny. "Some girls get right dewy when they're expectin' and others just turn green. You're the green sort at the moment, if you don't mind me sayin' so."

Jenny barely heard her. She was imagining William's reaction, and it frightened her. He'd want her to have the child in Seattle, which meant that the moment he found out he'd put her ashore at the very first opportunity, send her straight back to Mrs. Graves to wait out the birth of their baby—and probably the gold rush, as well.

William would want her safe, regardless of how she felt about it. He wanted a family, he'd told her so even before they married. He'd never allow her to take on this strenuous journey now that a baby was on the way. He'd been loath to let her come at all, even without knowing she was pregnant.

"You didn't realize, dearie?" Kitty patted her arm. "Takes a bit of gettin' used to, I s'pose. Not that I'd know meself, of course, never having been caught. Had friends who were, though. Fancy an orange? Or some tea—I've got a little spirit stove here somewhere. Albert made sure we brought all the latest things, bless his boring heart."

Jenny did want tea. The bitter bile taste in her mouth threatened to make her stomach heave all over again. The fat orange Kitty handed her peeled easily, and Jenny sucked the sweet juice from each segment, trying to figure out what to do. Pregnancy wasn't a thing you could hide easily, or for long.

Would she be endangering her child by following William to the goldfields? She thought of Mrs. Graves, of being trapped in the boardinghouse alone in Seattle month after month and she shuddered. She'd go mad. She'd never been alone in her entire life. She needed to be with William. She needed family around her.

Kitty soon had a pan of water boiling, and she dropped tea into it, let it sit a moment, and then poured them each a cup, adding tinned milk and generous heaps of sugar.

"Better now?" She sipped her tea daintily, little finger extended when she lifted her cup.

"Thank ye, I am." Jenny knew William could return at

any moment, and she blurted out, "My husband—William. He, umm, he doesna know about—about—" She gestured at her flat belly and felt her face burn. "If he finds out, he'll make me go back to Seattle. And I dinna want that. So if ye could just not—"

"I won't say a word, don't worry about that, duckie," Kitty assured her. "But he's liable to guess if you keep puking, don't you think?"

"I get the seasickness, I had it on the way o'er from Scotland." Now, however, she had to wonder if that was less seasickness and more early pregnancy. She remembered her stepmother being sick from the very beginning with the last of her brothers, little Frankie. A wave of terrible homesickness came over her, a longing for familiarity, even though she knew Nell wouldn't be any comfort. She and her stepmother had never gotten on. But her father—her heart burned with longing for him.

"I can't be more than a month or six weeks along," she said, more to herself than to Kitty.

"Then you'll have some time before you start to show, won't you, to break the news to him," Kitty said in a practical tone. "But I've heard this trip to the goldfields is a right bugger, 'scuse my French. Ye sure you want to give it a go? You look strong, and you're young, might make it just fine. How old are you anyways?"

"Seventeen."

Kitty wrinkled her pert nose and shook her head. "Still a baby yourself, ye lucky thing. Me, I'm twenty-five, not that I tell the gents that. Not to scare you, mind, but I don't guess there's doctors ready and waitin' for you up in the frozen north, should you need one come birthin' time. You need to think this through careful like, duckie. It'd be safer in Seattle. The boat could still put you ashore."

"I'd be alone all those months." Jenny lifted her chin and looked straight into Kitty's dark eyes. "I'm not goin' back, and that's that. I'd be obliged if ye'd not suggest it, aye?"

"Well, that's settled, then. So get that tea down you, and I'll dispose of this, and nobody's the wiser, huh?" Kitty winked and went out the door, basin extended in front of her.

Jenny gulped the hot tea, but inside she was icy cold and trembling. She vividly remembered her stepmother's agonizing screams when the babies came. Mrs. Macdougall, the midwife, had been there to help, and for Frankie, her father had had to bring the doctor because the birthing had stopped partway and not started again.

Frankie was something called breech; Jenny recalled the doctor explaining it to her father. He'd had to be turned while still inside Nell, and her stepmother had come close to death. Jenny had had to take over the care of the household and the new baby for a full six weeks afterward, because Nell could barely move.

What would she do, should her baby be backward like wee Frankie? Her trembling fingers clenched around the mug, and she had trouble getting her breath. It was no good thinking about it. Better to concentrate on the trip ahead of her, and try to keep William from knowing until they'd arrived in the Klondike. Or at least until it was too late to send her back.

After that, she promised herself, there'd be plenty of time for worrying. But William would be furious with her when he found out she'd deceived him. She shivered at the thought. And she didn't want to endanger her wee bairn, she really didn't. But Nell had had four babes without the need of a doctor, hadn't she? Birthing was a natural process; women did it all the time without the aid of doctors.

Jenny heaved a sigh. As a young girl, she'd dreamed about having a husband and, someday in the far future, babes of her own. It was the only way she could see of escaping from under her stepmother's nagging tongue and constant criticism. But she hadn't had time to get used to having a husband, never mind a baby. Being married seemed to involve one thing after the next, and not many were pleasant.

The boat trip turned out better than she'd expected, however, even though—or perhaps because—the captain and the purser both insisted there was nothing they could do about the crowded accommodations. The first night was difficult and embarrassing, with the women banishing the men from the cabin until they were in their nightclothes and safely tucked into the hard bunks. But everyone was thoughtful and very considerate, and after the first awkwardness passed, Jenny relaxed.

The next morning, Kitty imperiously ordered Albert to bring both her and Jenny tea and biscuits while they were still in bed, and that eased the nausea Jenny felt. When the men left the two women alone in the cabin to make their morning toilet, Jenny commented on how obliging Kitty's husband was.

"Oh, Albert's not my husband," Kitty said with a disparaging laugh. "Haven't got one of those and don't want one, either. Cramps a girl's style, don't ya think?"

Jenny was speechless, and her face must have revealed her shock, because Kitty laughed at her.

"It's easier to be Missus Fitzgerald instead of Kitty Boynton. I'm using his name for the time being."

"He's—he's very taken with you, though, is Mr. Fitzgerald," Jenny stammered. "And—and he seems a sweet
and biddable man, is he no?"

"Oh, boring Albert will do whatever I want him to,"
Kitty said, squinting into a small mirror as she used one
forefinger and a pot of rouge to put roses on her cheeks.
"He's a dentist, and he's got lotsa moola." She laughed at
Jenny's blank look. "Money, honey. The green stuff that
makes life worth livin'."

Jenny was watching the makeup process with fascina-
tion; she'd never known anyone who used makeup. "And
are ye in love with him?"

Kitty wrinkled her nose. "It's handy that Albert does
whatever I tell him, but that ain't what I want in a man. I fall
hard for the handsome dark ones, the dangerous ones. That
one of yours, now, he'd be more my choice were he available."

Jenny must have looked taken aback, because Kitty
gave her deep, raucous laugh and shook her head. "Not to
worry, any fool kin see he's mad for you, dearie. And I'm
not a husband snatcher anyways. It's not worth my while
when there's so many single ones runnin' around loose."
She tipped her head to the side and regarded her handiwork. "But your brother-in-law, now, he's single. He could
put his shoes under my bed any old night."

Jenny was shocked again, this time at the rawness of
Kitty's speech, but also by the fact that maybe she had a
mistaken impression of Robert.

"Robert's no the dangerous sort," she protested. "He's
gentle as a lamb, and kind as they come." As soon as she'd
said it, she realized that she couldn't honestly say the same
thing about William. Her husband had a dark side to him,
right enough.

"Oh, I think there's more under those lovely black curls than you imagine," Kitty claimed, putting the final touches to her blond hair. "But don't fret over me causin' yer men trouble, dearie. Old Albert's got money, and at the moment, that's what's needed, right? And will be needed even more if this old tub actually makes it to Skagway with the load it's packin'."

The boat *was* overloaded, which was frightening, and Jenny soon learned how very lucky she was that William had available money, as Albert did. Just as she'd discovered on the journey from Scotland, the plight of steerage passengers was horrifying.

Within days of the arrival in Seattle of the gold-laden *Portland*, thousands of people desperately tried to book passage to the Klondike. William had been smart enough to book immediately, and the *Utopia* was one of the better vessels making the northern trip.

But the *Utopia*'s owners, like all the others who owned steamships, had been quick to capitalize on the rush to reach the Klondike. They'd crammed in beds wherever they could, and when Jenny saw where Mae and Carl were billeted, she felt fortunate indeed—and terribly upset for her friend.

"Used to be the cattle pens, and it still smells like it," Mae informed her, showing Jenny the primitive compartments belowdecks with their rows of hastily constructed rough bunks reaching from floor to ceiling, not even separated by so much as a curtain. "There's six other women and a hundred men down here, snoring and farting all the living night long. And there's so many seasick the ones in the top bunks are puking on those beneath them," Mae reported with a shudder. "Carl and I take our blankets and sleep on the deck. I'd rather take my chances with freezing to death than die down here from the smell. You can hear the poor livestock, too, bellowing all night long. They're right next door in the hold."

Jenny had a handkerchief pressed over her mouth, trying not to gag at the stench. "It's disgustin'," she said when they were back on deck and she could breathe again. "I'm that sorry, Mae. If our cabin weren't filled to overflowing, I'd ask ye to join us. But there's nary an inch to fit another body inside."

"It's only for a couple more nights," Mae said philosophically. "Then we'll have wide-open spaces and more fresh air than we bargained for, I'll be bound. I can't wait to get out of this hellhole and start on the trail, can you?"

"Aye, ye're right." But now that Jenny knew she was pregnant, she was frightened and worried about the hardships ahead. She desperately wanted to tell Mae about the baby, but it felt like a terrible betrayal of William to confide in Mae without telling him. It was bad enough that Kitty knew.

"She seems a fancy sort to be heading north," Mae had commented after Jenny had introduced the two women. "I suppose she's a dance hall girl."

"Do ye think so?" Jenny also wondered about her cabinmate. She hadn't told Mae that Kitty and Albert weren't married. It bothered her to have so many secrets from her friend.

"Oh, I know she is," Mae said. "One of the other women told me so. She says dance hall girls can make a fortune in the Klondike. There's no women there except Indians."

There were only a handful of other women on the ship, and after the first day Jenny had deduced that more than a few of them were prostitutes, or soiled doves, which is what William told her such women were politely labeled.

Jenny glanced around and then whispered, "D'ye think a dance hall girl is the same as a prostitute?"

"Not much to tell the difference, I shouldn't wonder," Mae said. "They both take money for entertaining men, and who knows how far they go."

"Well, ye couldna find a kinder person," Jenny declared in defense of Kitty.

"Maybe so." Mae's voice was suddenly acerbic. "But if that poor man of hers was to fall overboard, there'd be a lineup waiting to claim her, and it wouldn't take her ten minutes to hook up with someone else." Mae sniffed. "She's no good, that one."

Mae's words made Jenny uncomfortable. She wanted Mae and Kitty to get along. They were her only two friends, and she had a strong suspicion she was going to need both of them before this trip was done.

Chapter Five

Three days later at eleven in the morning, sailing through thick fog that made it impossible to see two feet beyond the ship's railing, the *Utopia* arrived at the head of the Lynn Canal. The travelers who were taking the White Pass trail disembarked here at Skagway, while the ones who'd chosen the route over the Chilkoot Pass would leave the ship a few miles northeast of Skagway in Dyea.

William and the other men had discussed the two routes endlessly, trying to decide which was the best choice. The White Pass was ten miles longer but not as steep, and it was said that horses could be used to make the trip.

The Chilkoot, an ancient Indian trading route, was too steep for pack animals, which is what decided William and Carl. Albert had chosen the White Pass for exactly the same reason. William and Carl had bought several horses each to use on the White Pass trail, and Jenny knew that Albert had four. The animals were down in the hold of the ship.

Once again Jenny found herself being helped down an unsteady rope ladder and loaded into a crowded, flimsy boat. Skagway had no wharves where the steamer could land. It was raining, and if the arrival at New York's Ellis Island had been chaotic, this scene on Skagway's beach was utter bedlam.

Piles of gear, horses, dogs and black muck choked the tent town's main street. Everything permanent seemed under construction, and the noise of animals, hammers and men hollering was deafening.

Surging crowds filled the town's muddy streets, and an aura of excitement permeated the atmosphere. Stories on board had depicted Skagway as a wild and dangerous place, overrun with criminals who conned stampeders out of their money, and from her first glimpse of the sorry place, Jenny figured the rumors were right. She was relieved to have her tall, strong husband and her brother-in-law on either side of her as she made her way up the muddy street.

Behind them came Carl, with Mae on his arm, and bringing up the rear was Albert, with Kitty tucked protectively against his side. The four men had become friends on the boat and decided to travel together, which made Jenny happy. She figured there was strength in numbers, although Mae said straight-out she wasn't fond of going anywhere with the likes of Kitty. The two women struck sparks off each other.

Jenny looked around and came to the conclusion that Skagway was built mostly of tents. Every second one advertised something for sale on a board hung from the tent pole, and none of them looked the least bit inviting.

After a brief discussion, the men deposited the women in front of a rough wooden building whose sign said Skagway Hotel, Meals $3.

"We have to go back and claim our horses and our gear or they'll all disappear," Albert explained when Kitty complained about being abandoned in such a rough and rowdy place. "We also need to hire a pack wagon," he went on. "You ladies go inside and rest and have something to eat, we'll be back for you as soon as we can."

Jenny figured that wouldn't be very soon. Even though they'd brought horses with them, the men had to secure the use of more pack animals, and by the hundreds of frantic gold seekers milling around the streets, she guessed that was likely to be a challenge.

"Let's go inside and see if we can get a decent cuppa tea," Kitty said, leading the way through the rough wooden door and into a vast open room that looked far more like a barroom than the lobby of a hotel.

The arrival of the three women caused silence to fall upon the thirty or so men seated at tables and milling around the bar. With Kitty in the lead, Jenny and Mae made their way to the bar. The smells of tobacco and sweat and beer made Jenny gag. She swallowed hard and did her best to breathe through her mouth.

"We would like tea, lots of it, with fresh milk and sugar," Kitty ordered.

"We don't have fresh milk, ma'am," the bearded bartender said. "We only got tinned. But there's grub, beans and some rice if you want, three bucks a plate."

"No fresh milk? That's ridiculous. I'm sure I saw a cow or two outside, surely someone could milk them?" Kitty told him in her no-nonsense fashion.

A couple of men sniggered, and the barman was unimpressed. "Tinned or nothin', take yer choice."

"Some hotel," Kitty huffed. "All right, bring us a big pot of tea with your disgusting tinned milk, and we'll need sugar, and some biscuits with it, and extra hot water, as well."

She led the other two to a table that was hastily vacated to make room for them. Kitty sat down, fluffed her capacious skirts like some colorful, irate parrot, ignoring the rapt attention aimed their way by every man in the crowded room. Jenny and Mae were wearing their practical cropped-off skirts with their bloomers, but Kitty was in full-dress regalia, wide silk skirts, a fashionable small hat perched on her head and a fringed shawl which did nothing to conceal the low-cut bodice of her dress. She even had shiny teardrops in her ears, and a dainty gold locket around her throat.

It took nearly half an hour before a huge tin teapot and three enameled mugs were deposited on their table by an emaciated youth with pimples sprouting over every inch of his face.

"We had to boil the water, there's not much call for tea," he explained. He set down a tin of milk and a bowl of sugar and three rock-hard biscuits that looked and tasted like sawdust.

"Ugh. If this is any example, this godforsaken place could do with a proper bakery," Mae said, swallowing her single bite with difficulty.

Queasy as she was, Jenny left her biscuit untouched. Her stomach was unsettled, and as was happening regularly, she found herself feeling increasingly dizzy and disoriented.

Kitty snorted. "Needs a hotel with decent rooms, you ask me. I don't know if you noticed, but there's no upstairs here. It's a bar, plain and simple, calling itself a hotel. I wonder if there's a suitable room to be had anywhere in this place?"

Mae said, "Depends what you mean by suitable, I'd imagine. At least they know how to make a decent cup of tea. Even if they don't know how to milk a cow."

"I think the men are plannin' to get on the trail today, so it won't matter that there's no rooms," Jenny said, and felt faint at the thought of the ordeal ahead. She felt tired all the time, and could hardly sit for a few minutes without falling asleep. How could she possibly manage to walk forty-two miles over what looked like a towering mountain?

"You'll need to put on sturdier duds before we set out, won't you?" Mae said to Kitty, eyeing the other woman's green silk dress with its expansive petticoats and her dainty mud-stained shoes. "Carl says that even though the White Pass trail isn't as steep as the Chilkoot, it's still a hard climb and a long walk. You won't get very far in that regalia."

Kitty looked down her nose at Mae. "Oh, I ain't gonna walk. Albert promised me I could ride one of the horses, that's why he brought four."

"Ride, huh? Well, lucky you." Mae lifted her eyebrows and looked over at Jenny. "More fool us, aye? Never crossed my mind to tell Carl I was so delicate I needed a horse to ride. Or you either, Jenny, aye?"

Jenny knew Mae was alluding to the fact that it had been tough enough to convince their husbands to bring them, much less insist they had a horse to carry them. The horses they'd brought were strictly for transporting their heaps of supplies.

"Well, live and learn," Kitty sniped. "The trick with men," she said in a knowing tone, "is to tell them flat out in the beginning what you expect and how you want to be treated. If ye don't, then you deserve what you get, which'll be nothin'. They ain't much good without training, men."

"My, my." Mae rolled her eyes at Jenny. "*Ain't* it strange I never thought of that myself? But then, I probably don't have the wide experience with men that you do, Kitty."

The gibe wasn't lost on Kitty. "No charge for the advice, dearie," she sneered. "Just remember it when I'm riding and you're puffing your way up that mountain."

Jenny had had more than enough of the sparring. She waved at the serving boy and asked him to bring her a plate of beans and rice. Sick as she felt, at least a full stomach would give her something to get rid of when the time came. And maybe with a full stomach she could more easily abide two friends who disliked one another this intensely.

Mae and Kitty decided they, too, might as well eat, and the next hour passed in relative peace as all three women agreed on the poor quality of the food.

When the men finally came to collect them, Jenny caught the smug look on Mae's face when it became clear that pack animals were few and far between, and none of the horses they'd brought could be spared for riding.

"The information I received in Seattle about the trail out of Skagway was completely untrue," Albert said with a worried glance at Kitty, who looked mad enough to hit him. "I was told it was an all-wagon trail, that mules or pack wagons could carry us and our supplies all the way to Lake Bennett. But there are precious few animals for purchase or for hire, and I was laughed at when I inquired about wagons. It seems the trail isn't wide enough for a wagon."

William said, "We've managed to hire an Indian to help pack, he has four trained dogs and we've bought three mules. We're that lucky we have the horses. We'll need every last animal if we're to get our supplies over the pass."

Albert nodded, a worried frown creasing his broad forehead. "We did hire a wagon to take us the first few miles, but the trail narrows after that, and we have to ford a river. I'm sorry, but when we reach that point you'll have to walk the rest of the way, my kitten."

"Walk? *Walk? You promised* me I could ride all the way." The venomous look Kitty shot him reminded Jenny more of an enraged tiger than a kitten. Kitty grumpily exchanged her shoes for the pair of sturdy lace-up boots Albert had somehow procured for her, but that was her single concession to a more suitable wardrobe, and the way she flounced around and shot daggers at poor Albert embarrassed Jenny. After all, it wasn't his fault things weren't working out as he'd planned. Kitty was acting like a spoiled bairn.

It was late afternoon by the time the animals were harnessed, the wagon loaded and the packs arranged. A vote had been taken to decide whether or not the party should stay in Skagway until morning. The fact that the only available lodgings were either the filthy floor in the so-called hotel or a pallet in one of the large, equally dirty tents which they'd have to share with as many other gold seekers as could be crammed in decided them.

Sleeping in their own clean new tents seemed much more preferable. They set off with the wagon and driver, determined to travel until it was almost dark before they made camp.

Each of the animals was laden down with a huge pack, as was the silent Tlingit Indian guide. His native name was unpronounceable, so everyone called him George, and he simply nodded without really looking at anyone when William introduced the women. He stood with his arms crossed on his chest, back slightly bent under the incredibly heavy pack he wore.

The wagon was piled to overflowing, and each of the animals was also laden with heavy packs. Jenny wondered how it was possible to load the poor animals with any more provisions—but when the time came the things on the wagon would have to go somewhere.

She understood what William meant when he said, "We're hopin' to make the trail in only one go, without leaving things behind and comin' back fer them the way most others are doin', but that means the women may have to carry packs, too. Only what ye're capable of, mind. That way, we can maybe make it over the Pass and on to the Klondike before winter sets in."

"Winter?" Jenny was sure he was mistaken. "William, it's no but July, and the trail's but forty-two miles. Did ye no tell me that the boat trip on the far end would take another few weeks? Surely we can manage it before winter? You said it should take us but a month at the very most."

William shook his head, his face grim, and it was Robert who answered her.

"We talked wi' a dozen men who tried to make it to Dawson and turned back after three months. They say there's parts o' the White Pass trail so narrow a man's shoulders can barely make it through the rock, and so steep a heavy load on yer back could unbalance ye."

Jenny swallowed hard. How could she manage that, with a child growing steadily larger in her belly?

Robert was saying, "At the end o' this climb is five hundred miles more to go on water, some of it rapids which need to be forded. Freeze up is late September. We'll hae to make good time to reach Dawson afore the winter sets in."

Jenny felt fear, cold and bone deep, wash over her. What had she gotten herself into?

"We're fortunate to be traveling in the summer," Albert said, shooting uneasy glances at Kitty, obviously eager to put as good a face on it as possible for her sake. "Although when we reach the higher altitudes on the trail, we may well encounter snow. But George tells us he has relatives near Lake Bennett willing to take us by canoe and barge up the waterways, which is fortunate. But we still have to reach the lakes with plenty of time left for the remainder of the trip."

Kitty and Mae digested this upsetting information in silence. They climbed up and found a seat on the wagon amongst the piles of supplies.

Kitty looked down at Jenny. "Comin' up, duckie? Or have ye changed yer mind?"

Jenny knew Kitty was asking her more than just a simple question. This was the moment, the final moment, when she needed to make the decision as to whether she should chance the rest of the trip, or confess to William about the baby, endure his displeasure and take the boat back to Seattle.

She hesitated, and then grasped the side of the wagon. She'd come this far; she wasn't turning back now.

"Easy does it, lassie." William put his hands around her narrow waist and swung her up.

"It'll be our last chance to relax," Mae said, scrunching over so Jenny could sit down beside her. "I, for one, intend to take full advantage."

But after the first twenty yards, Jenny knew that walking was going to be far preferable to riding along this deeply rutted trail. The wagon dropped into one hole after the other and bounced out again, and she felt as if all her teeth were coming loose. She was afraid for the poor wee baby in her belly, so after a scant half mile, she got off and walked. Mae joined her, but Kitty stubbornly stayed in the wagon, clinging to the sides and cursing under her breath. She had an amazing vocabulary when it came to swearing.

Walking was pleasant despite the mud, Jenny decided, due in large part to the lack of corsets and the freedom of a short skirt and pantaloons. The air was fresh and clean, and the path wide, albeit rocky and rough. It wound gently upward, with giant trees on either side. Soon she was too warm for her shawl and tossed it on the wagon, wearing only her checked blouse. She and Mae discussed the landscape, eyeing the forbidding view of the mountain they'd have to climb and making halfhearted jokes about it.

Soon William and Carl joined them, and the two couples quickly drew ahead of the wagon, the plodding horses and the pack mules. George was ahead, tending the pack animals and the dogs. Voices were raised as dog harnesses tangled or the horses and mules needed urging through yet another huge hole. Carl and Mae speeded up, and soon they were a good hundred yards away from William and Jenny.

The quiet was restful, and Jenny enjoyed this rare opportunity to be alone with William. He held her hand in his, palm to palm, and her heart swelled with affection when he smiled down at her and gave her fingers a squeeze, stroking the back of her hand with his thumb.

"I'm that glad ye're here wi' me, Jenny. Ye were right to insist on comin' along."

She swallowed hard and tried not to think of how wrong she might have been, and how she was deceiving him about the baby.

He said, "I see now that it woulda been a verra long time

before I made it back to Seattle ta collect ye. Leavin' ye there would no hae been a wise thing. As it is, we're in this together, the way it should be wi' a man and his wife. And ye're a hardy wee soul, thank the lord, and not a complainer like yon Kitty in her frippery. The trip is no goin' to be an easy one, or pleasant, either, from what we learned in Skagway. But there's the two o' us, and together we'll manage fine."

"I'm that glad to be here, William. I'll do me very best to keep up, I promise ye that." She prayed silently that nothing would happen to interfere with that vow.

"I'd hae missed ye sore, lassie." He released her hand and put his strong arm around her shoulders, pulling her close for a moment. "And I'll be that glad to be alone in our own wee tent the night," he added in a husky whisper. "I've missed lyin' wi' ye, Jenny. I need ye warm and soft and willin' beneath me, lass. I miss the wee noises ye make, and the heat and wet of ye."

A surge of urgent desire sent warmth flooding through her lower belly. She ducked her head as the hot color rose in her cheeks, and as the warmth of the sunshine slowly faded and evening began to fall, she convinced herself that the trip would be an exciting adventure. William would forgive her deception, and the baby wouldn't come to any harm as a result of this journey.

In another hour, they reached the river they'd have to ford come morning and found a spot among the spruce trees beside the trail to make camp. The river was nearby and the trees formed a natural canopy overhead. The driver of the freight wagon they'd hired unhitched the pack animals while the men unloaded their supplies. Soon the horses and mules were tethered nearby, munching grass.

The freight wagons were soon bouncing back down the trail, leaving the gold seekers to set up their tents and make camp.

Jenny was weary from walking. She eased herself down on a handy flat rock while Robert and William set up the two small tents they'd brought. Carl had the same type, and set it up a short distance away. Albert's was much more elaborate, a large affair with netting and a porch entrance, and he struggled with it until the other men finished theirs and helped him. He wasn't exactly a handy sort, Jenny mused.

George took the dogs and set up his own shelter some distance away.

Kitty was in a temper, refusing to speak to anyone. She didn't join the other two women when they wearily unearthed frying pans, bacon and cans of beans for a hasty supper. But Albert offered them the use of the Yukon stove he'd brought, and soon the air was resonant with the smell of bacon frying. They'd bought loaves of freshly baked sourdough bread from a vendor in Skagway. Slathered with tinned butter, it made the simple meal into a feast.

Robert made tea over a campfire he and George had built and brought a mugful to each of the women. Jenny noticed that Kitty smiled at him, the first time she'd smiled since she learned she'd have to walk.

"Why, thank you, Robbie," she said in a flirtatious voice. "You're going to make some woman a fine husband."

Half-famished, Jenny bolted her dinner. The simple food tasted like the best meal she'd ever eaten. Afterward, she and Mae heated water in a pot and washed up the dishes, yawning until their eyes watered. Again, Kitty didn't participate, choosing instead to pour a good portion of the hot water into a pan and disappear into her capacious tent, presumably to wash herself free of the trail dust.

"I hope Her Majesty enjoys her bath," Mae muttered, scrubbing at a particularly stubborn stain on the frying pan. "I've half a mind to spill this dishwater into her boots, serve her right for being so lazy."

It was past eleven by the time the dishes were clean and the food packed away, with only enough left out for a hasty morning meal. It was still twilight, the long Northern summer day only now beginning to darken.

Jenny and Mae nervously ventured a short distance from camp to attend to their bathroom needs, and then washed hands and faces in their small basins.

Robert had found fallen tree limbs to feed the fire, and Jenny went to sit next to William in the flickering light from the flames. The men were discussing the trail ahead, and in a short time their deep voices lulled her to sleep. She leaned heavily against William, and he cradled her against his shoulder.

She woke only briefly when he half carried her to their tent, where she struggled out of her clothing and into her flannel gown. She was asleep again within minutes of crawling into the nest of heavy blankets William had arranged on the spruce boughs George had cut for bedding.

She was only dimly aware of William crawling in beside her a short time later. He wrapped his arms around her, kissing her neck, sliding his hands under the nightgown and cupping her breasts, but she was far too tired to do more than mumble.

She woke sometime before dawn, queasy and desperate with the need to piddle, nervous about venturing into the woods alone. She touched William's face with her hand, and he was instantly awake.

"Will ye come wi' me, please? I'm that scared o' the bears and the big cats I heard you men talkin' about."

He laughed softly and helped her locate her shawl. The air was frigid, and she shivered as she stuffed her feet into her icy boots.

Standing up, she caught her breath at the brilliance of the stars overhead. It was already growing light, and the campground looked bathed in silver, glowing as if each tent and tree was alive and giving off starlight.

William took her hand and led the way past the embers of the dying campfire, past the Fitzgeralds' large tent, silent and dark, Mac and Carl's much smaller one, and the small pup tent where vigorous snores signaled that Robert was sound asleep.

The dogs growled, but a low word from William silenced them.

Jenny squatted over a convenient log, and when she was done William led the way back to the tent. The fresh air had settled her stomach a bit, and she took a long drink of water from the stone bottle hanging on the tent peg.

Inside, she scuttled under the blankets, shivering until William folded her against him, her back against his warm belly and legs. His hands were cold against her bare skin, and when she flinched he tucked them into his armpits, warming them before he touched her again. Through her gown she felt him grow hard against her buttocks, and when she was warm she turned in his arms and kissed him.

He tasted of night air and sleep. Her breasts were swollen and ultrasensitive, and when he stroked his thumbs across her nipples bolts of sensation shot downward to her groin. She felt herself grow wet and she gasped and moved against him.

"Ahh, wee Jenny," he breathed, using his hand to open her legs, using his fingers to stroke and inflame her inside and out. "I'm that glad you woke up," he whispered in her ear, and then sucked on her earlobe.

As desire grew, the faint sickness in her belly faded, and when he propped himself over her, her legs came up to lock him into position. Her wetness made it easy for him to slide inside, and she gasped again at the feeling of urgency that grew rapidly as he began to rock against her.

She couldn't suppress the sound that rose in her throat, and as her climax reached its crescendo, she used a corner of her gown, now up around her neck, to muffle her cries.

He followed her only a moment later, clenching his teeth and shaking his head from side to side, silent and ferocious in the throes of ecstasy.

He collapsed beside her, holding her close. Their breathing was slowly returning to normal when Jenny heard someone stumble past the tent, and then Kitty's furious whisper and Albert's soft, placating reply.

Jenny pressed her mouth to William's ear. "D'ye think they heard us?"

"I wouldna worry about it if they did," he said with a chuckle. "It'll likely be us this night and the rest of them the next. If yon spitfire stops her gripin', that is."

But the following morning, judging by Kitty's stony face and Albert's downtrodden expression, Jenny thought it unlikely there'd be any joyful sounds in the nighttime from their tent. And she thought again of the exquisite pleasure she'd known in the darkness, here in the little tent in the Northern wilderness, and felt sorry for the other woman.

She looked at Kitty, at her petulant mouth, her narrowed eyes, and Jenny knew that she and William were blessed, as were Mae and Carl. They had love between them, a kind of love that Kitty and Albert were lacking, for all their money and fancy clothing.

Chapter Six

But after that first night, Jenny doubted that she would ever again have energy for lovemaking. It took every ounce of strength and stamina to get through the first day's climb, and she could barely move the following morning. She told herself each night that the climb would get easier, but instead it got worse with every new day.

It had been some strange quirk of timing that their group was alone that first night. The following morning, while they were still at breakfast, a steady stream of gold seekers caught up and passed them, and from then on, Jenny couldn't begin to count the number of people they encountered, men with only a very few women amongst them.

Most were heading to the Klondike, but there was also a disturbing, sizable number heading back to Skagway. Some were professional packers like George, heading back to bring another crew up and over, but most were beaten and broken stampeders, exhausted and penniless from their unsuccessful attempt to traverse the White Pass trail.

The four men Jenny saw coming toward them down the path one morning sent a shiver of fear down her spine and a sense of horror to her heart. Thin and dirty, carrying packs that bent them double, they resembled the walking dead, slowly putting one foot after the other in front of them as if it took every ounce of their energy just to keep going. Jenny pressed herself flat against the rock wall, and they passed with only a nod, hardly glancing at William and his party.

Behind her, Robert tried to stop one of the men, asking if they needed food or water, but the fellow only shook his head and kept going down the trail. It soon became abundantly clear to Jenny and her companions exactly how difficult the trip ahead would prove to be.

On the third morning, they'd been walking sharply upward for several hours. The path had quickly become a sea of sharp, jagged rocks, too narrow for two people to walk side by side. The horses stumbled and the mules constantly became entangled in their lines, making it necessary to stop and untangle them. It felt to Jenny that they were progressing at a snail's pace, and they'd just rounded a corner when the breeze became so foul her eyes watered and she gagged.

"Something's died," Robert guessed from directly behind her. William was somewhere ahead, leading the horses over the rough ground. He and Robert were taking turns tending the animals and, she guessed, keeping an eye on her.

"Four dead horses," Carl called from up ahead. "Breathe through your mouth."

But it didn't work. There was nowhere to go to avoid the stench, and as she drew closer Jenny felt as if her entire body was absorbing the awful smell. It grew stronger with every step she took, and then she couldn't hold back the vomit rising in her throat. She staggered to the side of the narrow gorge and began to heave. Once she started she couldn't seem to stop. Soon there was nothing left in her stomach, but still the convulsions continued, and she grew dizzy and fell to her knees.

When the dizziness passed, she was dimly aware of Robert holding her, gently wiping her mouth with his kerchief, his forehead creased in lines of worry.

"Try a sip o' water, Jenny." He held the stone bottle for her, and she managed to get a mouthful down, but the horrible smell seemed to permeate the water, and she gagged again. Shaking and weak, she finally made it to her feet, aware that she was holding up who knew how many people who were behind them on the narrow trail, other gold seekers unable to do anything but wait until she could move again.

She started to walk, and tried not to look when the dead animals came in sight, but they drew her eyes against her will. She found herself staring at empty eye sockets, bellies ripped open by carrion, and the gorge rose again in her throat, but there was nothing in her stomach left to expel.

After that, she walked on in a daze, aware only that she had to keep putting one foot after the other. The narrow trail was terrifying, leading steadily up the side of a mountain, a stone bank on one side with a steep drop-off on the other. Robert stayed close behind her, encouraging her with soft phrases, and whenever there was room, he moved up beside her and helped her along. He'd shouldered her pack as well as his own when the incline became too steep for her to manage.

As the afternoon wore slowly down and evening came, William took Robert's place. The path still led upward. They had to keep going because there was nowhere at all wide enough or flat enough to set up camp. It was nearly midnight by the time they finally conquered Devil's Hill and once again set up the tents. Trembling with weariness, the women unearthed the sheet-iron stove.

The men tended the animals as Mae and Jenny cooked supper, beans again, and a huge, fat freshly caught salmon Albert had bought from an Indian that morning. Jenny hadn't recovered from the nausea she'd suffered. She was trembling with fatigue, and she could only pick at her food, too exhausted and ill to eat.

After supper, the weary women headed for a clump of pines. Kitty came along this time. The blond woman was pale and bedraggled, her silk dress muddied to the knees, her hair tumbled down her back.

The moment they were out of earshot of the men, Mae turned on Kitty, hands on her hips, voice fierce.

"Listen here, my fine lady, either you start doing your share with the cooking and cleaning or you don't eat," she said. "Jenny and I aren't about to do all the work while you sit on your fat arse and watch us."

Kitty's face grew scarlet. "I don't happen to know how to cook," she said in a haughty tone. "I never had to learn."

"Well, it's time you got started, then, isn't it?" But it was plain Mae didn't have energy for quarreling any more than Kitty did. She sighed and started walking again. "If you can't cook, you can surely wash up afterward," she said in a quieter tone. "And no more taking hot wash water away to have a private bath, either. If there's hot water left over, we share it."

Kitty didn't answer. They found a suitable spot and squatted. When they were done, Mae led the way back toward the camp. Kitty took hold of Jenny's arm and held her back, waiting until Mae was some distance ahead before she spoke.

"I wonder," Kitty said haltingly, "would you have a spare pair of those knicker things? One more day trying to climb this damn mountain in a corset and a long dress, and I'll jump off the bloody cliff."

"There's a pair in my knapsack, you're welcome to them," Jenny offered. "I've got a pair of shears, if you've any dresses not so fancy, we could lop 'em off about your knees, make walking simpler."

"Thanks." Kitty stumbled over a tree root and fell to one knee, and Mae came back to see what was holding them up.

"Are you hurt?" Mae held out a hand to help Kitty up.

Kitty ignored it, scrambling to her feet by herself. "Bloody hell," she cursed. "I never imagined this gold thing would be this hard. To top it off I started my courses this morning, and my belly's been gripin' all day." She turned to Jenny. "At least you don't have that to contend with, chickie. How you holding up otherwise? Climbin' a mountain ain't what the doctor ordered for a woman in your condition, huh? I heard you pukin'. Those dead horses had me gaggin' and I'm not even pregnant."

"Pregnant?" Mae had started walking again, but she stopped so suddenly Jenny bumped into her. "You mean— Jenny, you're not *expecting?"* Her voice grew shrill. "Holy mother of God, why didn't you tell me?"

"Shush." Kitty held a finger to her lips and frowned at

Mae. "No need to let the world know, dearie. Her man's none the wiser yet, either, so keep mum about it." She turned to Jenny. "Sorry, I guess I should keep my big trap shut. I just figgered, you two being friends and all—"

But there was a sly tone to her voice.

Mae was looking away, and Jenny could see her friend was hurt.

"I only realized on the way up here," Jenny stammered. "Kitty guessed when I was sick on the boat. And I knew if I told William, he'd send me back tae Seattle. Ye know he wasna keen on me comin' tae start wi'. Ye mind how we both had tae struggle tae get them to bring us at all, Mae."

She added, her voice desperate, "So please, don't say anythin' tae Carl, in case he lets it slip to William. If William finds out he'll send me right back down that terror o' a trail. I've come this far the now, and I dinna want tae go back." She was on the verge of tears. "I won't go back."

"But it's terribly dangerous for you, Jenny," Mae hissed. "What if something happens? There's no doctor, childbirth can be—" She stopped short when Kitty shushed her.

"She's young and strong. She'll be fine," Kitty declared. "And perchance the worst of this cursed trail is behind us now. It'll get easier, I'll be bound."

But Jenny noted that there was no conviction in her tone. And the quelling look Kitty gave Mae had something sly and smug about it. She was pleased to have driven a wedge between Jenny and her friend.

For the rest of the evening, there was a strain. Jenny knew Mae felt betrayed and left out. Jenny had no idea what to do to mend the rift.

* * *

Kitty had no way of knowing how far off the mark her prediction about the trail was. Seven days later, slipping in mud up to her ankles as she and the others began the day's climb, Jenny thought that if any of them had guessed in Skagway what the ordeal ahead was going to be like, they'd have all turned and headed back that first day. Certainly she would have.

Far from getting easier, the trail had grown even worse, littered with sharp, jagged rocks, steadily climbing upward, so narrow in many places that a horse's shoulders—or William's, for that matter—barely made it through the openings in the solid rock wall. It became so steep in places Jenny felt certain her lungs would burst with the effort.

And even though they'd hoped to avoid it, the men each had to make several trips up and back again in order to get all the provisions to the campsite each night. The horses and mules simply couldn't manage, and the supplies had to be left behind. Sitting slumped by the campfire in the evening, drained and totally exhausted, Jenny marveled at the men's strength and determination, relieved beyond measure that she had only to climb the cursed trail once.

It had rained for several days and the track, bad enough when it was dusty, quickly became a quagmire. They'd camped the previous evening in the first possible spot they could find, and then spent an uncomfortable night in sodden bedrolls. Fortunately, the morning was sunny and warm, and they rose with the dawn and set out, rolling up wet packs and eating a cold breakfast of stew left over from the night before.

Jenny had somehow grown accustomed to the weary aching in her body, the pain of her blistered feet, even the roiling sickness that made it torture for her to smell bacon cooking or eat the porridge they made most mornings. Maybe a person could get used to anything if they had to, she thought. She often had the sensation that she wasn't really climbing the trail, but hovering somewhere high above it. It was peculiar, but also restful.

William noticed she wasn't eating, but accepted Jenny's explanation that it was exhaustion taking away her appetite and making her ill. He was bone weary, too tired himself to pay much attention to her. At night he fell asleep the instant he lay down.

Both Mae and Kitty assured him that they, too, were having a hard time eating, tired as they were, and Jenny was touched, grateful for the women's loyal, clumsy efforts at keeping her condition a secret, but shame and anxiety overcame her all over again for lying to her husband. And she also thought that Kitty had been overzealous, going on too long about her own loss of appetite—even as she spooned out a generous second helping.

Jenny hated to be suspicious, but ever since Kitty had managed to let Mae know about the baby, Jenny had distrusted her. Mae had been a little aloof since that evening, and Jenny felt very alone, achingly lonely. She and William didn't talk much. During each day's climb, no one talked. They simply put one foot after the next like the dumb animals accompanying them, hoping to make it through the day's challenges.

The worst thing by far was the terrible plight of the horses and pack animals of the other parties they encountered. Many of the stampeders had no knowledge of horses or mules or even of dogs, and their cruelty to the poor animals made Jenny weep.

Mae got angry. She screamed at one man, cursing him when he beat an exhausted horse with an axe handle and then put a gun barrel to its head and pulled the trigger just as they were going past.

"You cruel, heartless brute!" she shrieked. "You'll have the death of that animal on your soul forever. You'll rot in purgatory for what you're doing."

The man paid her no attention. He shouldered the pack the animal had been carrying and set out stolidly up the trail again without a backward glance.

Thanks to William, who'd worked with horses when he first emigrated to Canada, and also on the advice of George, their party had brought a generous supply of hay for the horses and mules and dried fish for the dogs. But others heading for the goldfields had relied only on pasture, or scraps from their own meals. They soon learned there was no grass for pasture beneath the dense forest. And food was at a premium, so scraps for the dogs were few and far between. The animals grew weak from lack of adequate feed. They broke legs slipping into deep crevasses, they drowned under the weight of their impossibly heavy loads during river crossings. Their owners seemed to think nothing of beating and shooting the poor, dumb beasts. Dead horses were a common daily sight along the trail, and Jenny never made it past that horror without heaving up whatever was in her stomach.

Fortunately, William and the other men had fallen in the habit of letting the women take the lead so as to avoid the dust and muck stirred up by the animals. The women, carrying only light packs, usually were some distance ahead of the rest of the party. They set their own pace and stopped when they needed to rest, so Jenny's violent spells of vomiting went unnoticed by William. Mae and Kitty offered water and damp handkerchiefs, and she always managed to resume walking before the men and the horses drew near.

William did notice she was growing thin, but so was everyone. And so far at least, Jenny was grateful that her belly wasn't yet expanding.

"By the time this is over," Kitty declared one night, "my waist will be the size it was when I laced my tightest. I may never have to wear a corset again."

By the time this was over, Jenny thought, she'd either be dead or so used to pain and sickness nothing would bother her. Her feet were a mass of blisters, every muscle in her body ached, and the nausea was constant.

She'd stopped even asking how much longer before they reached Lake Bennett, where George had promised he had relatives who'd arrange to have them taken by boat down the waterways to Dawson City. It was said that part of the journey would take them three weeks, but none of them believed anything they were told anymore.

But then one sunny day past noon—Jenny had no idea how long it had been since they'd left Skagway; it might have been a week or a year, each day seemed endless—she stumbled around a sharp, steep curve, lungs aching, legs sore, and stared down at a blue lake, far off in the distance.

They'd reached the summit at last.

Chapter Seven

Jenny stopped stock-still and caught her breath. The trail wound downward in a steep and steady arc. The lake far below was ringed by birches turning scarlet.

"Lake Bennett," Mae puffed. "Lake Lindemann's just a short distance from there."

"Thank God," Kitty breathed, coming to stand beside Jenny and Mae. "Much more of this climbing and I swear I'd get on bloody Albert's back and make him piggyback me. At least from here on we get to ride in a boat."

"It's beautiful, isn't it?" Mae was getting her breath back. "Doubly so because from here it's all downhill. Shall we begin, ladies?"

For the rest of that day, they slipped and slid down the trail with ease. That evening they walked for hours through the twilight in order to reach the lakeshore. For the first time in days, Jenny felt revived and even hopeful. She'd made it through hell, and she felt certain that nothing ahead could possibly be as terrible as the White Pass trail.

That night, they pitched their tents among dozens of others on the shores of the lake and Jenny slept soundly, waking in the early dawn to the cry of loons. William, his bearded face gaunt, snored as she crept out of the tent to have a look around.

Even at this early hour, men were heading for the saw pits where trees were being turned into lumber to make the boats needed for the long journey up the Klondike. The smell of campfires and brewing coffee filled the air, along with the odor that invariably made Jenny's stomach heave—frying bacon.

There was a crude latrine behind the row of tents, and she made it in time. When the heaving finally ended and the dizziness faded, she headed down to the lake for a basin of water to wash in, and by the time she got back to the campsite, Robert had a fire going and tea brewing.

"Mornin', Jenny," he said with a smile. "Are ye feelin' poorly, lass?" He studied her for a moment, taking in her pale face and trembling hands.

"I'm all right, thank ye, Robert." She was afraid for a moment that he'd guessed and she tried to smile as if nothing was wrong, but it was too much of an effort. "I'm that glad ta be on this side of those cursed mountains," she said, waving a hand at the trail behind them and shuddering at the memory of the ordeal they'd endured.

"And I," he said with feeling, filling a cup with tea, stirring in condensed milk and sugar before he handed it to her. "It'll no break me heart if I never see that cursed trail again."

Jenny nodded agreement, studying her brother-in-law.

Robert's beard, like William's had grown on the trail. His face was thinner, cheekbones prominent, features sharply drawn. His wide shoulders and long arms bulged with muscles that hadn't been apparent before the trip over the Pass. If anything, the Galloway brothers were even more handsome than before. And if Kitty and Mae were any indication, Jenny mused, she looked years older and much the worse for wear. It wasn't fair.

"How long d'ye think we'll camp here?" Jenny knew they had to go as soon as possible, but she longed for a few days rest before undertaking the rest of the journey.

"George is off right now looking for his cousin," Robert told her, taking a seat beside her on a handy log, sipping his own coffee. "It's already mid-August, and the latest that boats can leave here and reach Dawson before freeze-up is the middle of September."

"So we've plenty o' time."

Robert nodded. "Aye, we've time enough yet, but we don't want to be wastin' any, or we'll find ourselves spendin' eight months camped alongside the river some-where. The ice doesna break up till mid-May, allowin' travel to begin again." He pointed at the trail, where already tiny figures were beginning to descend. "There's many of those poor souls spendin' the winter here in a tent."

Jenny shuddered at the thought.

"Is there any more of that tea?" Kitty joined them, her face still puffy from sleep. But Jenny noted that she'd put her hair up and donned her corsets, along with a dark blue frock over a good number of petticoats.

Robert, always polite, got up and brought her a cup.

"Oh, dear, sweet man, thank you." Kitty looked up at

him and batted her lashes, making certain her hand stroked his as she accepted the tea.

Robert sat down again beside Jenny, and Kitty swooped over and plunked down beside him, her skirts and petticoats brushing against his knees.

"And how are you feeling, chickie?" Kitty leaned across Robert, giving Jenny a concerned look.

"Stiff and awful sore," Jenny said. She tried to sound casual, but Kitty was making her nervous. "I've a bad blister on me heel, and a bruise on me elbow where I slipped the other day. I was tellin' Robert I'm that pleased to be off yon mountain. It feels like heaven ta not have ta put boots on and climb today."

She knew she was babbling, and her nervousness increased when William, yawning, came out of the tent, filled a cup with coffee and took a seat on her other side.

"I was referrin' to your stomach trouble, if you take my meaning," Kitty said, and Jenny tensed. Her heart began to hammer. She knew that Kitty was deliberately baiting her.

Fortunately, George joined them, and Robert and William got to their feet and immediately began asking him about the canoes. The three men moved some distance away.

Jenny felt shaky, pitifully grateful that William's attention was diverted, but a wave of hot anger rolled through her as she turned toward Kitty. "Why did ye do such a thing?" Her voice was low, even though she felt like screaming at the other woman's duplicity.

"Do what?" Kitty feigned ignorance. "I was asking about your health, was all."

"Ye're no foolin' me, Kitty Fitzpatrick. Ye're threatenin' me, although I dinna know what yer purpose can be." Jenny got up and walked over to the cooking stove where Mae was pouring water into a kettle to make porridge and heating a pan to fry the bacon. She shot Jenny a curious glance, but didn't say anything.

Jenny busied herself helping, trying to subdue her anger toward Kitty, and it was some time before she realized the men were having a heated argument with Indian George. She stopped stirring the oats into the water and listened.

"But you assured us there'd be canoes to transport us," Albert was saying in a loud, angry voice. "And now you're telling us they aren't available?"

George shrugged, face impassive.

William said, "Kin ye find us other boats for hire, then?"

George shook his head, saying something to William that Jenny couldn't hear.

"Drat it all, it sounds like we're going to have to swim to get to Dawson," Mae said with a dejected sigh. She'd stopped slicing bacon to listen to what was going on. "Can't anything go easy and smooth on this trip?"

Jenny didn't say anything, and after a few more minutes of heated discussion, George walked away. The men, looking dejected, came back over to the fire just as Carl came out of the tent, yawning and scrubbing at his face with his palms. "What's going on?"

"We've no canoes," Albert said in a disgusted tone. "George says his cousin's taken another group down the lake, two days ago. I can't believe how unreliable these people are."

"So what are we going to do?" Mae had her hands on her hips, looking from one man to the other. "There must be other boats for hire."

"That's just it, there aren't any," Albert stormed. "Look at all these people camped here—they're busy building boats, that's why they're still here. If they could hire any, they'd be gone." He shook his head. "I think we should turn around and go back," he said, shooting a glance over at Kitty. Still sitting on the log on the other side of the campfire, she hadn't joined the others, but she was within earshot.

Jenny was surprised that Albert was actually voicing an opinion of his own. During the trip, Kitty had browbeat the poor man something terrible, blaming him for every hardship, throwing up to him the promise he'd made her about riding a horse over the trail. Jenny noticed that Albert had gradually begun to walk with a slight stoop, with a hangdog expression on his face, as if her constant criticism and complaining were physically wearing him down.

"Otherwise we're going to end up stranded here over the winter," Albert was saying. "And I, for one, don't want to suffer through ice and snow in a tent." He added as an afterthought, with a nervous glance in her direction, "And I'd never put Kitty through that."

Jenny couldn't help but think it was what Kitty would put Albert through that the poor man dreaded. She'd treated him abominably during the entire trip, and instead of putting her in her place, he just tolerated it and went on being kind and thoughtful of her comfort.

"We're no goin' back, Robert and I," William declared. "We'll just have tae build a raft, the way these other folk are doin'. George says he'll help us cut logs, and we'll make them inta lumber in the saw pits. We can sell off the horses and pack animals for the money we'll need."

"Yah, I agree wit you, Villiam." Like William, Carl's native accent became accentuated when there was pressure. "I vorked in a sawmill, I know how to make lumber," Carl said in his lilting voice. "And I saw boats being built in

Norvay. I know how to navigate on the water, ve made our living fishing, my family."

The other men stared at Carl as if he'd grown a second head. Older and less fit than the Galloways or even Albert, he'd seemed the least capable.

Robert clapped Carl on the shoulder. "Good lad. I'll go straightaway an' see if we can have the hire of a couple saws," he said, heading off toward the saw pit at a trot.

Mae and Jenny resumed their cooking chores, and William came over to Jenny and put an arm around her shoulders. "It's no altogether a bad thing, biding here awhile," he said. "There'll be time fer ye to have a wee rest, lass," he assured her. "Ye'll get yer appetite back and yer stomach problem settled before we go on agin."

From behind them, Jenny heard Kitty give a sarcastic sputtering laugh filled with derision, and for the first time in her life, Jenny longed to hit someone with a frying pan.

When breakfast was over with, Jenny and Mae washed the dishes. They'd long ago given up trying to make Kitty do her share. She simply made herself scarce when there was any work to be done. Mae was quiet for a time, drying the enamel plates and stacking them in the basket. But then she blurted out, "You want to watch out for her, Jenny."

There was no need to say Kitty's name. Jenny knew exactly who Mae meant.

Mae said, "She means you no good, she's got her eye on Robert and he won't give her the time of day. She'd try something with William, too, if she thought there was a chance. She's jealous of you, and she'll cause you and William trouble if she gets the opportunity."

Jenny nodded, up to her elbows in dishwater. "I have tae

tell William about the baby before she blurts it out, and I'm that scared tae do it," she confessed.

"What do you think he'll do?"

"Go clean off his head wi' anger. He may even insist on takin' me back o'er that trail to Seattle, givin' up on the goldfields. If he does that, he'll never forgive me," Jenny said in a miserable whisper. "I dinna think I can bear that, Mae."

"No, I couldn't, either. Maybe just tell him as soon as you can, though, because I wouldn't trust that one. Better you tell him than her spilling the beans for you."

Jenny knew Mae was right. She waited anxiously all that day for an opportunity to see William alone, but he was caught up now with the other men in the boatbuilding frenzy, and had gone out into the woods with George to fell and drag in suitable timber. It was dusk by the time he got back, and dinner was ready, fried fish with chips. She and Mae had traded with an Indian, salt for potatoes.

As usual, Kitty didn't make an effort to help with the meal. She'd wandered off among the tents, and Jenny could hear her raucous laugh as she flirted with a group of the Klondikers.

She was there to eat, however. She filled her tin plate and took a seat on the log beside William, playfully bumping him farther over with her hip.

Jenny filled her own plate, but a sense of foreboding took away every vestige of appetite. She sat on William's other side, and Robert made a point of squatting on the ground beside her instead of taking a seat beside Kitty.

Conversation centered around the preparation of the lumber and the style of the boat. Albert was still undecided as to whether he'd continue with the rest of the party.

"The rapids are very dangerous," he said when there was a lull in the conversation. "The outlet of the lake leads straight into One Mile River, and everyone says we'd have to portage around it because of the rapids." He chewed for a minute and added, "That means rowing to the end of the lake, completely unpacking the boat, portaging all the equipment on foot, skidding the skiff a mile over logs." Albert's voice had a whine to it that grated on Jenny's nerves. "I'm not sure I want to go to all that work."

"Ve could run the rapids instead," Carl suggested. "It's a matter of steering around the rocks. Ve need a strong sweep oar, but it could be done."

"That sounds like a fine adventure," Mae enthused, reaching out to touch Carl's shoulder.

Jenny could see that Mae was bursting with pride for Carl. The older man had become a valuable asset now with his knowledge of boats and waterways.

"You ladies could walk around the rapids and meet us when we reach the other side," William said. "It's one thing for us to get wet should we overturn, it wouldna do fer women."

Mae opened her mouth to argue, looked at Jenny and shut it again.

"I agree, the boat would be too dangerous by far for Jenny and the baby—" Kitty put a hand over her mouth. "Oh, sorry," she said, leaning forward to look at Jenny. Her eyes gleamed with malice.

Silence fell. It was as if the entire group held its breath. Jenny realized in that moment that most of the men already knew she was pregnant. But it was also obvious that William didn't know.

"The baby? What are ye blatherin' about, woman?" His voice was puzzled.

"I was sure Jenny had already told you the happy news," Kitty said in a mock contrite tone. "Me and my big mouth, aye? I know she wanted to be the one to break the news herself. Sorry, Jenny." She singsonged out the words.

Jenny felt herself grow icy cold and then burning hot. She felt the color rise in her cheeks, and she couldn't force herself to turn and look at William, even though she knew he was staring at her in disbelief.

Chapter Eight

Jenny got up, knees threatening to give way, entire body trembling. Without looking at anyone, she made her way past the others and into her and William's tent. She felt him following close behind, a large and formidable shadow.

Inside, she removed her shoes with shaking hands and crawled onto the bed of pine branches and blankets.

William was close behind her. It took a great effort of will to turn and face him. He knelt close to her and put his hands on her shoulders. His grip was hard, his eyes like a stranger's, hard and cold. She flinched.

"Ye must take me for a great bloody fool, Jenny," he ground out. "Surely the others do, because I dinnae even guess. Ye saw fit to share the news wi' everyone but me, aye?"

She didn't answer. She could hardly breathe, much less say anything.

"When did ye first know?" William's voice was soft, but there was that undercurrent of steel that terrified her. Why was she afraid of her own husband?

She cleared her throat and sat up straighter. "Yer hurtin' me shoulders, William."

He released her so suddenly she almost toppled over. She could hear him breathing, fast and deep, each exhalation like a horse blowing. His face was pale beneath the weather-beaten tan, teeth clenched, cheekbones standing out, green eyes dark now with rage. "When?" He spat the word at her, and she felt a new tremor of fear travel down her spine. "Answer me, woman," he roared.

"I didn't know until I was on the boat comin' here, William," she finally managed to stammer. Her voice didn't sound like her. It quavered and ran up and down the scale, and her throat felt constricted.

"On the boat. Ye could have gone back easily to Seattle, then." His tone had become soft and lethal. Jenny wished he'd holler again.

"I had nae wish tae go back, William. I wanted to come wi' ye, ye know that. I told ye so."

"And I had reservations about lettin' ye, ye know *that*. And you know as well I'd never hae let ye come on such a treacherous trip knowin' ye were carryin' our child. Ye do know that, Jenny?"

She bent her head. She did know all too well.

"Ye tricked me, Jenny. And what's worse, ye've endangered me wee bairn."

Her head snapped up. "My bairn, too, William."

He might not have even heard her for all the attention he paid.

"Climbin' o'er that trail, fallin' on the rocks, dog bloody

tired at day's end, it's a wonder ye ha' nae lost it already."
He stared at her until she met his gaze. "Is that what ye
want, Jenny? To lose me baby?"

Her mouth fell open in shock. She closed it and snapped,
"Dinnae be an idjit, William. I've no intentions of losin'
this baby."

"That's no how it appears ta me. Ye had no business
comin' over yon trail, ye should hae gone back to Seattle
when first ye suspected. Which is what ye're doin' now,
Jenny. Goin' back."

"No, I am not." She glared at him. "I've made it this far,
I'm comin' the rest o' the way."

Again, it was as if William didn't hear her. "I canna take
ye meself, I've too much money invested already in this
endeavor, and I need to be here and see the boatbuildin'
goes proper, but I'll speak to Robert directly. He'll take ye
back over the pass." He left the tent without another word,
leaving Jenny fuming, furiously angry not only at him, but
at Kitty. What she'd done was deliberate and malicious,
and Jenny felt a white-hot rage fill her when she thought
of the other woman.

But that was soon gone as terror took its place at the
thought of the long trip back over the horrible trail, and of
having the baby by herself in a strange place without her
husband there to comfort her. Terror gave way to tears, and
she was sobbing when a soft voice called out, "Jenny?
May I come in?"

It was Mae, and suddenly Jenny wanted nothing more
than to have her friend with her.

"Aye." She gulped. "Do come in, please, Mae." Her
voice trembled, and the moment Mae's narrow, kind face
appeared in the tent flap, Jenny began to sob even harder.

"He's—he's sendin' me back, he willnae listen to a thing I say," she wept. "I cannae bear that trail again, Mae. I'd rather die."

"There, there." Mae put her arms around Jenny and rocked her. "He's furious at the moment, but he'll calm down. He feels tricked, is all." Her tone hardened. "Damn that nasty bitch of a scheming woman."

"Why?" Jenny wailed. "Why did Kitty do such a rotten thing, Mae? I've never been aught but kind tae her."

"I told you, she's fair green with jealousy. You have two handsome, strong men doting on you. She despises Albert. It's obvious she's just using him for her own ends."

"But he's a kind, generous man, patient as Job wi' her."

"Women like her always want what someone else has. And when they can't get it, they turn mean as snakes."

"What—what can I do, Mae?"

"Bide your time. Find a moment when William's not so angry and try to reason with him. It's safer now to go on to Dawson than to risk climbing back over the trail, he'll see that when he calms down. Do you want me to talk to him?"

"No, thank ye." Jenny blew her nose and shook her head. "He'd be ravin' mad if he thought I'd asked ye tae intercede fer me. I'll—I'll do as ye say, but I know he's plannin' on sendin' me back straightaway."

"Plead exhaustion. It's not an untruth, either. After that horrible trip, you need a few days rest or you really will be ill. And take the first opportunity to talk quietly with William."

"I will, but I canna be around Kitty just now, Mae. I swear I'll do her bodily harm, I'm that angry."

"It would serve her right. But don't, she's bigger than you, and I'll bet she's a street fighter. No, Jenny, the best thing to

do is ignore her. Albert's still undecided about whether he'll
go on. We may be lucky enough to be rid of her soon."

"Aye, ye're right. No good would come of smackin'
her, though she richly deserves it. But I don't want to lay
eyes on her just now, so I'll bide me time here in the tent
the rest of the evenin'. Maybe by mornin' I'll feel better."

"Shall I bring you some tea?"

Mae's kindness brought tears. "I couldna swallow a
thing, but thank ye, Mae. Yer a true and loyal friend, and
I'm that grateful to ye."

When Mae left, Jenny tried to subdue the rising panic
that made her hands shake and her insides tighten. To
distract herself, she dug out her writing case. She hadn't
written to her father since leaving Skagway; she'd been far
too exhausted each night to do anything more than tumble
into asleep.

She extracted a fresh sheet of paper.

"My dear papa," she began, but then she sat for a long
while, rubbing away tears with her palms and wondering
what she could possibly say. She fingered the thick packet
of letters that had accumulated since Seattle. She'd thought
of trying to mail them in Skagway, but William had said
there was little chance of them ever being sent out. He'd
pointed out a telegraph office, where people were lined up,
eager to send messages to those they'd left behind. Curious
as to how a line could have been strung all the way from
Skagway, William had followed it out behind the busy
office, only to discover it ended a hundred yards away. The
people were being duped, and he felt the same would apply
from the tent labeled Post Office.

Well, now she could mail them herself when she got
back to the city, she thought, and new tears plopped down

on the paper at the thought. She hadn't heard from home, of course. Bruce would surely have written to the general delivery address William had given him in Seattle, and Jenny had taken pains to request that her mail be forwarded from there to Dawson. Now her father's letters would go there, and Jenny would be back in Seattle.

In this wild country, mailing letters was like flinging them to the wind. It was unlikely Bruce would ever get them, she thought, and that brought on a new flood of tears. So why not say what was in her heart? She blew her nose and considered the idea. It would help to write it all out, her fears, her heartache, her problems with William. In her previous letters, she'd been careful not to reveal how sick she'd been, or how lonely she felt. She'd never used a single word that might be construed as criticism of her husband.

Surely it was past time to be honest. She'd pretend she was writing a diary. She dipped the pen and now the words flew onto the page.

We've reached Lake Bennett safely at last. Dearest Papa, I have no words to describe the trip over the White Pass trail. The first day I thought I would die, and every day thereafter I knew I couldn't survive. The trail crosses over a huge mountain...

She explained exactly what had transpired, pages and pages of feelings and emotions that seemed to spill straight out of her heart's center. She told Bruce of her doubts about her marriage, about her homesickness and terrible loneliness, of Kitty's betrayal and Mae's friendship. By the time the letter was complete, she'd covered eight pages in cramped script, back and front of the paper, and her wrist was aching, her fingers cramped.

But she felt better. She folded the sheets and tucked them into an envelope. She addressed it, even though she'd never send this one. But she wasn't going to destroy it, either. She put the fat envelope with the others and closed the writing case. Her panic had subsided into a general feeling of depression, and she was bone weary. She had to use the outhouse before she could sleep, and she tugged on her boots again.

Outside, the day had slipped into the long Northern twilight, and although she listened intently, she couldn't hear any of the others talking. She stuck her head out of the tent and found the fire banked and the campground deserted. There was the sound of logs being whipsawed from the saw pit, but the rest of the tent city was quiet.

Taking this opportunity to visit the latrine and then wash herself in water still warm from the pail on the stove, she sat for a moment outside the tent, watching the stunning colors of the evening sky reflect in the long dark stillness of the lake. The sounds from the saw were like the buzzing of an angry swarm of bees, and the smells of food cooking over open fires and people talking at the other campsites were somehow comforting.

It was there that Albert found her. He came walking slowly, head bent, shoulders slumped, from the direction of the saw pits. When he saw her he called "Jenny" before she could bolt into the tent.

He came hurrying over to her.

"Jenny," he said again when he came close. "Jenny, please let me speak to you. I should like to apologize on Kitty's behalf. She spoke without thinking and feels very badly about divulging your, uh, your secret. Please say that you can find it in your heart to forgive her? She—that is, *we,* have decided to go on to the Klondike, and it would be very uncomfortable for her if you were to remain, umm, upset with her."

Jenny listened to his stumbling voice, knowing that Kitty had put him up to this. The woman wound poor Albert up like a clock and sent him ticking off to do her bidding.

Jenny thought of telling him that she'd be going back to Skagway, so there wouldn't be any problem, and then thought better of it. Whatever she said would be repeated to Kitty, and she didn't want to give the other woman the satisfaction of knowing she'd won. Not yet

"If Kitty has something to say to me, better she comes and says it herself, Albert." She saw him glance nervously toward his large tent, and Jenny knew that Kitty was in there, listening to every word.

Jenny raised her voice so her words would be easily overheard. "What she did was no accident, that I know. She has a viper's tongue, and I pity ye fer havin' to put up wi' it." She paused, and then added, "But ye don't have to, Albert, do ye? Ye're no married to her, ye could walk away any time ye chose, no?"

The dumbstruck look on his face told Jenny her words had hit home. She got to her feet and made her way to her own tent. And even from that distance away, she heard Albert's dejected sigh.

Emotionally exhausted, Jenny lay down on the make-shift bed and fell asleep. She woke briefly, aware that William had crawled under the quilts carefully so as not to wake her. He also made sure no part of his body touched her. That hurt deeply. They always slept curled into one another, for warmth and loving but also for comfort. She thought of trying to talk to him, but she didn't have the energy. Soon, she slept again.

She felt him stirring very early. By the time she was fully awake, he was dressing, pulling on his pants, buttoning his shirt. His back was to her. She sat up, dragging the quilt around her shoulders, shivering from nervousness as much as the morning chill.

"William, I have things that need said. Will ye listen, please?"

He heaved a sigh. "Aye, Jenny, I'm listenin'." He drew his belt through his trousers and buckled it, but he didn't turn around, and his voice was as cold as the air.

She'd thought about every devious way to make him give in, but now that the moment was here, she blurted out the truth.

"I'm afraid of bein' alone, William. It's why I dinna tell ye." Her voice trembled, and tears threatened. She cleared her throat twice before she could continue. "And I'm that afraid of havin' this bairn, too. I saw me stepmother laborin' to have me brother Frankie, and I know what to expect, which is why I'm afraid. But even worse than the pain would be havin' it somewhere I have no one of me own close to care whether the baby and I live or die. I love ye. I want ye near me when the time comes. Wi' me in Seattle and you in Dawson. It'll be months afore ye even know it's born."

The tears were streaming down her cheeks now, and she brushed at them with the back of her hand. "I have no one in this country but you, William, you and Robert. Ye're my entire family now, ye're my husband, and I have to be near ye—ye must see that. It's why I pleaded to come in the first place. I canna go back to Seattle alone, I canna walk back

over that cursed trail. If ye make me, the baby and I both
will suffer, I know it in me heart."

By the time she finished, she was shuddering, and it took
a long time before he responded.

"Do ye no see that it's fear wi' me, too, lass?" His deep
voice was barely more than a whisper. "I'm that afraid I've
made a mistake, bankin' all our money on this venture. I
dinnae understand fully how it would be, this travelin'
north. More fool me. But that fear is nothin' to the feelin'
that I've put your life in danger." He turned toward her, and
even in the dim dawn light, she could see the anguish on
his face. "I'd take ye back meself, lass, but I've spent most
of the savin's, Jenny. If I turn back now, we'll be hard-
pressed fer money. I wrote the railroad and told them I was
declinin' the job, ye see. So now I have no choice but to
go on and make me fortune in the goldfields."

"Then, please, William, *please,* let me come wi' ye."

She saw the indecision on his face and held her breath.

At last, his shoulders slumped and he gave the barest
nod. "All right, lass. All right, come along, then. Robert or
I will try and stay near, helpin' when we can, but it'll no
be easy." He heaved a heavy sigh. "It's said Dawson is a
thriven' wee city, wi' a bit o' luck there'll be a good doctor
there, and nothin' will occur in the meantime."

Jenny felt dizzy, giddy with relief. She fell back on the
bed, laughing and crying together. "Thank ye, William,
thank ye." She sniffled and he handed her his kerchief and
gave her head a clumsy pat. Then he pulled the quilts up
around her and tucked them tight.

"Stay there, lass, I'll make ye some tea and bring it to
ye. While this boatbuildin's goin' on, ye're to rest as much
as ye can. And eat, Jenny, ye must eat to keep up yer

strength. Ye're that thin, a good wind would blow ye away. Starvin' yersel' cannae be good fer the bairn."

"I will. I'll try. I promise, William." She'd have promised anything, she was that relieved and happy.

He left, and she curled into a ball, half-dizzy with relief.

She didn't hear him bring the tea. She slept for most of that day, waking only to eat, wash and use the latrine. She did the same for three more days, and when she finally fully woke up, it was as if a miracle had occurred while she slept. The awful nausea that had plagued her was totally gone, and her appetite was back in full measure.

It took a full week to build the boat, even with all four men working daybreak to dusk. It was now late August, and all the leaves were turning scarlet. For Jenny, those long autumn days were like a holiday, even though she knew how pressured William and the rest of the men were. They had to leave Lake Bennett by the end of August; freeze-up came in late September, and they had to be in Dawson before then.

Mae was thrilled that Jenny and William had come to terms. Kitty avoided the other women, wandering about the tent city and talking and flirting with whoever was available. Many of the men had resigned themselves to spending the winter there, so the urgency had gone out of their boat-building efforts. These were the ones who welcomed Kitty to their campsites. Mae and Jenny heard her raucous laughter during the day, but it was only when dinner was ready and the men were around that she appeared. She avoided being alone with the women, and Jenny and Mae pointedly ignored her. Albert, as usual, allowed himself to be bossed around as if he were her butler.

Kitty always tried to sit beside either William or Robert at mealtimes. Robert became adept at avoiding her, but William seemed oblivious to her ploys.

And he probably was, Jenny decided. William was no womanizer, but it made Jenny furious to have Kitty pressing up against her husband like a cat in heat at every opportunity.

The other men all looked to William as their natural leader, and she knew he felt it as a heavy responsibility. He paid little attention to Kitty as he and Carl and Robert endlessly discussed the finer details of boat making, and after they'd eaten the three men would hurry away to examine the day's accomplishments and plan the following day's work. Albert stayed behind, tending Kitty's needs, hauling water and heating it for her bath, making her cups of tea. Jenny pitied him. His love for Kitty had made him lose all self-respect.

The night before the launch, Jenny and Mae went along to admire the completed boat. Kitty followed along some distance behind, hanging on Albert's arm.

The vessel, properly called a skiff, was impressive. It was twenty-seven feet long, flat bottomed, pointed at the bow and square at the stern, large enough to carry everyone's bulky provisions. The sturdy, graceful vessel looked to Jenny's untrained eye as if it would be seaworthy, never mind capable of floating along rivers and lakes.

"It's beautiful," she breathed, but her quiet voice was drowned out by Kitty's loud squeals.

"Ooooooh," the other woman enthused. "Would you look at this lovely thing! You men are so clever, building this outta nothing but logs. Help me in, someone. I want to try it out."

She lifted her skirts higher than necessary, showing a great deal of leg and giggling girlishly as she attempted to climb into the boat, tottering precariously so that William shot out his arm and grabbed her in an effort to keep her from falling. She clung to him, looking up at him from under her long lashes, a winsome and seductive smile on her full lips. "You will allow me to ride the rapids with you, won't you? No fair to let gents have all the fun, I always say. What an adventure, I can't wait."

"Bitch, I hope she drowns," Mae murmured to Jenny. Mae had already offered to walk with Jenny around the rapids and meet the boat on the far side. They'd leave well ahead of the skiff's launch, so there wouldn't be a delay while the boat waited for them at the place where the rapids ended.

"If she drowns, so will they all," Jenny reminded her friend, and shuddered at the thought.

"They're not going to drown," Mae said firmly. "Carl is accustomed to boats, and William and Robert are strong and clever."

But they both knew that three boats in the past week had been broken to splinters on the rocks of One Mile River. Two men had drowned, and it was rumored that all along the river, wooden crosses marked the places where unfortunate fellow travelers had lost both their packs and their lives.

That night, Jenny was still awake when William crawled into the tent. When he climbed under the quilts beside her, she put her arms around him. She'd left her gown off, and she heard his quick intake of breath when he discovered she was naked. He lay quite still for a long moment, moving only his work-roughened hand, stroking her skin gently from shoulder to hip.

They hadn't made love since before the quarrel. Jenny

suspected that William still carried some resentment toward her for not telling him she was pregnant. It was important to her that they come together tonight, on the eve of the next stage of their journey together.

As her wandering hand moved down his body, it was plain that William was more than ready. "Are ye sure, lass? It willna harm the bairn?" His tremulous whisper tickled her cheek, and she smiled and kissed him instead of answering.

He smelled of wood smoke and resin and soap. He and Robert had found a secluded spot by a stream that fed into the lake. They'd hollowed out a bath where they washed the sweat from their bodies at the end of each long workday. Jenny and Mae had used it that afternoon, as well, one of them standing guard while the other hastily soaped and scrubbed.

William's hand came to rest on her abdomen where a small, hard bump indicated their baby was growing.

He whispered again in her ear, "It willnae hurt the wee one?"

"Nay." She was flattered he'd think her an expert on such things. The truth was, she didn't know and had no one to ask, but common sense indicated that men and women wouldn't abstain for nine entire months.

He heaved such an extreme sigh of relief she had a fit of giggles, and he made them worse by licking in places he knew were ticklish.

But soon the giggles gave way to sighs and soft moans of utter pleasure as he used tongue and teeth and fingers in ways he knew would bring her quickly to her peak. When the moment came, she arched and rocked her head from side to side, unable to subdue the cry that poured from her very depths. He caught it with his mouth, rising above her, entering her as her tender flesh still pulsed. His strokes roused her all over again, and she held his neck and tightened her legs around his hips, wordlessly begging him to take her with him.

When his release came, hers did, as well.

"Ahh, Jenny, love." William sighed deeply and rolled to the side so as not to crush her, but he went on holding her close. "Ye'd be the perfect wife, if only ye dinnae snore."

She cuffed him, and he gathered her even closer, smoothing her wild curls with one hand. She could feel his heartbeat under her palm, the hard band of chest muscle evident under hair-roughened skin.

"Ye'll be careful tomorrow in the boat, William?"

His cheek was against hers, his beard soft against her skin, and she could feel him smile. "Aye, lass, I'll be careful. I've too much to live for to take careless chances." He sighed and murmured, "This makes everything right, doesn't it, sweetheart?"

His words healed the last of the quarrel, and she savored them. If only they could always be this connected. But before she could answer, *he'd* begun to snore.

Jenny and Mae set out at daybreak, each carrying a small pack with lunch and a water bottle. Kitty had insisted on riding the rapids with the men, and although William and Robert objected on the grounds of safety, Albert, or course, had agreed. She'd smiled a sly smile and waved triumphantly at Mae and Jenny when they left.

"Enjoy the walk—we'll see you past the rapids," she called.

"The nerve of her, it's all I can do not to thumb my nose," Mae sputtered. "If Albert had any sense, he'd tip her overboard and count his blessings."

"He's the one needs to watch out," Jenny said. "I wouldna trust her wi' me back turned."

The men had estimated that it would take them four hours to walk the distance the boat would cover in one. The morning was cold but promising to be sunny, the path easy and clearly marked from all those who'd portaged.

The women made good time, stopping only once to rest and eat their bannock and cheese before they reached the slow water at the base of the rapids.

"We can watch them coming down if we climb up on that ledge," Mae suggested, pointing at a rocky bluff above the lake's outlet. The two of them scrambled up, and Jenny's heart began to pound when she saw the skiff come shooting out of the lake, flying straight into the rapids. Robert and Carl were pushing at the oars, and William stood at the stern with the long sweep oar held tight in both hands.

Albert and Kitty were crouched low in the boat, holding on to the sides. Jenny could faintly hear William hollering and Kitty screaming as the skiff shot into the white water.

"Oh, heaven help us," Mae cried. "They're headed straight for the rocks in the middle of the river." She grabbed for Jenny's hand and the two women watched in horror as the boat careened straight toward certain disaster.

Chapter Nine

The skiff tilted and seemed about to overturn.

Jenny prayed out loud, wanting to close her eyes but unable not to watch.

At the last possible second, when disaster seemed inevitable, she saw William, with a death grip on the long sweep oar, steer around the rocks and somehow maneuver the boat through the narrow channel of boiling water.

Robert and Carl, using their oars as leverage, managed to keep the skiff from hitting the steep rock walls on either side of the canyon.

And then the boat was through the rapids, safe in calmer waters, and the women heard the men's shouts of triumph.

"They made it, oh, thank God they made it." Jenny unclenched her hand from Mae's fierce grip and the two of them hugged one another hard.

They climbed down and raced along the shore until they reached the quiet inlet where the skiff was already tied to a sapling. The men were standing on the lake-shore, waiting for them.

"Carl, that was utterly brilliant, my dear." Mae flung herself at her husband, nearly bowling him over. "I'm that proud of you, you're a hero!"

Jenny didn't say a thing. She flew into William's arms, and she could tell by the tension and fine trembling in his body that the trip had been nerve-racking. He was soaking wet, but he held her tight, and when he released her with a long kiss full on her mouth, Jenny caught the spiteful expression on Kitty's face. It was only there for an instant, because as soon as the other woman saw her looking, Kitty assumed a sneering smile.

"You two *ladies* missed all the fun," she jeered. Her dress, too, was soaked, pasted against her body so that little was left to the imagination, but she made no effort to cover herself with her shawl. "I can't wait for the next set of rapids at Five Fingers. But next time, Albert had better walk along with you ladies, hey Albert? Nearly screamed me ear off, he did."

Albert didn't answer. He was sitting on a fallen log, and Jenny could see his entire body shaking. His face was ashen, and his Adam's apple bobbed as he swallowed every few seconds. It was obvious the rapids had frightened him nearly senseless, and Jenny despised Kitty for making fun of him.

"Only a proper fool wouldna be afraid o' such a ride," Robert said in a steely tone, staring straight at Kitty. "And it's no a thing any sane person would choose to do fer entertainment, ye ask me."

His words were a direct rebuke, but Kitty pretended she didn't hear. She was rummaging in her carpetbag for dry clothes, and she flounced off into the woods to change. The men, too, unearthed dry clothing and disappeared. When everyone returned, they all climbed on the skiff and the men took up oars.

Jenny was seated on a pile of tents. After the exertions of the White Pass, it seemed almost sinful to relax and let the water transport her.

"Together now, vun, two and three." Carl called out the cadence as the heavily loaded boat began its journey down the wide lake.

She felt excitement build as the sturdy skiff skimmed over the deep water. She knew there were more rapids ahead, and undoubtedly more challenges for all of them to face on the five-hundred-mile water journey to Dawson, but for the moment, she had nothing to do but sit and watch the Canadian wilderness slip past—and battle the mosquitoes and the other ravenous insects that were so plentiful here. She slapped at a blackfly that had just taken a generous bite out of her wrist, then looked toward the shore, where deep green pines climbed up toward the timberline, and the morning sun shone on magnificent snowcapped peaks. Ahead, the dark waters of the lake stretched as far as she could see, and the rising sun warmed the sweet-smelling air. It was growing colder as the autumn advanced, and the night before, for the first time, they'd seen the Northern Lights. Bands of shimmering color danced across the darkened sky, green and rose and yellow. Jenny had stared up at the heavens, awestruck. The breathtaking display was evidence of the vastness and mystery of this strange land. William had taken her hand, and she felt the fine tremors in his body as he stared up at the heavens. He was silent, but she could sense that he, too, was overwhelmed by wonder.

He turned now from his labors with the paddle and gave her a fond, crooked smile, and a feeling of great peace and happiness descended upon her. He'd forgiven her. They were together, and for the moment, at least, that was all that mattered.

Three long weeks later, the skiff rounded one last rocky bluff and from her perch on top of the provisions, Jenny saw the city of white tents, frame houses, hotels and warehouses that comprised Dawson.

"We made it." Mae let out a whoop, and the others joined in.

The skiff pulled into the dock, and Jenny stepped off, stiff and sore from hours spent immobile on the boat, but thrilled to have finally arrived at this place they'd struggled so long and hard to reach.

The men made the boat fast with ropes, and then William took Jenny's hand and they walked along Front Street.

The town was situated at the very foot of a dome-shaped mountain, its side scarred by a landslide. It was a confusing and noisy scene to Jenny, accustomed as she'd become to the sounds of the river, the silence of the wilderness.

It seemed as if hundreds of miners swarmed this town, and signs advertised restaurants, saloons, bakeries, mercantile establishments. It was so noisy she felt like holding her hands over her ears. There were yapping dogs and braying mules, neighing packhorses and countless men hollering to one another. Just as it had at Skagway, everything in Dawson seemed under construction, and the sound of hammers and saws added to the general din.

Jenny and the two other women attracted enormous attention, even flanked as they were by the four men. It wasn't difficult to figure out why; in the time it took to walk from one end of the bustling boomtown to the other, Jenny only saw two other women.

One was a respectable-looking older woman heading into a restaurant with a basket loaded with wonderful-smelling loaves of bread, and the other was undoubtedly a dance hall girl. She came out of the Globe Saloon. Her hair was an unbelievable shade of yellow, her red skirts shockingly short, her bodice tight and extremely low. Around her neck was what looked like a fortune in gold nuggets suspended on a chain.

"Hey, handsome." She wriggled her fingers and batted her eyes at Robert. "Come in and join me for a drink?"

"Thank ye, no." Robert was, as always, polite. "We've only just arrived and need ta get settled, ma'am," he said, his face slowly turning brick red under his tan.

"Too bad. See ya around, then." She pranced off in the opposite direction.

William jabbed an elbow into Robert's ribs. "Ye great dumb gorrum, why did ye no go wi' her?"

"It's no whiskey I'm after, it's food," Robert replied in a dignified tone. "I'm right famished."

"And me," Jenny said. "I'm that hungry, William. Can we no go into one of these places and have somethin' to eat?" Jenny's formidable appetite had returned with a vengeance, and she spent a great deal of time wondering when and what she could next eat.

"Aye, we can, lass, and then we'll find a boardin' house, until we can locate somethin' to rent," William decided.

Carl and Mae came into the Pioneer Café with them, but much to Jenny's relief, Albert and Kitty didn't.

"We'll catch up to you later," Albert said. "Kitty wants to find a suitable hotel and a proper dining room."

"She ought to try the rooms above the Globe Saloon," Mae whispered to Jenny as they found a table in the crowded cafe. "It's where she belongs."

The food was wonderful, but horrifically expensive. After more than six weeks on the trail, having yeast bread, a thick steak and a fresh salad was heavenly. They finished their meal with big slabs of apple pie, and when the bill came, Mae gasped.

As the men paid it, Mae said to Jenny, "Well, that'll be our last meal at a restaurant until we stake a claim and get rich. We only had twenty dollars left, and I'll wager we just ate up ten of it. Not that it wasn't worth it. But we're going to find a spot to pitch our tent. We can't afford to take a room."

Jenny had been looking forward to sleeping on a real bed with a mattress, and she knew Mae must have been, as well. "We'll likely be joinin' ye, if the rooms are as dear as the food." But she said it to make Mae feel better, not really believing it.

It turned out that not only were the rooms expensive, but there were none to be had at any price. William inquired at all the hotels and boarding houses in Dawson, but the influx of gold seekers had filled every available space. He and Robert and Carl found a relatively private spot alongside a creek and set to work pitching their tents.

Bitterly disappointed, Jenny found herself once again arranging quilts over a springy bed of spruce boughs. The only consolation was that Mae was nearby and Kitty wasn't. She and Albert had retrieved some of their belongings from the skiff and disappeared without even a goodbye.

"That'll be the last we see of them," Mae predicted. "Not

that I want to speak to Kitty ever again, but I did like Albert. He's probably spending a fortune finding a room that woman deems suitable."

The men had gone to a saloon, not to drink but to find out all they could about staking claims. Mae and Jenny were hauling water from the creek and trying to get enough heat out of the campfire to make tea and do the washing up. They were feeling the loss of Albert's stove.

Mae stuck another piece of wood in the fire and lowered the trivet to speed up the process. She was still thinking of Kitty. "And I'll wager she'll have him out on his ear the moment she finds a man with a good supply of gold nuggets, don't you agree?"

Jenny did. "There must be plenty o' that sort around here," she replied. "They say the gold is lyin' out there, for anyone to take."

It was what they'd heard on the long, exhausting journey, but the next morning, Jenny found out exactly how mistaken that idea was.

The men hadn't come home until long after Jenny and Mae were in bed asleep, so at breakfast the women were eager to hear what had been learned from the men in the saloon.

The first thing William told them was that Dawson would soon have a hospital. According to the saloon gossip, a missionary called Father Judge was bringing in nuns as nurses, and bullying miners into donating money for a building to house it. There was already a doctor in town, Dr. Ichabod Perry. William sounded vastly relieved when he said, "He's a drinkin' man, but apparently when he's sober he's verra good at what he does."

Jenny knew that William was trying to reassure her about the baby's arrival. It was comforting to know there was a doctor and some hope of a hospital, although Jenny couldn't help but wonder about the doctor's drinking habits.

William went on, "As for the gold, d'ye want to come along to see the diggin's? Carl and Robert and I have the loan of a wagon and a horse this mornin' to take us out to Bonanza Creek and Eldorado." William added with a note of pride in his voice, "And our Rob's got a job already, workin' a claim fer one a the miners. He's promised twenty dollars a day. The experience will benefit when we have our own claim."

"Never." Jenny was amazed. "Twenty dollars, Robert! Ye'll be a rich man in no time." In Seattle, the average daily wage for a man doing hard physical labor was two dollars. "But it'll no be for long, ye'll find a likely place and work it yourselves, no, William?"

"Aye, lass." William nodded and smiled at her. "But we're a wee bit short o' money, and Rob had the job handed tae him. One o' the workers broke his leg yesterday. Rob will file a claim along wi' Carl and I, and I'll work his as well as me own fer a wee while." He went on to explain that there was a rule that claims had to be staked in person and could not be left unworked more than three consecutive days during the mining season.

Jenny and Mae, eager and excited to see the place where gold nuggets were as thick as hens' eggs, quickly abandoned the dishes and climbed up on the wagon. They clattered over the wooden bridge spanning the Klondike River. They headed up the Bonanza Creek Road, and Jenny gasped when they topped a hill and looked down on the diggings.

"Merciful heaven," Mae exclaimed after a moment of shocked silence. "It looks like Dante's Inferno."

Jenny didn't know what that was, but if it was part of
hell, Mae was certainly right. She stared at the unfolding
scene in horror.

Huge piles of dirt and gravel were everywhere, and
tents, lean-tos, privies and the occasional cabin were
scattered among them. All the hills had been stripped,
and there was not a trace of greenery anywhere. Instead
there was raw and ravaged earth and what appeared to
be tons of machinery randomly scattered along a
winding creek, and men, hundreds of them, working
sluice boxes, shoveling dirt and gravel, winching huge
buckets from holes that William explained were vertical
mine shafts.

"Most of these men are working for wages," Carl explained. "The claim owners pay them to do the dirty work."

"Dirty work, clean money," Robert said with a grin.
"I'm workin' fer a man called Krauss, let's see if anyone
knows where his claim lies."

They rode down the hill, and the first group they came
to pointed them along the right way and went straight
back to work.

After several more inquiries, they arrived at the proper
spot, which to Jenny's untrained eye looked exactly the
same as every other spot along the desolate creek—until
Robert asked for instructions as to what he should do.

One of the people bent over the sluice box turned
around, and Jenny realized it was a woman. She was
wearing men's clothing—pants and a flannel shirt, tall
work boots and a brimmed brown hat that covered her hair.

Her face was sweaty, with clear-cut, bold features. She
looked to be about forty, but there was an air of enormous
energy and enthusiasm about her. She lifted her hat for a

moment, revealing dark brown hair tied up in a knot at the back. She mopped her brow with the red bandanna tied around her neck.

"I'm Belinda Krauss," she said, taking off her gloves and extending a hand to Robert. "I expect an honest day's work. You'll get paid at week's end. You had any experience at gold mining?"

"No, mistress, but I'm willin' to learn." Robert must have been as shocked as Jenny was to find his boss was a woman, but he hid it well. He introduced the rest of them to Mrs. Krauss, and she nodded curtly. It was obvious that she, too, had no time for idle chatter.

"You'll learn soon enough, that's certain, or you'll go packing. If you make it through the day, you can bunk in with Larry and Jimmy in the shack over there. Work begins at daybreak and ends at dark." She pointed at a crude log hut. "Come with me." She turned and headed for the workings, and before William had the horse turned around, Robert was already busy with a pick and shovel.

"Imagine," Mae said in a reverent voice. "A woman working a claim. That's what you and I should do, Jenny."

"I'd like to oblige ye, but I'm otherwise engaged just at the moment," Jenny whispered, rolling her eyes and patting her stomach just to make Mae giggle.

The realities of gold mining were a shock to all of them. They were quiet as they made their way back to their camp. That afternoon, William and Carl headed out on a scouting expedition to see if they could locate likely spots to stake claims.

Grumbling about the difficulty of keeping the campfire hot enough, Jenny and Mae laboriously heated up buckets of water and filled several washtubs. Then they set about the backbreaking job of scrubbing the mounds of dirty clothes and bedding that had accumulated on the long trip.

They used carbolic soap, their washboards and a great deal of effort. They strung up several drying lines from a length of rope and hung the clothes up as they were rinsed. By evening they'd filled the lines as well as every convenient bush with drying laundry.

"I'm as worn out as that dishrag," Mae confessed when they were finally done. "It'll be sardines and baked beans again for dinner if those men ever decide to come home. And they have to fashion a decent latrine for us to use. I'm through hunkering over a log. Living in a tent is one thing—not having a decent privy is quite another."

Jenny nodded weary agreement. She felt too tired to even talk. She and Mae slumped on the ground, their backs resting against a log as they drank a mug of tea and rubbed lard into their red, swollen hands.

"Isn't that Albert?" Mae sat up straighter and pointed at a figure making its way toward them. "He's on foot. And oh, dear me, he's carrying the stove. Oh, please God, let's hope he plans to let us use it. I'm that sick of trying to cook over a campfire."

"Well, it's no a thing Kitty would have any use fer," Jenny remarked. "It's queer he's walkin' wi' it, though."

The women struggled to their feet just as Albert reached them. He was puffing hard, and he looked both exhausted and utterly miserable.

Usually scrupulously clean and well-groomed, he hadn't shaved and his eyes were bloodshot. When she got close to him, Jenny could smell stale whiskey. He had a pack on his back, and she could see blankets and the sleeve of a shirt hanging from it.

"Albert, it's that good to see ye," she said. "Can we get ye a cuppa tea?"

"Please. I'm about done in." He had the stove under one arm and the pipes under the other. He set them all down and collapsed beside them.

"And where's Kitty?" Mae tried to be polite, but her tone revealed how little she cared.

"Kitty has left me," Albert said in a strange, high voice. "She met a prospector yesterday evening, someone called Diamond Jim, and she's gone off with him. I'd gone downstairs to bring her tea this morning—she likes it first thing—and when I returned with it she was gone. Whatever am I going to do without her?"

"Oh, Albert." Jenny reached out a hand to touch him, but he covered his face and started to sob.

Chapter Ten

Mae and Jenny exchanged a knowing look as they tried to comfort Albert. Jenny filled a mug with hot, sweet tea and held it out to him. But Albert's hands were shaking, and half of it spilled down the front of his trousers before he got it to his mouth. Normally a fastidious man, he didn't seem to even notice.

"She left a note. She said I was a coward and a weakling," he went on after he'd had a few gulps. "If only I'd been braver on those rapids—"

"Balderdash, you mustn't blame yourself," Mae told him in a firm tone. "It's nothing to do with you, it's that—" she bit back what she'd been about to say, substituting, "You are a good, kind, brave man, Albert, and you'll soon meet someone else who'll appreciate you properly."

Jenny thought that was highly unlikely in Dawson, considering that they'd seen only two women amidst the hundreds of men, but she nodded enthusiastic agreement.

"I don't want another woman. I just want Kitty," he wailed, and he started weeping again, choking on his sobs. Apart from handing him a clean handkerchief and patting his shoulder, Jenny couldn't think what to do to comfort him. She hadn't seen a man cry before, but she couldn't see any point in standing up while he sat there sobbing, either, so she sank down on the ground beside him.

Mae followed suit on his other side, and for several moments she and Jenny were quiet.

"Are you going to stake a claim, Albert?" Mae obviously thought it was best to distract him. "Or you could set up shop as a dentist. I imagine you'd do very well. Everyone needs a dentist."

But Albert wasn't able to answer. He wept and mopped at his scarlet cheeks, and Jenny couldn't think what to do for him.

Eventually, however, he stopped crying and over another cup of tea, he asked, "Where are the men?" It was obvious he'd only just noticed they were absent.

Jenny explained about Robert having a job and William and Carl searching for a good location for a claim.

"They'll likely be along anytime now," Jenny added. "Ye'll stay and have supper wi' us, will ye?" She saw Mae eyeing the stove again with a covetous expression.

"Thank you, it's very kind of you. I have nowhere else to go," Albert confessed with a hitch in his voice. "You see, Kitty took all my money. I had it in a belt that I wore under my clothing. I left it in the room when I went out this morning and it was gone when I came back."

"She stole yer money?" Jenny was horrified. She

knew Kitty was untrustworthy, but she hadn't thought the other woman would stoop so low as to steal. "Why, the nasty bisom."

"Did you tell the Mounties?" Mae was always practical. "You must tell them right away, in case she decides to leave town. They'll get it back for you."

"No, no, no. Oh, no, I wouldn't do that. They'd arrest her, you see."

"Which is exactly what she deserves," Mae snapped.

"No, no," Albert insisted again. "Kitty's had a hard life—I couldn't do that to her. I have money, in a bank in Seattle, although it'll take me some time to get funds sent up here. Kitty has nothing to fall back on."

"Except her back," Mae muttered.

Jenny felt it wisest to change the subject.

"And where are ye stayin, Albert?"

He blew his nose and took several deep breaths. "Well, that's just it. I wondered if perhaps I could camp here with you? I paid the hotel bill when we registered, which was fortunate, but of course I can't stay there any longer, I can't afford it." He gestured at the stove. "I couldn't bring all my supplies along, I couldn't carry them, but I thought you might need this more than anything else."

"We do, bless your heart. And of course you'll stay with us." Mae got up and began to assemble the sturdy little cast-iron stove. "Give us a few minutes and we'll have supper ready on this little beauty."

Jenny helped, and soon they had the pipe in place. Jenny had become adept at shaving thin slivers of kindling from a larger log, and soon the little stove was sending off rays of heat. They warmed beans, and Jenny made bannock.

Mae stirred up a kind of pancake using dried potatoes, dried eggs and some wild sage she'd found.

Albert sat quietly watching them, sipping a fresh cup of tea and sighing periodically. Having the stove to cook on gave Jenny a fresh surge of energy, and she could see it was doing the same for Mae.

It seemed as if the smell of the cooking food lured William and Carl home, because just as it was ready they arrived. They were in high spirits and they greeted Albert with enthusiasm.

"Good to see you, my friend," Carl said, shaking Albert's hand and giving him an affectionate punch on the shoulder. "And where's Kitty?"

Jenny saw the raw pain on Albert's face and was relieved when Mae immediately recounted what had happened, tactfully sticking to the facts without adding her opinion of Kitty. "So Albert will be staying here with us," she concluded. "He couldn't bring his gear, we'll have to figure out a makeshift bed for tonight."

"Ye can use Robert's wee tent, and in the mornin' we'll go wi' ye and bring yer supplies over," William decided. "But first, we need to go to the land office and register our claim," he added, smiling at Jenny.

Thinking so much about Albert's problems, she'd forgotten to ask if they'd located a promising site. "Ye've found a place to mine, William?"

"Aye, we found a wee spot along a tributary of Bonanza that no one has filed on. We'll claim it in the mornin' and take our chances along wi' everyone else."

"We'll need to get started right away, so we're not digging in frozen ground," Carl explained. "And we also learned that a man named Joseph Ladue owns all this land around Dawson City. He filed on it as soon as the news got out about the gold strike on Bonanza. We'll have to either buy land from him to build a cabin or move a distance away from the town."

Jenny said, "And are we on his land right now, then?"

William nodded. "He's no so concerned about tents, but if ye want to build, ye have to buy the piece. It'll be a wee while before we get around to a cabin, so we've got breathin' room."

Jenny was disappointed. She'd expected William would build a cabin right away, but she knew their money was running low. Mae and Carl were nearing the very end of theirs. Buying a piece of land at the moment was out of the question, and moving away from the town wasn't appealing, if the camps they'd seen that morning were any indication. It looked as if it was going to be quite some time before she slept in a proper bed again. She knew William was doing his best, so she hid her reaction.

"I have that large tent," Albert said. "Why don't we set it up as a kitchen and living area, and use the smaller tents for sleeping?"

"There's a canny thought," William agreed. "It's very generous o' ye, Albert, thank ye."

Mae made everyone laugh when she said, "And do we have to buy a piece of land to build a privy? Because we absolutely need one, I'm fed up with heading off into the woods."

"We'll build one tomorrow," Carl promised.

"I have witnesses," Mae said, eyes twinkling. "You all heard him. By tomorrow evening, we'll have the finest outhouse clever men can devise, or know the reason why, right, Jenny?"

They ate and then spent the rest of the evening around the campfire, talking about the claim and the hopes they all had for finding gold. Jenny noticed that Albert didn't join in. He sat with his shoulders hunched and his hands clasped in front of his chest, a lost expression on his face as he stared into the flames.

Kitty had broken his heart. When hearts broke, did they ever mend again? Jenny looked over at William, talking in an animated way to Carl about sluice boxes and rockers. She hoped the day would never come when they broke one another's hearts.

She put a hand on her belly, the way she'd started doing whenever she was relaxed. The baby was only a small, hard lump, and she'd felt no movement yet, but it was very real to her now.

She hoped and believed this new life she and William had started would bind them together in an entirely new way, more firmly than ever before. She looked across at Mae, sitting close beside Carl. His arm was around her shoulders, and the other woman had a radiant look, as if she was exactly where she wanted to be.

Jenny envied her friend that absolute certainty. She still felt as if she didn't belong in either the world she'd left behind in Scotland or in this new one. She was too tired tonight, but tomorrow, she'd write another letter to Bruce, reassuring him about this strange, wild place she'd arrived at. And maybe soon there'd be a packet of letters from him.

There was a post office in Dawson, one that William said she could trust. Although there hadn't been any letters there waiting for her, she'd sent off her own thick packet of letters, including the one she'd written on the trail. She'd had time to think about it, and she'd come to the conclusion that total honesty was the only way to maintain the closeness she'd always treasured with her father. What would be the point of lying to him? She didn't want Bruce to edit what he told her—how else would she know how things really were with him and her brothers? And she, in turn, would be honest with him.

She wasn't as desperately homesick now as she'd been on the trail, partly because she and William were close again, but she longed for letters from home with news of her brothers and assurance that everything in her old life was continuing as it always had. Knowing that would somehow forge a link, a bridge that would perhaps allow her to travel all the way across and embrace this strange new world.

But it was two weeks and three days more before Bruce's letters finally arrived. Jenny had gone to the post office every day, hoping, trying not to be disappointed when the strange little man who ran it told her there was nothing for her.

His name was Bartholomew Fieldstone, and he'd greeted her every day with the same sad shake of his large, round bald head. They were now on friendly terms. He'd asked her to call him Bartholomew, but when she told him her name was Jenny, he'd blushed fiery red and gone on calling her Mrs. Galloway.

This afternoon, however, he beamed at her and held out a thick packet wrapped in oilskin. "One of the packers brought these in not an hour ago, Mrs. Galloway," he crowed. "I couldn't wait to give them to you. I know how eager you've been for news from home."

"Oh, thank ye. Thank ye so very much, Mr. Fieldstone."

Jenny held the packet to her heart, and she had the absurd urge to throw her arms around Bartholomew's scrawny neck and hug him. She didn't, because she was fairly certain he'd swoon.

"I trust they'll bring good, cheerful news of your family in Scotland, Mrs. Galloway," Fieldstone called as Jenny rushed off with her treasure.

She hurried back to her tent, and for the first time she was pleased that Mae wasn't at the campsite. Money had become a pressing issue for her and Carl, so Mae found a job waiting tables at the Pioneer Café. She was gone from early morning till late at night, and ordinarily Jenny missed her badly. But not today. She wanted privacy, to savor her treasure. She went into her tent and sank down on the raised bed William and Robert had made for her the week before. It had a mattress made of striped ticking stuffed with dried moss, and Jenny had spread her clean sheets and quilts over top, thinking it the best bed she'd ever slept on.

Her hands were trembling as she undid the oilskin covering. Inside were eight letters addressed to her, six in her father's handwriting and two in childish scrawls, from the oldest of her brothers, Geordie and Johnny.

She picked up the envelopes and held them to her nose, trying to detect a whiff of home. But they smelled only of the oilskin they'd been wrapped in. She moved them from her nose to her heart, squeezing her eyes shut and imagining Bruce sitting at the small writing desk in the corner of the living room, lamp guttering as he dipped his pen in the inkwell and wrote her name. And the boys, bent over the table in the kitchen, tongues stuck out the side of their mouths as they labored over their letters.

A wave of terrible homesickness overcame her, and she

doubled over from the intensity of the ache in her chest. When it eased, she went through the envelopes, trying to determine the order in which they'd been written by the date on the postmark, sniffing and trying not to let her tears smear the ink.

She found the first one and carefully slit it open.

Jenny, sweetheart,
I'm just back from seeing you off on the boat. My dear Daughter, it's very hard to let you go so far away, even though I trust that William will care for and protect you. I mind the first time I let you go down the lane and along the road to Mrs. Abernathy's house, you were maybe four, I had this same fearful feeling in my belly....

"Oh, Da. I miss you, too, something fierce," she whispered. Outside she could hear the faraway din of the town, the sound of the wind in the trees, the calling of some strange bird. All were alien sounds, not the familiar noises of home that she so longed to hear—a meadowlark in the hedge, the lowing of cattle, her father's voice calling to one of the boys.

Bruce wrote,

All is well here, the same as usual. The boys have a new puppy they've named Jock, they'll be telling you all about him. He's not allowed in the house at the moment as he gets carried away and is prone to piddle on the rug. Also, wee Frankie will chew on his ears, which makes Jock nip him and causes great turmoil.

Jenny gave a choked giggle even as the tears trickled down her cheeks. She read each word, savoring it, going slow to make the letters last. Bruce's words drew comforting pictures for her, and again she held the paper to her nose, imagining she could smell her father—hay, peat smoke, the faint pleasant scent of cows and farmyard and good honest sweat mixed with the tobacco from his pipe.

She opened her brothers' letters next and their painful efforts made her laugh aloud.

Dear Jenny, Da says we have to write you, so how are you, I am fine too, we have a dog named Jock, he likes to eat horse turds, I love you, Geordie Cameron.

Johnny's was longer. He'd always felt the responsibility of being the oldest of the boys and tried hard to please his father.

Dear Jenny, Da says by now you're out on the sea I wonder what it feels like in a boat he says they take horses on it and I wonder what they think when they're on water like that I want to come and see you when I get older we have a dog now he's really clever except he ate mother's slipper and now he can't come in the house. I hope you get to the New World without getting ship recked. Love, John.

One after the other, she devoured the letters, and when she was done she began again with the first one. Bruce wrote of homely things, of Daisy, the cow she'd liked best, of weather, always a concern to a farmer, of her brothers and their antics, of an old neighbor, Jock Stanfield, who'd died suddenly. At the very end of each letter he added,

> Your Mother sends her love and good wishes, and hopes that you are well and happy.

Jenny knew very well that Nell had no part in that message. She doubted her stepmother even gave her a passing thought, apart from being glad she was gone, but Bruce had always tried to soften the antagonism Nell held toward Jenny. In his clumsy man's way he'd tried to make peace between them, and been frustrated over and over again when it didn't happen.

Now, in these letters, there was a freedom to his words and feelings. He didn't have to censor or hide his love for her so as to keep Nell from being jealous. He had the gift of writing as he spoke, and it was profoundly comforting.

"Thank you, Da," she whispered as she got up from the bed. Her legs were stiff from sitting so long, and she felt drained by the storm of emotion the letters had brought. When she went outside she found she'd let the fire go out, and the afternoon was fading into evening. The days were getting shorter, the nights cooler. Everyone would be coming back soon, Robert, as well, because tomorrow was Sunday, the only day the miners didn't work.

Jenny started the fire again, using shavings from a piece of birch, chopping kindling from a larger log. When the little stove was glowing, she set the heavy cast-iron frying pan on top and sliced bits of bacon from a slab, browning them carefully. Then she poured bannock batter over them, and set the beans she'd cooked early that morning to warm. She'd found a sizable patch of edible berries near a small creek and made them into pies, mixing them with the dried apples they'd brought as part of their supply list. The pies were on the wooden table the men had hammered together, and Jenny felt proud and pleased, looking at the result of her labor.

The men had also made rough chairs and done a fine job of the two-seater outhouse, so now the campsite had the appearance of permanence. They'd promised that tomorrow they'd start on the cabins.

William and Carl had made an agreement with Joseph Ladue, whom they'd found to be a reasonable man. They'd put down a small amount of money for the land they were on, with a promise to pay it off when their claim proved profitable, or else to turn it back over to him, with the improvements they'd made, if they left Dawson.

Jenny was putting plates on the table when Mae came hurrying down the path from town, red hair blazing in the last of the sunlight. She'd grown even thinner since they'd come North, and the lines around her mouth and eyes had deepened, but she was enthusiastic as ever.

"Jenny, you'll never guess what!" She hurried the last few steps, smiling a thank-you for the mug of tea Jenny always had ready for her, setting the parcel of leftover food, which was part of her wages, on the wooden table and sinking down on a chair for a moment's rest.

Jenny joined her, loving these few moments before the men arrived. The work at the restaurant was hard, cooking, serving, cleaning up, and Mae was on her feet all day, but she was always cheerful, always full of some fascinating bit of gossip.

"I overheard two miners talking about Kitty," Mae announced. "That man she left Albert for, that Diamond Jim?"

"Aye?" Jenny nodded eagerly.

"Well, he has set her up as a dance hall girl in the Savoy Theater. He must not have as much gold as she thought he did, because now she's working for him."

"Never." Jenny was shocked. "What sort o' man sends his woman out to entertain other men?"

"The very kind our Kitty deserves," Mae declared with satisfaction, pursing her lips. "She'll get her own back for what she did to you and for breaking poor Albert's heart, you watch and see if she doesn't."

Kitty's meanness to her was in the past, but Jenny thought of Albert and shook her head. "He's still not himself, is our Albert. He's drinking his life away."

Albert hadn't set up a practice at dentistry. He'd stayed with them until his money arrived from Seattle, and then he'd moved into a room in town. He'd given them the bulk of his elaborate outfit, refusing to take anything for it.

Jenny and Mae fed him to try and make up for his generosity, and he came to visit every few days, but each time they saw him he reeked of alcohol. His nose was red, his eyes bloodshot and his grooming more haphazard with each visit.

"He'll have to know about Kitty. There are no secrets in this place," Mae said, draining her teacup. "I only hope he stays away from the Savoy. He doesn't seem the jealous type, but who knows?" She got to her feet. "Now, what needs done for supper?" She stirred the beans and lifted the cloth Jenny had put over the pies.

"Jenny, how brilliant of you. Berries and apple? Oh, yummm. The men are going to be over the moon when they see these."

Jenny smiled at Mae's enthusiasm. "I got a packet o' mail from home today." She took the bannock off the stove and sliced it into neat triangles.

"Jenny! And here I am going on about that awful Kitty."
Mae grabbed Jenny around the waist and did a whirling
two-step. "How wonderful. Quick now, tell me all. Are
your brothers well, and your father? Is your wicked stepmother ill with the grippe, as she deserves to be?"

Jenny giggled. She'd told Mae all about her family.
"Ye're that bad, Mae Sundstrom. They're all healthy, Nell
included." She told Mae about the puppy.

"Oh, I'd love to have a puppy," Mae said in a wistful tone.
"Maybe we can get one later on, when we're more settled."

"They're a terrible lot of trouble, are puppies," Jenny
said. "Almost as much work as a baby, what with their
chewing and making messes where they shouldn't."

"Well, of course I'd choose a baby any day over a puppy,
but it doesn't seem as if Carl and I are having much luck
in that regard." Mae busied herself setting out dishes on the
table and didn't look at Jenny.

"You're so lucky to be expecting. I know it's been hard
for you, and it's not getting much easier, what with all the
work there is here, but I'd give anything to be in your
shoes. I'm quite jealous, truth be known."

Jenny was surprised and touched. "I dinnae know ye
wanted a bairn, Mae."

"Of course I do." Mae smiled at Jenny. "I'd love to have
one soon, so our wee ones could grow up together."

Jenny grinned at her friend, feeling mischievous. "Ye do
ken what starts 'em, do ye no? Maybe ye just need more
practice at it?" Jenny knew Mae and Carl had a passionate marriage. Living in tents so close together, the two
women had few secrets from one another. She and Mae
were like sisters.

Mae giggled. "I'll be sure to suggest that to Carl."

They were still laughing when the men arrived, grimy and weary from their day's work on the claim, full of talk about the nuggets Robert told them came out of the claim he was working.

"Ve'll be next," Carl pronounced as they stripped to their undervests and washed in the water basins Jenny and Mae had warmed for them.

Jenny noticed that William wasn't as optimistic.

After the meal, they sat around the fire. Jenny wrapped a warm shawl around her shoulders and leaned against William. The nights were cold now, and everyone predicted snow very soon.

Mae told the men what she'd heard about Kitty.

"Daft bloody woman," William growled. "Albert's a fine man. She'd ha' done well fer hersel' if she'd settled wi' him."

Carl agreed, and then the men discussed the cabins they'd start building the following morning. Jenny wanted to tell William about her letters, but she wanted to be alone with him when she did. Finally, the fire burned down and everyone headed for their tents.

Burrowed under the warm quilts, held close in William's arms, she told him all the news from home.

"Does he know about the bairn?" William had one large hand cupped on Jenny's belly.

"He will when my letters reach him. But that may be a while—he'd no received any when this bundle was sent."

"He'll be put out wi' me when he learns I've brought ye to this place, lass. Yer da wasnae overly keen on lettin' ye wed me."

"He just dinnae want me to leave Scotland."

"He wanted ye tae wed fearsome auld Graham Cameron." Jenny giggled. That was the truth. Cameron's land adjoined Bruce's, and to her father it had seemed a good match.

"And do ye sometimes wish ye had, Jenny?"

William had never asked her that before.

"Wed Graham? Never." She thought back to the night she'd first laid eyes on William, resplendent in his kilt. He'd bowed low and asked her to dance a quadrille at Robina Macgregor's wedding feast.

He was a bonny dancer, and afterward, when he brought her a cup of ale and told her dashing tales of cowboys and cattle and land for the taking in America, where he'd spent the past four years and made a fortune working on the railroad, William had seemed the answer to her fervent prayer that she not be forced to wed dull old Graham Cameron, who was at that minute glowering at them from across the room as if Jenny was already his.

"And do ye ever wish ye'd never wed me, either, Jenny?"

She knew he was only half teasing. She thought of reassuring him, but then she blurted out the truth.

"Aye," she confessed, "on that cursed White Pass, I wished often I'd never laid eyes on ye, William Galloway. But now, I'm content. Or I will be when the cabin's built. I so long for solid walls around me."

"And ye shall have them, lassie." William yawned. "We'll begin at first light."

In a moment, he was snoring. Jenny lay curled against him. As his hand slackened and fell away from her abdomen, she was aware of a fluttering inside, a movement so tentative she wasn't sure at first she'd really felt it. But as she lay still, waiting, it came again, stronger now.

The baby was moving. *Her* baby was moving.

She waited, heart pounding, and when the tiny flutter

came again, and then again, Jenny felt a wave of powerful emotion wash over her, wonder that a living being could be growing in her belly, and for the first time, a feeling of profound love for this tiny creature.

Before this moment, the baby hadn't been real. When she first realized she was pregnant, it had been nothing but a terrible, worrying problem, the cause of violent illness, the reason for her weariness and lack of energy. And there was the fear that woke her sometimes in the small hours of the morning, the memory of her stepmother's terrible screams.

The fear was still there. It would be with her until the child was safely born, but now the fear wasn't only for herself. She thought now of her baby's safety, as well.

She considered waking William and telling him her news, but he couldn't feel what she did. The movement was too faint for someone else to detect. She lay still, waiting, dozing off, waking again when the fluttering came. For the moment, it was her secret, hers and the bairn's, and Jenny cherished it.

Because she'd been awake half the night, she overslept the next morning. William was in the habit of bringing her a cup of tea first thing, but this morning he'd obviously thought it better to let her rest.

Raised voices awakened her. Excited voices. She opened her eyes, aware of a strange muted light streaming in through the tent's canvas walls. And it was shockingly cold. She shivered as she got out of bed and tugged on her clothing, trying all the while to make sense of the scraps of sentences she heard.

She left her hair down, streaming over her shoulders, and clutched a wool shawl tight around herself as she opened the tent flap and gasped at the sight that awaited her.

"Snow," she breathed, reaching out a hand and letting the fat, cold drops melt on her skin. The world was white, covered in several inches of fluffy snow, with more floating down in thick clumps. The air was frigid, and the first lungful made her cough.

William heard her and came hurrying over, and one look at his pale and somber face told her something was terribly amiss.

She said, "William, what is it? What's wrong?"

"Jenny, there's bad tidings," he said. "Albert has shot the man called Diamond Jim, and then turned the gun on himself."

Chapter Eleven

"Oh, William, no." Shock and horror made Jenny stagger, and William came close and put an arm around her. "Is Albert alive? Is there any way we can help? Should we go to him?"

"Robert and Carl and I are goin' to see if there's aught we can do. A workmate o' Robbie's stopped by to tell us—he knew we were friends. He said Diamond Jim was dead, but he wasn't certain about Albert. He thought maybe they'd taken him to hospital."

The men hurried off and Jenny moved over to the cook tent and sat down heavily, feeling as if her legs wouldn't support her. It was relatively warm inside; the stove Albert had given them was roaring. Mae brought a mug of hot tea for Jenny and one for herself.

"A shame he didn't turn the gun on the one who

deserved it," Mae said bitterly. "If Albert lives, he'll have to stand trial for murder, and it's her fault, not his."

"Poor, poor Albert. If only he'd stayed here wi' us, mayhap we might have been able to talk sense to him." Jenny warmed her icy fingers on the steaming mug. The baby did its little feathery slide, but this was no time to confide the good news to Mae.

Snow swirled and melted outside, and the trees were laden with white frosting. It might have been beautiful, but Jenny couldn't appreciate it. All she could think of was Albert, maybe dying in this desolate corner of the world, far from all he understood and held dear. She wondered if she'd always associate snow with bad news.

"It might be best if he doesn't survive," Mae said in a hushed tone, and Jenny had to agree.

"There's hot porridge," Mae said, but Jenny couldn't eat.

"D'ye think she feels responsible at all, Mae?"

"Her?" Mae blew a raspberry and shook her head. "The likes of her don't know what responsible is. She's a selfish, cruel woman, and all she'll be upset about is having to find another foolish man to take her on." Mae was silent for a while, and then she said in a rush, "My own mother was very like Kitty. That's how I know exactly what she is. My mother ran off with a traveling salesman when I was six. I remember her standing at the door with her carpetbag, laughing and telling me to be sure and tell my dad she wasn't ever coming back. I knew she didn't care about me. I'd always known. By the time I was four she had me cooking and cleaning like a housemaid. My dad was heartbroken, though. In spite of how badly she treated him, he loved her. Just like Albert. Only Dad was lucky, he met Gladys and she was wonderful to both of us. She insisted I learn to read and write. It was really thanks to Gladys I got an education. She was the only real mother I ever knew."

"Ahh, Mae. Ye never told me. Here I've blathered on about Nell and never asked ye much about what sort o' childhood ye had. I'm that sorry for bein' so selfish. And sorry as well ye had to have a mother like Kitty."

"I didn't tell you to make you feel bad, Jenny. I just wanted you to know." Mae got up and stoked the stove with wood, then refilled their mugs with tea. "You're the best friend I've ever had. This entire trip would have been horrible without you."

"Or you, Mae. I thank God every night to have met ye and ha' ye as my friend."

Together, they cleared away the breakfast things. It was several hours before the men came back, and one look at their somber faces told Jenny the news was bad. Mae reached for her hand, and Jenny clutched at it.

"Albert died, poor man," William said with a heavy sigh. "We were wi' him when he passed, Doc Perry and Father Judge, as well. The doctor and the holy sisters did their best but Albert dinnae want to live. Perry said he's seen it before, when a man has no will to live and gives up."

Jenny began to cry, and so did Mae.

"We cannae send his body back to Seattle, so we'll bury him here," Robert said. "Albert was a Protestant. We arranged wi' Reverend Bates for a wee service tomorrow mornin', ten o'clock. As long as the Reverend is sobered up in time."

It was general knowledge that Bates preached more sermons drunk than he did sober. Like Dr. Perry, alcohol was the minister's downfall, although many said that Bates was much better at speaking when inebriated.

Perry, on the other hand, was useless at doctoring when he'd had too much.

"It must be done quickly before the ground freezes," Carl added. "We'll build him a box now."

The men bought lumber from the sawmill and spent the day fashioning a coffin. Jenny and Mae lined it with one of Jenny's linen sheets, and it was ready by the time darkness fell early that afternoon. While Carl finished the coffin, Robert and William made their way to the cemetery to dig Albert's grave. It was still cold and snowing, and Jenny wondered if she'd ever be warm again.

A heavy weight of sadness hung over the entire group all that day. She couldn't imagine it getting any colder than it already was, but overnight the snow stopped and the temperature plummeted far below freezing level. When she awoke the next morning, her hair was stuck to the pillow with frost from her breath and the floor of the tent was white. The air even inside the tent was so cold it hurt to breathe. In the cooking tent, the little stove turned cherry red with the wood they fed it, but a few feet away there was no heat at all. They ate a hurried breakfast and set off to Albert's funeral.

They made their way into town, and the men carried the coffin to the cemetery. Reverend Bates wasn't exactly sober, but he was able to conduct a brief service, mostly asking for forgiveness for Albert's grievous sins.

Bates, Dr. Perry and the five of them were the only ones at the graveside. It seemed that Diamond Jim had been a showy and popular figure in Dawson, and public sympathy was against Albert.

The cemetery was outside of town, on a lonely and barren hillside, and Jenny wept for this kind, gentle man being laid to rest so far from his family and friends.

Jenny had wondered if Kitty would show up, but there was no sign of her. Jenny shivered throughout the short Bible reading and the few words Bates spoke, standing with William on one side and Robert on the other. Carl kept a protective arm around Mae. Dr. Perry, a thin little wisp of a man, stood huddled inside a long black overcoat that looked two sizes too large for him.

William spoke when the reverend was done.

"Albert Fitzgerald was a kind, honorable and generous man," he began. "He was our good friend, and shall be sorely missed." And then, in his deep and stirring baritone, he quoted Scotland's favorite poet, Robbie Burns.

Should auld acquaintance be forgot,
And never brought to mind?
Should auld acquaintance be forgot,
And days of auld lang syne?
But seas between us braid hae roared,
Sin auld lang syne.
And there's a hand, my trusty friend,
And gie's a hand o'thine:
We'll tak' a cup o'kindness yet,
For auld lang syne.

There was silence when he finished. Jenny's chest and stomach hurt from sobbing, and she saw tears trickling from the men's eyes as they took up their shovels. The sound of the earth falling on the coffin had to be the loneliest sound on earth.

When the grave was filled, they hurried back to the campsite. Everyone had to go to work, and Jenny hurriedly fixed food for them to take with them.

Afterward, alone at the campsite, she spent the morning huddled under the bedcovers trying to get warm, alternately feeding the stove, and composing a sad letter to Bruce, telling him the story of Albert and Kitty. Every now and then she felt her baby move, which lifted her spirits—and made her sad at the same time. Albert's death had consumed everyone, and there hadn't been a convenient moment to tell William. She'd tell Bruce instead.

She wrote steadily for several moments, and when she looked up, she noticed there were icicles hanging from the tent flaps. It struck her then how vastly different her life was from what she'd envisioned when she wed. She'd imagined this life in the New World as one of, if not luxury, at least comfort. She'd never dreamed she'd be living in a canvas tent in the far North in the winter, with only a small woodstove for warmth. The terrible memory of the White Pass was always with her, and she knew that even should she want to leave, she'd have to go over it again. She was trapped here, as limited as she would be were she in jail.

She'd been faithful in her resolve to tell her father the absolute truth in her letters, but it was difficult to convey the depths of the cold and the extent of the isolation. It was something that needed to be experienced firsthand.

The stove needed wood again, and she crawled from the nest of blankets and shoved another length of wood into the voracious little beast.

She remembered William's poignant recitation at the graveside today, and the words of the poem played in her mind.

"Should auld acquaintance be forgot—" Would there come a time when her memories of Scotland grew faint, her longing for her father and brothers and her home gone from her memory for days or weeks at a time? It seemed impossible. But oh, what a blessing should it happen.

At some point every day, her heart grew heavy and sore in her chest with homesickness for Scotland. She still wore her gold locket day and night. Her dreams were often of her father and home, and waking on the other side of the world to this icy cold and the drudgery and terrible effort that daily existence demanded made her want to weep and never stop.

You've made yer bed, now lie in it.

Nell's vindictive voice was so clear in her mind that Jenny started and looked around. Of course the words had only been in her mind, reminding her that she had to make the best of it.

There was nothing else to do, Jenny knew. And although it was early afternoon, it was already growing dark, which meant that everyone would be home soon. She needed to get up and put on a pot of soup, make bannock, start the rice pudding.

And count her blessings? She thought of Albert, in his dark and icy grave, of Kitty, who'd caused the death of two men with her careless actions. And dear Mae, who longed for a baby, who spent long dreary hours waiting tables and washing dishes because she and Carl didn't have money. Then there was William, a good and honest man, even though he wasn't as attentive as she might like. And dear Robert, the best brother-in-law ever.

There were so many ways in which she was blessed, Jenny told herself firmly. She'd try and remind herself of that when the next wave of the loneliness overcame her.

Chapter Twelve

There was a delay in finding a suitable stovepipe, and then a winter storm made further building impossible, so it was mid-November before the two cabin roofs were finally on.

The morning they were to move from the tents into the cabins, Jenny and Mae were beside themselves with excitement. Living in the tents had been terribly hard these past weeks as the wind shrieked and the temperature dropped below freezing and then plummeted lower than Jenny dreamed a thermometer could go.

Every morning, hoarfrost covered the inside of the tent's canvas, and even buried beneath quilts in bed, it wasn't warm or even anything bordering on comfortable. Actually having a sturdy roof over her head and four log walls surrounding her made Jenny giddy. Mae had danced around the campfire the night before, clapping her hands when Carl and William announced the women could move into the cabins the following day.

The morning of the move was cold but sunny, and after a hurried breakfast, Carl and William fitted the chimney pipes to the new Empress cookstoves they'd just bought at an exorbitant price from an enterprising man who'd hauled a dozen of them over the Pass. Their claim had yet to produce more than a few ounces of gold, and William had loaned Carl the money for the stove, insisting that it would only be a matter of days before the claim proved itself.

But Jenny knew that William had serious doubts about their chances of striking it rich; he'd told her so in bed one night as they lay trying to get warm, huddled as close as two spoons. He whispered to her of the many men who worked themselves half to death, only to give up in defeat, selling off their supplies and heading back to civilization. He wasn't at all certain the claim they'd filed would pay out. It was pure luck, whether they hit pay dirt or not.

But Jenny didn't care about getting rich, not this morning. Her new home was a compact one-room structure, with a Yukon heater in the center of the room, and wonder of wonders, the shiny Empress, snugged against the back wall. In both cabins, the men had fashioned work shelves beside the cookstove with shelved cupboards below, and in the far corner of each room were the beds they'd made. There were root cellars out back of each cabin to store supplies. To Jenny, the small dwelling was a mansion.

The moment the stovepipe was in place and the door hung, the men hurried off to work the claim. The ground would soon be too frozen to dig and they had to take advantage of every minute.

Alone in her new house, Jenny lit both the Yukon and the cookstove, piling each lavishly full of wood, and in only a few moments, the well-chinked little cabin was deliciously warm. For the first time in weeks, she was able to take off her coat and her woolen shawl. She hummed under her breath as she arranged dishes and food on the shelves, made up the bed and strung up a curtain to partition off a bedroom. She put a pretty cloth on the table and set a pot of water boiling for tea. Then she hurriedly made a pan of biscuits, thrilled with the oven on the Empress.

The moment they were out of the oven, she wrapped her shawl around her and stepped outside. Mae's cabin was only fifty feet away. Jenny walked over and knocked on the sturdy door. When Mae answered, she said, "Missus Sundstrom, I'm your new neighbor, Jenny Galloway. I wondered would you care ta join me for a cuppa tea?"

Mae's eyes danced, and she suppressed a giggle. "Why, I'm so pleased to meet you, Mrs. Galloway. I'd be delighted, just step inside while I get my shawl."

Mae had done exactly the same as Jenny. Both stoves were glowing, and the cupboards were neatly stacked with pots and pans. A colorful shawl covered the table, and in the center was a jar with a few green sprigs from an evergreen. The room was cozy and inviting.

"Oh, Mae, it's that bonny in here."

"And warm, can you believe it? I'm actually warm, Jenny. I thought my bones would stay frozen till summer came. I felt as if they'd break like twigs if I bent over too fast."

Being so thin, Mae felt the cold even more than Jenny had. She stoked both stoves with wood and damped them down. Then she wrapped a woolen shawl around her, and they hurried to Jenny's cabin.

Mae looked around. "I must say, Mrs. Galloway, you have a beautiful home."

"Very like yer own, wouldn't ye say?"

They wrapped their arms around one another and giggled like schoolgirls. When Mae was seated at the table, sipping her tea, she said, "Remember what you told me about practicing?"

"I don't recall." Mystified, Jenny frowned and shook her head.

Mae's cheeks were fiery red with excitement, and her eyes were dancing. "You said that maybe Carl and I weren't getting enough practice to start a baby. Well, guess what?"

Recognition dawned. "Ye're not—oh, Mae, are you—?" Jenny leaped to her feet, spilling her tea in the process. *"Ye're expectin'?"*

"I am. Our babies will play together after all."

"Oh, Mae, I'm that glad for you. And for me, as well. D'ye know when?" Jenny grabbed a rag and mopped at the spill.

"I think early July."

"July? And mine's in March, near as I can figure. Three months apart is all they'll be. Ach, I can hardly fathom it— it's a miracle."

Mae's thin cheeks were flushed with joy. "It is that. I was beginning to think I was barren. Carl's beside himself, he wanted this so much."

Always practical, Mae began planning. "We'll have to get the men started making cradles. And I wonder if there's any flannel for diapers in this town. We'll have to get busy hemming nappies and making gowns. And knitting, heaven help us, we'll have to knit some blankets and woolies or the poor little things will freeze. But I'm not very good at knitting, are you?"

Jenny was. She'd knitted countless small bonnets and coats for her brothers, as well as socks for her father. "I'll do the knitting if you sew. I'm no a seamstress by any means. And I'm ashamed to say I've not even considered all that yet." Jenny put a hand on the swelling at her middle, and the baby kicked hard, as if to reprimand her for not planning better for its arrival.

"We'll scour the town tomorrow for wool and suitable fabric," Mae decided. "I'm lucky, I'm not sick at all yet, touch wood."

"And I'm over it, God be praised." All of a sudden it dawned on Jenny that she was no longer alone in this endeavor. The deep-seated fear she'd carried along like heavy baggage eased a little. She and Mae were both facing childbirth in this rough and raw environment, and somehow, with two of them it no longer seemed as terrifying. They'd get through it; they had each other.

"I should go home and put wood on my fires," Mae declared. "And tea will be at my place tomorrow, I have two more days before I go back to work. I told Eli I needed time to get settled in my house. Now I'm going to set a batch of sourdough. The cook at the café gave me some starter and told me how to do it. I'll bring you over a cupful and you can try, as well. Carl and William will think they've died and gone to heaven when they smell fresh bread baking."

Jenny felt as if she, too, had found a piece of heaven. For the first time, instead of numbing fear at the thought of childbirth, she felt a glimmer of anticipation at the thought of her and Mae with their babies. She envisioned warm sunny days, and fat little angels, and her and Mae sharing the joys and the problems. All they had to do was get safely through the winter in their snug little houses.

Chapter Thirteen

By the time December arrived, Jenny had learned that housekeeping in the North was a task far harder and more frustrating than any work she'd ever done. The Northern winter had settled in with a vengeance, harsh and icy cold and worst of all, dark. There were only two hours of daylight in early December, and as Christmas neared, even that window narrowed. That meant the paraffin lamps needed cleaning and filling every day, and the smell permeated both clothing and bedding.

The creek froze over, and every drop of water had to be melted. The stoves needed stoking every half hour because the wood was soft and burned quickly, and although William and Robert chopped and stacked huge piles for her, there was only so much she could keep inside the small cabin. Jenny had to run out and replenish her supply a dozen times a day, which meant donning boots, coat and mitts against the bone-searing cold.

Wash day was a horror. There was ice to melt to get wash water, the endless scrubbing on the board to get the soil out, and then the wet clothes froze the moment they were hung on the line. They had to be brought in, stiff as boards, stacked by the stove to thaw so they could be handled, and then strung up all over the cabin until they dried, which meant two or even three days with the cabin damp and cold no matter how much wood she piled into the heater and the cookstove.

Each of Jenny's fingertips split and bled, and her knuckles were permanently scabbed from the washboard. Cooking was a time-consuming chore as everything in the root cellar had to be thawed before it could be used. Knitting, which should have been a pleasant pastime, ended up being a gigantic task—as William's socks and sweaters wore out and needed mending and replacing—and she'd barely even started the baby clothes.

As Christmas neared, Jenny knitted more and more frantically, because she wanted to have socks and mitts to give Robert and William and Carl. The items were not only practical, they were necessary. Her knitting needles flew, but she found she was so bone weary that many times when she sat down to knit she fell asleep.

Somehow, by Christmas Eve, she managed to get everything finished. She'd made a pretty blue scarf for Mae by unraveling her own favorite sweater, and she was pleased with the stack of mitts and socks for the men.

Mae was no longer working. The café wasn't busy because miners who'd counted on striking gold found themselves short of money, unable to afford the exorbitant restaurant prices. Eli was apologetic about letting Mae go, but as she told Jenny, it was a blessing, because in her third month of pregnancy she'd become horribly ill, vomiting not only in the morning but most of each day and even during the night. Always thin, she grew so emaciated and weak everyone was worried about her. Carl insisted she go to Dr. Perry, but Mae refused. Jenny suspected it was because there was little money to pay him, although Mae insisted there was no need for a doctor to tell her she was suffering a particularly bad bout of morning sickness.

It had been snowing off and on for a week, but Christmas Eve day was cold and clear. Despite the bad weather, the men had worked their claims every day, and were working them today, as well. So far, they'd taken out just enough gold to live on, but the claims hadn't yielded the riches they'd hoped for. William was working both his and Robert's, because Robert was still working for wages from Belinda Krauss. Her claim was a lucky one, and Jenny could see how it depressed Carl and William, hearing about the riches taken out of the Krauss workings. But Robert's wages were a godsend.

Jenny had invited everyone for Christmas Eve dinner. She'd perfected making sourdough bread, and she'd traded an Indian woman three crusty big loaves for a wild turkey, which she stuffed with rice and wild onions. It was in the oven now, and she checked it anxiously, basting it with its own juices. The smell made her ravenous.

She'd been determined they'd have this one meal without beans, which they'd eaten nearly every day since arriving in Dawson. Butter, milk, fresh vegetables and sugar were in short supply. They cost a small fortune, but even if there was money enough to buy them, the stores were running out.

Jenny had hoarded several precious tins of butter, and she'd set one out for today's meal. She formed bread dough into buns and set it to rise, and then fashioned pies out of dried apples, being lavish with the sugar for once—they'd just have to make do without it until spring.

The table was laid with the white linen she'd been given as a wedding gift. It was the first time she'd used it.

Jenny arranged evergreen boughs around tall candles as a centerpiece and the gifts she'd made were wrapped in newsprint and tied with red ribbon. They were tucked under the small evergreen in the corner. Robert had cut it for her last Sunday, and Jenny decorated it with acorns and wild berries strung on thread to make garlands.

She stood back now to admire her handiwork. The cabin was warm and cozy and festive, and she felt excited and proud of herself.

"It'll do." She nodded, giving an excited little skip. The baby heaved around, and Jenny grinned and patted her protruding belly. "Dinnae fret, my dearie," she soothed. "Ye'll be old enough next Christmas to ha' a wee taste o' the turkey." She'd fallen into the habit of talking to the baby when she was alone. She knew it was mad, but there was no one around to hear her.

The turkey was done and she was taking the buns out of the oven when Mae arrived.

"Happy Christmas," she sang out as Jenny hurried to relieve her of an armload of food and wrapped packages so Mae could take off her coat and shawl. "Oh, Jenny, everything looks beautiful, and it smells heavenly in here."

"Thank ye. This can't ever be fruitcake?" Jenny sniffed at the heavy fragrant loaf. "How ever did ye manage that, Mae? And steamed pudding, oh, we always had that at

home at Christmas." She set the food down on the cupboard
and turned to embrace her friend, trying not to be alarmed
at Mae's fragility. "And ye weren't supposed to raise a
finger, sick as ye are."

"Balderdash, I can't lie about like a lady in my satin
nightdress doing nothing, now can I? Eli gave me a bag of
dried fruit and nuts as payment for a shirt I sewed for him,
so naturally I thought fruitcake and pudding."

Mae's face was painfully thin, but her wide grin was the
same as always. "And before you ask, yes, I'm actually
feeling a bit better. Hungry. Now what can I do to help?"

The two women put the finishing touches on the meal,
and it wasn't long before William and Robert arrived,
knocking snow off their boots outside the door, bringing
in a rush of icy air as they crowded into the small cabin and
took off their heavy coats and hats and gloves.

"Ahhh, it smells that good in here," William said. "Carl's
just gone over home to wash up. He'll be here straightaway."

"Happy Christmas, bonny lassies," Robert said with a
wide smile. "I'd gie ye each a Christmas kiss, but I'm no
exactly clean."

"Here ye go." Jenny had curtained off a corner near the
door as a wash place, and she took a kettle of hot water over
to the men and a spare towel for Robert. William was
always filthy from the diggings when he came in, and
Robert was as bad. They stripped off their shirts, washed
up and changed into clean clothing in the curtained-off
bedroom, and Carl arrived just as they reemerged, bringing
chairs so everyone would have a place to sit.

"We'll hae a wee dram to celebrate the season," William
declared, pouring whiskey for the men and sherry for the
women. "To absent friends and family," he said, lifting his

glass. Jenny sipped the sweet liquor with tears in her eyes, thinking of her father and brothers, and of Albert. He should have been here with them tonight. She'd heard nothing of Kitty, and neither had Mae.

The food was ready and they gathered around the table. William asked the blessing. "Thank ye for good health, Lord, for good friends, and a sturdy roof o'er our heads. Bless this fine food, and all those less fortunate. And for the promise o' new life, we're verra grateful, Lord."

Under the cover of the tablecloth, Jenny cupped her hand over her belly and felt the baby's movement. She met Mae's eyes across the table, and the smile they shared was blissful. Carl and William were having a discussion about some piece of mining equipment they needed, but Robert had caught the interchange between the women. Jenny saw a wistful expression in his green eyes. He was a fine man, was Robert Galloway. Surely there'd be a woman who'd appreciate him.

After dinner, which everyone praised lavishly, Robert took out his harmonica and played carols, and they all sang. Toward midnight, they opened their gifts.

The men were greatly pleased with their socks and mitts. Mae had made them each large white linen handkerchiefs with their names embroidered on a corner. She wound the scarf Jenny had knitted around her throat, exclaiming at its softness and beauty.

"It's the same color as that sweater of yours, the blue one I always admire," she said.

"I was that fortunate to find the yarn," Jenny lied as she unwrapped her package from Mae. Inside was a small meticulously cross-stitched picture of flowers done on burlap. Underneath it were the words, Friends Like You Mean A

Day's Glad Start, With A Brighter Brain And A Lighter Heart. It was stretched on stiff board and carefully framed in twigs.

"Oh, Mae." Tears welled up and overflowed. "Oh, dear friend, I'm that touched. Thank ye so very much. It'll hang on me wall forever."

"Carl did the framing for me." It was obvious Mae was thrilled with the pleasure her gift brought.

They lingered until the small hours of the morning, telling tales of other Christmases. They all agreed that none had been as special as this one.

When Mae and Carl put on their coats and headed out the door, Mae looked up at the sky and said in a breathless voice, "Oh, come out and see the lights, they're wonderful tonight."

Since that first time on the trail, Jenny had often stood in awe and watched the Northern Lights play across the night sky, but she'd never seen them as majestic and vivid as they were tonight. William wrapped his arms around her from behind, warming her with his body, and they all stood gazing up at the heavens, spellbound.

Brilliant green light played in bands across the dark sky, and ribbons of pink and yellow wound across it, brighter and then dimmer, wider and then narrowing.

"It's the angels putting on a show for us," Mae whispered. It was as good an explanation as any.

Goose bumps rose on Jenny's skin, more from the lights than the cold, but William noticed and turned them toward their door. Calling good-night to Carl and Mae, they went inside.

Jenny spread quilts and pillows on the bear rug for a bed for Robert as the two men brought in wood for the night. As they stoked the stove, Jenny went behind the curtain and put on her warm flannel nightdress and crawled into bed. She was weary from the long, busy day, but she was also happy.

William and Robert talked in low voices about money and equipment and how to tackle the next excavation at the mine, things that concerned men. Their voices were soothing, and she lay snuggled in the bed, drowsily thinking about her first Christmas as a married woman.

Tomorrow she'd hang Mae's wonderful gift. There was enough leftover food that she wouldn't have to worry about cooking. The men had fashioned a sled, and they talked about going to a nearby hill and trying it out. While they were gone, she'd write a long letter to her father. Mail hadn't left Dawson for some time, and none had arrived. She knew Bruce would send her Christmas greetings; they'd arrive whenever the next mail did, and she had that to look forward to.

A few more months of cold and darkness, and spring would be here, she reminded herself. She imagined green buds bursting on trees, grass instead of snow, blue skies and sunshine that lasted as long as the darkness did now. She'd plant a garden, preserve the harvest, make certain there was plenty of food for the following winter. This one was challenging, but life would get easier. She just had to endure until spring came.

Contented, warm and happy, she drifted off to sleep.

By the last day in February, Jenny could barely remember how it felt to be comfortable or to feel a spring in her step. Her back ached, her chapped, sore hands throbbed from washing clothes the day before, and dinner would have to be soup made from dried peas again. She sighed at the thought. She was that tired of peas and beans, she could hardly force them down. She'd begun to dream of greens, lettuce, kale, even leeks and cabbage. There were none to be had. Food was in frighteningly short supply, and greens of any sort were nonexistent.

She still had a decent supply of tea, and she'd made a pot for her and Mae this morning. But Jenny couldn't allow herself to drink much of it because the baby was pressing on her bladder, and she had to run to the privy so often it seemed a waste of time to even take off her coat.

As for her feet, they were so swollen she could barely lace up her boots. She wore William's soft carpet slippers in the house, longing for the time when she'd get her body back again.

Mae, on the other hand, was blooming. The sickness had passed, and she'd sprouted a round little bump that she was proud of. Sitting at Jenny's table this morning, she warmed her hands on her mug and did her best to make Jenny smile before she picked up the small gown she was finishing.

"Just think, only two more months and yours will be outside instead of in. No more bashing your ribs and turning somersaults when you're trying to sleep. I'm the one who'll be left moaning then." Mae's baby was moving, which thrilled her.

Jenny rubbed goose grease into her hands and picked up her knitting needles. "I'm tired of it all. How do women go through this over and over?" She felt particularly dispirited today. William had told her the night before that he was giving up on gold mining come spring. There was talk of a railroad to be built from Skagway over the Pass to Lake Bennett, and being a qualified steam engineer, William was certain he could get a job with the developers.

After the baby came, Jenny would have the choice of

traveling back over the Pass with him and settling in Skagway or staying here in Dawson. Either choice meant that she'd not see William for weeks, or more probably months, at a time. She couldn't say anything to Mae yet, because William wanted to be certain of his plans before he broke the news to Carl or to Robert, but the prospect depressed her.

"I knew a woman who had twenty-three children," Mae was saying, carefully fashioning the ties on the back of the miniscule gown. "She said it gets easier as you go along. I suppose what happens is you just get used to it."

"With twenty-three how could she remember what it was like wi'out a bairn in her? And what could the poor lass look like after that many?"

Jenny had only a small, wavy mirror, but she could see enough in it to know that her face was puffy, her eyes dull, her hair without luster. It was a wonder William still wanted her in his bed. He did, though, and she was glad, because something about being with child had turned her insatiable when it came to loving.

She wanted to ask Mae if expecting had made her hungry for Carl's loving, but of course she didn't. She and Mae had skirted around discussions of that sort, although they'd never addressed such things openly.

Still, Jenny was curious. Was it an ordinary effect of pregnancy, or was she totally unnatural?

"Bein' this pregnant makes me frachetty," she said, laying down the knitting. "I wouldna want to spend most of me life this way."

"Or me. But three or four, maybe even half a dozen, that would suit me fine."

Jenny snorted. "I'm thinkin' mebbe two at most. About five years apart."

Mae giggled. "You'll change your mind once you're through this rough patch. Besides, I don't think it's something you can decide on."

"Aye, yer right there. Although I've wondered about the fancy women. How is it they don't get caught?" She was thinking of Kitty.

"I've heard they know ways to stop it from happening. And there's those who'll help them get rid of a child, but a lot of the poor women die in the process." Mae's mouth tightened. "And then there's some that richly deserve to die, and don't."

"Hae ye heard anythin' about her?" Jenny didn't have to name names. They were talking about Kitty.

"She's working as a percentage girl at the Savoy. She gets a cut of what they charge for drinks and dancing, but I'm sure she earns much more on her back after hours."

"I wonder does she ever think of poor Albert?"

Mae snorted. "Not that baggage. She doesn't think of anyone but herself."

But Kitty had been kind to her on the boat, Jenny remembered, even though it was an offhand type of kindness which involved having poor Albert bring tea and biscuits in the morning.

"Bein' a fancy woman cannae be a bed o' roses," Jenny remarked. "Ye must hae to go wi' whoever asks ye, and many o' the miners are that rough and dirty."

Mae snorted. "You won't catch me feeling sorry for the likes of her."

The talk veered to more pleasant things—the tiny sweater Jenny was knitting, the stack of diapers they'd hemmed, the number of gowns a baby needed.

Mae went home soon afterward, and Jenny forced herself to put a pot of soup on and bring in firewood. It took incredible effort, and her stomach was roiling so she couldn't eat anything. Her back was hurting something fierce; it had been all day. In the early afternoon she lay down on the bed and fell quickly into a fitful sleep.

She woke with a cry of agony when a small pain in her abdomen swelled instead of subsiding. It was already dark, but she'd forgotten to wind the clock beside the bed and it had run down, so she had no idea what time it might be.

She tried to sit and realized there was a pool of sticky wet warmth between her legs, and panic seized her when she found it was bright red blood.

"The bairn," Jenny gasped. "It's coming, and it's too early."

She had to get Mae. She struggled off the bed, half falling, and managed to shove some towels inside her pantaloons. She shoved her feet into William's slippers, unable to get her shawl around her properly. She managed to stagger to the door, bending double as the pain intensified to unbearable proportions.

Sweat broke out on her forehead. Shouldn't there be time between? She remembered her stepmother in labor. Certainly the pains had started much less violently than this. There'd been time to prepare the bed, go for the midwife.

She opened the door of the cabin and stumbled outside. Somehow, gasping and staggering, she made it across the short distance to Mae's door. She didn't bother to knock, but when she opened the latch, the cabin was dark and empty.

Too late, Jenny remembered that Mae had told her she was walking into town to see if she could find any blue embroidery thread to finish the tiny gowns she was sewing.

Panic grew along with the pain, which now became an all-consuming animal, tearing her apart.

She was going to die. Gasping and moaning, Jenny knew she couldn't make it back to her own cabin. She had to lie down. She doubted she could even get across the room to the bed in the far corner.

Shuddering with a combination of icy cold and utter terror, Jenny managed to shove the door closed, shutting out the cold before she sank to the floor in front of the heater. Mae had woven a rag rug and spread it there, but still the chill from the floorboards penetrated Jenny's clothes, wet from the blood.

Jenny lay shuddering, rolled in a ball around her rigid belly. She wouldn't have believed the pain could get any worse, but it did. She screamed and writhed in agony as hot daggers tore through her back and abdomen, and in the seconds between, she prayed desperately.

She was barely conscious of Mae bending over her, holding a candle.

"Jenny, oh, Jenny love, hold on, my dear. I'm going to wrap blankets around you and then go for help."

"No. Dinnae leave me, *please,* Mae," she gasped. "Dinnae leave me, I'll die here alone."

"But I don't know what to do." Usually low, Mae's voice was a tinny shriek. "I've got to get help. Your baby's coming too fast and I don't know what to do."

Another wave of agony swept over Jenny before she could reply. Through a haze of red, she thought she heard Mae at the door of the cabin, shrieking for help at the top of her lungs.

Afterward, Jenny learned that an old trapper had heard Mae's screams and gone running for Dr. Perry. Unfortunately, Perry had been drinking for days, and it took over two hours before he sobered up enough to get on a horse and come to Mae's cabin.

By then, William and Carl had come home from work, and Jenny was clean and washed, nestled in a nest of blankets on Mae's bed, shivering uncontrollably from shock and blood loss.

Grief would come later. Her tiny, dead baby boy was lying on the kitchen table, wearing a gown with blue embroidery, wrapped in one of the small white blankets Jenny had knitted for him.

Chapter Fourteen

For Jenny, one horror built on another in the days that followed. Her baby, whom William named Jamie, couldn't be buried until spring thaw because the earth was too deeply frozen. He had to lie in a shack at the back of the hospital with other bodies, also waiting to be buried, and Jenny feared she'd go mad, thinking of that little body abandoned there. William and Robert made him a wooden casket, beautifully carved and finished, which Jenny insisted they line with pale blue satin cut from the skirt of her wedding gown.

She was terribly ill after Jamie's birth, both emotionally and physically. She couldn't seem to cry for her lost baby. She felt frozen inside, weak as a kitten from blood loss, sick at heart. Her breasts filled with milk, which seemed a cruel joke when there was no baby to suckle them. They became inflamed, hard as the frozen ground but hot with fever.

Jenny was so angry and bitter toward Dr. Perry, she wouldn't tolerate him anywhere near her. Shamefaced and apologetic for not being sober when Jenny needed him, he sent one of the nuns from the hospital, Sister Pauline, and the sister took charge immediately.

"Hot and cold compresses, morning and evening," Sister Pauline said. "You have milk fever, child, you must take care of yourself." She applied the compresses, making Jenny grind her teeth and cry out from the pain.

Sister Pauline then wound long strips of a wide bandage around Jenny's painfully tender, grotesquely swollen breasts. She pulled the bandages tight to the chest wall, and Jenny bit her lips and panted to keep from screaming. "It'll take a week to subside, try not to drink overmuch."

When William was at work, Mae took care of Jenny's cabin as well as her own, stoking the fires, making pots of soup, washing the dishes and the soiled clothing. She was there now, paying close attention to what Sister Pauline said.

Mae said, "She's not drinking or eating, Sister." She didn't add that Jenny wasn't talking much, either.

Sister Pauline patted Jenny's hand and sighed. "You have to try to get beyond this, my dear, for the sake of your husband and yourself. Losing a little one is a terrible thing, but you must remember it is God's will. And there will be other babies. You're young, Mrs. Galloway. This pain will fade with time."

Jenny turned her face to the wall and kept it there until after Sister Pauline left. Then she said to Mae in a stony voice, "I dinnae want that woman in this house ever agin'. She knows nothin'. She's never laid wi' a man or lost a bairn."

Mae sighed. "She's only trying to help, Jenny. We all

are. You have to forgive us when we don't know what to do for you or what to say to comfort you."

Jenny didn't say so, but the only person she wanted comfort from was William, and it wasn't forthcoming. She knew he blamed her for the loss of his firstborn son. Not that he said so. He didn't have to. Jenny knew from the polite and distant way he acted, the silences, the things he didn't say, the way he turned away from her at night in their bed.

And she knew he was right. Losing Jamie *was* her fault. She'd insisted on coming here over that cursed White Pass, she'd begged and pleaded with William not to send her back. He'd given in, against his better judgment. And their son had died as a result. It was something she'd have to find a way to live with for the rest of her life, but for now, she couldn't see how.

Breakup came early that spring, in late March.

When it was possible to dig, William and Robert made a small grave up on the hillside, not far from where Albert lay. The day was blustery, with an icy wind blowing from the North. Jenny huddled in her coat and shawl, knowing it would ease the painful knot in her chest if only she could weep, but the tears didn't come. Mae stood on one side, William on the other, but she hardly knew they were there. All she was conscious of was the tiny wooden box set in the raw hole of this foreign earth.

The reverend read from the Bible. When he was done, Jenny wondered if William would speak, as he'd done at Albert's funeral. She hoped he would say something that would ease the pain.

But when she looked at him, she saw tears trickling down his cheeks. He didn't wipe them away. Instead, he stepped forward and bent over to place his right hand, palm down, on the top of the tiny casket.

Jenny couldn't stand any more. She couldn't bear to hear the earth falling on her baby's coffin. She turned and almost ran down the hill, to the wagon William had borrowed to bring them all here. Mae came after her, and together they sat on the wagon seat and waited until the men came. Jenny rocked back and forth in silent agony, and Mae wept.

In bed that night, Jenny couldn't stand the distance any longer. "William, I'm that sorry," she choked out, her agony overcoming her silence. "I— I know I should have listened when ye told me it wasn't safe fer me ta come here. I should hae gone back to Seattle, the way ye wanted."

She had to clear her throat before she could go on. "But wishin' can't change what is. Will ye no forgive me? *Please,* William."

He sighed and didn't answer for several endless minutes. When he did, there was no warmth in his tone or his words.

"It's no a matter of forgiveness, Jenny. Forgiveness willnae bring the wee boy back, will it? The loss of me son is tearin' me heart in two. It was no a wise thing, climbin' o'er that cursed mountain, an' you wi' the baby startin' in ye. I knew ye should go back, I told ye so, but ye're that stubborn."

His words were like lashes on an open wound. She curled into a ball with her back toward him and lay as if frozen to stone. She couldn't sleep, that night or the nights that followed.

Things didn't improve between them. William remained polite and distant, like a stranger. The following week, a letter arrived confirming his new job as an engineer with the railway which was being built from Skagway to Lake Bennett.

The following day, he packed his gear. He gave Jenny money.

"Robbie'll see ye have whatever ye need. He'll be workin' the claim while I'm away. He's found lodgin' in town wi' two other single men, so he'll be close should ye need him. I'll be back when I can, but it's a long journey. We'll talk then about whether or no ye want to move to Skagway."

The kiss he gave her was perfunctory. He shouldered his pack and walked out the door.

Jenny had the feeling he was pleased to be leaving.

Robert came by that evening. He chopped a pile of wood, emptied ashes from the stove and carried in buckets of water from the stream. When he was done, Jenny made them dinner.

"This is good, Jenny." He lifted another forkful of the meat pie she'd concocted from tinned beef. The supply boats had arrived, so there was more choice now, not that she cared for herself. She still had no appetite.

Her dresses were loose on her, her arms thin. She'd lost strength along with weight; she had to struggle now with the heavy wood and pails of water.

"Carl and I hae great plans for the claims," he told her. "We'll surprise Willie when he gets back. We'll hit a rich stream o' ore and be up to our elbows in gold dust, see if we don't. Serve him right fer goin' off to build a bloody railroad, hey?"

Jenny knew he was making an effort on her behalf, trying to make her smile. "Have ye ever given more thought to the brewery ye want to start, Robbie?"

"Nay." He shook his head. "Although here would be the place, what wi' the miners and their liken' fer the drink. Mebbe when we strike it rich, lass. Then I'll be a gentleman o' leisure, free to do what I please."

She wondered would the day ever come when he'd balk at doing William's bidding. He was so good-natured, William took advantage of him, or so it seemed to her.

Robert was kind and gentle. He helped her with the dishes and made sure there was kindling for morning. Ready to go out the door, he turned and said in a concerned voice, "And are ye feelin' any better in yourself, Jenny? Ye've grown overthin, and ye're pale. I'm that worried about ye, lass. Is there ought I can do to help?"

His voice and William's were nearly identical. If only her husband had said those words to her. She looked at Robert's handsome face, his green eyes also like William's, but gentler, warm and caring, anxious about her well-being. Robert had loving eyes.

"Aye, Robbie, I am better. Thank ye fer asking." It was a lie she'd told many times in the past weeks whenever anyone asked, but tonight the words were no sooner out of her mouth than a wrenching sob rose in her throat, taking her by surprise. She clapped both hands over her mouth to hold it in, but another came, and another.

It felt as if something hard had suddenly cracked open inside her chest, and the tears poured out like rain, tears that she hadn't been able to shed for so long, for months, ever since her poor wee baby was born. They were physically painful, hurting her chest and stomach, but she could no more hold them back than stop her breath. The sobs grew harder, tearing at her ribs, ripping her throat, breaking her heart. She could hear the high keening sound she was making, and it embarrassed her, but she couldn't stop.

"There, there, lassie." Robbie took her arm and gently led her to the table. "That's the way, let it out." He helped her sit, found her a handkerchief, crouched at her feet. "There, there," he murmured, awkwardly patting her shoulder. "Let it come, Jenny. Do you good to cry it out, lass."

She couldn't stop, and after a while she gave up trying. She cried until her throat was raw, her skin scalded. The sounds she made echoed from the corners of the cabin, raw, terrible cries that didn't sound like her at all. Her burning eyes would barely open, her cheeks were stiff from salt.

Robert brought a cold washcloth and she held it to her face, and still she cried. Her chest ached and she wondered in a panic if she'd ever be able to stop. She kept expecting him to leave, because she knew William hated it when she cried, but Robert stayed. He knelt beside her, took her hand and held it cradled between both of his. He waited patiently, rewetting the cloth from time to time, smoothing her hair back when it stuck to her cheeks.

And finally it was over. Her breath hiccuped and she blew her nose on the fresh hankie he presented. She drew in several sobbing breaths, and the tension in her body eased. She slumped back in her chair.

"Better now?"

She nodded, unable to speak. She was exhausted, drained, wrung dry. Her eyes were so swollen she could barely see. She felt dizzy, but the horrible weight of guilt and sorrow had eased.

"Best lay your head down, lass. Sleep will do ye good." He got to his feet, put a log in the stove and turned the damper down, then patted her shoulder one last time and headed for the door.

Just before he reached it, she cleared her throat and managed to croak, "Robbie? Thank ye, Robbie. For—for stayin' wi' me."

He gave her his sweet smile. "No thanks needed. See ye in the mornin', Jenny." The door closed gently behind him.

She staggered to the bed and managed to get her clothing off and her gown on. She crawled under the quilts and slept for fourteen hours, and then she got up only to light the fire and visit the outhouse.

She was dimly aware that Robert came by, stoked the fire, made her tea and left again. For four days, Jenny slept twenty hours out of every twenty-four. On the fifth day, she woke up ravenous. Mae had brought her a loaf of bread and some soup and left it on the counter, and she ate every scrap. She warmed water, bathed and washed her hair, trembling with weakness. Mae or Robert had left her sourdough starter, and she added flour, kneaded it and set a batch of bread to rising.

When the cabin was tidy and the bread in pans baking, Jenny took her writing case and sat down at the table.

"Dearest Papa," she began in a shaky hand unlike her own.

I have sad news. My dear wee baby was born too soon and didn't live. His name was Jamie. I held him only for a moment but he was beautiful with dark hair and I think a forehead like yours, Papa.

Tears came again, but these were gentle tears, sad and accepting. She wrote about the funeral, and William's new job building a railroad.

As always, telling Bruce what was happening in her life took some of the pain out of her heart. Writing cleansed and healed her heart, and made it possible to go on.

Chapter Fifteen

Mae's labor was short, a scant two hours, and she was clutching Jenny's hand and screaming, nearly breaking the bones, when her baby girl popped like a cork from between her legs, howling even before the umbilical cord could be tied and cut.

The baby was small, but fully formed and loud. She had a crop of hair as red as her mother's, and her outraged shrieks made both women laugh through their relieved tears. Even the red-eyed doctor smiled. Jenny had run for him when Mae's pains began.

"She's a fine, noisy specimen," he declared, packing up his bag, wincing when he bent over. "That'll be twenty-five dollars," he said, although as far as Jenny could see he hadn't done a thing except catch the baby and cut the cord.

Jenny saw the look of concern on Mae's face, and she ran

to her cabin and took the money out of the generous amount William had left her the last time he was home. She shoved it at the doctor and hurried him out of Mae's cabin.

Mae looked up at her, thin face glowing. "Thank you, Jenny. Carl will see you get the money back."

"Nay, it's me welcome gift for this sweet wee babe," Jenny insisted, cradling Mae's daughter in her arms.

"It's too much, Jenny. Carl will want to pay you back."

"He cannae return a gift, it would no be polite," Jenny said, glad that at least money wasn't a problem for her and William. He'd quickly been made a supervisor on the railroad, and he told her in his infrequent letters that he was making more money than he ever had before.

Carl, on the other hand, was still working long days on his claim, barely making a living wage but still hoping against hope that it would prove out and make him rich.

She handed the baby reluctantly to Mae. Holding her had made Jenny realize how hungry she'd been to hold a warm, squalling bairn.

"What's her name to be?"

"Sophia, after Carl's mother."

"Sophia Sundstrom. Bonny wee Sophia," Jenny crooned, leaning over to kiss the scrunched-up little face.

Jenny had sent word for Carl to come home, and they heard him now, hurrying up to the door. He opened it hesitantly, his face rigid with fear as he took in the blood-stained sheets Jenny had stripped off the bed and set outside the door to take home and wash.

"Mae?" It came out in a high-pitched squeak. "My Mae, is she—?" He gulped and stood swaying in the doorway.

Jenny smiled and gestured toward the bed. "She's fine. Come see fer yerself."

"Carl, dearest, come and meet our daughter." Mae held the baby up, and he looked down at the wrinkled, red face with an expression of awe.

"Ahh, so beautiful, like an angel," he breathed reverently. "Like her mother. I must vash before I touch her," he said. He was covered with mud from the diggings. "I came as fast as I could. I'm so sorry I vasn't here sooner, Mae."

"Jenny took such great care of me, and of the baby, as well."

"My thanks. My very great thanks."

"No thanks needed." Jenny realized the family needed to be alone. "I'm off home now, but if there's anythin' I can do, holler. I'll be back to check on ye a wee bit later."

Her cabin was orderly and silent. Empty. With the door open to the summer warmth, she could clearly hear the wailing of the newborn next door, and it brought to the surface her own terrible yearning for a baby of her own.

For several weeks now, since summer came, she'd realized she was ready to try again. But as she'd once jokingly told Mae, starting a baby took a certain kind of practice. And that practice wasn't possible with William far away.

He came home only once, toward the middle of summer, and then for only three days before he left again. And even when he was home, his attention wasn't on her. He talked, ate and slept the White Pass railroad.

He'd turned to her the first night with the hunger of a healthy young man, but although Jenny welcomed him into her arms, something was lacking between them. She couldn't seem to recapture the passion that had burned in her before she lost her baby. The burning desire to have him make love to her was entirely gone. She must still love him—he was her husband—but that feeling, too, had changed. Resentment was more powerful than love.

He'd never once told her he forgave her for Jamie. He never spoke of it, and Jenny wasn't brave enough to bring it up. It lay between them like a huge stone stuck in the middle of a narrow path. It was a barrier for her that she couldn't seem to get past. She was relieved when he left.

As the summer days grew shorter, William wrote and suggested again that Jenny move to Skagway. With the advent of the railroad, the rough town was becoming civilized, he insisted. Robert could easily find work on the railroad, William urged, and it would be easier for him if they lived in Skagway. They could make it over the Pass if they left before freeze up.

Jenny refused to move. In Dawson, she had Mac, and baby Sophia, whom she adored. She had a home, and she was making other friends among the few women in the town. Her horrible memories of the journey over the Pass were still fresh in her mind, and Skagway had been the beginning of it. She blamed that trip for the loss of her son. She wanted never to make the journey again.

William was not pleased. "Ye're a stubborn wee woman, Jenny," he wrote in his next letter.

"Aye, ye've called me that before," she murmured, reading the letter.

"Have it yer own way, then," he wrote near the end of the page. He sounded resentful and angry.

She wondered if it was only her, or if Robert, too, wanted to move. Was he staying in Dawson solely to care for her? When next she was alone with him, she asked.

"If I had me choice, lass, I'd likely go back to the city," he said. He smiled at her. "I like the cities more than this wilderness. But beggars can't be choosers, aye? If Willie tells me to move to Skagway, then that's what I'll do. But I'm as good here as anywhere. Dinnae fret o'er it."

Sometimes Robert irritated her by being so agreeable with William. Surely he must resent having his brother make all his major decisions for him? But if he did, Robert never showed it.

Jenny persisted. "But what is it you'd *like* to do, given yer druthers?"

"Make beer." The reply came instantly, so she knew it was something he'd thought a lot about.

"Make beer?" Jenny was taken aback. "But ye don't drink much at all, either you or William."

Robert laughed and shook his head. "It's no the drinken' of it that interests me, Jenny. It's the process of makin' it. When I was a wee boy, I used to get sent to the ale shop to bring Da home his pint, and it always interested me, the makin' of the stuff. I found a book on it. There's a lot to it, more than ye'd think there is, to the makin' of good beer and ale."

"So ye'd have an ale shop of yer own, then? Is that what ye'd do if ye had choice and the money to start?"

"Aye, and if wishes were horses, beggars would ride, no?" He laughed again softly and stretched. "It would take money, and it's a gamble, however you look at it."

She wondered if William even knew about Robert's dreams. Her husband was ambitious, single-minded, incredibly strong, determined in his decisions, while Robert, just as strong physically, was more passive, willing to go along, to agree. But obviously he had his own secret dreams and desires.

No question, William was the dominant brother, making

decisions for all of them, and it irked her. It was also plain Robert held no resentment toward him for it. There was love between the twins, a palpable deep bond that she'd recognized the moment she saw them together, in spite of the difference in their natures.

"What was it like at home for the two of ye?" Jenny knew precious little about her husband's life, and she was curious. William had told her only the barest of details, that his mother, Maggie, had died when the twins were babies. A housekeeper named Mrs. Ferris had raised them, and William had spoken highly of her. He hadn't done the same about his father, Colum, who was a butcher in Edinburgh, and who hadn't bothered to come to their wedding.

William had left home at thirteen, found a job at a factory and somehow convinced the owner, Mr. Sprague, to take him on as an apprentice. Colum had been less than pleased about it—when he found out he'd kicked William out of his house. He saw no reason why his sons should be anything other than butchers and shopkeepers, as he was.

Now Robert told Jenny how he'd begun working at twelve in the butcher shop with Colum. There'd been a disagreement and a fierce quarrel, and Robert, too, had left home, just a year after Willie, traveling to Glasgow where he found work on the docks.

"It was a hard go for a half-grown lad," he said with a grimace. "But a damned sight better than workin' wi' the old man. God himself couldna get on wi' Colum Galloway when he'd a drop o' whiskey in him. Which was most of the time."

Robert turned his head and stared out the window, and Jenny knew from the tension in his body that he wasn't seeing the Dawson landscape. He was remembering, and from the set of his shoulders the memories weren't pleasant. After a minute, he shrugged and turned to her again.

"Willie was ever a talker. He got knocked about a good bit for it by our da. Stood up fer me, time and again, did Willie. He'd say his piece to the old man, and get knocked flat and climb right back on his feet and go at it all over agin. Me, I'd button my lip, knowin' if I didna I'd get a clip on the ear hard enough to deafen me, but our Willie, he never gave in. Never let up for a minute, which is how he got the trainin' he did, he just kept on and on at Mr. Sprague, always wantin' ta learn more and still more. Sprague wore down and took him on as apprentice, which is how Willie got to be a qualified steam engineer."

The story explained a great deal about both her husband and her brother-in-law.

Chapter Sixteen

During the endless summer daylight, Jenny found that, just like the other Dawson residents, she needed much less sleep. Robert was working the claim, but he came during the long evenings to chop her wood, carry in water, weed the garden. Of course Jenny made dinner for him, and he always helped her with the dishes afterward.

They began having a game of cards after the dishes were washed. They talked together easily, about the small happenings of the day, but also about the books they read, the ideas they had, the dreams they harbored. He played his mouth organ for her and told wild tales of the goings-on in Dawson.

"Last Monday, Mad Joe Pickering offered the dance hall girl named Lola her weight in gold dust if she'd marry him," Robert said one evening. "And Lola's no a light-weight by any means."

Jenny giggled. She'd seen Lola. "And what was her answer, then, Rob?" She laid down a queen of hearts, trumping his ten.

"She told him she didnae fancy washin' any man's socks and underwear, so unless he agreed to send his clothin' out to the laundry, the answer was no. And he agreed, signed a statement to that effect, witnessed by half the men in the saloon. Weighed out the gold, and when the Reverend sobered up enough, he married them." He laid his cards down. "Ye've gone and skunked me agin, Jenny Galloway. Ye missed yer callin'—ye could make a fortune at the gamin' tables."

"I'll keep that in mind should I decide to take up a career." She got up to cut them a slice of the fruitcake she'd made that day. "And d'ye not ever feel tempted to offer one of the lassies their weight in gold, Robbie?"

Although more women had made the trek North, there was still a chronic lack of young marriageable ladies in Dawson.

"Never, even if I had the gold." He laughed. "The rate I'm goin', I'll be an old man by the time I hae that much to spare."

"Anywhere's else, ye'd have the lassies offerin' fer you," Jenny declared. "Mebbe ye should think o' goin' back to Scotland and findin' a bride, the way William did me," she suggested, pouring him tea and stirring sugar in the way he liked it.

When it came, his answer was soft. "Ahh, but there's only the one like ye, Jenny."

She thought he was teasing, but when she looked over at him, he wasn't smiling. His green eyes met and held hers, and she felt her cheeks grow hot at the raw yearning she saw there. An awkward silence fell between them. For the first time, Jenny felt self-conscious with him.

Alone in bed that night, she thought about the look she'd seen on his face. It wasn't really for her, Jenny assured herself. It was bein' in this unnatural place where there weren't suitable brides for young men such as Robbie. He was lonely, which was why he spent so much time with her.

She was lonely, too. Robbie was her husband's brother, he was family, it was only natural that they'd find comfort in each other's company.

As for Robbie, he needed a wife.

She'd talk to him again about going out before freeze-up came. The claim wasn't a rich one, but surely William could afford to pay for a trip for Robbie. William was making enough to send his brother to Seattle, even Scotland perhaps.

It wasn't right that a bonny man like Robbie should waste his young years tending his brother's wife, Jenny mused. He needed a family of his own. You'd think William would realize that. But Jenny was beginning to suspect that William didn't see much beyond his own needs and wants.

In the next letter Jenny broached the subject.

William wrote back impatiently.

I can't spare Robbie, no as long as you're set on staying in Dawson, Jenny. It's a rough town, and you need someone to care for you. Before the winter comes again, I want us to have a decent house, and I want Rob to see to the building. I am writing him forthwith with the plans I've drawn up.

Jenny was tempted to lash out at William. He had no right to blame her for staying in Dawson. After all, coming here had been his idea in the first place. But the thought of living in a decent house kept her silent. The cabin was certainly better than a tent, but to live in a real house—that would be heaven. Especially if—*when,* she corrected firmly, for surely it was only a matter of time until they had babies. *If William was ever around long enough to make it possible.* After his short visit, she'd hoped—and wept when her courses came right on schedule.

William sent detailed plans and Robert began construction when he wasn't working the claim. The house would be set closer to the creek than the cabin, but still not far from Mae's cabin. It would have two stories, with a living room, large kitchen and pantry, a small bedroom down, and two large bedrooms upstairs. It sounded like a mansion to Jenny, and most exciting of all, Robert had located glass for the windows. Glass was in short supply in Dawson, because bringing it in was so hazardous.

Robert began building immediately. William told him to hire a man to help him, and Robert hired Carl. The two men worked at the claim half the day and the other half was spent on the house, so the construction went ahead quickly.

On a warm autumn day in early September, it was nearly finished. Carl was splitting shakes and Robert was hammering them onto the roof, but Carl kept falling behind, bent double by bouts of violent coughing.

"He's been coughing all summer," Mae said with a worried frown. "I've poulticed his chest and made him swallow enough chamomile tea to float a boat, but it doesn't seem to help." She and Jenny were preserving wild blueberries, cooking them in a huge kettle. They were working outside, using the stove Albert had given them so as to keep the cabins relatively cool.

"Summer grippe is the worst," Jenny said, checking on baby Sophia. The infant was sleeping in the cradle she and Mae had lifted outside. They'd covered the top with cheesecloth to keep the bugs away. Jenny was hoping she'd awaken soon. Sophia was smiling now, and Jenny never tired of holding the sweet baby.

She realized she was only half listening to Mae, and felt guilty. "Kate Nutchalna, who traded me the turkeys at Christmas, once told me there's a bush called devil's club. Ye use the bark, peel it and boil the outside piece into a tea. I think she said it was good for grippe. I'll see if I can get a piece o' it fer Carl."

"I'd be grateful, Jenny. I'm that worried about him."

Jenny got the root, and Mae boiled it up into tea, but Carl went on coughing.

William came home the following week and stayed for two. He and Robert finished the roof and the inside walls. They moved into the house the day before William left again for Skagway. Jenny made a celebratory dinner and invited the Sundstroms to join them, but they left early because Carl wasn't feeling well.

That night in bed, Jenny was the one who teased and stroked William, enticing him until he made passionate love to her. He fell into a deep sleep afterward, but she lay awake, dreaming of the baby they'd maybe started.

William left at dawn, and that night Jenny was awakened by Mae, pounding on the door. She was in her nightdress with a shawl around her, and there was terror in her blue eyes.

"Jenny, come quick. Carl's coughing blood and it won't stop. I'm going for the doctor."

Jenny pulled on shoes and a dressing gown and hurried over to Mae's cabin.

The baby was asleep in the cradle. In the corner curtained off as a bedroom, Carl was propped up on pillows. His eyes were closed, his face drained of color. He held a towel to his mouth, but the pillowcase and bedding were bright red with blood and there was a sizable puddle on the wooden floor. He opened his eyes and tried to say something, but the coughing stopped him.

"Be still, rest now. Mae'll be back wi' the doctor straightaway."

But Jenny was shocked and frightened. The stove was hot, and she stirred honey into warm water and gave it to him to drink, but after the first swallow, the coughing became violent. Soon the towel was drenched with blood. Jenny found him another, praying the doctor would be sober and that he'd hurry.

It seemed a long time before the door finally opened and Mae rushed in, followed by Dr. Perry. Jenny could smell spirits on him, but he seemed sober enough. He took his top hat off and extracted a stethoscope from his black bag, setting it on Carl's chest and listening for a long time. Then he put a hand on Carl's forehead, studying him closely, looking into his eyes and smelling his breath.

Jenny took Mae's hand in hers as they waited. When his examination was done, Perry turned to Mae.

"I believe your husband has consumption, madam."

Mae put a hand over her mouth, shocked speechless.

Jenny said, "What can ye do fer him?"

"There is no known treatment. Keep his head high, give him warm liquids. Rub his chest with camphor. I would advise immediately leaving Dawson for a warm, dry climate. Many of the natives here have consumption. The harsh Northern air is not good for such ailments."

Mae stammered, "But—but he'll get better, won't he? If—if we go somewhere dry and warm, he'll get better?"

"I am not God, madam." Perry put his hat on and adjusted the brim. "I can make no promises. I know only that once the bleeding begins it's usually not long before the patient succumbs. That will be ten dollars, please, or an equivalent amount in gold dust."

Jenny wanted to slap him. She glared instead, but he didn't even notice.

Mae's entire body was trembling. She went to a corner, fumbled a small sack out of a tin and handed it to him. Perry took it, weighed it in his hand, shrugged and went out the door.

The coughing finally subsided and Carl fell asleep, breathing heavily.

Sophia started to wail, and Jenny lifted her from the cradle. Her clout was sopping, so she found a dry flannel and pinned it on the baby, talking softly to her all the while and wondering what she could say or do to help and comfort Mae.

"Give her here, she's likely hungry," Mae whispered, sitting down in the rocking chair Carl had made and opening the front of her gown. She nursed the baby automatically, staring out at the room with frightened unseeing eyes.

Feeling helpless, Jenny put wood on the fire, made a cup of tea and brought it to Mae. In a quiet voice, so as not to disturb either Carl or the baby, Jenny said, "Dinnae take what that scoundrel says to heart, Mae. He could be wrong. As he admits himsel', he's no God, much as he'd like to be."

Mae looked at Jenny with stricken eyes, her narrow face parched white. "It's all my fault," she whispered. "I was the one who insisted we come here." Her chin wobbled. "Carl was perfectly healthy before I made him come to Dawson. And now—oh, God, Jenny. If something happens to him—oh, Jenny, I couldn't live without him."

"Ye willnae have to," Jenny said stoutly. "If the Indians hae consumption like yon idiot says, they'll also hae some treatment fer it. I'll find out from Kate. He'll get well, wait and see."

But Mae shook her head. "We'll have to go, Jenny." She was looking down at her baby. She slowly raised her head and met Jenny's eyes. Hers were desolate and brimming with tears. "We'll have to leave before freeze-up. As soon as we can. There's a party leaving next week, we'll have to leave with them. It may be Carl's only hope."

Jenny's legs gave way and she sank into a chair. She wanted to argue, but reason told her there was no point. Mae was right. They both knew consumption was a horrible disease. Carl deserved any chance, regardless how faint.

But oh, what would she do, alone in this place without her best friend? She wrapped her arms around her chest, feeling as if she couldn't breathe.

Mae got up and gently put Sophia in her arms. Jenny cuddled the sweet, warm bundle as her heart broke. She was going to have to say goodbye to this dear wee one whom she loved as her own. She was going to have to learn to live without Mae, as close as a beloved sister.

"I hate this place," she whispered fervently. "It takes all that I love and gives me nothing back."

Chapter Seventeen

Barely a week later, as dawn was breaking over the mountains, Jenny and Robert waved goodbye to Mae and Carl and Sophia. As the boat they were on grew smaller and smaller, Jenny felt more alone than she'd ever felt in her life.

"God go wi' them," Robert said. He put a comforting hand on Jenny's shoulder. "I'm sorry, lass. Ye're going to miss them something fierce."

Jenny swiped at the tears running down her cheeks. She doubted she'd ever see Mae again, in spite of Mae's parting words.

"We'll meet again, Jenny. We're sisters of the soul, nothing will keep us apart. I'll write as soon as we're settled. God bless and keep you, dear one."

Robert walked Jenny back to the house, but then he headed off to work the claim and she was truly alone.

Slowly, she made her way up the path to her house, feeling sad and drained, old and weary to the bone, barely able to put one foot in front of the other. The Sundstroms' cabin sat empty and deserted. She could barely stand to look at it. The other one, Jenny's first home here in Dawson, at least had smoke curling from the chimney.

Robert had moved into it, preferring to live alone rather than with the two miners. He was Jenny's nearest neighbor now, and for that she was grateful.

But when she went inside, the new house was too big and too empty.

As a farewell gift, Mae had given her the armless rocking chair Carl had made. "To sit and nurse your babies, dear Jenny. They'll come soon, just wait and see."

But this morning Jenny didn't think so. She felt withered and barren and cold. She walked from one room to the next, desolate, unable to settle.

At last she took her writing case from the shelf in the living room and sat down at the new dining table William had instructed her to buy. She took out her pen and inkwell and smoothed the clean sheet of paper.

"Dearest Father," she began.

I have written often of my best and dearest friend, Mae. Today she and her husband and dear baby Sophia left on the boat, heading for Seattle. I cannot put into words the sadness and loneliness I feel, Papa. They will not be coming back. Carl has the Consumption....

The words poured out on the paper. Once again, she found that writing down her feelings helped her. She knew that by the time Bruce replied, whatever crisis she was

going through would long be over, although she still found
his words comforting. Putting them down in black and
white seemed the key. She wrote,

Perhaps now I will find the courage to do as William
wishes and move to Skagway, where he is still working on the new Railroad. It will mean traveling the
terrible White Pass trail once again, and I have not the
heart to think of that now. Perhaps in the spring?

She paused, daring to hope that by spring she'd have a
baby to love and care for.

In the meantime, I thank God for Robert, who takes
wonderful care of me while William is away.

Robert did take care of her, and with Mae gone, he
became even more attentive, planning drives out of town
in a rented buggy so she could see the fall colors of the
countryside, cleaning and tilling the garden patch in preparation for the winter, finding a patch of the rose hips
which Kate said the Indians used for grippe, bringing the
bright red seedpods to Jenny.

She had no idea anyone in town noticed that Robert was
attentive until the afternoon she stepped out from behind
a stack of fabric bolts in the general store and saw Kitty
coming in the door.

She obviously hadn't known Jenny was in the store, and
for an instant, her face betrayed her feelings. It was obvious
from her expression she wouldn't have come in if she'd
known Jenny was there. But she recovered quickly.

"Well, well. Hello there, stranger." Kitty was dressed in

an elaborate scarlet satin gown, with heavy gold jewelry at her throat, ears and wrists. She gave Jenny's simple gown an up-and-down glance as she wriggled her fingers at her. They were covered in black lace gloves.

"Good day to ye, Kitty." Jenny had seen her more than a few times in town, but always some distance away. She had the feeling Kitty deliberately avoided her, and certainly Jenny had no desire to seek the other woman out.

"So, Jenny Galloway, I hear you've a fancy new house up there on the hill."

"I wouldna call it fancy. It's warm and verra comfortable." And Jenny had no intention of asking the other woman over to see it.

"And I also hear your handsome husband has left you in the tender care of your equally handsome brother-in-law," Kitty sneered. "Nothing like keeping it all in the family."

Jenny felt her face flame. There were others in the store, and she could feel them looking at her. She wanted to ignore Kitty and walk out the door, but she knew she had to confront her or tongues would wag.

It took all her courage to lift her chin and say in a level tone, "And what exactly d'ye mean by that?"

Kitty purred, "Why, only that you're fortunate to have two fine men so concerned for your welfare, Mrs. Galloway."

Jenny kept her tone polite and her voice soft, but the words had been in her far too long to hold back. "Ye had the love of one of the finest men I ever knew, and he was also concerned for your welfare, was he no? Albert Fitzgerald was a good man, and ye treated him verra poorly, I'd say. Ye dinnae even see fit to come to his funeral."

It was Kitty's turn to flush deep red. "I go where and when I choose. What I do is none of your concern."

"And neither are my doin's any of yer affair." Jenny paid for the skein of wool she'd chosen and walked out the door with her head high. But inside she was trembling. The encounter was upsetting, and she sensed she had a spiteful enemy in Kitty. At least now the enmity was out in the open, she told herself as she walked home. But it had been disturbing. If only she had Mae to confide in, it would make it easier.

In the days that followed the confrontation with Kitty, Jenny was lonelier than she'd ever been. She waited for a letter from Mae, but none came. William had promised he'd try and come home once more before freeze-up, but September was already gone.

Early one morning Jenny woke to find the upstairs bedroom window white with frost. The temperature had dropped to well below freezing overnight. Ice would soon prevent any movement of boats on the river. Unless he hurried to Dawson, she wouldn't see her husband again for many months.

Jenny lit the stove and raced up the stairs and back to bed, huddling under the bedclothes until some warmth crept into the room. She'd been trying not to even hope, but this morning she needed something to lift her spirits.

Her courses were late. They hadn't come since William's last visit home. She put her hands on her abdomen, closed her eyes and let herself dream of a baby growing there.

Chapter Eighteen

When the cramps started the following afternoon, Jenny tried at first to ignore them, but it was soon abundantly clear there would be no baby. Now there was only the long, dark winter ahead, with no hope of the child she longed for.

Jenny was beyond tears. A heavy darkness seemed to settle on her body and her brain. She abandoned the bread she'd set, ignored the fact that the stove needed wood, and went to bed, seeking oblivion in sleep. She'd moved to the small downstairs bedroom because it was warmer there.

She woke to Robert's voice. The room was dark and icy cold. He'd lit a candle, and she could see him, hovering in the doorway to the bedroom.

"Jenny? Jenny, are ye feelin' poorly, lass?"

"I'm a bit out of sorts, is all," she managed to say as she struggled to sit up.

"I'll make ye a cup o' tea, shall I? I'll just get the fires goin', it's that cold in here. Stay there, I'll be in directly."

She had no intentions of moving. Her body felt heavy and she shivered, despite the heavy quilts. Her belly was cramping painfully. She lay back on the pillows and dozed until Robert brought in a lamp, and then a tray with tea and soup and toast. He set it on the bed and plumped her pillows so she could sit upright.

"Ye gave me a fright, lass, what with the house dark and cold and no sign of ye. It's Mae goin' has ye upset, is it?"

"It is, Rob." He was family, but he was also a single man. There was no way she could admit what was really wrong. "That, and knowin' William won't be comin' home now till breakup, I was hopin' ta see him soon." She took a sip of tea and the warmth was comforting. "Mebbe I made a mistake, Rob, insistin' on stayin' here. Keepin' you here, as well. Mebbe we should hae gone to Skagway, as William wanted."

"Nay, never worry about me, Jenny. I'm content, doin' what I'm doin'."

"Which is spendin' much of yer time takin' care o' me. And I'm afraid it's causin' talk in the town." She hadn't told Robert about meeting Kitty, but she did now, repeating exactly what Kitty had said, adding, "She was that put out wi' me, and she's vicious. I fear there'll be more lies told in the town, thanks to her."

"She's a nasty woman, that one," Robert said. "And as fer talk, there's always gossip in a place the size o' this. Dinnae let it bother ye, Jenny. I'll hae a wee word wi' her."

Jenny thought that over. "Mebbe better not. My father used to say, 'The more ye step in a skitter the broader it gets.'"

Robert laughed. "Might be he's right. Better to ignore it. Now eat yer soup whilst it's warm, lass."

She wasn't hungry, but she didn't want to hurt his feelings. He was the most thoughtful, kind and caring man she'd ever met, with the exception of her father. To please him she spooned the soup up, and gradually she began to feel a little better.

He sat on a chair beside the bed, telling her about his day at the diggings, saying nothing that demanded answers from her.

After a while he pulled his harmonica out of his pocket and began to play, tunes from home and some he'd picked up since coming to Dawson. The haunting music filled the little room, and the music eased her soul.

"I'll be off home now. I'll stoke the fires and come back o'er later to add wood, no need fer ye to rouse yoursel'. Rest, lass, and ye'll feel better tomorrow."

He took the tray and the dishes, and she heard him in the kitchen whistling as he washed them.

She got up later to use the outhouse. The house was warm, and he'd hauled in water and filled her big copper pot. He'd set it to heat in case she wanted a bath. She scooped water into a basin, put the latch on the door and stood beside the stove, slowly sponging herself down. Tonight she longed to lie in a man's strong arms, just for the closeness, the comfort, the assurance she wasn't alone. And not for the first time, she found herself guiltily wondering what it would be like to lie with Robert.

Wednesday of the following week, Bartholomew Fieldstone waved a packet of letters at her as she walked past the post office.

"Mrs. Galloway, look what I have for you." He was breathless with excitement. "One of the packers dropped these off this morning."

It was an unexpected gift. With freeze-up imminent, it could be the last mail she'd get for six months.

"Oh, bless ye, Bartholomew. I'm that pleased, thank ye." She gave him a wide smile, and he turned deep red all the way to the top of his shiny bald head.

There were two fat letters from her father, and one burlap wrapped bundle from William. She raced through her shopping and hurried home through the late-afternoon sunshine.

She opened William's packet first, cutting it open with her scissors. Inside was a thick wad of money and two pages in his scrawling hand.

"My dear Wife," he wrote,

I hope this finds you well, as it leaves me. I enclose money, which I trust will reach you intact and will be sufficient to see you through the winter. I received your letter of the 7th with the sad news of Carl's illness, and indeed I saw the Sundstroms for an hour, the day they passed through Skagway. Carl was poorly, very thin and tired from the trip across the Pass. Mae was as ever, and the child hale and hearty. They asked that I send their regards, and Mae promises to write as soon as they are settled.

Jenny shook her head, impatient with William's reporting. Could he not have found more to say about beautiful baby Sophia than hale and hearty? And Mae, as ever. What

did that mean? Was her friend exhausted from the cursed
White Pass? Was she worn down by worry?
She read on.

The weather is becoming inclement, and between
the demands of work and the possibility of an early
freeze, I doubt I will be able to make the trip to
Dawson again before spring.

Well, Jenny had guessed as much. But seeing it written
still gave her a pang. How could their marriage be expected to flourish, with him so far away? How could she
have the baby she longed for?

The work on the Railroad goes ahead as quickly as
possible, which means I must be on hand to supervise. The quality of the workforce is poor, we lose
men and tools in equal proportions. I have been approached by several businessmen who have asked me
to run as a Delegate to represent Skagway in the
coming election. The idea is an interesting one, the
political arena is where change is truly possible.

Politics. Her father had always said it was a dirty
business. It was man's business, and it interested Jenny not
at all. And she suspected it would be one more reason to
keep William away from her.

I very much miss the comforts of home. The rooming house where I stay is serviceable and the food
adequate, but it tends to be cold and noisy. I miss you
and trust Robert is taking good care of you. Jenny, I

would again like you to consider the possibility of moving here to Skagway in the spring. I should like us to establish a home where we could be together.

Always your loving Husband,
William.

A home where they could be together, indeed. They had a perfectly good home, but he chose not to live in it with her. Jenny tossed the letter down on the table. She was being a little unfair to him, she knew that. He'd gone to Skagway to make money. She sifted through the thick pile of bills, counting them. He'd sent her more than enough to last the winter, and she was grateful to him for that. And he'd said he missed her, but almost as an afterthought after all the blarney about his work and the politics.

She knew by now that William didn't write love letters, but surely he could at least express a little more concern for her welfare than this?

With a feeling of glad anticipation, she slit open one of the envelopes from her father.

"Dearest daughter," he began.

I received the sad news of your wee baby's passing, and my heart is heavy for you. I so hate to burden you further, my darling Jenny, but I must also tell you that here we have suffered great loss, as well. I can hardly bear to put the words on paper. There was a Fever in the countryside, and your Mother suffered greatly and passed away two weeks ago, God rest her soul. And wee Frankie followed her not two days later. Johnny and Ian were also terribly sick, but they recovered, although still weak. I escaped entirely, which is a blessing in that I was able to care for the others, but I would gladly have given my own life for that of my beloved wee son and my wife.

Jenny couldn't seem to get a breath. When at last she did, she let out a long, keening wail, crossing her arms across her stomach and rocking back and forth.

"Frankie," she sobbed. "Ahh, Frankie, me wee toad."

She felt badly for her father for the loss of Nell, but she and her stepmother had never been close. But Frankie's death was pure agony. He was the baby she'd rocked and soothed and bathed and fed when Nell had been too sick after his birth to care for him. He'd turned to Jenny, thinking her his mother. It was like losing her own baby all over again. She rocked and moaned and wept, unaware of Robert until his big hand came to rest on her shoulder.

"Jenny, what is it, lass?"

She handed him Bruce's letter, and he scanned it quickly.

"Ahh, Jenny. I'm that sorry. Ye've told me often about the wee boy, and how ye missed him."

Desperate for comfort, hysterical, Jenny stood and flung herself into his arms. The feel of his strong body against hers, the warmth and security of the muscular arms that slowly came around and then held her tight brought consolation and the knowledge that she wasn't alone.

"Ahh, Jenny." Her name came out on a long sighing breath.

She ought to pull away, but it felt so good to be held. He was solid, reliable. She was starved for simple creature comfort. He smelled of soap and clean sweat. After a moment she relaxed into the curve of his shoulder, letting her tears wet the front of his blue cambric shirt. She wept bitterly, and he rocked her. At length as her sobs subsided, she realized he was murmuring soft undefined sounds of comfort and caring, his mouth pressed against her hair, one hand rubbing gently between her shoulder blades. It felt so good, so safe.

She lifted her drenched face up to thank him, and his mouth came down on hers, hard and sweet. The shock of it froze her in place, but the kiss warmed her in a way that was dangerous.

She was much shorter than he, and with one arm around her waist he lifted her, pressing her close against him, crushing her breasts against his chest. There was no mistaking his arousal. There was no denying her own.

She knew she should pull away. And she would, in a moment. But his mouth was soft and warm, insistent, and for this one small instant, she succumbed to it—to him.

His tongue slid between her lips, opening her mouth, wanting her. It had been so long since anyone had wanted her wholeheartedly. A shiver of need uncurled in her abdomen. God, the man could kiss.

This was Robbie, the man who'd taken care of her for months now. She couldn't, in all honesty, say that she hadn't fantasized about him. Looking at his well-made body and wondering how it would be with him. He was a bonny man, inside and out. She'd been alone for a long while, and she was young and healthy. She wanted him. Suddenly, she was wild and hot with wanting.

Unable to stop herself, she moved her pelvis against him, her breath quick and shallow, her heart hammering against her ribs.

That was all it took. With a muttered oath, he swept her into his arms, shouldered his way into the small bedroom where she'd been sleeping. He set her down on the tumbled bed, his breathing ragged.

"Jenny. Aaaach, Jenny, my God, I love ye, lassie." The fervent whisper answered some need in her for adoration, for passion untouched by pain. "I've loved ye from the moment I first laid eyes on ye. Ye're that bonny, so soft and rosy."

His fingers were deft on the buttons of her bodice. He slid her dress down, unfastened the ribbons of her chemise, slid it over her shoulders. When his lips closed around her hardened nipple, she was lost. She gasped and bucked, fumbling at the buttons of his shirt, and he stripped it off over his head, undid the fastenings on his flies and stepped neatly out of his trousers.

His naked body was both familiar and strange, like William's, and not. He pulled her clothing off gently and she helped him. He straddled her, and his big workman's hands traced her, touching throat and breasts and belly. She could see how aroused he was, and every stroke on her skin inflamed her, until she could bear it no more. She spread herself for him.

"Jenny. Are ye sure?"

She could only guess what it cost him to hold back long enough to ask.

"Please, Rob." It came out like a prayer. "Please."

He groaned and slid into her, stretching her, inflaming her, and before he was fully inside she convulsed wildly, threshing her head from side to side, body taut as a bow, her abandoned cry echoing from the corners of the small room.

She lay sated, boneless, in this one short moment free of memory or sorrow, a body overflowing with peace and joy. She expected him to quickly follow her, but instead he waited, holding himself taut with arms that quivered, letting her shuddering stop before he began again. He looked down at her, straight into her eyes, his green gaze intent.

With each long, slow stroke, he whispered to her.

"Ye're beautiful, Jenny. Ye're so beautiful, Jenny." Over and over, until she found herself rousing again, anticipating the slow, wet glide, the tantalizing withdrawal, the whispered words. Soon she was moving with him, loath to have him withdraw even the slightest bit. She moaned, driven wild by his hardness and heat, desperately reaching for the place that eluded her. But not for long.

When her climax came, his did, as well. They clung together, shuddering, their voices mingling in the slowly darkening room.

When the trembling subsided, he rolled to one side, never letting her out of his embrace. He pulled the sheets and quilts up over them and turned her so she was spooned against his body.

"Rest, wee darlin'. I'll go fix the fires in a while, but for now, lay down your head and sleep."

She knew she ought to feel remorse and terrible guilt for what they'd done, but she didn't. Instead, peace filled her, and a quiet, all-consuming sense that at this moment in time, in this room, all was well.

With Robert's arms holding her close, she closed her eyes, limbs heavy, mind drifting.

She didn't hear the door in the kitchen open and close, and Robert mustn't have, either, because when William appeared in the bedroom with the lantern, they both bolted up.

Chapter Nineteen

"So it's true." William was breathing hard, and the look on his face was frightening. "I wouldnae believe it if I didn't see it wi' me own eyes. The two of ye—" He let out a wild roar, rage and pain mingling.

Jenny clutched the sheet to her neck, making small indecipherable whimpers.

Robert sprang out of bed and was pulling on his pants when William punched him in the face, knocking him to his knees. His nose spurted blood, and Jenny screamed, scrambling out of bed, dragging on her shift. The lantern was on its side on the floor, and she grabbed it before the spilled coal oil could catch fire, setting it on the dresser.

"William," she begged. "William, dinnae blame him, it's not him—"

But William was beyond hearing. "Bastard," he roared,

eyes blazing and face contorted. "Friggin' bastard, me own brother, cuckoldin' me with me wife."

Robert got to his feet, swiping at his dripping nose with one hand, and William swung again, catching him on the side of the head. Robert went crashing down, taking a small table with him.

"Stop," Jenny screamed. "William, will ye stop, it's no his fault—"

But William was dragging his brother to his feet, drawing back a fist, smashing it once again into Robert's face, sending him backward onto the bed.

Jenny hollered, "Stop, stop it, William, will ye stop now!"

She could see that Robert wasn't fighting back. And when William reached down and dragged him up again, she flung herself at her husband, clawing at his arms, trying to restrain him.

William shook her off and she fell backward against the edge of the door. It struck her in the back, and the pain took her breath away. She crumbled to the floor, gasping for breath.

"Dinnae lay a hand on her," Robert bellowed as William tackled him again, dragging him to the floor, pinning him down and punching first with one fist and then the other, hitting face and body. The sound of the blows was sickening, and Jenny knew if she didn't do something, William would kill Robert.

She struggled to her feet, grabbed a heavy stoneware pitcher from the dresser and raised it with both hands, bringing it down with all her strength on her husband's head.

There was a hollow thunk, and the handle flew off the pitcher as William gave a grunt and slowly toppled to one side. He lay shaking his head, stunned by the blow.

"Get up." Jenny grabbed Robert's hand and tried to tug

him to his feet. He was covered in blood, his forehead split open, his nose off to one side, obviously broken and bleeding in a gushing torrent.

Jenny babbled, "Go, Robbie, ye have to go, please, get up and leave us, *now*."

He shook his head. He panted, "I willnae—leave—ye alone—wi' him."

Jenny was hysterical, wringing her hands, barely able to even talk. "Ye have to go, please, please, Rob, go. He will nae harm me, just go, *please,* for God's sake."

"Come wi' me." Robert was on his feet, staggering but upright. His face was swelling. It looked like raw meat in places. He swiped a hand across his nose, smearing blood over his cheeks. "I'll no leave wi'out ye, Jenny. Leave him and come wi' me."

"I cannae. He's me husband, ye know I cannae." Jenny found his shirt and shoved it at him. "Leave us, Robbie, I'm beggin' ye."

"I love ye, Jenny. I'll take care wi' ye, should ye come wi' me."

At that moment she saw the full scope of the damage she'd caused. She stared at him, appalled at what she'd done. "Robbie, I cannae. I love William, he's me husband. I've made a terrible mistake, and I've hurt ye somethin' fierce, and him, as well. I'm that sorry."

One of his eyes was swollen nearly shut. He studied her with the other, the clear green gaze trying to fathom whether what she said was the truth. There must have been something in her expression that convinced him, because he gave a small nod.

"It wasnae you, lass. Dinnae go blamin' yerself. It was all my doin'. And I'll never be sorry. If ye should change yer mind, I'll be waitin'." He limped toward the door, pulled on his boots and went out, closing it softly behind him.

Jenny was shaking. She'd have to go and see to William, but she needed a moment alone to collect herself.

"Lyin' bitch."

The low, vicious words came from behind her, and Jenny whirled. William was clinging to the door frame, legs braced, blood trickling down his cheek. The look he shot her was contemptuous.

"Lyin' whore, Why don't ye go as he asks?"

She swallowed hard. "Ye willnae speak to me that way, William Galloway."

"I'll speak to ye any way I please. Ye're no but a slut."

She walked over to him, drew back her hand and slapped his face as hard as she could. Her palm stung with the force of the blow. She'd been terrified and ashamed, but now she was angry, as angry as she'd ever been in her life. And it felt good.

"Ye have no idea what I am, William, because ye've never bothered to learn. Ye're so busy wi' yer own wants and needs, ye've not taken any time fer me."

"Liar." His face was scarlet where she'd hit him, and his eyes were those of a wild animal. His fists were clenched, but even though she was trembling, Jenny refused to step back, refused to let him intimidate her.

"I've been workin' like a fiend, livin' rough in Skagway, makin' money so life would be easy fer ye, and in return ye've been friggin' Robert all along."

"Robert never laid a hand on me before this night, not that it matters." She stepped away from him, over to the table. She rested her hands on the smooth wood, looking straight at him. "What we did was wrong, but ye're no blameless, either, William." She was afraid to say all the things that she'd held back all these months, but she knew they had to be said. "Ye're not in Skagway because o' me, but fer yerself. Ye put me in Robert's care because ye couldnae be bothered wi' me, grievin' as I was for our bairn. Ye blamed me for his loss, and at first I believed ye. Now, I see that it wasnae my fault. Some bairns are no meant to stay here."

He gave a disparaging snort. "Dinnae try and lay any o' this at my doorstep, Jenny, aye? I'm no the one rollin' around in bed wi' someone else, am I?"

"Mebbe not, but then ye don't give a thought *to* anyone else, do ye? Comin' up here was what you wanted, William. Yer choice, not mine. Goin' to Skagway was your choice again, and yet ye blame me fer not followin' ye. Ye've never once asked Robert what he wants to do wi' his life. Have ye? As fer me, it was easy fer ye, leavin' me here, orderin' yer brother to build this house and do the chores ye're too preoccupied to do, what with yer engineerin' and now the politics. Even when ye're here, William, yer attention is elsewhere."

It was wonderfully freeing to put into words the things she'd been feeling.

His eyes were wild. She should be afraid, but she wasn't.

"Yer mad, woman. Yer a cheatin', lyin' hussy, and ye want to pass the blame to me. It's only fortunate someone thought to warn me what was happenin' here behind me back."

She hadn't stopped to wonder what had brought him back. She wasn't about to go into it now, because it would veer away from what needed said. She'd come to a decision, she wasn't certain exactly when, but it was clear in her mind what she needed to do.

"I'm going back to Scotland, William."

She could see his face change. He hadn't expected that.

"I'll write me father straightaway and tell him the honest truth of what's happened, never fear," she went on. "I've just had a letter from him, ye see, and me stepmother has died, and—" She choked up, and it took a moment to regain control. "And wee Frankie, as well, God rest his soul. Da will be that glad to hae me back, takin' care o' him and the boys. And if ye cannae see yer way to payin' my fare, I know he'll send it to me."

It would mean waiting till spring, but she could bear that. She could endure another winter here, knowing she'd be leaving when the ice broke. She got up and found a shawl to wrap around herself. The fire had gone out and it was cold in the kitchen. She went to the stove and carefully laid in twigs that Robert had gathered for her. She lit them, waiting for just the right moment to add larger wood.

"Ye'll want a divorce, and rightly so. I'll sign any papers ye need. I want nothin' from ye, William, but my freedom."

She put a bit of kindling on, and then a larger log before she turned to face him again. It was the first time she'd ever seen William at a loss for words. He stared at her, and then dragged a chair away from the table and collapsed on it. The fight seemed to have gone out of him. When he finally spoke, his tone was quiet.

"I dinnae know about wee Frankie, Jenny, or yer stepma, either. I'm sorry."

She nodded in acknowledgment and sat down herself. The tension between them had eased somewhat, and she was grateful for that. She was shivering, part from cold and part from emotion.

William cleared his throat. "I heard ye tell Robert ye didnae love him. Is that the truth, Jenny?"

"I wouldnae hae said it otherwise."

"Ye said—"

She could tell it was a struggle for him to get the words out. She waited.

"Ye said it was me ye loved. Can that be true, Jenny?"

"Aye. I've made terrible mistakes, William, but I'm no a liar."

"Then will ye stay, Jenny?"

It took her by surprise. "Why would ye want me to? Ye saw me with—"

"Dinnae say his name." It was him now who got up and tended the fire. He filled the kettle from the water bucket and set it to heat. When he sat down again, his voice was husky. "Ye're my wife, ye belong wi' me."

"And have ye throw up me sins in me face every time we quarrel? Nay, William. It's better if I go."

"Think about it, Jenny. Dinnae decide this minute. I'm home fer a week, we'll talk again." He got up, put on his coat and left the house.

Jenny hurried to the window. William headed straight for the cabin where Robert was, and she clasped her hands to her chest and prayed that there'd be no more fighting between the brothers. But if there was, there was nothing she could do to prevent it.

The kettle was steaming, and she washed herself and then set about straightening the bedroom, scrubbing away the blood, putting the pitcher away to be mended. She stripped the sheets and washed them, and then sat down to write to her father. She told him everything, just as it had happened.

That night after a silent dinner, Jenny went into the small downstairs bedroom and closed the door. She heard William go up the stairs, and she heard the bedsprings creak overhead. She lay wakeful, trying to think how her life had taken the turn it had. She'd made the wrong choices, that was plain, perhaps first by marrying William, and certainly now by making love with Robert. She could think of it no other way than that; what they'd shared was lovemaking.

She had no idea what had transpired between William and Robert. William was away until late, and she hadn't seen Robert again. It pained her badly to know that she'd caused a breach between the brothers, and she wondered if they'd ever make it up. Perhaps after she was gone. She was going over the things she'd have to do to prepare for the journey, mentally packing her few belongings, when she heard William coming down the stairs.

Her heart began to hammer.

The knock on her bedroom door was tentative. She sat up. "Jenny, can I come in?"

"Come." The word was little more than a breath, but he heard. The door opened. He stood by the bed, and she could hear him breathing as if he'd been running.

"Jenny," he said. "I've considered what ye said about the way I've treated ye, and ye're right about much o' it. I'm sorry, lass. Sorry fer the names I called ye, and sorry that I've not been the husband I ought to have been. If ye'll take me back, I'll do better. I don't want to lose ye, Jenny. I love ye."

It was the last thing she'd expected, the declaration of love. In the dark of the room, she couldn't see his face, and she needed to. She slid out of bed and lit the lamp, crawling back under the covers because of the chill.

She watched his face, searching for the truth. "It would always be between us, William. It's no a thing ye can forget easily." Certainly she couldn't, so how could he?

He sat down on the bed, took her hand in his, caressing it with his thumb. She saw a humility in him that had never been there before.

"I'd do me best, lass. I'd never speak o' it again. I kin see how I was to blame, leavin' ye here, makin' ye feel the loss of the bairn was all yer own fault, not givin' ye any comfort when ye needed it. I've been a bloody fool, Jenny, selfish and thoughtless, just as ye said. I'm askin' ye for another try at it. See if mebbe I could get it right this time, aye?"

"And what of Robert?" She had to ask. They had to have things out in the open.

A shadow passed over his face. "He's leavin' Dawson, probably tomorrow."

"And where's he goin'?"

"He didnae say. I've given him what money I can spare, enough for his fare back to Scotland, should he choose."

"Ye said someone told ye about—" She stopped, not knowing how to phrase it, and suddenly the answer came to her. "It was Kitty wrote ye, wasn't it, William?"

"Aye, it was. The letter came and I went mad wi' rage. I traveled day and night to get here."

If only he'd chosen to come home for different reasons. But there was no point in regrets.

"Should I stay, and I'm not sayin' I am, mind, would we live in Skagway?" She knew they'd leave Dawson, there was nothing left here for either of them, except the tiny grave up on the hillside.

"I've been thinking about that, lass. It's somethin' we'd need to talk over together, but I think it would be best to make a fresh start, somewhere away from here. There's a place out on the water in southeastern Alaska, in Prince William Sound. The town's called Valdez, it's the start o' the all-American route to the Klondike. They'll be buildin' a railroad from there to the Interior."

"Prince William Sound." She found a small smile and offered it to him. "The name's right for ye, anyway."

"I'm no exactly a prince, lass, as well ye know." His answering smile was no bigger than hers had been. "I've had the offer of a job there, though. When the present railroad contract ends, they'll be constructin' a railway line from Valdez into the Interior. I've heard it's a bonny place, on the ocean and all and rich with fish and game. We'd need to think it over, the two o' us. But mebbe ye'd rather go to British Columbia, the way we'd planned to do in the beginnin'? I could still find work on the railroad there."

Jenny thought it over, noticing that he was asking her instead of telling. "I like this North Country fine, William." It was the truth. In spite of everything, the beauty of the wild land had lodged in her heart. "It's no a place I care about, one's as good as the next, if we're happy. It's—it's knowin' I'm loved and cared for, William. That means everythin' to me."

He nodded, and by the intense look on his face he'd actually heard her and understood. "I'll need to finish me contract with the railroad, which will be next spring. Plenty of time to decide, Jenny. In the meantime, would ye no consider comin' away wi' me, stayin' in Skagway for the winter?"

She knew it was the only thing to do. With Robert gone, there was no way she could stay on in Dawson alone, and she had no desire to do so.

"We'd have to go right soon. Freeze-up is comin'." She dared not even think of the harrowing trip across the White Pass.

"Aye, we'd have to leave within the week." He guessed what she was thinking. "It's no so hard goin' back, Jenny. The trail is much improved, and with the railroad nearly done, ye can ride from the summit down to Skagway. I've the use of horses. It'll be much easier this time."

Whether she stayed with him or went back to Scotland, she had to make the trip to Skagway, regardless. "I've no reason to stay on here. I'll begin the packin' in the mornin'."

He nodded, still holding her hand. Barely above a whisper, he said, "And will ye no come up to bed wi' me now, Jenny? Please?"

Here it was, the real moment of decision. If she went upstairs, it represented a commitment. It would mean staying with William. Should she climb the stairs or stay where she was?

She looked into his green eyes, and she saw sadness and remorse, and a humility she'd never before associated with William. The anger was gone. There was love there, she was certain of that. She knew it would be wrong to turn away from him, because in her heart, she loved him in return.

It was a different sort of love than the kind she'd felt for him in the beginning. That had been a young girl's dreamy kind of adoration. Now, she saw him as he was—a strong man with as many flaws as she had herself. She loved him in spite of them.

"Aye," she whispered. "Aye, William. Let's go on up to bed, then."

Tears shimmered in his green eyes, and an expression of immense relief flickered across his strong features.

"Ye'll no be sorry, Jenny. I promise ye that."

Chapter Twenty

September 8, Prince William Sound, two years later

"C' mere, ye wee scamp."

Jenny caught the sturdy baby up in her arms, just in time to prevent him tipping over the water bucket for the second time that morning. Bruce William stiffened and kicked, squealing to be put down so he could finish the job.

"He's a fierce mind of his own, this one," she told William, handing the struggling boy over so she could finish cooking the breakfast oatmeal and eggs.

"Here, laddie, let's get ye into dry breeks. Ye're soppin' wet." William wrestled the baby out of his britches and nappies, expertly pinning on a dry flannel, holding Bruce down with one hand and somehow shoving small, frantically threshing feet into fresh trousers.

The baby screamed throughout, insulted at being re-strained.

"Put him in his chair and give him a crust," Jenny directed. Food was the one thing that would distract the rascal and keep him from mayhem.

William did, and then scooped out a generous spoonful of porridge, added milk and a pat of butter, and began shoveling it into Bruce's willing mouth. The greedy boy screeched between mouthfuls, too impatient to wait even the time it took William to fill the spoon.

"He's starvin', poor wee man," William said with a teasing grin at Jenny.

"Aye, that's because he only had me awake three times last night to nurse instead of five." She was going to have to wean him before the next one was born, but she'd wait as long as she could. Bruce was eleven months; it would be good to go on feeding him for another seven. Milk was a scarce commodity in and around Valdez.

She hadn't told William yet about the small presence in her belly, and he hadn't guessed because she wasn't sick this time. She'd been surprised herself because she'd heard that a woman couldn't get pregnant as long as she was nursing, but obviously it wasn't always so. It would mean two babies not two years apart, but she was thrilled, and she knew beyond a doubt that William would be ecstatic. His dream was to have a house full of bairns.

Bruce took another huge mouthful of oatmeal and then blew it out, spraying William and the tablecloth. If all her babies were to be the same nature as her first, she'd be sat-isfied with a lot less herself.

She watched the two of them in between turning eggs and buttering toast. The boy had the handsome look of the

Galloways, although his curly hair was exactly the color of hers, a rich chestnut brown instead of their gleaming black. It was the only feature he'd inherited from her, though. His eyes were summer-grass green, Galloway eyes, with long, sweeping lashes. And when his little round face matured into manhood, it would have the distinctive high cheekbones and strong jaw of his Highland ancestors. Like his father and his uncle.

The features that marked the baby as Robert's child were subtle, but she'd seen them right after Bruce was born. His tiny ears had the same distinctive fold that Robert's had, and even at birth his little chin was deeply cleft. She'd agonized the entire time she was pregnant, knowing that the baby she carried could have been fathered by either man. And her worst fears were realized when she looked at her son the first time and knew beyond a shadow of a doubt.

William knew, as well; she was sure of that, although he'd never acknowledged in so many words that Robert had fathered the boy. She'd watched closely at first, waiting for any sign of rejection. But there was none. From the first moment, he'd adored the wee boy, surprising her by taking on chores that most men wouldn't, like changing nasty nappies.

"Donald's takin' the boat into Valdez this mornin'. We're in need of nails and tar paper. Is there anything ye need, Jenny?"

"Aye, I'm low on flour and sugar. And it would be grand to have some fresh milk, should there be any."

Donald Cameron, an unsuccessful gold seeker turned fisherman, had come to work for William a few months ago. The grandiose plans for the new railroad had fizzled soon after they'd arrived in Valdez, which was disappointing because Jenny and William were loath to move yet again.

They'd settled into a little cabin in town and fallen in love with the wild, extravagant beauty of ocean and glaciers, but there was the matter of earning a living to consider. William had decided to start a business.

Fishing was one of the area's mainstays, and the king salmon were huge and delicious. But there was no way to get them to market—the trip south was long, and in the summer the fish rotted, while in winter the passage was too perilous.

William saw the need for a fish cannery and set about designing and building one. He found land at a price he could afford in a secluded bay, forty minutes by boat from the town of Valdez. They were living in a cabin that he'd built for them while the cannery was under construction, but now that it was done William was constructing a luxurious new house, on a rise overlooking the Sound.

"Here's a bundle of letters to post, and Donald's to ask would there be any mail for me," Jenny instructed. She still wrote weekly to Bruce, describing his small namesake's latest accomplishments and confiding her innermost thoughts and feelings.

Her father would be married again before these letters reached him, and Jenny was happy for him. A neighbor had been killed in an accident a year ago, and Bruce and the widow, Lizbeth, were courting. He confided to Jenny that it would be a marriage of convenience because Lizbeth had two small daughters to raise, and Bruce badly needed help with the boys and the house. But she was a kind and generous woman, he added, and comely, as well. He was a fortunate man, he wrote.

Jenny felt Lizbeth was the fortunate one, to find a man like him.

In the mail Jenny was sending out were several letters addressed to Mae. She and Carl and little Sophia had made their way to Idaho, where the dry climate seemed to be helping Carl. Mae had gone back to teaching, and when he was able, Carl took care of Sophia and made furniture in a small workshop behind the house they rented.

Jenny sorely missed Mae. She'd tried to make friends with Donald's wife, Imogene, but the woman was quiet and standoffish. There wasn't much time to be lonely, however, not with Bruce into everything he could lay his little paws on.

Every time mail arrived, Jenny flipped through the envelopes searching for a letter with Robert's handwriting, but none had ever come.

She'd never seen him again, and she wouldn't know he was in Australia except for the note the postmaster, Bartholomew Fieldstone, handed her the day she left Dawson. She'd gone in to say goodbye, and to ask him to send whatever mail might arrive for her back to Skagway.

"I'm terribly sorry to see you go, Mrs. Galloway," he'd said. "I shall miss your lovely smile." He turned tomato red at his own daring, and then glanced furtively around. Seeing no one else in the building, he reached a hand under the counter and then slid an envelope toward her with one finger.

"I was asked to give you this personally," he hissed, leaning so close she could smell onions on his breath. "To no one *but* you."

Jenny thanked him, feeling herself tense when she recognized Robert's bold handwriting. Walking home, she stopped and sat down on a fallen log, tearing open the envelope with trembling fingers.

"Darling Jenny," he wrote. The salutation brought tears to her eyes. She whispered, "Oh, Robert, I wasnae fair to ye. Or to William, either."

It was knowledge she'd have to live with for the rest of her life.

She read,

> By the time you receive this, I will be on the trail back to Seattle. I pray you are safe and well. I'm that sorry for the trouble I caused you, Jenny, but I shall never be sorry for the time we spent together. I love you, lass, and shall as long as I draw breath. Willie told me you'd chosen to stay with him. He wants no more to do with me, but I want you to know that I'll wait for you in Seattle until spring, should you change your mind. I'll leave a note for you every week at the Post Office, so you can find me should you come. Jenny, I pray you do, but if not, then next spring, probably May, I'll sign on as deckhand on a ship heading for Australia. It's a place I've read much about. But if you should come to me, we'd decide together where to live. I wouldn't care where on this earth it was, should you be with me, Jenny.

She still had the heartbreaking letter, tucked inside a hidden pocket in her writing case. She couldn't bear to throw it away, because she suspected it was the last she'd ever hear of Robert. William wouldn't speak of him. Once, when she hesitantly asked him about his twin, William turned away, fists clenched.

"I have no brother," he said, in a voice so fierce and terrible she never dared bring the subject up again.

It was the one dark spot in an otherwise happy existence. Jenny tried not to dwell on it. There was no changing the past, and no point in spoiling today's joy by remembering past mistakes.

"Come out wi' me, Jenny, will ye, and tell me have I got it right, where ye want the rooms in the new house."

"Aye, I'd like that." They'd been through it many times already. Jenny knew it wasn't accuracy that William was after. He wanted her to share his excitement, his delight in every detail. He'd taken no interest in that first house in Dawson, leaving the building to Robert. Perhaps she wasn't the only one needing to daily choose joy over regrets.

She bundled Bruce into his little coat and wrapped her cloak around her, because the early September mornings were chill.

"Gie him here." William took the baby as they stepped out of the cabin. The days were already growing short, and the sun was rising behind the snowcapped Chugach Mountains. Behind their peaks the glaciers shone, so bright they hurt her eyes. Sunbeams glittered in a dazzling display on the waters of the narrow bay, and as always, Jenny's breath caught at the sheer grandeur and beauty of this place that had become her home.

The cabin was nestled in a thick stand of spruce and hemlock. The cannery stood some distance away at water level, situated so the prevailing wind would blow away the powerful smell of fish. William had hired six single men to work in it, and he'd had a long, low bunkhouse built for them on the other side of the cannery.

There was a gentle incline from the water up to the level of the cabin, but higher still, on a large level shelf of land, was the site they'd chosen for the house. William had cleared it, and laid logs on the ground to outline its massive size and shape. It was huge, two stories, as large as any manor house Jenny had ever seen in Scotland. She'd objected at first to the size, her Scots thriftiness horrified by two floors and so many large rooms, but William had insisted.

"It's to be our home, lass, and our children's after us and mayhap our grandchildren's, as well. We'll grow into it, and I'd have it worthy of them. And of you, Jenny." He reached out a finger and touched the gold locket at her throat. "I did promise your da I'd make a fine home fer ye. I intend to keep me promise."

Standing now in the golden sunshine, shading her eyes as she gazed out at the water and then up to the site of her new home, Jenny understood what William meant.

At some point in the last two years, the terrible longing for her father and her homeland had eased and then disappeared without her even noticing. Her allegiance had changed. She was William's wife, her baby's mother, but most of all she was Jenny, a woman grown strong, with a heart that had broken open and bled and healed again.

Her love for her father and for Scotland lived on in her soul, and would until the day she died. Love didn't diminish with use. It expanded, growing stronger and ever larger, encompassing the tall man at her side, the child in his arms, the one in her belly, and this unforgiving foreign land, harsh and new, incredibly beautiful. The birthplace of her children, living and dead, born and unborn.

She belonged here, and here she would stay. There was no way of knowing what tomorrow held. For today, there was bread to bake, Bruce William to chase, knitting to finish, letters to write. It was more than enough.

She looped an arm through William's and walked with him toward their future.

* * * * *

Happily ever after is just the beginning...

Turn the page for a sneak preview of
DANCING ON SUNDAY AFTERNOONS
by
Linda Cardillo

Harlequin Everlasting—
Every great love has a story to tell.™
A brand-new line from Harlequin Books
launching this February!

Prologue

Giulia D'Orazio
1983

I had two husbands—Paolo and Salvatore.

Salvatore and I were married for thirty-two years. I still live in the house he bought for us; I still sleep in our bed. All around me are the signs of our life together. My bedroom window looks out over the garden he planted. In the middle of the city, he coaxed tomatoes, peppers, zucchini—even grapes for his wine—out of the ground. On weekends, he used to drive up to his cousin's farm in Waterbury and bring back manure. In the winter, he wrapped the peach tree and the fig tree with rags and black rubber hoses against the cold, his massive, coarse hands gentling those trees as if they were his fragile-skinned babies. My neighbor, Dominic Grazza, does that for me now. My boys have no time for the garden.

In the front of the house, Salvatore planted roses. The roses I take care of myself. They are giant, cream colored, fragrant. In the afternoons, I like to sit out on the porch with my coffee, protected from the eyes of the neighborhood by that curtain of flowers.

Salvatore died in this house thirty-five years ago. In the last months, he lay on the sofa in the parlor so he could be in the middle of everything. Except for the two oldest boys, all the children were still at home and we ate together every evening. Salvatore could see the dining room table from the sofa, and he could hear everything that was said. "I'm not dead, yet," he told me. "I want to know what's going on."

When my first grandchild, Cara, was born, we brought her to him, and he held her on his chest, stroking her tiny head. Sometimes they fell asleep together.

Over on the radiator cover in the corner of the parlor is the portrait Salvatore and I had taken on our twenty-fifth anniversary. This brooch I'm wearing today, with the diamonds—I'm wearing it in the photograph also—Salvatore gave it to me that day. Upstairs on my dresser is a jewelry box filled with necklaces and bracelets and earrings. All from Salvatore.

I am surrounded by the things Salvatore gave me, or did for me. But, God forgive me, as I lie alone now in my bed, it is Paolo I remember.

Paolo left me nothing. Nothing, that is, that my family, especially my sisters, thought had any value. No house. No diamonds. Not even a photograph.

But after he was gone, and I could catch my breath from the pain, I knew that I still had something. In the middle of the night, I sat alone and held them in my hands, reading the words over and over until I heard his voice in my head. I had Paolo's letters.

* * * * *

Be sure to look for
DANCING ON SUNDAY AFTERNOONS
available January 30, 2007.
And look, too, for our other
Everlasting title available,
FALL FROM GRACE
by Kristi Gold.

FALL FROM GRACE
is a deeply emotional story of what a
long-term love really means.
As Jack and Anne Morgan discover,
marriage vows can be broken—
but they can be mended, too.
And the memories of their marriage have an
unexpected power to bring back a love
that never really left....

HARLEQUIN® *Romance*®

From reader-favorite

MARGARET WAY

Cattle Rancher, Convenient Wife

On sale March 2007.

"Margaret Way delivers...
vividly written, dramatic stories."
—*Romantic Times BOOKreviews*

———————

For more wonderful wedding stories,
watch for Patricia Thayer's new miniseries
starting in April 2007.

Rocky Mountain
BRIDES

This February...

Catch NASCAR Superstar *Carl Edwards* in
SPEED DATING!

Kendall assesses risk for a living—so she's the last person you'd expect to see on the arm of a race-car driver who thrives on the unpredictable. But when a bizarre turn of events—and NASCAR hotshot Dylan Hargreave—inspire her to trade in her ever-so-structured existence for "life in the fast lane" she starts to feel she might be on to something!

Collect all 4 debut novels in the Harlequin NASCAR series.

SPEED DATING
by *USA TODAY* bestselling author
Nancy Warren

THUNDERSTRUCK
by Roxanne St. Claire

HEARTS UNDER CAUTION
by Gina Wilkins

DANGER ZONE
by Debra Webb

On sale
February
2007

REQUEST YOUR FREE BOOKS!
2 FREE NOVELS PLUS 2 FREE GIFTS!

HARLEQUIN®

Super Romance®

Exciting, emotional, unexpected!

YES! Please send me 2 FREE Harlequin Superromance® novels and my 2 FREE gifts. After receiving them, if I don't wish to receive any more books, I can return the shipping statement marked "cancel." If I don't cancel, I will receive 6 brand-new novels every month and be billed just $4.69 per book in the U.S., or $5.24 per book in Canada, plus 25¢ shipping and handling per book and applicable taxes, if any*. That's a savings of close to 15% off the cover price! I understand that accepting the 2 free books and gifts places me under no obligation to buy anything. I can always return a shipment and cancel at any time. Even if I never buy another book from Harlequin, the two free books and gifts are mine to keep forever.   135 HDN EEX7 336 HDN EEYK

Name	(PLEASE PRINT)	
Address		Apt.
City	State/Prov.	Zip/Postal Code

Signature (if under 18, a parent or guardian must sign)

Mail to the **Harlequin Reader Service®:**
IN U.S.A.: P.O. Box 1867, Buffalo, NY 14240-1867
IN CANADA: P.O. Box 609, Fort Erie, Ontario L2A 5X3

Not valid to current Harlequin Superromance subscribers.

Want to try two free books from another line?
Call 1-800-873-8635 or visit www.morefreebooks.com.

* Terms and prices subject to change without notice. NY residents add applicable sales tax. Canadian residents will be charged applicable provincial taxes and GST. This offer is limited to one order per household. All orders subject to approval. Credit or debit balances in a customer's account(s) may be offset by any other outstanding balance owed by or to the customer. Please allow **4** to 6 weeks for delivery.

Your Privacy: Harlequin is committed to protecting your privacy. Our Privacy Policy is available online at www.eHarlequin.com or upon request from the Reader Service. From time to time we make our lists of customers available to reputable firms who may have a product or service of interest to you. If you would prefer we not share your name and address, please check here. ☐

HSR07

Romantic
SUSPENSE

Excitement, danger and passion guaranteed!

Same great authors and riveting editorial
you've come to know and love
from Silhouette Intimate Moments.

Silhouette®

Desire

Millionaire of the Month

Bound by the terms of a will,
six wealthy bachelors discover
the ultimate inheritance.

USA TODAY bestselling author

MAUREEN CHILD

Millionaire of the Month: Nathan Barrister
Source of Fortune: Hotel empire
Dominant Personality Trait: Gets what he wants

THIRTY DAY AFFAIR
SD #1785 Available in March

When Nathan Barrister arrives at the Lake Tahoe
lodge, all he can think about is how soon he can
leave. His one-month commitment feels like solitary
confinement—until a snowstorm traps him with lovely
Keira Sanders. Suddenly a thirty-day affair sounds like
just the thing to pass the time…

In April,
#1791 HIS FORBIDDEN FIANCÉE, Christie Ridgway

In May,
#1797 BOUND BY THE BABY, Susan Crosby

Flirty, humorous and sensual, these four stories from four national bestselling authors offer hours of reading pleasure!

TORI
CARRINGTON

JULIE ELIZABETH
LETO

LESLIE
KELLY

JULIE
KENNER

On Sale February 2007

*Available wherever books are sold,
including most bookstores, supermarkets,
discount stores and drugstores.*

www.eHarlequin.com

RCBTC0207